Sea Sonata

Libby Jacobs

Aurora Corialis Publishing

Pittsburgh, PA

SEA SONATA

Copyright © 2025 By Libby Jacobs

For more information, address cori@auroracorialispublishing.com

This is a work of fiction. Names, characters, businesses, places, events, locales, and incidents are either the products of the author's imagination or used in a fictitious manner. Any resemblance to actual persons, living or dead, or actual events is purely coincidental.

Paperback ISBN: 978-1-958481-94-3

Ebook ISBN: 978-1-958481-95-0

Printed in the United States of America

Cover designed by Karen Captline, BetterBe Creative

Edited by Sarah McKnight

Praise for Sea Sonata

"*Sea Sonata* reads like a warm sea breeze that whispers across your face. Author Libby Jacobs has crafted a beautiful and lyrical story that is steeped in Irish folklore. It follows a young woman who loses herself in pain, grief, and disappointment but finds strength again through the power of new love, her passion for music, and a mystical bond with her deceased grandmother, whose young life unexpectedly intertwines with her own. After reading Sea Sonata, I now believe in the "Good Folk." I highly recommend."
~ Ann Howley, Author of *The Memory of Cotton* and *Confessions of a Do-Gooder Gone Bad*

"Libby Jacob's *Sea Sonata* follows a family of musical savants through three generations of heartache and loss. It explores forbidden love, the stories told to replace disappointment, legends falling from good graces, and the importance of friendships—especially those that withstand the fiercest storms. Lyrically musical at moments, this tale of myth merging with reality is a solid first novel."

~ Jill Cullen, Voted Best Writer in Best of PGH 2024 *City Paper* Reader's Poll, Author of the *Flirting* Series

Chapter One
Weeping Willow (*Salix sepulcralis*)

April 27 – 28, 1998

The grand piano sat abandoned in the artificial night of the music room. A scarf of Irish lace shrouded the closed lid, the covered keyboard.

Jane Bell stood outside the room. Her forehead rested against the door; her hands clenched in tight fists by her sides. The piano had been her voice, an extension of herself, but now the liquid heat of Mozart, the erotic pulse of Rachmaninoff, the veiled seduction of Brahms were gone. She reached out and locked the door, threaded the small key onto a chain, and fastened the chain around her neck. She glanced at her hands with their bitten nails and ragged cuticles made more unkempt by the past few days of packing boxes and sorting and stacking music. She was pleased that her hands looked ruined, so different from her hands at the keyboard when everyone had watched them. Perhaps no one would recognize her now.

She held her breath and listened for a banshee shriek, the funereal keening that should accompany any good Irish lament for the dead, but the only cries she heard were from children playing in the park next door. She closed the window and lowered the blinds, but not before she caught sight of a young girl about seven, braids bouncing in time to the jump-rope song she chanted. Jane closed her eyes, capturing the image. Delicate wrists traced circles in the air as they arced the rope over the child's head, then under her navy blue sneakers. The pattern in her plaid jumper blurred as it lifted up and down, its hem fluttering as it caught the air, inches above white knee socks. Her face was raised to the spring sun, and wisps of hair, as dark as

Jane's, clung to her cheek. The rope slapped the pavement with the rhythm of a muffled heartbeat. A few feet away, a young woman watched proudly, protectively, from a park bench.

Jane turned from the window as the metallic sound of the buzzer echoed in her Manhattan apartment and erased the jump-rope song from her mind. A few minutes later she opened the door for Ken, her agent and best friend. For the past sixteen years, since she was twenty-one, he only slightly older, he had scheduled concerts, negotiated recording contracts, and kept the press away when he knew she needed to rest.

Now he dangled a set of car keys in front of her. "You've got one shiny black Jeep downstairs. Have you named it yet?"

"Sister Theodora," Jane said.

Before she could take the keys he closed his hand around them. "North Carolina?"

She nodded.

"You can get to Connecticut a lot sooner. Rob and I opened the cottage last weekend. Take the keys and relax there for a week or two."

Jane stared past Ken.

"It's a long way to Wilmington and you don't know anyone there," he said.

He waited patiently for her to respond, both of them used to her silences. Over the past few years the piano had become her voice. The spoken word was now a halting second language to her.

Jane pulled a key ring from her pocket. "Trade?" she asked. Ken had arranged to sublet the apartment to friends with the understanding that the small room with the piano would remain locked. They exchanged keys and he held her hands for a moment. She could see the concern in his eyes when he noticed the marks her short fingernails had imprinted on her palms.

"Saint Jane?"

"A little leaving-the-nest anxiety," she said. "Not stigmata." She pointed to the boxes of books and two suitcases. "This is going to take a couple of trips."

"Sure you don't want to take any CDs? Sheet music?"

Jane ignored him and picked up a carton. He followed her with another box of books.

As they packed the SUV, the doorman handed Jane a much-taped cardboard box. "Ms. Bell, I know you're headin' out of town. Good thing I saw you. This was delivered yesterday and never got out of the mailroom."

Jane smiled when she read her parents' return address. "My mother probably sent me cookies for the trip."

Ken tucked the box in the back of the Jeep and returned to where Jane stood beside the open passenger-side door, arranging and rearranging the Thermos and maps Ken had placed on the seat. He finally turned her around to face him. As they stood inside the angle of the open car door, he braced his arms on either side of her shoulders so that she would look at him. "You going to be okay?"

"Sure."

She was whispering and wouldn't meet his eyes, and Ken leaned close to hear her. They would have looked to anyone passing by like lovers, but they were closer in many ways. Ken had proposed to her years before, a conditional but very sweet proposal. "If you weren't married and I weren't gay, I'd marry you in a minute," he had said. Her marriage to Alex fell apart, or rather faded away, more than a year ago. But Ken remained her best friend, the brother she'd never had. Now he cradled her chin in his hand and turned her face to his, as though she were deaf, as though he sensed words were slipping away from her.

"Call me when you get settled. I'll come visit when you're ready for company. And if you want to come home, just turn the map upside down, follow it back to New York and stay with me until the sublease is up." He reached into his pockets and pulled a CD package from each. When she tried to stop him, he explained, "They're books. Hours of books to listen to."

She put the CDs on the seat and hugged him.

"Have a safe trip." He kissed her on the forehead. "Call me."

Getting out of the city and onto the expressway occupied her mind for the first hour of the trip. Strong coffee and an Agatha Christie mystery kept her awake. After she passed a Welcome to Virginia sign, she left Route 95 and stopped in a town whose business district seemed to stretch only as far as the single block between its two traffic lights.

Outside the café where she ate lunch, the sun struck Jane with inseparable sensations of heat and light. She twisted her hair into a coil and held it away from her slender neck. It seemed to press on her with more than its physical weight, as though made heavier by a burden of memory, of the past.

Next to the café, a young woman jiggled a key in the lock, opened a shop door, and flipped the Back-in-10-Minutes sign to its Open side. Jane followed her into Chez Beauty. "I want you to cut my hair," Jane said.

The beautician's cropped, purple hair shimmered as she nodded, and Jane sat down, swiveling to face the mirror.

"Shampoo?"

"No. Just cut it. Please. I don't have much time."

She reached for a comb. "Shoulder length?"

In the mirror Jane watched as her hair, like jet-black silk, cascaded through the hairdresser's fingers. "Shorter," she whispered. "Like yours." She closed her eyes.

When Jane was little, Nana was the only one with the patience to do her hair. Her grandmother brushed out the tangles and transformed the wildness into a neat braid or twist, diverting Jane with stories made music by her heavy brogue. "Your mane's all snarled. For sure that must be your Other Side. Are you a girl or a faerie horse today?" Stories about the Other Side were always told in whispers.

The snipping stopped.

Jane opened her eyes. Reflected in the mirror, her eyes seemed larger, a more vivid green, fringed by the new bangs. Pixied wisps accented her cheekbones. She smiled, and paid the woman twice her asking price for the haircut.

Walking past her car, she sat for a moment on one of the park benches that flanked the statue of a Confederate soldier. Through half-closed lids she watched a rabbit approach a tuft of clover near her feet. He was small but brazen. A few hops, then motionless except for the twitch of his leathery nose, then a few more hops toward her. Each leap brought an old memory closer to the surface. She was about five. They were beside a lake. Her mother stacked up paper plates shiny from fried chicken and stained crimson by pickled beets, and packed them in a wicker picnic basket. Jane sat on the edge of an old quilt and Nana stood nearby as they watched a rabbit nibbling scraps of lettuce Nana laid out for it.

"What is it you're seeing?" Nana spoke so softly that her voice seemed part of the breeze.

Jane matched the whisper. "A bunny."

"What is it that's there?"

She knew the grownup word. "A rabbit."

"Look harder. Look deeper."

Jane stared into the rabbit's eyes. It blinked and in the limpid surface of the globes she saw her own reflection, her strange green eyes. "Nana, I see something!"

The startled rabbit hopped away from the blanket. Nana told her stories every night about the magical creatures who shifted from one form to another, who transformed from human to animal and back again according to rules as ancient as the rocks Jane collected in her pocket. Could this be one of those mythical beings? She turned to ask her grandmother, but stopped when she saw her mother with a hand on Nana's elbow as though the older woman were a misbehaving child.

"Mother, you've got to stop filling Jane's head with that Irish malarkey. She believes everything you tell her."

Nana pulled her arm away and twisted long silver strands into the knot of hair from which they had escaped. "Sorry, Bridget."

Jane stood and took the quilt to her grandmother.

"Jane," Nana said. "A rabbit is just a rabbit." Jane and her grandmother shook out the quilt, their hands meeting and moving away from each other like dancers as they folded it. "Sometimes," she winked at Jane, her voice returned to the whisper of *si-gaoith*, the faerie wind, "sometimes a rabbit is just a rabbit."

A car horn honked at the intersection and Jane saw a streak of white as the rabbit bounded into the tall grass beside the parking lot. *Coinín.* The Irish word for "rabbit" drifted into her mind, planted long ago by her grandmother's bedtime stories. She got into the Jeep and headed south.

***

Jane arrived in Wilmington, North Carolina, and found a hotel on Wrightsville Beach about midnight. She grabbed her small overnight case and the battered box from her mother and locked the rest of the things inside the car. After she checked in, she collected real estate brochures from the counter and sat down at the hotel bar. Over a Jack Daniels, she skimmed the pictures; none of them was what she wanted, but she found the name of an agent, Mike Tyler, appearing time after time, and circled the agency phone number.

Jane crunched on the last ice cube in the tumbler, left a tip on the bar, and gathered her things. As she stood to leave, she was surprised to see that three other people were in the room. Each of the men sat alone, one at the far end of the bar and two at small tables. They all smiled at her, the one at the bar almost embarrassed, the other two phony friendly. Jane walked quickly out to the elevator.

As she opened the window in her room to hear the surf, she noticed the box. It looked battered, bandaged, as though it had traveled much farther than its trip from Florida to New York. Tempted by the thought of homemade cookies, she peeled away the tape and opened the package. Inside, wrapped in sheets of bubble wrap, nestled a green cloth-bound composition book and a flute case. A note was taped to the plastic.

I found these in an old trunk of Nana's. I don't know anything about the flute. I think she would like you to have them.

I wish you had decided to stay with us for a while in Florida. Know that you are welcome here. I'm not sure what else to say, except that your father and I love you and we're here if you need us. Let us know how you are doing and where you are staying. Love, Mother

Jane put the flute case back in the box and covered it with the cushioning plastic as if that might shield her from any music the flute still held. She crawled into bed and brushed her fingers over the composition book, pleased that a keepsake from Nana accompanied her.

For the few seconds it took for her to fall asleep, she was aware of the sensation of still traveling down the highway. She knew she had not yet arrived.

***

Her travel alarm woke Jane from fragmented dreams of a sleazy real estate agent who looked like one of the men in the bar the night before. He had tusks, subtle but threatening, which he kept polishing with a white cotton handkerchief. He showed her dozens of houses, all missing walls, and she woke up wondering, as she had in the dream, how they could possibly protect her.

Jane turned off the alarm and let the sound of waves outside wash the abrasive noise from her mind. After quick calls to her mother and Ken to let them know she had arrived safely, she phoned the real estate office, and the receptionist put her through to Mike Tyler. "My name is Jane Bell and I'm in from New York and I'm looking for a house on the ocean to rent for about six months and I wondered if you could help me." She hated using the telephone and wished for a second that Ken were there to do the phoning as he always did in the city.

"I'd be glad to do whatever I can, although I usually deal in sales rather than rental properties."

"I might be interested in renting with an option to buy."

"Do you know the area at all?"

It was one of those simple questions that didn't have a simple answer. How could she explain that she remembered a day here, an ocean too cold to plunge into, a beach filled with sun and seashells, and wind that drove everything else away. And she wanted to be erased like that now.

"Ms. Bell?"

"I performed here once a long time ago," she explained quietly. "I want to stay for a while."

"Well, I've lived here all my life and I know exactly what you mean." Jane heard the flip of pages on the other end of the line. "I've got appointments scheduled for the next couple of hours. Tell me a little more about what you're looking for, and I can get some things lined up and meet you around three."

Another one of those not so simple questions, Jane thought. "I want to be on the ocean, away from people, maybe with a little yard, and it doesn't much matter what it costs. I mean I'm not a millionaire or anything but—moderate range." No wonder Alex or Ken had always wanted to handle financial matters.

Mike managed to sound as though she had been most helpful. "Okay. That gives me something to go on. Where are you staying?"

"The Atlantica."

"I'll meet you at the front door at three."

Jane was eager to see some of the city and the beach. As she passed through the lobby, she glanced into the coffee shop and almost laughed out loud at the sight of the tusked real estate agent from her dream, now quite tuskless, napkin tucked into his collar as he enjoyed a bowl of oatmeal. He was probably a harmless salesman debating with mixed feelings his return to a wife and four kids in Shreveport.

She eased out of the parking lot and found Route 17, which would lead her along the coast. She drove around for about two hours, chasing little back roads, then finding her way to the main highway before she could become completely lost. She had decided to head back to town and look in some of the shops when she noticed a sign: Aria 2 mi. Unbidden, the haunting melody of the fifth movement, the Aria, of Guerre's *Sonate* whispered in her mind. Jane had played the violin music when she was thirteen; now she rolled down the window and let the wind drive the music away. The sign pointed in the direction of the beach. Jane didn't remember the name from any of the real estate maps, but she headed onto the side road toward Aria.

She had driven about a mile, dodging the deeper craters in the hard packed sand, when she came to a fork. The left was clearly marked with another old-fashioned sign to Aria. She took the narrower road to the right that would take her toward the ocean. The warning of a Private Property sign was overruled by the lure of a hand-painted sign announcing House for Sale.

As she drove, Jane felt pulled apart from the rest of the world, protected as though the horizon had gently curled in at the edges to hold her. Gulls flew overhead and tipped their wings to her. She could hear the sea whispering in the distance. She slammed on her brakes, sliding a few feet on the sandy surface, to avoid hitting a mailbox that appeared to have been planted in the middle of the road.

"Shit." The road ended at the mailbox. She laid her head back on the headrest and looked up through the sunroof. Waving across the intense blue of the sky were the green ribbon branches of the tallest weeping willow she had ever seen. It reminded her of the willow in her favorite aunt's yard. All the cousins called it the "faerie tree." When the huge tree fell in an ice storm, Jane was sure that the faeries had scattered to live in the hedges and lilac bushes that surrounded the yard. She still believed that as much as she could believe in any magic.

Jane turned off the engine. A huge shadow crossed the hood of her car and she looked up to see a prehistoric-looking bird with a wingspan of at least six feet soaring overhead. The pelican nodded to her and she took it as a sign to go on with the adventure. The worst that could happen, she thought, was that she would get shot for trespassing.

She climbed out of the car and walked to the mailbox. The door hung open on one rusty hinge. The box was empty except for straw remnants of an abandoned nest. A scraggly climbing rose left a warning scratch on her wrist as she reached to examine the tiny buds. Tightly wrapped, warmed by the sun, they teased with their perfume and let her glimpse the pale pink of blossoms still days from opening.

Reaching down to pick up the red flag that had broken off the mailbox, she noticed faded letters spelling out S. Nevin scratched or burned into the post. The letters were neat and squared off, stacked on top of each other like a child's wooden blocks. She traced the letters with her finger and wondered about the name. Sam? Susan? She slipped the flag inside the opening, careful not to disturb the deserted nest.

Jane searched for a few minutes before she found anything that looked like a path. Scrub pines, lilacs, and bushes she couldn't identify tangled in a nearly impenetrable wall. After about thirty feet, she was stopped by a picket fence, armed like the mailbox with thorns of climbing roses. The fence, once painted white, was now scraped down to bare wood in most places by the sandblasting of the beach winds. In the shady spots, moss had tinted it a pale green. The gate, unlike the door on the mailbox, hung fast to the hinges, and a shiny new padlock suggested that someone was keeping watch on the place.

She spent a few minutes pacing the length of the fence to get a glimpse of the house but could see little beyond the pines. Glancing at her watch, she was surprised to see that it was nearly two o'clock. She dashed back to the hotel, proud to find it on the first try. In her room, she cleaned the rose thorn scratches, then headed downstairs to meet the real estate agent.

A black Lincoln pulled into the circle outside the hotel. The driver's door opened, and a sandy haired man about her own age got out.

"Ms. Bell?"

She nodded and shook the hand he extended. "Please call me Jane."

"My secretary saw your name on my calendar and bet me fifty cents that you're the pianist."

Jane withdrew her hand and nodded again.

"I have to apologize for not recognizing your name this morning. It sounded familiar but I couldn't place it. But my secretary set me straight right away. She heard you play a few years ago right here in Wilmington, and she called my wife because she knows that she—my wife, that is—has about every record you ever made. Except that I guess they're not records anymore. Everything is on CDs now."

"Thank you. But I'm really here to get away from all of that."

He nodded. "We get lots of movie stars and famous people down here, and we understand the need for privacy." He opened the passenger door. She slid into the seat and he closed the door for her. "Actually, two of the places I've picked out for us to look at are on a private island, discreet guards at the gate house, absolute quiet. Might be perfect for you." He maneuvered the Lincoln into the stream of traffic.

"I really was thinking of something not too large."

"Well, I figured that you'd want a place big enough for a piano and maybe some entertaining. And I hope you don't mind, but my secretary—she's so excited that you're here—took the liberty of checking around about piano rentals. There don't't seem to be any concert grands, which is what she thought you'd want, but she found —"

Jane felt as though he had put his hands around her neck and was slowly strangling her. She had a brief panicked thought that if he slowed the car a little more, she could probably jump out as they rounded the next curve without hurting herself too much. "Mike," she said, forcing her voice up loud enough for him to hear her, "I don't want a piano, and I won't be entertaining."

"Okay." He seemed to be at a loss for words, maybe for the first time in his real estate career.

"I don't play the piano anymore. I brought a flute along and might try taking lessons on that." She didn't know why she had said anything about the flute, except that he seemed to be upset by the piano confession.

"My daughter plays flute. We took her to hear James Galway in Raleigh. She doesn't practice much but likes to play in the band, and we go to a lot of the football games to hear her."

The Lincoln pulled onto a side road that led to a four-story apartment building. "Now this is one of the condos that overlooks the ocean." Mike seemed relieved to change the subject back to real estate. "It may not be exactly what you were thinking about," he said, "but it helps to get an overview of what's available."

The condo, with its bland, cookie-cutter façade, reminded Jane of the place in Florida where her parents stayed for a few months every winter since her father's retirement. "Let's skip this one. When I was out driving around this morning I did see something that interests me."

"Great!" He pulled a cell phone from his pocket. "Tell me where it is and the listing agent if you saw that on the sign and we'll set up an appointment."

"It must be close to a place called Aria. I didn't see a regular listing sign but the name on the mailbox was S. Nevin."

"Jackson handles that." He slipped the phone back into his pocket. He was looking closely at her. "How did you find that place?"

"I followed the willow tree."

"Nobody can figure out how that thing grew so big out there. Did you see the house?"

"No. I couldn't get past the front gate and the trees are all grown up around it."

He smiled, but his eyes were serious as he glanced over his shoulder. "You don't want to see it. It's a mess. Been vacant for years."

Now Jane felt like she wanted to wrap her hands around his neck. "*Mallaigh.*" Nana's mild curse escaped her lips. She hadn't come six hundred miles to be told what she did and didn't want to see.

Mike seemed to sense the meaning of the Gaelic "damn." He pulled the phone back out of his pocket and reached over her to find a small leather address book in his glove compartment. He opened the book and dialed a number. Jane could hear the ring faintly. He let it ring eight times, then gave her a look and lifted his shoulders as if to say, See, I tried. As he was ready to break the connection, the phone was answered. "George?" Mike was practically shouting into the phone. "George Jackson?" He apparently heard an affirmative response. "This is Michael Tyler." A pause. "Tyler. Seth Tyler's boy." He listened again. "No, I've been out of school for quite a while." A pause. "I'm selling real estate now." More muffled sounds from the other end. "Sure, I know you're still in the business. I've got a client here wants to look at the Nevin place."

Jane could hear dead silence at the other end of the line. "George?" There was a short question from the other end. "A woman." Mike listened again. "No, she's going to be living by herself but she seems pretty respectable as far as I can tell." Mike winked at her. There was another brief pause followed by more words from George. "Of course I remember where you live.

Right by the candy store." He listened for a minute and laughed. "Damn, George, how do you remember that? Those root beer things were my favorite. Haven't thought about them in years." He put the phone back in his pocket.

"Mr. Jackson sounds like a character."

"He's at least eighty, but he still remembers that I was crazy about those root beer barrels."

"So you know Aria?"

"Sure." Mike pulled out of the parking lot. "I rode my bike out there all the time when I was a kid. It's a sleepy beach town that was popular with tourists until the highway passed it by."

"What can you tell me about the Nevin house?"

"From what I remember, it's real small. Must be close to falling down by now."

Jane felt like they had traveled back forty years in the four or so miles to Aria. "How often do you come here?" she asked as they turned onto Main Street and she caught her first glimpse of the dozen buildings that made up the downtown.

"I probably haven't been here for ten years. No reason to." He seemed to reconsider. "Of course my wife wouldn't agree. She's out here every couple of weeks in the summer and even more often in the spring."

He parked the Lincoln in front of a two-story brick house. Crocus and forsythia bloomed along the walk and crimson azaleas reached nearly to the upper windows. Green metal porch chairs, the kind that bounce gently on bent pipe legs, formed a cozy sitting area on the porch. The grass curled around the bottom of posts that held a multi-paneled sign ornately lettered in Old English script. "George Jackson, Esquire, Attorney at Law" read the top and largest panel. Below it hung a panel announcing "Licensed Real Estate Agent." Suspended from that one was a sign declaring "Justice of the Peace." The smallest sign brushed the grass and further described Mr. Jackson as a "Notary Public."

Mike nodded toward a frame building next door. "She drives out here with friends to shop at the candy store. Of course it hasn't been a candy store for years. An Irish woman turned it into a garden store, and Marci comes out here all the time."

An Irish woman? In the breeze Jane heard whispers of Nana's humming. "I'd like to do some gardening." Glancing up, she saw a figure standing in the front window of the Jackson house. "I think Mr. Jackson is waiting for us."

As they walked together up the stairs to the porch, she noticed subtle signs of age and wear. Delicate tendrils of dark green paint curled away from rough spots on the porch chairs, revealing earth-colored rust stains. Autumn leaves nested in the seats.

The heavy oak door swung open as they reached the top of the porch steps. Jane heard Mr. Jackson's voice and caught the warm spicy scent of Bay Rum before she saw him in the darkened hallway. "Michael Tyler," he laughed, "You've grown up."

"It's been many years, sir." The men shook hands and Jane's eyes, adjusting from the sunlight, perceived her host as an image etched in softly gleaming silver. His eyes were a steel gray, his hair pure silver, thick and brushed straight back from his forehead. He wore a shirt of pearl-colored silk, open at the throat, gray slacks, and a matching cashmere cardigan. "Jane, I'd like you to meet George Jackson. George, Jane Bell."

She had a sudden fear that he might melt into a puddle of mercury at her feet. Quicksilver, Nana had called it. Jane extended her hand, and George took it in his, seeming to gain substance, energy, from the contact. Still holding her hand, George led them toward the living room. "Would you care for some iced tea? It's real. Sun tea, not a mix. Although everything else these days seems to come in little instant packages."

The few steps from the hallway transported them into a garden-like room. Hand-crocheted doilies lay like Queen Anne's Lace on the back and arms of a love seat and armchairs covered in jade green velvet. Mirrored shelves along the walls and half a dozen ornately carved tables seemed weighted down with hundreds of fragile flowers. Porcelain roses bloomed beside a crystal orchid. A tear-shaped paperweight cradled violets in a nest of bubbles. The faded wallpaper trellised the room with pale roses, and a worn oriental carpet covered the floor in spring-grass green with accents of pink, like blush petals fallen from the roses on the walls.

As George released her hands, she thrust them into the pockets of her jeans to keep from reaching out and caressing the rosewood baby grand in the center of the room. A book of Chopin preludes was open to the B minor, a corner of the page bent over to mark the place. Jane closed her eyes and heard the music playing in her head as though the strings still resonated, the left hand pushing to a crescendo through the falling notes of the melody, the right hand giving life to the piece with a *sotto voce* heartbeat.

"My sister played the piano, too." George spoke in a whisper, and Jane didn't know if he knew about her own career, or meant that his sister had played the piano in addition to her other interests.

"I was very sorry to hear about Mary Ellen..." Mike seemed uncertain about how to continue.

"Thank you." Here, in this room in this light, George looked as fragile as the translucent teacup on the sideboard, ivory bone china graced with a single violet. "A female cancer took her two years ago."

Although Jane understood what he meant, she had the sudden bizarre image in her mind of a malevolent female sprite whisking away the sister George had loved and hiding her behind the rose trellis, trapping her forever in the walls. But Jane knew that the music had never stilled in the piano. If Mary Ellen lingered behind the trellis, that was exactly where she chose to be.

"Has Michael told you much about the little house, Miss Bell?" George glanced from Jane to Mike and back again.

"He told me very little, actually."

"There's not really much one can say about it," George said.

"He seemed to think it might not be what I am looking for."

"An honest man." George seemed to lose his train of thought. "Did I offer you tea?"

"Tea sounds wonderful, but I'm eager to get to the house," Jane said.

"Yes, of course. Always easier to see it before dark. Michael, come into the kitchen with me, and get the key and some lightbulbs. Take the stepladder, too. You can leave it on my porch on your way back." George gestured for Jane to sit in the garden room and ushered Mike through a dark green lacquered door.

Jane did not intend to sit down. She thought she would move to the sheer curtains covering French doors that must lead outside, perhaps to a real garden. But it was so warm in the room, and the velvet love seat seemed closer than she remembered, and the flowers of crystal and porcelain were intoxicating her with the sweetest scents. She sat and closed her eyes.

A breeze even warmer than the air in the room caressed her face and she turned toward the French doors. A woman stood in the doorway. Behind the woman, framing her in a blur of pastel blossoms, was the garden Jane had imagined. The woman's long dark brown hair was tied back. She wore a simple white cotton dress which ended mid-calf. Her feet were bare. Her face might have looked unremarkable, plain, in a black and white photograph, but in the sunlight, she glowed with the colors of an impressionist painting. Her eyes were a deep blue; her lips and cheeks had stolen hues from poppies. She held her hands in front of her.

"Selena says get rid of those awful pine trees in front of the windows. And pull all of the weeds in the garden by hand." She narrowed her eyes and stared at Jane. "Selena doesn't think you're strong enough for this, but I think she's wrong." She turned as though to leave through the open French doors.

"Wait!" Jane wanted to jump up and run to her but felt her body held down by the heaviness of the air in the room.

The woman started through the door, then turned back. "I'm not supposed to, but I'll send this one out to the house for you. You must promise to feed her." She released a hummingbird into the air and Jane saw a flash of iridescent blue and purple before the door closed.

"Jane." Mike was standing beside her. "Are you sure you want to see the house today? You must be tired after that drive yesterday." Had she dozed off for a minute?

"Let's go." Jane stood to shake hands with George. "Would you mind if I looked at the garden before we leave?" she asked, nodding toward the French doors.

"You're welcome to look, but nobody's done anything out there since Mary Ellen passed away." George struggled for a minute with the door handle, then shrugged his thin shoulders apologetically. "Must be rusted shut." He held the curtain aside so Jane could look into the yard. A cloud covered the sun and Jane gazed into the gloomy tangled remains of Mary Ellen's garden, somber with the sepia and gray tones of an old photograph.

"I'm sure it was beautiful once. I can picture how it must have looked." As Jane walked past the piano and out the front door, she heard the final chord of the prelude still vibrating, anchored in the bass, the treble floating a third and fifth echo over it. Hovering. Like the hummingbird.

Chapter Two
Da Capo (It.) From the Beginning

1960 – 1971

Her father had been a violinist, but Jane had never heard him play except in dreams where she saw him only as a shadow and heard muted music so sweet that she woke up with tears on her pillow. She could never remember the pieces he played and knew only that they had no beginning and no end.

He had studied at Juilliard and met Bridget, Jane's mother, in an Italian restaurant in Manhattan where she waited tables and he wandered with slicked down hair and a passable Italian accent through the maze of seated customers as he played his violin. Bridget was near the top of her class at NYU, one of the few women accounting majors, but she left school after two years to marry Jack Bell and follow him to his home in Cleveland. Jane knew that there were several years when her grandmother, angered by their three-month courtship and marriage outside the Roman Catholic Church, refused any contact with Bridget and Jack. But the ice between them thawed with news that Bridget was pregnant, and Bridget's mother left her apartment in Boston and stayed with them to help with her first grandchild. And so it happened, her grandmother would say, "through the wisdom of God and the intercession of the Blessed Virgin who watches over mothers and children," that she was there with Bridget when they received word of the Accident.

It was always capitalized in Jane's mind. She had heard the story so many times that she felt it was her own memory, one that she somehow overheard from inside the womb. Her father rushed out of their apartment that morning, violin case in his right hand, briefcase of sheet music in his left, pausing to kiss

Bridget on the forehead and leaning down to rest his lips on her pregnant belly. She stood in the open doorway for a few seconds, listening as his footsteps and a soft humming of whatever piece he would be playing faded, then stopped with the percussive closing of the outside door.

Jane's grandmother always maintained that a keen sense of foreboding wakened her early that morning. Bridget was in the kitchen filling the teapot with boiling water when a crescendo of thumps up the steps, punctuated by calls for "Mrs. Bell, Mrs. Bell —" had Nana at the apartment door as Mrs. Winton, the landlady, reached the landing. Hers was the only apartment in the building with a telephone and usually a phone message was announced to all six apartments by a bellow that echoed up the stairwell. Her voice was now drained by the effort required to move her body up the stairs. She held her arms crossed in front of her huge bosom as though she feared her labored breathing might thrust her heart right through her starched white blouse. Mrs. Winton grabbed Nana's arm. "Thank God you're here."

Anticipating bad news, Nana tried to close the door between Mrs. Winton's message and Bridget, but the landlady's wide, trembling body blocked the door. "There's been an Accident. Mr. Bell's been crushed in the bus. They've just took him to the Clinic —" Her message was cut short by the metallic clatter of the teapot hitting the stove. Both women turned to see Bridget wrap her arms around her swollen belly as though she were trying to block the news from the ears of her unborn child. Nana said that what happened next was a miracle as Mrs. Winton "flew like an angel" to Bridget's side, cradling her in her arms and cushioning her fall to the floor. Bridget sat in the landlady's lap as though sound asleep in the safe embrace of a slightly wobbly, overstuffed chair.

"My door's unlocked. Call the ambulance. I'm not moving another inch."

She was right there on the floor holding Bridget when Nana led the ambulance attendants into the apartment minutes later. Bridget was conscious and in the first stages of premature labor.

While waiting for the ambulance to arrive, Nana called the hospital for news about Jack. As the attendants lifted Bridget onto the stretcher and carried her down the steps to the ambulance, Nana told her daughter that Jack would be all right. His left hand and arm had been injured in a bus accident, but the best surgeons at the Cleveland Clinic were working on him and he would be out of surgery soon. She couldn't bear to quote the exact words of the nurse who had spoken to her from the hospital. "They're working to save his arm." When Bridget asked if Jack would be able to play the violin again, Nana could only pat her hand and answer that it was in God's hands now and her job was just to think about the new baby.

With Nana at her side, Bridget was rushed to the maternity ward where ten hours later, and three weeks prematurely, she gave birth to Jane. In the hours before and the long night after the birth, Nana bustled through the corridors between the maternity and surgical wards, reassuring her daughter and whispering news to her son-in-law. When the nurses who attended him tried to convince her that he would not begin to regain consciousness until the next morning, Nana smiled at them tolerantly and leaned down to deliver her message, careful not to dislodge the white bandages that encased his left arm, shoulder and part of his chest.

The next day Nana commandeered a wheel chair, helped position her daughter in it with newborn Jane swaddled in blankets and held in her arms, and pushed the chair to Jack's room. Jack opened his eyes and winked at Bridget as the chair rolled in. "I knew it would be a girl."

Nana rolled the wheelchair to Jack's right side and glanced smugly at a startled nurse. "I told you he could hear me. Let's leave them alone for a bit." The nurse started to protest that she wasn't supposed to leave her patient, and was still trying to explain as Nana led her into the corridor.

"Let me hold Jane for a minute," Jack said, nodding toward his right side.

"Can we name her 'Jane'?" They had discussed girls' names for weeks with no decision. Bridget wanted "Jane" after the heroine in her favorite novel and Jack favored "Elizabeth" because that had been his maternal grandmother's name.

"'Jane' she is," Jack said, curving his right arm away from his body, creating a nest.

Bridget laid the newborn in the crook of his arm. "Jane Elizabeth," she whispered, "meet your daddy."

As Jane reached out, fingers clenched in a sleepy baby fist then stretched wide to touch the world, a different nurse strode into the room carrying a thermometer and tiny pleated paper cup of pills. She was followed by an irate Nana who had tried to delay her entrance.

The nurse nodded toward Jane and shook down the thermometer. "Look at those long fingers. With hands like those, that child will either be a pickpocket or a violinist." Bridget burst into tears, and the poor nurse looked bewildered.

"We're hoping for a violinist," Jack said. "Every family should have one."

During the following week in the hospital, Bridget and her mother pieced together the story of the accident from Jack's account and a newspaper article carefully clipped from the *Plain Dealer*. The clipping, later folded and tucked into the back of Jane's baby book like an obituary recording a death no one wanted to remember, reported a freak accident that crushed the left arm of the city's most promising young violinist. Jack had entered the bus at a run as he did every morning, swinging his violin over the handrail to his friend, Michele, a flutist with the symphony. She cradled his violin for him as he searched his pockets for change for the bus. This morning, before he could move his left arm and shoulder into the bus, the bus was struck from behind, pinning his arm in the grip of the heavy metal door. Surgeons at the Cleveland Clinic Hospital were optimistic that they had been able to save his arm, the reporter noted, but doubted that he could continue his musical career. The article ended with mention that a baby girl had been born to the Bells on the day of the accident.

The story made the front page of the local section of the paper. Centered above the headline was a picture of Jack Bell in his tuxedo, violin tucked under his arm. He was smiling with an expression of confident amusement at the camera. On the bottom of the fourth page, where the article concluded, was a slightly out of focus photo of Bridget in a wheel chair holding a swaddled bundle that was Jane. Nana had been standing behind the wheelchair and the photographer or editor had cut her off just below her ample bosom. She was present only as a matronly midriff and hands, which even in blurry outline were beginning to show some swelling and crippling, resting with gentle strength on her daughter's shoulders.

Before she could express the idea to herself in words, Jane grew up believing that she was a part of some preordained cycle which, like the layout of the newspaper article beginning with her father's photo and ending with hers, linked her birth with the death of her father's career as a violinist. With a child's need to find order in the world, she thought there had to be some reason that her life began with the death of Jack Bell's dreams of becoming concertmaster.

Long before she began violin lessons, Jane heard the recorded music of Bach and Beethoven and Mozart in concert with her father's voice whenever he was home. A few weeks after the accident, he accepted a position teaching music history in a local university. Her father's arm healed so well that by the time Jane was a few years old only a slight stiffness of movement and an inability to completely straighten his left arm remained as outward evidence of the accident. When the family vacationed for a week each summer on the shore of Lake Erie and Jack swam and relaxed shirtless in the sun, Jane would trace the scar that wandered from his shoulder to mid-forearm like the raised indication of a mountain range that snaked along a stretch of globe, marking the division of one part of a country from another, dividing one part of his life from another.

Jane knew there were deeper scars that had never healed as completely as the flesh of his arm. She knew there were slashes in her father torn open every few months when he lifted his violin out of the case, unwrapped it from a butterfly print silk scarf that had been his mother's and tried to find his music again. Once when she was about five years old, the ritual tuning sounds woke her; she crept out of bed and sat on the floor by the door of her bedroom, her long, slender fingers crossed for luck, hoping that this night the strings would sing for him and the music would soar. After a few minutes of music and more minutes of silence, Jane heard her father sobbing in her mother's arms, and she knew that she would never hear a more terrifying and heartbreaking song.

The next day, he greeted her with his usual smile and kiss on the cheek as the three of them sat down to breakfast. They were living in a different apartment by then and Nana was still with them, but her arthritis slowed her down in the mornings. After breakfast, while her father went to say good goodbye to Nana, Jane found his briefcase, checked to be sure it was locked so the papers wouldn't fall out, which Jack assured her was a very important part of her job, and waited beside the front door for the game to begin.

Her father came out of Nana's room, tossed his raincoat over his arm and stopped in front of Jane, who tried to hide the briefcase behind her little body.

"Who's seen my briefcase?" Jack made a great show of looking around the living room.

"What will you give me for it?"

"A kiss?"

"More than that."

"A hug?"

"Nope."

"What will you trade for it?"

"A music word," Jane sang or sighed or squealed, depending on her mood.

"Awfully low on words today. Would you settle for a big diamond ring?"

"Nope."

"You drive a hard bargain, young lady." Then reaching around her to grab his briefcase, he threw her a word. "*Presto*," he called, dashing from the room. Or sauntering out the door, he would drawl, "*Largo.*"

He left her with a physical cue and a magic music word, and before he reached his car, Jane dragged her mother or Nana to the music dictionary to search for its meaning. All day long she rolled the word around in her mind like a smooth lucky stone. When her father arrived home at six, she met him at the door intoning an incantation composed of word and definition. "*Presto*. Quickly."

"Cherman?" her father joked, exaggerating the word "German" with an accent.

"No, silly. Italian!" After a hug, Jane hauled his briefcase to the desk while Jack went to greet Bridget and Nana.

Jane had been asking for violin lessons for years, and on her seventh birthday she received the three-quarter-size violin that was her father's first instrument. She began to study with David Cohen, Jack's teacher until he left for Juilliard. Cohen had played with the symphony for years but was now semi-retired and concentrated on teaching. He hadn't accepted a beginning student in twenty years, but made an exception for Jane. It would be fun, he told Jack, to help shape a second generation, and he missed the challenge of watching a student take her first musical steps. So much of his career had been spent correcting another teacher's mistakes that he looked forward to an unspoiled pupil. Jack assured "Poppa Cohen," as his students called him, that he hadn't even taught his daughter how to tighten and rosin the bow, and Poppa Cohen found space for a lesson on Fridays at five.

Looking back on those early lessons, Jane remembered the total quiet of the book-lined study where she stood in front of a heavy black metal music stand which somehow made her music books seem more significant than they did on her skinny metal folding stand at home. They moved to the living room with its baby grand piano when she advanced to pieces with piano accompaniments, and as her teacher played the piano, in the background Mrs. Cohen seemed to float wraithlike around the dining room preparing for their Friday Sabbath dinner.

Jane remembered the tears cried in frustration at not being able to play as well as she wanted to. When the tears slid down her cheek, without a word Papa Cohen handed her the clean white handkerchief he always carried to place on his chinrest, and she wiped the tears away, finding comfort in the muted scent of the starched and ironed cotton square. When she was ten years old, Poppa Cohen lent her a full-sized violin, and she began to study her first Bach violin sonata.

While Jane practiced, Nana rocked and crocheted and hummed. Before she went to sleep, Jane stopped in her grandmother's room to say goodnight and listen to stories about *si each*, the faerie horse, the riches of the Good Folk, and Nana's own crossing from Ireland.

"You married Granda right before the trip, and he died on the crossing?" Jane never tired of the story.

"And I never heard the banshee keen for him over the sound of the wind and waves." At mention of the banshee, Jane gripped her grandmother's hand tighter. "The spirit is nothing to fear, Jane. She comes to lead us to the next world."

"Nana, I want you to stay here with us forever."

"That would be a bad thing."

"But why?"

"*Is ón saol a thagann an chiall.* Life will give you the wisdom to understand. Be patient, little one."

"I don't want the spirit to ever lead you away." Jane knew that her mother had taken Nana to the Cleveland Clinic to see several heart specialists. Late at night she heard the concern in her parents' voices as they talked about murmurs and damaged chambers in her grandmother's heart, and Jane would fall into half-dreams of ruined caves where magical creatures drew labored breaths.

Now Jane leaned closer to her grandmother and tangled her fingers in the silk fringe of the scarf that Nana had draped around her shoulders. "This was your wedding present."

"It will be yours one day soon. After I'm gone."

"Soon?" She had never used that word in the many retellings of the story.

"Don't fret, child. Time is a most strange thing." She settled the scarf closer around her shoulders. "Now get me a drop of the Dew to keep the chill away 'til morning."

Jane knew to ask her father, not her mother, for the whiskey. He poured a bit into a china teacup and let Jane carry it back to Nana.

That night, the temperature dropped and the wind rose, whistling in the eaves. Jane heard, or dreamed that she heard, an unearthly wail, and she crept to Nana's room. Her grandmother's eyes were closed and she whispered, "*Fan liom.* Stay with me." Jane fell asleep in the chair beside Nana's bed.

She woke up the next morning as Jack lifted her from the chair. "Jane, your grandmother died in her sleep last night. I'm going to take you back to your room."

"I heard the banshee call her. She'll lead Nana—"

"I don't ever want to hear another word about those ignorant superstitions." Jane was stung by the grief and anger in her mother's voice.

Jack tried to soothe both of them. "Your mother is very sad. She's not upset with you. An ambulance will be here soon for Nana."

"May I sit with her until it comes?"

"We'll all stay," her father said. He put her back in the chair and held Bridget in his arms. Jack had closed Nana's eyes, and her mouth was open a bit as though death had caught her in the middle of a sigh or in the final measure of a song she had been singing. Jane reached out and touched her hand. It was cool and smooth like a piece of ivory satin that had been laid near a window and cooled by a spring breeze. Jane held Nana's hand in hers until a knock at the door announced that the ambulance had arrived to take her grandmother away.

One Sunday a few months later, they passed a small brick home with an Open House sign on the neatly trimmed lawn. Before Bridget could reach over to touch Jack's arm and ask him to stop, he had pulled the car to the curb. After ten minutes inside the house, all three were in love with it.

Bridget and Jack explored the basement and paced off the cozy dining area and kitchen that overlooked the back yard. A narrow driveway connected the back alley to a one-car garage next to the kitchen. Neither of them realized that Jane had slipped away from them until she grabbed their hands as they were about to investigate the garage. She whispered, "I found my bedroom!" and started to lead the way at a run, then stopped, turned to her parents and said in her most serious grownup voice, "There's a room upstairs that has definite possibilities as a bedroom for a young person," and continued at a much more moderate pace toward the steps between the dining room and living room.

Jack gave Bridget a puzzled look.

"You told her that buyers weren't supposed to seem too excited about a property they liked because it sometimes drives the price higher. She's just looking out for your interests," Bridget said.

"Good advice. We ought to keep it in mind."

Jane led them up the narrow steps and turned to face them when all three had reached the attic floor. "Ta da," she sang, spreading her arms wide as though she had made the room appear as the finale to a grand magic trick.

The ceiling was low, no more than seven feet high. The walls sloped down on two sides where the roof embraced the room. Two dormers faced the front of the house, and windows in the dormers and at each end of the room filled the room with sunlight.

"It's big enough to divide into my bedroom and a workroom for you," Jane said to her mother. "You could have an accounting desk and space for your sewing machine and everything."

"Just think," Jack said, "tax time without boxes and papers on the kitchen table." They walked around the room, their footsteps echoing in the open space, then he and Bridget started back down the steps.

Jane followed, watching the patterns the sunlight made on the bare wood floor.

At the bottom of the steps, Bridget asked Jane if she wanted to look at the back yard. There was a swing set next door and they might be able to get an idea of how old the children were. "May I stay in here if I'm careful and don't touch anything?"

"Sure," Jack said. "We're going out through the garage and into the back yard. We'll be back in a few minutes." Jane watched them leave through the kitchen door that led to the garage, pleased that they were holding hands. Then she made her way through the house full of adults into the living room.

When her parents returned to the house, Jane met them in the kitchen. Her eyes were solemn, her voice low and intense. "I can't believe it."

"It is a lovely attic space," agreed Bridget.

"More than that," said Jane, as though she had almost forgotten about the wonder of a bedroom hugged and shaped by the roof. "The house comes with a piano."

Jack knelt down in front of her to meet her eye to eye. "Honey, the people who are selling the house will take everything when they move to their new house. If there's a piano, the people will take it with them."

"No, Daddy, Mr. Daniels is selling the house and the piano was Mrs. Daniels' mother's and he would sell it with the house and he knows who you are and he would like you to have the house and the piano." She stopped to take a breath.

"Jane, the people selling the house probably aren't here now. Someone called a real estate agent handles showing the house to people who might be interested in buying it."

"But he is here," Jane protested, starting to move toward the living room, leading her father by the hand.

A few feet away, they were met by a middle-aged man. "I am here, although I gather it's not considered good form. The agent is a bit miffed, but I promised my wife I'd stick around and personally attend to the open house."

"Mr. Daniels, this is my father, Jack Bell, and he would like to see the piano even though he doesn't believe it's for sale with the house. And we really, really like the house but we're not supposed to act too excited in front of the real estate —" she paused and looked to her father for help.

"Agent. Real estate agent." Jack glanced with some embarrassment at Mr. Daniels.

He seemed not the least put off. "I understand completely, Jane. I try not to act too excited in front of her either." They had entered the living room, which was considerably less congested by this time. "Here is the infamous piano." He gestured to a spinet tucked into a corner. "According to family legend, it came from a bar downtown. My wife says it was delivered in a snowstorm, and she remembers the piano movers cursing on each step as they carried it up from the sidewalk. My mother-in-law mostly played hymns on it. And carols at Christmas time." Mr. Daniels laughed. "I guess I sound a little like a used car salesman."

Jack moved to the piano and played a C major scale with his right hand. Mr. Daniels sounded apologetic. "It probably hasn't been tuned for twenty years."

Jane stepped closer to the piano and brushed her fingers over the keyboard, not depressing the keys hard enough to make a sound, hearing the music in her head. "The E and A are a little flat, but it does have a lovely tone."

Jack seemed as surprised as Mr. Daniels, who asked, "Do you play the piano?"

"No," she responded with equal parts pride and hesitation in her voice, "I'm studying the violin."

"Just like your father."

Jane lifted her fingers from the yellowed ivory keys as though reluctant to break physical contact with the piano. She took her father's hand in hers. "Yes," she said. "'Like my father."

"Try not to act too excited," Mr. Daniels said. "Here comes the real estate agent now."

An exuberant woman in her mid-fifties with Bridget in tow extended a business card to Jack. "Your wife says that you're interested in the house. I know you need to think it over, but at this price and in this neighborhood, it won't stay on the market long." She paused for a second. "My name is Mrs. Small, Jo Small, and you can reach me at this number almost anytime."

Jack took the card and shook hands with her. Then he shook hands with Mr. Daniels. "We'll be in touch."

Mr. Daniels smiled at Bridget and then addressed Jane. "If you buy the house, the piano is included in the purchase price. But you will have to promise to have it tuned." Jane nodded and extended her hand in agreement. Jack and Bridget always talked about that handshake as the gesture that sealed the negotiations.

In three weeks, on a rainy Easter weekend, the Bells moved into the little brick house with a spinet in the living room. That Monday morning, the piano tuner arrived.

***

Jane's commitment was to the violin, and she practiced for an hour or two after dinner while her father read the paper, dozed in his chair, or prepared his lectures. Every Saturday she took her place as the youngest member of the youth symphony. But right after school, when her mother chatted in the backyard with their next-door neighbor or watched soap operas in the den, Jane sat at the piano with the sheet music and old hymnals that had been left in the piano bench, and matched up the notes to the keys. Playing the music was like solving a wonderful and complex puzzle.

Their first Christmas Eve in the house, the living room glowed with candlelight. The three of them had spent hours decorating the fat tree that stretched almost to the ceiling with barely enough room at the top for the angel that had crowned Nana's tree since Bridget's childhood. After a few Christmas cookies and before they left for church, Jane asked her parents to sit on the sofa, which had been pushed against her father's chair to make room for the tree, and she sat down at the piano to play Christmas carols for them.

The melody lines sang out, harmony floating gently underneath. There was none of the new pianist concentration on playing note by note. She found the phrases and breathed with them as they rose and died away. Her long, slender fingers curved naturally over the keys, pressing into them, caressing them.

Jane finished "Silent Night" and swung around on the bench to face her parents. Bridget applauded and wiped her eyes. "Nana would have loved that."

Jack sat for a second without speaking. Jane turned around and quietly closed the lid over the keyboard. "I didn't do it very well, did I?" She started to put the hymnal away, pulling out the red and green strips of construction paper that had marked the carols she wanted to play. "We probably should get started for church."

"No, Jane, honey, it was wonderful! You just surprised me. I didn't know you could do that." He rushed to give her a hug then opened the lid over the keys. "How did you learn to read the bass clef?"

"*Simplement.* We have music classes in school, you know, and they taught us what notes go with those lines. When I get stuck I count down from the violin clef."

"She gets that gift from you, Bridget." Jack opened his arms to include his wife in the hug.

"It's true, Mom. A lot of music is really math."

"Well, I'm glad I could contribute something. And because I'm really good at math, I know that we have half an hour to get to church, and it's going to be very crowded tonight."

Soon Jane sat between her parents near the back of the church. She closed her eyes and concentrated on the tangled web of organ music that she felt rumbling up from the stone floor of the church as much as she heard it, the scent of incense and pine boughs adding grace notes and overtones to the songs. Jack cast his eyes down, focusing on his daughter's hands clasped in prayer. As though she could read his thoughts, Jane turned and whispered to him, "The piano is just for fun. I still want to be a violinist."

In the morning, the cookies left for Santa were gone and Jane's Christmas stocking was filled. They exchanged and opened gifts, including a present from Nana. It was the Irish lace scarf edged with fringe as soft as the fur of a kitten.

When all the gifts under the tree had been opened and the mountains of paper cleaned up, Jack pretended to remember something. "Oh, there is one more thing your mother and I thought you ought to have this Christmas. But you have to sit on the sofa and promise not to look." He disappeared into the den. Jane sat on the sofa and closed her eyes. "Ready?" he asked a few seconds later.

"Ready," responded Jane and her mother in unison.

Jane knew what the present was as soon as she felt its weight on her lap and her father guided her hands to balance it, but she didn't open her eyes. Her hands traced over the hard leather violin case, caressing the gentle swell of the top, the hard angles of the hinges, the secure rectangle of the lock with its tiny keyhole, the worn oval handle. Finally she opened her eyes and slid back the brass lock. Her father's violin rested inside, wrapped as she remembered it in the butterfly print scarf. She looked up at her father and mother, unable to speak.

"If it's not the right color we can return it," Jack said.

"It's perfect," Jane whispered, "but I can't play well enough yet. I don't deserve it."

Jack sat beside her on the sofa. "You deserve it. Poppa Cohen and I are both impressed with how well you're playing. The violin ought to be played. It's not good for it to lie around in the case." He gave her a hug. "It will please me to know that you're playing it."

"Do you mind if I practice for a while?"

Jack and Bridget laughed. "We'll work on brunch and call you when it's ready."

* * *

At Jane's lesson that week, she returned the borrowed violin to her teacher and proudly played the one that had been her father's. When the lesson was over, Mr. Cohen met her father at the door and welcomed him in. Then he told Jane to go into the kitchen and try some of the pastry his wife was baking. Its sweet and spicy fragrance filled the house. Jane carefully wiped rosin from the violin and bow, put them in the case, and ran to pull up a chair at the kitchen table, straining to overhear the conversation between her father and her teacher.

"She sounds good," Jane heard her teacher say. "The instrument fits her just like it fit you." She knew that each violin was different. Each had its own character, its own voice, its own soul. In the minute of silence that followed, she could picture Mr. Cohen carefully folding the handkerchief he placed on his chinrest when playing and tucking it neatly into his pocket. "You know that Jane is teaching herself to play the piano?"

"She played carols for us on Christmas Eve."

"Sometimes when she's playing she seems to almost forget about the violin and concentrates on listening to the piano part. She asks me to play certain passages over and over until she figures out how the piano lines interconnect. You won't be able to keep her away from the piano, and she's going to develop some bad habits if she plays much longer without a teacher. Habits that will take years to correct."

There was a longer silence, and Jane wondered if her father or her teacher could be angry about her playing the piano.

Poppa Cohen cleared his throat. "Teaching Jane is fun for me, you know. It reminds me of years ago when you were in her place. It's not a chore like with some students. Hardly worth charging full price for her lessons. I think half price would be about right. Or even less if Bridget wants to do my taxes for me."

"Thank you, David, but it's not the money. I was wondering how Bridget would feel about it. She worries that Jane is already spending too much time with music and not enough time doing—whatever it is girls do."

"So what is she supposed to do? Be a cheerleader or take up knitting? She has friends, right?"

"Lots of friends."

"She's a musician. It would hurt her more to take the music away from her."

Jane quickly finished the last crumbs of pastry and thanked Mrs. Cohen. She didn't want to interrupt the conversation, but she had to hear the answer to her father's next question.

"Who should teach her?"

She slipped back into the living room and settled on the edge of the sofa beside her father. He patted her hand, and her teacher smiled at her. A carafe and two wine glasses sat on a glass table in front of the men.

Poppa Cohen rubbed a shadow of rosin from the calluses on the fingertips of his left hand. "There are lots of good people around. Roger Pope, Nancy Berkner. You know most of them. Someone who can get her started right."

"Joseph Lamb?"

"Ah, Joseph. You studied with him for a while before you went to New York."

"About a year, but I haven't seen him for a long time."

"*Wunderkind* and infamous bad boy." The teacher shrugged. "I don't know if he is teaching right now, but I did hear that he's composing again."

"That's great! Who told you?"

"Actually he called me a few weeks ago and said he was working on a piece and planned to premiere it with a group at the university with a couple of us old timers mixed in."

"What did you tell him?"

"I've got to be crazy, but I said I'd love to." He stared into the crystal wine glass as he swirled the last drops in the bottom and watched them sheet like waves of purple honey on the slanted sides. "I really miss that. The excitement of new sounds, the wild ideas flying, extra measures with the ink still wet being tossed on the music stand five minutes before you go on." He emptied his glass and reached for the decanter. "Maybe you and Jane would like to come to a rehearsal. I'm sure Joseph would love to see you again."

He glanced up at Jack as he lifted the wine to pour it and started to apologize, but Jack covered his wine glass with his hand. "No. Please," he said quickly. Jane sensed he was refusing both the wine and the sympathy. She squeezed his hand and both of them stood. "We would love to come to a rehearsal," he said.

Poppa Cohen handed her several music books and her violin. "Take good care of that fiddle and remember to slow down when you practice the new etude. You've got to get the notes in your fingers before you can play it up to tempo."

"Okay," Jane said. She was almost out the door when she turned to ask, "But what if I do get it up to tempo by next week?"

"That will be wonderful. But start out slowly."

"I will. And thank you." She couldn't wait to show them that the etude could be played correctly and at tempo the following week.

That night at the dinner table, when their plates were nearly empty, Jane's father said, "Mr. Cohen thinks Jane should start piano lessons soon so she doesn't pick up too many bad habits from trying to teach herself to play." Her mother finished a last bite and took her plate to the sink. "I thought I might see if Joseph Lamb is taking any new students," he added, warning Jane with a shake of his head not to add to the conversation.

"There's some vanilla ice cream for dessert, and then, Jane, you should get to your homework," was her mother's response.

When Jack got home from work the next evening, Jane was waiting in the open door to meet him. "I'm going to start piano lessons next week!"

"Who's your lucky teacher?"

"Sister —" she looked to her mother standing behind her for help.

"Sister Helena."

"Yes. Sister Helena at the convent."

"That sounds wonderful," Jack said.

"She has a master's degree from Oberlin, and she's supposed to be excellent with young students. I think she'll be an appropriate teacher for Jane." Bridget's tone left no room for negotiation.

Jack gave Jane a hug. "We'll have the piano tuned this week."

Chapter Three
Lilac (*Syringa vulgaris*)

April 28, 1998

Mike seemed unusually quiet after they left the Jackson house. George had followed them out to the porch, then waved goodbye as they pulled away. Through the back window, Jane watched as he sat in one of the porch chairs, not bothering to brush away the leaves pooled in the metal seat.

"Mr. Jackson is wonderful. A classic southern gentleman."

"He is. I can't believe how much he's aged since I saw him last. But it was a long time ago." He didn't seem to want to pursue the conversation.

"What does the 'S' on the mailbox stand for?"

Mike took his eyes off the road and looked at her for the first time since they had gotten into the car. "Why?"

"Just curious."

He stared out the windshield again. "Selena." Jane would have bet money that his answer would be the one he spoke in a hushed voice, but when she heard the name, she wasn't sure whether to laugh or ask Mike to take her back to the hotel immediately. She had the feeling that the latter request would please him.

"What do you know about her?"

Mike cleared his throat. "I don't know much, really. Mostly rumor. She grew up around here. She was a couple of years older than me. Her daddy was a preacher. Real strict." He paused for a minute. "More than strict. All our fathers were strict. Hers was mean. He was the kind of man who saw the Devil everywhere and seemed to think he had special permission from God

Himself to whip his kids whenever they might be getting close to finding pleasure in something."

"Did you ever meet her?"

"Like I said, she was a couple of years older than me. But my older sister, Patti, made friends with her at school, probably about the only friend Selena had, and Patti brought her home for dinner a few times. Selena loved my mother's cooking." Mike smiled, but it was a hard smile, more ironic than pleasant. "I remember apologizing to her one night about not having dessert after dinner because our whole family had given up dessert for Lent. She made a joke about the hardest thing for her family to do was find something to give up for Lent because they had already given up everything. We laughed, but we knew it probably wasn't a joke at all."

The car turned off the main highway onto the rough road Jane had found earlier that day.

"What else do you remember about her?"

"I think she was very beautiful, but that didn't occur to me until later. She always wore hand-me-down dresses that went to her ankles. She wasn't allowed to wear any makeup and she pulled her hair straight back in a ponytail or one long braid. She had huge brown eyes that were never still. It was like she was always glancing around expecting to see her daddy or God or the Devil in a corner watching her." Suddenly the car was skidding in the sand to avoid the mailbox at the end of the road. They came even closer to hitting it than Jane had.

"I feel much better about my driving this morning." She wanted to hear more about Selena, but was equally eager to see the house. "What happened to her?"

It seemed like he wasn't going to answer her question. He asked Jane to grab the lightbulbs from behind the seat while he got out of the car and opened the trunk for the stepladder. He met her at the gate with the flashlight and key in his hand. For a few minutes, he struggled with the padlock. When it popped open, he dropped the key into his pocket, straightened up and spoke very quietly, as though there were someone nearby eager to overhear Selena's story. "I never saw her again. A few days later, Patti came home in tears. Her teacher had skipped Selena's name during roll call that morning and when Patti asked after school about her friend, the teacher said that Selena was gone. She had run away and her father sent word to the school that as far as he was concerned, she was dead. Take her name off the roll. And they did."

"But what about this house?"

Mike seemed hesitant to talk at all now. "She came back a few years later but I never saw her." They were struggling to find the path that led through the overgrowth to the house. "She had money with her, but I never heard where it came from. She bought this land and drew plans for the house and had a local carpenter build it for her." The rest of the story came out in a monotone rush as though Mike wanted to be done with it before they reached the door of the house. Jane could make out the outline of a wooden porch through the trees. "Selena died and the house has been empty ever since."

"What was the relationship between Selena and Mary Ellen?" Jane asked, aware that she had lowered her voice, too.

Mike almost dropped the stepladder he still carried. He set it carefully against the porch rail. "I'll tell you what I know when we get back to the car." He seemed afraid to talk here. Jane felt something, too, but it didn't make her afraid. She felt warm and connected to the house.

They had walked through a small yard overgrown with coarse grass. The house was one story tall. Its squarish front and triangular roof line, simple door set in the center, and wooden spindles of the porch railing that stretched across the width of the house, gave it the air of a child's drawing. Windows flanked the door on both sides, the left slightly smaller than the right, as though the house squinted a bit. On the left side of the house, scraggly pine trees and huge tropical weeds reached six or eight feet into the air, covering any windows that might be on that side of the house. Jane thought about the cryptic message she had been given in the dream, if it had been a dream. Had it been Mary Ellen who talked to her?

She walked up the two wooden steps to the porch. The porch floor seemed sturdy, but the left corner of the roof over the porch dipped lower than the right. The post that should have held it up was splintered, and Jane couldn't tell if it was from insect damage or pure exhaustion. The other three columns looked secure. The outside walls of the house had once been painted white, but, like the board fence ringing the yard, had succumbed to an earthier palette of brown, gray, and moss green. One shutter hung by a single hinge. Other shutters were piled in a corner nearly covered by scraps of faded newspaper, rusty cans, and unidentifiable trash.

Mike was struggling with a larger key on the ring that George had given him. Jane was not usually good with keys and locks but took it from his hands. As the bolt slid back, the click of a different lock, the one that secured the piano room, echoed in her mind. She slipped the ring into her pocket.

Jane opened the door and walked into the house before Mike could turn his flashlight on. It was almost six o'clock in the evening, and the daylight that remained was filtered through a layer of dirt on the windows. Jane stood still until Mike had flashed the thin beam around the room. Neither of them could make out more than disconnected images of rubbish caught in the stripe or circles of amber light that raked the walls and paused in the corners.

"There's really no point to this —"

"I want to see it."

Mike released his breath impatiently. "Then wait outside while I find the main cutoff switch for the power. George said it's near the right front corner of the house."

"I'll stay here."

"There are probably rats."

"And spiders and bats," Jane added.

Mike handed her the flashlight without another word. Jane heard him muttering, "Jesus," under his breath as he left the house.

Jane stood still, her back to the front door. They had entered a living room with a stone fireplace on the right wall. Small windows that must have been shuttered on the outside flanked the fireplace. In front of her, an archway opened to the kitchen. The back door lined up with the front. On the left side of the house, three interior doors stood closed, two opened into the living room, one into the kitchen.

In spite of Mike's warnings about rats, Jane closed her eyes and drew in the odors of the house. It had a tired smell of damp newspapers and mildew, but Jane felt comfortable wrapped in it. She had forgotten about the flashes of lilac she had seen this morning, but now their pastel sweet scent, the gentle bite of salt air, and the muffled sound of the ocean embraced her.

About two minutes after some rustling in the bushes at the side of the house, Jane heard a metallic snap and opened her eyes. A reluctant mechanical hum began near the back of the house. Mike walked into the doorway and stood outlined in the evening light. He had picked up the stepladder from the porch. He flicked the light switch inside the door. The room remained dark.

"Lightbulbs?" Jane asked.

"Lightbulbs. The power is on, anyway."

Jane directed the flashlight beam over the dried leaves and trash on the floor while Mike set up the ladder under the bare bulb in the center of the ceiling. "I heard a motor go on in the back. Must be a refrigerator or something."

"Can't wait to see that," Mike grumbled from his perch on the ladder. He unscrewed the old bulb, trading it for the new one that Jane handed him, and turned it gingerly.

The switch was still in the on position. George had given them two hundred-watt bulbs and the unshaded flash of light temporarily blinded both of them. Jane grabbed Mike's hand to steady him on the ladder. For a few seconds both of them looked around the room. If Mike saw stained walls, paint peeling off windowsills, carpet rotting on the floor, Jane saw walls that wanted to protect her, windows that would let light into her life after so much darkness.

Mike wet his fingers and reached up to unscrew the bulb. "Don't!" Both of them seemed surprised at the vehemence in her voice. "At least use the switch."

He got down off the ladder and started toward the switch on the wall. "You can't want to see any more of this."

Jane stepped between him and the switch. "I want to see all of it."

She couldn't tell if he was more amused or annoyed. But he nodded assent at the same time he seemed to be shaking his head at her obstinacy. He launched into his real estate salesman's banter. "A charming little cottage, bit of a fixer-upper, a real handyman's special. Needs some work and a woman's touch in the decorating department." He moved to the door on the left side of the living room, kicking trash out of the way as he walked, leaving a trail for Jane to follow. "Here we have the first of two charming bedrooms." He pulled open the door and Jane stepped inside.

She felt as though the air had been squeezed out of her lungs and it took a second to fill them up again. This room had not been trashed like the other or had been cleaned more recently. It was empty of furniture. A trick of the light coming in through the door they had opened, reddened by the approaching sunset outside and filtering in through the pines at the side of the house, suffused the room with a rosy glow. They could barely make out the remains of tiny pink roses on the walls and, hanging in tatters at the windows, scraps of matching curtains in patterned cotton.

"This could be a study," Mike said.

"Yes. This could be a study."

They left the door open and moved to the second door opening off the living room. Inside, a shade was mostly ripped off its roller, and the single window let in enough light to reveal an old-fashioned footed bathtub that had been ringed by a plastic shower curtain now heaped on the floor. A simple pedestal sink and a toilet with a cracked seat completed the bathroom. Mike walked over to the toilet and pushed the handle. With a hesitant watery roar and gurgle, it flushed. "It's kind of gross," he announced, sounding like a high school kid, "but it seems to work." He turned the handles for the hot and cold water and a stream of dark, rusty water gushed out. "I thought the water might have been turned off. George couldn't remember." After they walked out of the bathroom, Mike closed the door behind them as though afraid of what might follow them into the living room.

"Kitchen next?" he asked, getting his flashlight ready. But as they walked through the arch, red light from the sunset streamed in windows at the back and side of the house and through a window in the back door. In spite of layers of dirt and salt and grease on the panes, they could make out the counter and sink against the far wall to the right of the back door. The once white stove and bravely humming refrigerator took up the right side wall. Against another wall that separated the kitchen from the living room, open shelves held cracked jars, a few chipped plates, rusty cans and mounds of leaves, dirt, and small animal nests. A square table was on its side in the center of the room. One wooden straight-backed chair had been shoved into a corner.

Mike laughed. "I forgot to mention that this one comes furnished. Would you like to see the master bedroom as long as we've come this far?"

Jane didn't wait for Mike to open the third door on the left side of the house. Stepping inside the bedroom, she felt at home. Windows on the side of the house were blocked by the pines as she had known they would be. But the wall at the back of the house consisted of two sets of French doors that opened onto a narrow porch. More scrub pine and dense weeds topped a sand dune. She could see and smell the lilacs growing wild around the overgrown yard, and, as the breeze from the ocean picked up, branches from the willow brushed across the ground a few feet from the French doors.

"I want it." As Jane turned to face Mike, who was standing in the doorway, she noticed a bed, mattress stained and torn, springs dangling from beneath. A chest of drawers lay on its side against one wall, three of its four drawers dumped upside down and scattered in various places around the room.

"It's a wreck," he said, but sounded as though he knew he couldn't dissuade her.

"How much for rent? Or rent with an option to buy or whatever?"

"Three hundred a month."

Jane started to laugh, thinking that three hundred a month wouldn't cover the rent on her bathroom in Manhattan.

"All right. It's a mess. But there is a lot of land. Two fifty."

"I'll take it. Where do I sign?"

"We'll take care of that in a minute. Let's go see the sunset first."

As they pushed through the heavy grass in the yard, following an overgrown path of bricks that led toward wooden steps over the dune, Jane caught sight of Venus in the darkening sky and began to chant under her breath the child's rhyme her mother had taught her, "Star light, star bright, first star I see at night —" But she never finished the poem. She reached the top of the dune and saw the ocean spread out in front of her. Even close to high tide, about twenty feet of beach stretched between the dune and the reach of the waves. Jane looked back toward the house. The sun had slipped halfway below the horizon like a conjurer's coin sliding into a magic bank. When she turned again to the waves, her tears blurred the boundaries between the darkening sky, the paler blue of the ocean, and the reflection of the setting sun, and she felt as much as saw the intensity of the colors.

She heard Mike exhale beside her. "You never quite get used to it." They stood without speaking until the sun had disappeared. "Most likely you'll get lots of the sunrise in that bedroom window. If you still want the place."

"Just try and let someone else have it!" She watched sandpipers advance and retreat in a skittish dance at the water's edge. "I don't understand why this didn't sell years ago."

Mike sat on the top step leading over the dune to the beach and patted it to suggest she sit down, too. "You don't want to try to get down these steps when it's this close to dark. They're all overgrown and most of them are probably rotted out." She sat beside him. "Everything else around here has sold. It's not really as isolated as it looks. There are big, fancy golf and tennis condos on both sides."

"How much land is with the house?"

"The last six acres."

"What 'last six acres'?"

"I don't know all the details. What I understand is that Selena bought up about fifty acres when she came back to town. That was when property was still pretty cheap and the development boom hadn't started. When she died, George was named executor of the estate. The land went on the market, but there were some real strange, but perfectly legal, conditions in the agreements. George had to personally approve the buyers, and special restrictions applied to the house and the six acres around it. The outside land was eventually sold with arrangements to protect the land and the wildlife."

"Selena must have been a little ahead of her time."

"I guess she was. Anyway, the last and best parcel could only be sold if the purchaser agreed to keep this house. All the other ocean front around here was being developed with million-dollar beach homes, and nobody was crazy enough to want the property with that shack on it." He stood up.

Jane stood up beside him and brushed the sand off the seat of her jeans. She looked at Mike to see if he realized what he was suggesting about her sanity.

He seemed to know exactly what he was saying and didn't look like he was going to back away from the assessment.

"How do you know George will approve me?"

Mike led the way to the house in the growing darkness. "When he took me into his kitchen to get the lightbulbs, he told me to accept any offer you made. If you need money to fix the place up, he'll deduct it from the rent, which means that he'll probably owe you money."

"What does that do to your commission?"

"Don't worry about it. With this deal, I'll either be the laughing stock or golden boy of the local real estate market."

"My agent used to say, 'As long as they're talking about you.'" When they reached the back porch, Jane noticed a tarp-covered object in the corner of the porch and identified it as a wooden rocker from the delicate new moon curve resting on the porch floor. It looks like a lady's slipper peeking out from under a petticoat, she thought as she walked back into the kitchen, and wondered if the chair could be saved.

They walked through the house without speaking, checking the back door and turning off lights.

Jane took the key from her pocket and locked the front door, then handed the key to Mike. She supposed there was some formality about making deposits and signing papers before the keys were left in her possession. He started on ahead as she whispered goodbye to the house and walked across the yard and through the gate. Mike relocked the padlock on the gate. When she reached the car, Mike was holding the passenger door open for her. "What about the ladder?" she asked, getting into the car.

"George said to leave it in the house if it looked like you were going to need it." He walked around to the driver's side and slid in. "Looks like you're going to need it." He hesitated for a moment before reaching into his pocket for the little ring with two keys on it. "I'm really not supposed to do this. I mean usually I wouldn't do this. But I think I may as well give these to you now."

Jane clutched the keys in her hands like a talisman that would guide her on a special quest. She imagined she could feel the metallic caress of another key suspended from the chain around her neck.

"When do we sign the papers?" she asked when they reached the main highway and even the willow had disappeared from sight.

"I'll clear everything with George as soon as I get home tonight. The papers can be drawn up tomorrow morning and I'll bring them to your hotel by noon."

"Not until noon?" Jane realized that she must sound like a very spoiled child.

"There's not much you can do until then. Go spend a couple of hours on the beach in front of your hotel." Mike paused for a moment. "Sometime tomorrow I can get Steve out there with his pickup to start clearing out the trash and maybe get some of the yard work done. But the inside cleaning and painting are going to take at least a week, maybe two, even though it's a small place. So you're looking at ten days to two weeks before you can think about moving in."

"I'm thinking about moving in in a day or two, and I want to do most of the work myself."

In a maneuver that reminded Jane of Manhattan cab rides, Mike glanced over his shoulder and dashed across two lanes into the parking lot of an abandoned custard stand. He turned off the motor and looked at her. "I feel somewhat responsible for this although God only knows why." Jane was again aware of the softening of the vowels and the music in his accent that made his statement sound less patronizing than it might have. "That place is a mess. There might be snakes out there. There are certainly rats. And you're going to need some help. You've got to have plumbing inspections and electrical inspections and termite inspections —"

"I want do most of it myself. I need to do it."

"Let me send Steve out there to help move the heavy stuff, and I'll schedule the inspections with people I know."

"Okay. But I do most of the work."

He shook his head and started to turn the key in the ignition. Jane reached out and stopped his hand. "You said you'd tell me what you know about Selena and Mary Ellen."

Mike dropped his hand and leaned back in the seat. His voice sounded sleepy, like he was going to tell a bedtime story late at night. "When people live mostly boring lives in a little town like Aria, they talk a lot about people who seem to live more interesting lives. Pretty soon those more interesting lives, which probably aren't really all that interesting, get to sound more and more exciting with the things the boring people make up about them.

"People had always speculated a lot about George and Mary Ellen. He was a brilliant young lawyer, graduated top of his class from UNC law school, dated all the most eligible debutantes, could have married and gone into politics, but he stuck around Aria, winning all the cases he tried, but never even going for a judgeship. There was gossip that he was queer, maybe. That was how it was whispered about then. It was talked about like something that couldn't happen in good families in the South.

"Then Mary Ellen returned from finishing school, made her debut at the cotillion, dated a couple of guys from the right kind of families, and then pretty much kept to herself. When both their parents died and George and Mary Ellen stayed on at the house, the rumors leaned toward how he loved her more than a sister, whispers about incest. Of course, Mary Ellen was active in several of the charities and founded the garden society so people never said too much out loud. Selena came back into town and somehow became friends with George and Mary Ellen. Selena would visit them in Aria and the three of them spent afternoons at Selena's beach, and people heard them laughing and thought they were having more fun than anyone else, and the rumors got nastier about all of them."

"What do you think was going on?"

"I think they were bright, interesting, mostly ordinary people who felt pushed away by the rest of the town, and they found each other and probably did have more fun than anyone else."

"Thank you."

"My pleasure," he said. "Anything else you want to know?"

"Do you think I can see the ocean from the bedroom?"

"Probably, after you get some of that trash cleared off the dune. But I'm going to send a landscaper friend of mine out to look at it before you cut anything down on the dunes. They're fragile, and you may need to plant some sea grass to hold the sand. That's what Selena would want you to do."

"Are there shells on my beach?"

"Tons of them."

"Can I pick them up and take them in the house?"

"You can do whatever you want with them. Anything else?"

"Where can I get some heavy limb cutters?"

Mike laughed as he started the engine and pulled into traffic. "Lowe's. You'll need a couple of pairs of heavy work gloves, not those cotton gardening things, a good sturdy rake or two, and boxes of heavy trash bags. And that's just for starters."

"How late are they open?"

"Nine or maybe ten."

"Can you tell me how to get there from the hotel?"

"I'll draw you a map." Neither one of them said anything else until they pulled up outside her hotel. He drew a simple map on a sheet of paper and slipped it into the folder with the other real estate papers. "You might want to keep this. It's got some interesting information about the area." He held out his hand and she shook it. "I'll call you before I bring the papers over. I'll make it as early as I can."

"Thanks for everything." Jane got out of the car before Mike could start around to open her door. She stepped back as the car pulled away from the curb, her tired feet tracing the ghost of a clog step Nana had taught her so long ago.

Chapter Four
Entrada (It.) Introduction

1971 – 1973

Sister Helena had most loved the waltz. Jane thought that the nun breathed in three-quarter time: in-two-three, out-two-three. When Jane played on the convent piano during her lessons, Sister stood beside the bench swaying in time to the dance music, the hem of her habit brushing the floor in a graceful swing like a contessa's heavy satin gown making romantic arcs across a marble ballroom floor.

Lessons passed in a whirl of waltzes and endless scales and arpeggios, each repetition underscored by Sister Helena's admonition to slide her thumb swiftly under her hand to begin the next octave. Jane practiced the move even when away from the piano, to the occasional distraction of her classmates. She raced through elementary piano books, taking on twice as many of the little pieces as Sister assigned each week.

Always she returned to the violin. At the end of her Friday violin lesson a few weeks after her thirteenth birthday, Poppa Cohen again approached the subject of Joseph Lamb's new composition. "Tell your father that Mr. Lamb has finished his concertino and we're going to rehearse tomorrow at noon in the music building on campus." Jane handed her teacher folded bills from a wrinkled envelope to pay for her lesson.

She told her father about the rehearsal as soon as she slid into his car waiting for her outside the Cohen house. It was a warm evening near the end of June and her father had been dozing in the driver's seat. He pulled a small appointment book from his pocket.

"Damn." Jane hardly ever heard her father swear. "I've got to show up at a faculty picnic at noon tomorrow. Wait here a minute." He left the car, ran to the house, and rang the bell. Poppa Cohen came to the door. They talked for a few minutes and Jack returned, waving goodbye to the violin teacher. As he started the car, he said, "Mr. Cohen will pick you up at 11:30. I'll meet you at the university if I can get away in time. If not, he'll drop you off at home after the rehearsal, and you'll have to tell me all about the piece."

Saturday morning started off with an argument between Jane and her mother. As he did every morning, Jack had called to waken Jane, then fixed breakfast for both of them. This morning Jane had been out of bed for an hour. She had showered and washed her hair and dressed in jeans and a tee shirt.

As Jane finished her toast, Bridget wandered in from the bedroom. "I thought you were going to a rehearsal with Mr. Cohen."

"I am. He's going to pick me up at 11:30."

"You're not going to wear jeans when Mr. Cohen picks you up."

"Musicians don't care what other people wear." Jane dropped the last of her toast on the plate and carried it to the sink. "Not that you'd know anything about that."

Jack gave Jane a warning look. "What do you think she should wear?" he asked Bridget.

Bridget addressed Jane directly as though Jack hadn't interceded. "I stayed up last night and ironed your white blouse with the Peter Pan collar and laid out your navy pleated skirt. I thought you might want to borrow the pin you gave me for Christmas to wear on the blouse."

"It's not a tea party, Mother." Jane caught the admonition in her father's eyes. "Fine."

Her stomping up the stairs was echoed a few minutes later by the pounding out of scales on the spinet. After every few repetitions, Jane looked out the front door, and she called goodbye to her parents when she saw Poppa Cohen's car pull up at the sidewalk. Her father followed her to the car and reminded them that he would try to join them later at the rehearsal.

Jane carried her teacher's music case and he carried his violin into the rehearsal hall. Mirrors and ballet barres lined three sides of the room, and for a moment she thought enough seats for a full orchestra were set up inside. Poppa Cohen led her to a row of folding chairs. He opened his violin case and asked her to get the new music out of the worn leather folder. Jane pulled out the manuscript paper, marveling at the neat hand-inked notes that raced across the bar lines and climbed and fell from staff lines. As she read the first violin part, hearing its melody sing in her head, she glanced up toward the front of the room and saw Joseph Lamb, the man and his mirror images, reflected like a visual theme and variations.

There was no mistaking his role as conductor, composer and soloist. Several musicians far older waited to ask questions about the manuscripts in their hands. He focused some attention on each one in turn, humming a melody buried in a few measures of the score, shaping sound patterns in the air with his hands as though the music were as substantial as clay that he was driven to model into a new sculpture. Jane could sense that his intense concentration focused inward on the music in his mind, and she felt his impatience to begin the rehearsal and give the music life.

His hands were never still and played out rhythmic patterns against the podium, against the smudged surface of a doorframe as he paused to talk to a clarinetist who mumbled around a reed in his mouth. Most often, Joseph's hands fingered silent passages against his own chest, rising and falling metronomically with his breath. Jane wondered if his fingers pressed out dream songs on the feather keyboard of his pillow as he slept, practicing music not yet played, as a child in the womb might kick gently, rehearsing steps not yet taken. Poppa Cohen took the music from her and moved toward the front of the room to take his seat close to the concert grand piano that waited for Joseph.

A few minutes later, her violin teacher stood and led the small orchestra in the tuning ritual that signaled the start of the musicians' work. Joseph stood at the podium beside the piano, his intense brown eyes closed. He wore a white shirt open at the collar, sleeves rolled up to the elbow. It was warm in the room and a single drop of perspiration trailed from his wavy dark hair to the edge of his jaw line. Almost unconsciously, he wiped away the drop with his right thumb and brushed it against his lower lip as though the salt might wake him from the sweet dream of the music in his head. Jane was in love with his hands with their strong, restless fingers.

When he opened his eyes and spoke, she was surprised by his voice. It was softer and higher pitched than she had expected, a sleepy velvet tenor. He told the musicians that he wanted to hear the first few sections without piano, then he picked up the baton, waved the tempo for the first movement, and coaxed the solo flute into a silver call with which the music opened. Muted violins breathed a shadowed harmony under the flute and Jane watched Joseph hum the piano entrance. She was soon lost in the music, directed as much by his pulling and caressing and shaping and fondling of the music in the air as were the members of the orchestra. She felt physically jarred when he cut off the music mid-measure to question the timpani player about an entrance.

The young percussionist held his drumsticks loosely and continued the hollow tapped heartbeat of the music as he studied the score. "It's on the third beat of measure twenty-seven, sir."

He had played the music as written, and Joseph asked him to mark the entrance two measures later and replace the original entrance measures with rests. As the musician took a pencil from his music stand and corrected the score, Joseph joked with the orchestra about these rehearsals being the chance for the composer to figure out where all his mistakes were. Jane watched his reflection in the mirror. He was sweating more profusely now and wiped the sleeve of his shirt across his forehead. It unsettled her to see drops of perspiration dampening his neck and the hair on his chest. Her father's chest was lightly muscled and brushed sparsely with ginger-colored hairs that were always covered by a clean white cotton undershirt. Jane found herself wanting to tangle her fingers in the thick black curls on Joseph's chest.

She was warm, too, but with a heat that seemed to come from inside her. Her blood had rushed with intense and distinct waves into the bottom of her belly, filling her with a pressure that was at the same time an equally compelling emptiness and hunger. She pressed her thighs more tightly together as though to hold the warmth inside. She had read the "racy" passages in her mother's books and in the paperback novels passed around by her friends and had been aroused by their descriptions of bodice-ripping passion, but never had she experienced this intense breath-taking and irrational desire for a man. Jane lifted her hand to her mouth and brushed her index finger across her lips, wishing it were his finger that touched her; for a brief moment she sucked the salt from her finger, wishing it were his skin she tasted.

Then, without warning, Joseph stopped the music in mid phrase, thanked the orchestra, and told them to take a fifteen-minute break. After the break, they would go back to the beginning of the piece with the piano. Jane was enchanted with the music and had to remind herself that she had heard only the orchestra part, as though she were admiring the elaborate and delicately entwined silver filigree of a Victorian friendship ring before a jeweler had set the stone in place.

During the break, Jane checked the street to see if her father's car was parked there, but the picnic must have gone on longer than he hoped it would. Back in the rehearsal hall, she met Poppa Cohen wiping off his violin, getting ready to continue the rehearsal. "Would you like to meet Joseph Lamb?" he asked. Jane wondered how he could even pose the question so casually. "I don't want to bother him." She wished she were wearing something other than the babyish outfit her mother had chosen for her.

"He won't be bothered." Poppa Cohen held his bow and violin in his right hand and led her by the elbow with his left. Near the podium the conductor had finished a conversation with one of the cellists. From across the room her teacher called, "Giuseppe!" Joseph turned and moved with open arms to embrace the violinist. Then Poppa Cohen stepped back and introduced Jane. "This is Jane Bell, Jack's daughter and one of my favorite students."

Jane felt another rush of warmth when Joseph took her hand. He didn't shake her hand so much as hold it in his as if measuring it, looking for her father there. "I haven't seen your father for years. We were good friends once. I hope he'll be able to hear this work sometime."

"He wanted to come today, but he had a meeting. He told me to tell him all about it when I get home."

"What will you tell him?"

Jane wondered if he would even hear an answer. He seemed to be listening to music she couldn't hear. "I'll tell him that it's amazing. I can't wait to hear it with the piano."

He smiled almost shyly, as much for the music as for her, she thought. Then he released her hand, dismissing her, and turned away, reaching for a cigarette from a pack stashed inside the podium. Poppa Cohen touched Jane's shoulder and nodded for her to go back to her seat, and he began to rearrange the music on his music stand. Jane glanced over her shoulder and saw that Joseph was studying the manuscript on the podium, his head and shoulders wreathed in smoke.

She wished she had thought of something to tell him about the music, some brilliant and perceptive comment about a slight weakness in its structure or how it longed for one more repetition of the melody line, and his eyes would have met hers. He would have taken her hands in his and whispered his thanks. He would say that he had known that there was some tiny emptiness in it and she had shown him what it was. He would take a minute, clouded in smoke, to follow her suggestion and make a few simple but significant revisions in his manuscript. He might even dedicate the piece to her, might ask if she would sit beside him during its premiere, turning the pages she had helped to shape. As she took her seat, Jane almost laughed out loud at the silliness and pretension of her fantasy and contented herself with remembering the warmth of his hand holding hers.

A few minutes later, when all the musicians were in place, Joseph nodded to Poppa Cohen to begin tuning.

Jane watched him move from behind the podium to his place on the piano bench, reminded of seals she had seen who transformed themselves from awkward land mammals into the swiftest swimmers, clearly delighting in an element in which they were completely at home. She heard her grandmother's voice whispering tales of selkies, shape-shifters who donned sealskins to morph from human to sea creature. Abandoning his baton on the podium, he set the tempo for the movement and coaxed in the solo flute with his right hand. He nodded to the violin section, then dove into the waves of the piano part, immersed in the liquid sound.

Jane felt as though she held her breath throughout the piece.

The music moved more intensely, more cohesively as the orchestra became familiar with its shapes and demands and began to sense how the piano line nestled into and played against their parts. Near the end, the solo flute waited for the dying breath of the cellos, then sighed the three-note pattern with which the movement had begun. Joseph brought the piano in with a leaping virtuosic finale that intensified the joy and delightful sense of humor laced throughout the piece.

No one moved, no one seemed to breathe for several seconds. Then Jane heard the gentle tapping on stands and foot beats on the floor by musicians as they signaled their approval of a fellow artist, and she knew she did not want to live in any world but this one.

Poppa Cohen was beside her in a few minutes. Jane longed for a last look at Joseph, but he had disappeared behind a mass of admiring orchestra members who draped themselves around his piano like a heavy stage curtain.

Jane wished Mr. Cohen would tell her more about Joseph, but they spoke little on the way home. She thanked him for the chance to attend the rehearsal and told him how much her father would have enjoyed it. Perhaps he could hear it soon in performance. When they reached her house, she paused for a second before opening the passenger door, then asked the question that had been haunting her for hours. "Does Mr. Lamb teach piano now?"

"He takes a few select students." He shook his head as if reading her mind and disapproving of what he saw there. "But it would take an act of God to get your mother to agree to your taking lessons from him."

"Thank you," Jane whispered. "Thank you, and I'll see you on Friday." She raced up the sidewalk and into the house to tell her parents about the rehearsal. After that, she would practice the piano until she could play the Chopin waltz up to tempo. Then she would work on scheduling "an act of God," which couldn't be much more difficult, Jane thought, than perfecting the Chopin.

***

At her next piano lesson, Jane told Sister Helena about the rehearsal. The nun looked wistful and confessed that she had heard Joseph play years earlier and would never forget his genius. Then she brushed her hand across her eyes as if to rid herself of some unbidden memory. "You know, Jane, Mr. Lamb has led a life of indulgence and dissipation and ought not be a model for a young girl in anything but his performance of music."

"And his creation of music."

"Ah, his creation of music," the nun echoed. "I heard him once, playing jazz improvisations in a club. We were both very young and I had not fully responded to the call of my vocation, but I remember thinking that either God must have touched his hands and mind, or the devil was having some fun there."

"Surely it must have been some heavenly power that influenced those gifts," Jane suggested, almost choking on the sanctimonious tone she had adopted. "He was so polite and controlled and—proper—at the rehearsal. If he has chosen to turn his life around, wouldn't God want us to forgive and forget the past and offer him another chance to use his music? Perhaps to the glory of God?" Jane wondered if this last had been a bit too much even for the nun.

But as if Sister Helena had been drawn too close to memories she dared not examine, she cleared her throat and asked Jane to begin with the Chopin. Jane did, and flew through the waltz with a sureness and lilt and joy that left her teacher breathless.

***

The following week, at the end of her piano lesson, Sister Helena walked with Jane to where Bridget waited. "Mrs. Bell, I was wondering if it would be possible to meet with you and your husband for a moment after Jane's lesson next week."

Bridget stood up and asked if there was something wrong. Jane wondered if her teacher might be sick or planning to retire from teaching. But the nun bowed her head in dismissal after Bridget agreed to bring Jack along. If his schedule didn't permit a meeting then, Bridget would call, and they could find another time to talk.

All week, Jane worried about the unusual conference. Her preoccupation distracted her from her practice, and when the day came for her lesson, she felt that she played everything badly, but Sister Helena made no comments. At the end of the hour, the nun closed Jane's music books on the piano and asked her to bring her parents into the music room. As she approached the bench on which both her parents sat, Jane shrugged to indicate that she still had no hint as to the reason for the meeting. The three of them filed into the little room like children who had been summoned to the principal's office.

Sister Helena stood, a tiny but substantial column of black and white, clasping the music books in her hands. When the Bells were lined up shoulder to shoulder in front of her, she sighed and handed the books to Jane. "I'm sorry to tell you that I can no longer accept Jane as a piano student."

What had Jane done to so alienate her teacher? She had tried her best and Sister Helena had never expressed displeasure with her work. Had she been so upset by Jane's talk about Joseph?

Jack Bell recovered from the announcement first. "Sister, could you tell us why Jane can no longer be your student? Has she done something wrong?"

"Oh my goodness, no," replied the nun, apparently realizing the effect her words had had on the three of them, especially Jane, whose eyes had filled with tears, which made the room seem to shimmer. She reached out to give Jane a hug. "She's done nothing wrong and everything right. I've taught her all I know. Now she needs to find a better teacher who can continue her training. She has a real gift that must not be wasted."

Jane held her breath while her father asked the question, "Who do you think should be her teacher?"

Sister Helena looked into Jane's eyes. "Joseph Lamb is the best. I would send her to him to continue her studies."

Bridget jumped into the discussion. "But surely with his past he couldn't be considered the right teacher for a young girl!"

"He is the best teacher," the sister repeated. "I have it on very good authority that he has been behaving quite respectably. He'll give her more instruction in theory than I can, and Jane is already starting to compose interesting pieces of music that I can't begin to critique the way he could." Jane's father glanced at her. She had kept her compositions a secret from him because the pieces seemed so elementary and silly to her. Jane could not imagine ever showing them to Mr. Lamb.

"She deserves to have the best teacher." Sister Helena spoke with finality, ending the discussion. "Jane, I will see you again next week. It may take a while for Mr. Lamb to be able to fit you into his teaching schedule. I'll do my best until he can take over."

The Bells started to leave the room, and Jane thought she caught the slightest curve of a smile directed at her by the usually serious nun. Sister Helena turned toward the piano, making the sign of the cross as though praying that she had indeed given them the right advice.

Chapter Five
Sage (*Salvia officinalis*)

April 29, 1998

Jane paced in front of the window watching the sunrise. With each step, her room service coffee sloshed like a microcosm of the ocean waves outside. She couldn't sit around and wait until noon for Mike to bring the papers. She had the keys to her house and new tools in her car; she was ready to work.

She called the real estate agency and left a message.

"Mike, this is Jane Bell. I'll be out at the house until five or so. Hope you got in touch with Steve about doing some of the heavy work and trash hauling. Leave a message at the hotel desk about when we can meet to sign the papers." She hoped he would understand.

She had purchased cleaning supplies and a small cooler the night before and bought food on the way to Aria.

This time she was quite prepared for the mailbox in the road and stopped a safe distance from it. Mike had identified her prehistoric bird friend, and she paused for a minute to watch a formation of pelicans fly overhead, letting her mind drift with the waving of the willow branches above her sunroof. She needed a plan of action because there were so many things to do. The path to the house needed to be cleared to make it easier to carry things inside, but that would be a huge job that might take days. A few trips from the car to the house to unload would trample a temporary path so she could start some of the cleaning.

Jane unlocked the padlock on the gate and grabbed her first load of cleaning supplies and a broom from the back of the car. Walking down the path, she was glad she had worn jeans rather than shorts even though it would probably get very warm by afternoon. Brambles and briars tugged at her legs as she made her way to the house.

The house looked even more dilapidated and pathetic in the bright morning light than it had wreathed in the warm glow of last evening's sunset. The front porch roof seemed to slant at a more desperate angle. The one remaining shutter appeared poised to drop to the porch at the slightest breeze, and Jane thought that the piles of leaves and branches and trash in the corners had grown considerably since the night before. Undeterred, she struggled up the tilting steps with her bags and broom, almost stepping on a bouquet of wild flowers and lilacs that lay in front of the door like a pagan offering. As she wondered at the welcoming flowers, a tiny hummingbird dashed across the porch like a fragment tossed from a rainbow, and hovered by an ancient wisteria that splashed purple near the side of the house.

She put down her bags and unlocked the door. She let it stand open to the sunlight and hiked back to her car for the next load. When the car was empty and the porch littered with bags full of equipment for the job ahead of her, Jane marched through the living room and across the kitchen to open the back door. She watched the ocean, stunned as before at its beauty, wishing that the steps over the dune were strong enough to allow her to walk on the beach. But she realized there would be time for shell gathering soon enough; now she had work to do.

On the back porch, she pulled the weathered tarp from the rocking chair, apologizing out loud to the few spiders she dislodged. Both rockers were intact, and the chair looked quite at home when she set it right side up. Jane couldn't resist trying it out. The arms could use some sanding, she realized, and made a mental note to add sandpaper to her next shopping list.

After one more look at the ocean, she went back to the kitchen, leaving the door open behind her. Both the front and back doors had screen doorframes still attached, but the rusted screens were ripped and useless. Jane wondered if that was something she could fix by herself.

She searched through the bags for her heavy work gloves and a box of trash bags and went to work clearing off the shelves and counters in the kitchen. Mike had said that he would try to get Steve to stop by today to take some of the trash away and help with the heavy yard work, and she wanted to have as much trash bagged as possible. She had filled two bags with cracked jars, rusted cans and a few chipped plates from the open shelves when she discovered a delicate little milk pitcher shoved into a corner behind a pile of crispy leaves on the top shelf. As Jane carried it down the steps of the little ladder George Jackson had provided, she remembered the flowers that had been left in front of the door.

She brushed some leaves and scraps of newspaper out of the kitchen sink. The old plumbing replied with an alarming rattle when she tried to turn on the cold water, but brown water gushed out and splashed into the stained porcelain sink. She let it run while she went to the porch to get the bouquet. By the time she returned, the water was clear, and she rinsed off the pitcher, filled it, and arranged the flowers.

Returning to the sink, she tried the hot water faucet. It required all of her strength to budge the handle. Finally, dark water burst forth. Jane let the water flow as she began to sweep piles of trash from the corners to the center of the room. By the time she had accumulated a neat pile on the floor, she was surprised to notice a small cloud of steam hovering over the sink. The little hot water heater in the corner of the kitchen must have turned on when Mike threw the switch on the main power box. That would be a big help when she was ready to begin the real scrubbing.

She dropped a full trash bag in the front yard beyond the edge of the porch railing, reaching out to test the steadiness of the wooden structure. Satisfied, she leaned against it for a minute, closing her eyes and tilting her face to the morning sun.

As she passed through the living room, she stepped across the trash on the floor and stopped in front of the windows that flanked the tiny stone fireplace. The glass on both windows was filthy but intact. The sashes refused to move upwards no matter how hard she struggled.

She marched around to the right side of the house, dragging the stepladder behind her. The shutters covering the fireplace windows on the outside were secured with rusty bolts that eventually yielded to her persistent prodding. The first shutter swung open with a piercing screech, and a bird behind her seemed to answer the noise with its own shriek and flurry of activity in a lilac bush.

Back in the house, Jane was pleased by how much brighter the room looked with the light entering from the unshuttered windows. Diffused as it was, filtered through the grimy panes, it made Jane even more eager to remove the impenetrable pines that shaded the bedroom side of the house. She had purchased a wicked looking chainsaw at Lowe's and would ask Steve to remove the trees as soon as he arrived. Dream or not, Selena had been right about that priority.

Jane righted the square oak table and single chair in the kitchen. She wiped over them with oil soap and water, enjoying the scent that brought back memories of her grandmother and cleaning days. Nana would have loved this little house.

Jane examined the ragged linoleum on the floor, then sighed and armed herself to do battle with the bathroom. If she was going to move in soon, the bathroom would have to be functional. After dumping prodigious quantities of bowl cleaner into the toilet, she began wiping mud and scraps of newspaper and other trash out of the tub. Even streaked with dirt, the footed tub pleased Jane with its graceful curves. The porcelain appeared unblemished. With a good scrubbing and a new rubber stopper for the drain, it would hold Jane and lots of hot water. She discarded the torn and filthy plastic curtain that had ringed the tub, but the oval rod suspended from the ceiling seemed sturdy enough to hold a new shower curtain. The heavy pedestal sink sported a chip and one crack behind the tarnished brass cold-water knob. The linoleum on the floor was in even worse condition than that in the kitchen. Patches of splintery, stained wood showed through ragged edges of the flooring around the base of the tub and sink.

It took only a few minutes to pick up the leaves and scraps of paper that had blown into a corner of the little front bedroom and add them to another overflowing trash bag. Jane opened the window that faced the front porch and placed a rusty expandable screen in the opening. A gentle breeze swept into the room. In the sunlight filtering through the pines, particles of dust swirled and sparkled like would-be snow in an upturned globe.

It was getting hot. Jane glanced at her watch as she pulled a can of soda from the cooler. It was only ten thirty but felt much later. She hoped Steve would be here soon to start work on the trees and haul some of the trash away. If she worked quickly, she might be able to clear out the living room and larger bedroom before she stopped to have lunch.

As she wiped leaves and dirt from the windowsills and mantel in the living room, she thought about what she would be doing if she had stayed in New York. There had been endless rehearsals, practice time by herself and with orchestras around the world. Hours, days, weeks of travel she had grown so tired of. Lost nights stretching into mornings that surprised her with their unexpected arrival as she composed new music, sonatas that had become lullabies that had become a dead silence. Jane wiped the cool metal of the can across her forehead and squeezed her eyes shut to close off the memories. She pulled her mind back to her task in the living room and began to sweep as though fueled by an intense and unspeakable anger.

But she could not stay angry long in this place. Two more bags had been filled and hauled to the yard, and Jane was ready to tackle the larger bedroom. She opened the French doors facing the sea. Heavy wooden shutters to protect the glass in a storm were folded against the outside walls of the house. She leaned for a minute against the doorjamb and closed her eyes again, this time breathing in the perfume of the lilac bushes and the crystal salt scent of the sea. She felt her shoulders relax as the wind from the ocean caressed her face. Cries of seagulls filled the empty places in her mind.

She turned, feeling drugged by the sun, and gazed through heavy-lidded eyes at the double bed that seemed to occupy most of the floor space. The mattress, torn and discolored, leaking stuffing like a fatally wounded animal, would have to be discarded. But the filigreed brass headboard that arched over the head of the bed was exquisite. She hadn't noticed it in the quick tour of the room the night before. In the darkness, the tarnished metal had blended in with the dirty wall behind it.

Jane shuffled her way to the bed, wading through the leaves and crumpled newspapers that littered the mildewed carpeting. She reached out and touched the warm metal. Straight vertical bars were intersected by arched pieces of brass that seemed to mirror the curved limbs of the willow tree outside the French doors. Tiny leaves decorated the ends of a few branches as though the artist who made the headboard had captured the essence of the willow in springtime. A gust of wind sent branches gently clacking against the windows. With leaves swirling around her ankles from the breeze, Jane grabbed the broom and began to reclaim the room. When the trash had been bagged, she carefully wiped out the four drawers and replaced them in the oak dresser.

By the time the final trash bag had been dumped into the yard, it was after noon. Jane was tired and hungry and more than a little annoyed that Steve had not appeared to chop down the scrub pines and haul away the old mattress and trash bags. She pulled off the leather work gloves and washed her face and hands in the warm water from the kitchen sink. Grabbing a container of yogurt and an apple from the cooler on the front porch and gazing at the work she had accomplished, she wandered through the tiny house to the back porch. She left the door to the kitchen open and settled into the oak rocker.

As she rocked and ate her lunch, Jane surveyed the little yard between the house and the dune. Most of the thirty by fifty-foot area was clearly very sandy soil covered with tangles of desert-like vegetation. Heavy vines clung to huge yucca plants and a few ferociously needled cacti. Clumps of sea grasses fought for a hold in the hard ground.

Between the willow to her left and the overgrown path that bisected the yard and led over the dune to the beach, knee-high grass—looking like a field she might have run through as a child in Ohio—glowed a rich emerald green. A circular patch of weeds and wildflowers surrounded a rotten tree stump just outside the shadow of the willow. Jane put her empty carton and plastic spoon on the porch and walked into the yard. She sat on the stump to get a closer look at the grass and nearly toppled over. The stump had been cut from somewhere else and placed on the ground in the middle of what appeared to be overgrown narrow brick walkways.

Jane knelt in the circle and began pulling out weeds and grass that grew over the pattern of bricks, uncovering the mystery of the brick puzzle. She had left her gloves beside the kitchen sink, and soon her hands were raw, nails caked with rich topsoil from the little garden. Her face streaked with earth, she leaned back on her heels for a moment, then stretched out on the ground. She rested on her elbows and gazed up into the lyrical waving of the willow branches.

A brushing sound in the grass separated itself from the delicate touch of wind-caressed branches on the ground. Thinking that the footsteps must belong to Mike or the eagerly awaited Steve, Jane rolled over onto her stomach and peered like a jungle cat through the tall grass at her visitor. The young man who appeared around the corner of the house and stood staring at the ocean was certainly not the real estate agent. It must be Steve. His pickup truck was probably parked near the mailbox.

Jane had a sudden shocking impression that a faun had stolen into her domain by the sea. He moved with a relaxed and easy grace that seemed in stark contrast to the dark intensity of his gaze. The ocean breeze played through curly black hair that reached nearly to the collar of his blue work shirt. A slightly unruly beard kept his mouth a secret and gave him a serious, almost severe expression, but Jane felt that he was smiling at her, that he knew exactly where she was hiding in the grass, that he would continue to stare over her head until she made a move to show herself.

Now she was in the awkward position of having to explain lying in the grass watching him for a few moments, and the longer she lay stretched out on the ground, the more embarrassing the encounter would become. She took a deep breath, stood up, and brushed the dirt from her hands onto her filthy jeans. Meeting new people had become increasingly difficult for her in the past year. She blurted out the first thing that came into her mind. "I'm Jane Bell and I was sitting down working in the garden and then you were there and I thought I saw you change ..."

A look of near panic crossed his face. He must think that he's stumbled upon a mad woman, Jane thought. "I mean I thought you were a faun or something."

At that, he relaxed and Jane was treated to a warm smile. "Deer fawn or myth faun?"

"I've never been sure that they were myth, but yes, the ones with cloven hooves and reed flutes."

He laughed out loud and lifted his right foot, encased in a worn leather loafer. "Ten toes, no hooves." He held out his hand. "Mike suggested that I stop by."

Suddenly, Jane realized she could not take the hand he extended. She brushed past him toward the side of the house feeling foolish and on the verge of tears. "The first thing that needs to be done is cutting down these ugly scrub pines that cover the windows. Can you do that for me?"

He looked bewildered. "Do you have any tools here?"

"I got a chainsaw last night. It's right there on the front porch with a can of gasoline. And there are some safety goggles there, too. The guys at Lowe's said they'd be a good idea."

"I'll get started on it." The shy smile reappeared. "Cut them off at ground level?"

Jane nodded and headed toward the garden again. "There're cold drinks in the cooler. Haven't gotten the refrigerator cleaned up yet. I'll be out by the garden." Still flushed with embarrassment, she rounded the corner and headed toward the garden circle. There was so much to do inside, but she was fascinated with the plot of rich earth defined by the brick pathways. She sat down on the ground again and watched a fat earthworm she had dislodged with her weeding burrow back into the soil.

The metallic barks of the chainsaw startled her. After two short false starts, the machine hummed. A few seconds later the tenor of the mechanical voice shifted as the blade bit into the trunk of the first tree. Jane stared at the corner of the house until she heard the soft brushing thud that meant the tree had been felled. She could not see even the shadow of the work and knew he had begun with the pine closest to the front porch and would work his way to the ocean side of the house.

Jane returned her attention to the garden. The earthworm had completely disappeared. For the next few hours, Jane was lost in her project, pulling out the plants that she assumed were weeds, trimming those which looked like herbs or pretty wildflowers, resetting with her trowel the bricks that had been pushed furthest from their places in the emerging pattern. She found a clump of tangled leggy mint, chewed on a dark green leaf, and wondered about making tea with it. She grew used to the background droning of the chainsaw and the muted thumps of the falling trees.

Movement drew her attention to the corner of the house. He had pulled off his denim shirt and, holding the chainsaw at his right side like a weapon, he wiped his face with his left forearm. Sweat darkened the waistband of his jeans. Jane watched him as he attacked the last standing pine. He was slender, with a build that her mother would have called "wiry." She was fascinated by the play of muscle in his arms as he lifted the heavy metal saw and leaned in to press the blade against the trunk of the tree. The longest branches reached to his chest and bent against his legs, and Jane wondered if some woman tonight would search the dark hair on his chest and belly for tiny wounds to soothe with her fingers and mouth.

He jumped backwards as the tree fell. He moved around the tree and planted a foot on it, raising the chainsaw in the air, a victorious warrior saluting his lady over the body of a vanquished foe. She wondered if he knew all along that she had been watching him from the garden. He laid the chainsaw in the grass, disappeared for a few seconds, and returned wearing the denim shirt, wrinkled, sweat-streaked and unbuttoned. Jane hoped he was ready to load up the trash and the old mattress, and she wanted to ask him about the best way to clear the high grass away from the path and parts of the yard.

Jane stood up and stepped out of the garden circle. He walked toward her, wiping his hands on his jeans, wincing when he scraped a tender section on his palm. When he reached her, Jane realized he was only a few inches taller than her height of five-foot seven. He had seemed taller battling the pine trees. His look was almost sheepish, apologetic. "The pines are down," he told her. Jane wondered if there might be a hint of a brogue under the North Carolina accent that sweetened his voice. "I'll put the chainsaw back on the porch but I'm afraid that's all I have time to do today. Maybe I can come by for a while on Friday."

Were two hours of work all she could expect out of workers in North Carolina? She would ask Mike to recommend someone who would stick to a job until it was finished. "There's still a lot of trash to haul out of here."

He looked at his watch. "I really have to get cleaned up a little. I have to be somewhere at four but I might be able to get back Friday morning if that would help."

Great, Jane thought. He's on an every other day work schedule. "Mike didn't tell me how to pay you," Jane said, exasperated. "Do you get paid by the hour or by the job? I've got my checkbook inside."

At that, he looked still more sheepish. Jane thought she saw a hint of amusement in his gray-green eyes. "I usually get paid by the lesson. Ten dollars for half an hour or twenty for an hour."

"A lesson?"

"Actually, I stopped to talk to you about flute lessons." He wiped his right hand on his shirttail and extended it to Jane. "I guess I never properly introduced myself. I'm McCue Cairncross. I ran into Mike this morning, and he mentioned that you were moving into the Nevin place. He said you told him that you were thinking about taking flute lessons. I've been a fan of yours for years. I heard you play a couple of times." He stood with his hand out, smiling at her. "I thought I would stop by and meet you and see if you were serious about the flute lessons."

"Oh my God," Jane whispered. "I'm so sorry." She wiped her palms on her grimy jeans and took his hand to shake it. Several quarter-sized red spots marked places where the handle of the chainsaw had rubbed his palm. "And I've given you blisters." She held his hand for a moment, letting herself be comfortable with him, not threatened, embarrassed that she had taken advantage of him this afternoon. "I thought you were Steve somebody. Mike said he would send him over to help with the yard and haul trash and when you showed up, I assumed you were Steve."

"That's okay." He took her hand in his, squeezing it for a second to show that he meant it. "You're probably waiting for Steve Humbolt. He's a good guy with a big pickup truck, and he always shows up about three hours after you expect him. But he's a good worker."

"Can I pay you for the work you did?"

"No, but you can forgive me for having to leave right now. I've got to give a lesson at four, and I could use a shower." Both of them smiled at the understatement. "And I would like to help on Friday. Thursdays I teach out of town."

"I couldn't ask you to do that."

"You don't have to. I asked you. I'm glad to see that someone is caring for the place." He looked into her eyes again, and Jane wished that he didn't have to leave. Then she felt herself closing off, willing herself to pull away from him. "I really do have to go," he said, as if he had sensed a change in her. He nodded toward the neater circle of the garden. "You got a lot done this afternoon."

McCue's comment reminded Jane of the stump in the center of the circle. "Do you have time to help me with one thing before you leave?"

"Sure."

"Can we move that rotten stump out of the center of the garden? This probably sounds stupid, but I don't feel like it belongs there."

"Not stupid at all," he said, stepping closer to the cleared circle. "I think I can roll it into the woods. Is it okay if I step in and get it?"

What an odd question, Jane thought. But it was true that she would not want just anyone inside the circle. After one day, she felt possessive about the house, the yard, and especially about this small garden plot.

"Yes, it's all right to go in." There was something quaint about his requesting and her giving him permission to enter the space. "I've never had a garden. I haven't lived in a house with a yard for years. What do you suppose this was for?"

McCue crossed to the stump and tipped it on its side. He began to roll it toward the woods at the side of the property, taking care not to dislodge the bricks. "My guess is that it was an herb garden." He stopped for a moment and pointed to a sprawling, scraggly plant with furry, silvery leaves. "That's sage," he said, and rolled the log into the thick layer of leaves in the shade of the trees. "You really need to talk to Moira and Kaeth if you want to know about gardens." He walked back to the edge of the circle and stood watching Jane as she knelt near the flattened round spot where the stump had been.

"Who are Moira and Kaeth?" Jane asked, not taking her eyes from the ground where her fingers dug at a flat circular stone that lay half buried there. McCue stepped into the garden, knelt at the opposite edge of the stone and began to work to release the other side from the earth that seemed to hold it in a tenacious grip.

"Moira runs the garden store in Aria beside George Jackson's house. And Kaeth is —" He paused for a second, as if at a loss for the right word to describe her. "Kaeth is like her sister. Moira, Kaeth, and I share the building. Part is the store and part is my studio and there are two apartments. Mine is a little one on the first floor, and Kaeth and Moira have the whole second floor."

"Then I might see you there when I go to the store?" Jane hadn't meant to ask the question and felt immediately embarrassed. She began to dig even more aggressively at the ground around the stubborn rock.

It was McCue's turn to seem disconcerted. "We're usually there on different days. Monday, Wednesday, and Friday I teach there and do repairs in the studio while Moira and Kaeth go off to hunt for herbs. Tuesday, Thursday, and Saturday the garden shop is open, and I'm off teaching in the hinterlands. Sundays, it's anybody's guess who you'll find at home." Suddenly, with both of them prying the stone loose, it seemed to jump from the ground, spraying them with dirt. Jane started to lift the stone in her hands, but McCue reached out, put his hands over hers, and replaced the stone in its original position.

He moved his hands away from hers and brushed loose dirt from the surface of the stone. Jane saw the mark he pointed out. She had thought it was a scratch in the stone, but as McCue wiped it clean, she saw that it was an arrow, shaft radiating from the center of the circle. McCue picked up a few pebbles and positioned them near the point of the arrow on the edge of the flat rock.

"What does it mean?" Jane asked.

"I haven't the foggiest idea, but you might want to put it back in the same spot. I think it points due north." He lifted the rock and handed it to Jane. As he tipped it to lift it from the ground, she noticed more marks on the underside of the rock.

"Wait," she said, turning the stone over as McCue held it. She brushed her hand over the surface, and letters scratched into the rock appeared as the loosened dirt was swept away. Jane thought of automatic writing and magic tricks. They read together as the letters spelled out "Faerie Cyrcle."

At the unspoken question in Jane's eyes, McCue shrugged. "Maybe that's what Selena called the garden."

Jane realized she was delaying McCue but couldn't help tracing the uneven letters with her fingers as though she might be able to know the writer from the marks left behind. "Did you know her?"

"I was gone most of the time she lived here—at Eastman and then playing in Atlanta for a couple of years." They started walking past the fallen pines to the front of the house. "She and Moira were close." He nodded to the stone in his hands. "What do you want to do with this?"

"I'm sorry. Put it on the front porch and I'll clean it up."

"And put it back again?"

"I think I'd better. Arrow pointing due north, name up this time. Do you think that would be okay?"

"I'm sure of it. Do you believe in faeries? They might come back if the stone is face up again." He sounded quite serious.

"My grandmother was Irish. She believed in faeries and leprechauns —"

"And fauns?"

"I was right about the flute playing part, wasn't I? Nana believed in all those things." Jane ran her fingers through her hair and looked off toward the ocean. "I don't believe in much of anything anymore."

As McCue placed the stone on the floor of the porch, they heard a voice from the road. "That's Mike, and I think he's got someone with him. Maybe you can get some of the trash moved out."

Jane extended her hand to him. "Thanks so much for your help. I'm really embarrassed about putting you to work like that. Are you sure I can't pay you?"

"Positive. And I'll try to get over for a while on Friday." He had taken her hand in a firm handshake but didn't release it immediately. "Are you interested in flute lessons or did Mike misunderstand?"

"I said it to change the subject, I guess." She withdrew her hand from his.

"That's all right."

"I brought a flute with me, but it was sort of an accident. I don't play music anymore."

"It's really all right."

The real estate agent, carrying a briefcase in one hand and a basket in the other, entered the yard. With him was a red-haired man who looked to Jane like a giant coming out of the woods. He pulled his right hand from the pocket of his tent-like overalls and waved a greeting. McCue returned the wave and headed toward the men.

Mike shook hands with McCue and asked if he had signed up another flute student. "Haven't convinced her yet. Might show up Friday to ask her again." He disappeared through the woods toward the road.

"Good," Mike called after him. "She's going to need a lot of help." He and the giant in overalls had reached Jane at the porch. "Ms. Bell —" Mike caught Jane's look and corrected himself, "Jane, this is Steve Humbolt. Steve, Jane Bell." The red-haired man, at least a foot taller than the real estate agent, placed the index finger of his left hand over his mouth and glanced at Mike as though reminding him of something. Then he extended his huge right hand to Jane.

As Jane reached out to shake hands, Mike said, "Steve is mute so you won't have to worry about any back talk when he's around." Steve's grin broadened as if this were a favorite old joke. Still holding Jane's hand in a grip that was gentle, almost tender in spite of the obvious power in his hands, he flexed the muscles in his left arm in a body builder pose. "He wants me to tell you that he is the strong, silent type," Mike added.

Steve released Jane's hand. He must be fifty, Jane thought, but his clear blue eyes reminded her of a mischievous ten-year-old. Something clicked in her mind. "Can you hear? Do you read lips?" He pointed to his ear and nodded yes. "Did you help Selena build this house?"

His eyes filled with tears that seemed to surprise him as much as it did Jane.

"I'm sorry —"

He held up his hand to stop her and pulled a small rumpled spiral notebook and a tooth-marked pencil from the center pocket of his bib overalls. Finding a blank page about half way through the notebook, he began to write, forming the letters carefully as a child might to prepare an assignment for a favorite teacher. When he was finished, he handed the notebook to Jane. The handwriting seemed familiar. "It was my first house I built," he had written. "I still miss Selena."

Jane handed the notebook back to him. "This is my first real house, too, and I'm so glad that you're here to help me with it." Steve nodded and replaced the book and pencil in his pocket. He turned away for a second and wiped his eyes with a cotton handkerchief.

Mike had stepped onto the porch and was peering around to the side of the house. "Did McCue do that?" he asked, nodding toward the pines that lay like corpses on a battlefield.

"I feel terrible about it, but I thought he was Steve, and I put him to work before I realized he was here about flute lessons."

"Not bad for a musician." Mike looked at the filled trash bags lined up in the yard. "You've been busy. Steve can start with those while we get some papers signed."

Steve had already grabbed four of the stuffed bags, two in each hand. He nodded to her as he carried them in the direction of the road and his truck.

"Is there any place to sign these inside or should we do it here?" Mike asked.

"Actually, we can go into the kitchen and sit at the table."

Mike stepped away from the front door to let her enter. As he followed her inside, she heard an appreciative whistle. "You just might make this work." Both of them paused for a minute, taking in the sunlight that now poured into the house from all four sides.

"It's a start. Nothing is even scrubbed yet."

"I thought by the time I got out here this afternoon you might have had second thoughts."

"You couldn't tear me away from here."

"Then I guess I ought to give this to you now." He handed her the basket he had been carrying. Jane lifted the blue and white checked cloth that covered the wicker basket. Nestled inside, she found a bottle of white wine, several pieces of fruit, and nuts in the shell which reminded her of Christmas treats when she was a child. A corkscrew and nutcracker were tucked in one corner. "It's a little house warming present."

"Thank you," she said, running her fingers over the intricate braiding of the basket handle. "I'll put it in the kitchen." She led him into the room facing the ocean and placed the basket on the table. "I've only got one chair in here right now. But we could bring in the rocker from the porch."

Mike pulled out the chair for her. "You sit down so you can write, and I'll stand." Jane sat, suddenly realizing how tired she was. He laid his briefcase on the counter, opened it, and took out a small stack of papers. "George had these drawn up as agent for the estate. The arrangement is a bit different from the usual contract."

"Different in what way?"

"Well, he's written it up as a rent with option to buy, but there's no specific purchase price, just the rent we had agreed on. The final clause states that details will be discussed at a later date."

"Is that a problem?"

"Not to me. I talked with my boss about it, and he was a little leery. Just because he wanted to protect your interests," he added. "But everyone around here knows and respects George Jackson, and they know how he feels about the property. It's clear from what you've already done how you feel about it."

Jane felt herself blushing as though Mike had revealed that he knew about a secret crush she had on someone. "I love it. Let's sign the papers."

He spread them out in front of her, and she read through them. "He says that I'll be reimbursed for repairs? I wouldn't ask him to do that. This is the most exciting thing I've done in years."

"Well, keep the receipts. I have a feeling this could add up to lots of money." He handed her a pen with the company logo and pointed to blank spaces at the bottom of the last page on both copies of the contract. Jane signed her name and gazed out the open door toward the ocean while Mike stacked the papers, putting one set in his briefcase and neatly arranging the other on the oak table. The sun was nearing the horizon, and Jane held her breath for a moment, lost in the intense blue of the sky, which the sun had streaked with peach and lavender clouds. "It's different tonight."

"It's different every night." Mike walked to the doorway and leaned against the jamb. Jane crossed to his side. Both watched as four pelicans flew by in formation. Suspended on an invisible air stream, they played connect-the-dots with the first stars appearing in the evening sky. He turned to her. "I've got to get home. Steve will be here for a little while. Is there anything you need?"

"I think I'm all set. And thanks again for the basket. It makes me feel like I'm at home." She turned to walk back into the kitchen and tripped on the ragged edge of the linoleum. Mike caught her before she fell.

"What are you going to do about the flooring?"

"I haven't the vaguest idea what I should do with it."

Mike bent down and tugged at a section near the baseboard. The stained covering broke off in a jagged piece in his hand. "This is shot, but you've got an oak floor under here." He stood up and brushed his hands on his slacks. "Talk to Steve about ripping up the linoleum and refinishing the wood. I mean, it's just an idea, but it's what I would do."

"That sounds wonderful. But I don't need Steve to do it. I can rip it out myself."

The agent shook his head. "That's a huge job. Did you get a pair of work gloves?" Jane realized he was focusing on her hands, raw and dirty from her hours in the garden. She nodded to the heavy leather gloves beside the sink. He raised his eyebrows but didn't say anything.

Both of them started toward the living room. "Everything seems to work? Electricity, plumbing?"

"I even have hot water. The refrigerator works but it's pretty rusty inside. Burners work on the stove, but I haven't done any baking yet so the oven is still a mystery."

"Call me when your first apple pie is ready. Or peach pie. You can't beat the peaches here."

"It's a deal." They had reached the front porch and Jane extended her hand. Mike shook it then reached into his coat pocket. "Here's my card." He took out another company pen and wrote on the back. "This is my number at home if you have any questions or need anything. Marci said to tell you to call if she can help. She knows the best places to shop for whatever you need."

The trash bags had been cleared away from the yard. Mike nodded a greeting as Steve passed by the porch dragging a fallen pine in each huge hand. "I've scheduled inspections on Thursday afternoon for plumbing, electricity and the roof. I hope that's okay with you. Couldn't reach you by phone, and I thought you'd want them taken care of as soon as possible."

"That's great. Thanks again for the basket and for bringing the papers out. I just had to get started."

"I guess I would have been surprised if you had waited. But you don't have to finish it in one day. Take some time to relax and enjoy it."

"I will." Jane spotted the mysterious stone. "I did spend some time in the garden this afternoon."

"Relaxing?"

"Mostly trying to *find* the garden. But I do want to get to the beach as soon as I can."

"That's the other thing I wanted to tell you. I can give you the name of a good local contractor to fix the steps to the beach and anything else that needs to be done, but Steve is just as good a carpenter as anyone you'll find around here."

"I'd like to have Steve's help." As she mentioned his name, he rounded the corner of the house, overalls flapping slightly in the breeze. He reminded Jane of the tall ships she had seen in the New York harbor, mammoth but blessed with an undeniable grace.

"Steve," Mike called to him. "Would you be interested in fixing the steps to the beach and doing some other things around the house?"

His face had been turned away from them and both Mike and Jane were surprised when he took several seconds to face them. His eyes were intensely sad, their blue darkened by several shades. Jane moved down the steps to the yard and put her hand on his arm. "Are you all right?"

Steve dropped the trunks of the pines he had been dragging and breathed a sigh so deep it might have been comical if it hadn't been so heartfelt. He reached into the pocket of his overalls for the little spiral notebook and opened it to the page he had started with their earlier conversation. "Fine." The pencil hovered over the lined page. "I had put her out of my mind & now she is back & it hurts."

"I'm sorry," Jane said, her hand still resting on his arm. "I can find someone else to do the work."

He reached out and patted her hand. Jane noticed that beside his hand, hers, large for a woman's hand with an enviable reach at the keyboard, looked like a child's. Then he finished writing. "I would like to help. Working on this house, this garden, heals us."

Jane removed her hand from his arm. She experienced the familiar sensation of cutting herself off from human contact, snipping some vital and precious connection with very sharp blades, of wanting the empty darkness inside that had become safe for her. She didn't even know who he meant by "us," but she didn't want it to include her. "I don't need to be healed. I just want to get it fixed up so I can move in." Jane heard and hated the hardness in her voice. It was as though her sound echoed against the brittle shell she had erected around herself.

Steve looked into her eyes, then back at the paper in his hand. He underlined the sentence, "I would like to help." Then added, "Don't be angry with me."

"I'm not."

Steve turned to the next page in his notebook and waved to Mike, who had retreated to the far corner of the porch, giving them some privacy for their conversation. When the real estate agent joined them in the yard, Steve wrote, "Finishing project for Mrs. Daley —"

"How is her husband doing?"

Steve shook his head slowly in answer. "Not good," he wrote. "Made screened porch with ramp so Mrs. can push him there in wheelchair."

"Don Daley was the town pharmacist for as long as I can remember," Mike explained to Jane. "Just about everybody owed him money at one time or another. Whatever you needed when you or your kids were sick, Don got for you. Samples whenever he could wheedle them from the drug reps. Regular bottles and tubes when that was what he had. Seemed to know who had the money to pay for it and who didn't. And when you didn't have it, Don would point to his big bald head and say he was keeping tabs right there and when you had the money send it over."

Mike looked back to where Steve was writing on his tablet.

"Should be finished there Fri. Can pick up lumber & start steps Mon. OK?"

"That would be great," Jane said. "But I don't know if I can wait that long to go down to the beach."

"Got to get started on your seashell collection," Mike said. "That reminds me. I forgot to tell you that I talked to the landscaper. He'll be over sometime Friday to look at the dune and beach and give you some advice. If you need to get down there before then, don't take the steps. If they're as weak as they look, one is sure to give way and you'll break an ankle or a leg and nobody's likely to hear you screaming for a while. Put on jeans and sneakers or duck boots and go carefully down the overgrown places near the woods. That will give you something to hang onto on the way up and down. Okay?"

"Okay." The idea of walking on the beach was exciting, but she was beginning to realize how tired she was from cleaning and gardening all day. She felt her energy ebbing with the remaining daylight.

Mike glanced at his watch. "I've got to get out of here. I promised Marci I'd go along to the PTA meeting. The junior high band is playing." He shook Jane's hand again. "I'll be in touch.

And do call if you need anything. If I can't get you at the hotel, I'll figure that you're working out here." He shook Steve's hand. "Glad you're going to be helping. Please tell the Daleys that I send my best." He turned and walked up the path toward the road.

Steve wrote again in his notebook. "Good man." He nodded toward Mike's retreating figure. "Will take last trees to truck. Anything else?"

"I couldn't carry the old mattress from the bedroom. If we get that out, I can order a new one." Steve nodded as he pushed the notebook back into the center pocket of the overalls. He lifted the trees and started toward his truck. They heard the sound of flying gravel as Mike's Lincoln peeled off down the road. Jane moved around to the side of the house. The tree outlines were fainter in the waning light. The house looked a bit naked and Jane knew it needed some flowers around the foundation to dress it up. She took a few more steps toward the ocean side and was pleased to see how neat the garden circle looked in the still shaggy yard.

Jane heard Steve mounting the steps to the porch and she returned to the front of the house. He stood in the doorway, one hand on either side of the opening, his head bent forward. Dwarfed by his huge body, the doorway seemed like the entrance to a child's dollhouse. He leaned into it as though encountering a force field he needed to break through to get inside. Jane wasn't sure whether the force came from the house itself, or from the man who had so steeled himself from thinking about and remembering this place that he had to gather all his energy to acknowledge and enter it.

Jane stepped up to the porch and touched his left hand. He jumped, startled at the contact, then took her hand in his and followed her into the house.

In the living room, he relaxed and released her hand. Even though the sun had set, the room was brighter, more hopeful than it had been. Steve nodded toward the windows flanking the fireplace. "Yes," Jane said, "I got the shutters open, but it wasn't easy. Will you check the fireplace and chimney for me sometime in case I want to build a fire?"

Notebook in hand again, Steve wrote, "Sure & will bring back pine cut for firewood. Chilly some nights." Both of them heard the old refrigerator whir to life in the next room. "Still working????"

"It seems to run, but it's pretty grizzly inside. I don't know if it will ever come clean. It's really rusty." Grizzly. She hadn't thought of that expression for years. Her grandmother had used it to describe something incredibly dirty, almost beyond redemption.

"If 2 grizzly, try Sears. For mattress 2." He paused for a second, then added, "If can afford new 1."

"Good idea. I think there's money for that in the budget."

They walked into the kitchen and Jane noticed the jagged edge of the linoleum where Mike had pulled a piece away. The hole looked like some hungry monster had chomped on the flooring and found it too nasty even for his taste. "Mike says there's a good oak floor under here. Do you think I could tear out the old flooring?"

Steve moved his hands apart in a smooth horizontal gesture. Did she want to put down new linoleum?

"I'd like to refinish the wood underneath. Just shine up the oak."

"Good oak floors everywhere," Steve penciled. "You'd need help & I'd be glad 2. Get rid of fridge 1st."

"OK, but the mattress goes now." As Steve moved toward the bedroom door, Jane again had the feeling that he pushed his body against a physical barrier to reach the side of the bed, as though the air in the room had become a substance as dense as his memories of Selena. When he stood beside the mattress, he reached out to touch the headboard and Jane suddenly pictured two bodies naked on the white-sheeted bed. The man, immense and powerful, cradled a woman who looked like a china doll in his arms. His face was hidden in her long auburn hair and with one finger he traced the line of her shoulder, her slender arm, her breast, with the same tenderness and sense of wonder that Steve caressed the filigree of the headboard.

He pulled his hand away and looked at it as though his thoughts might have left a residue on his palm like the dust from a butterfly's wing in a child's hand. Now there was just the ruined mattress on the bed, and he swung it to his shoulder.

Jane stepped aside to let him pass out of the room. She heard him cross the porch and go down the steps. She stood in the room, holding her breath, trying to find again the figures she had seen. But of course she had imagined them. She was tired and there were shadows playing in the room, tossed there by the willow branches outside waving in the last light of the day. She pulled the French doors closed and locked them.

She had the back door locked when Steve came into the house carrying most of the tools from the front porch. "Let's put them in the little room for now." In her exhaustion, she had forgotten about cleaning up. She followed him to the door of the room. On his way out, he carefully tore an inch wide scrap from one of the few remaining strips of rose bud sprigged wallpaper on the wall. He held it up and gestured questioningly around the room. "I'll have to steam the scraps of wallpaper off," she said, proud that she knew that much from her parents' frequent remodeling ventures. "And then I think I'll paint it white." She laughed. "My husband always said my solution to any decorating problem was to paint it white."

Steve started to reach for his tablet and pencil but Jane anticipated his question. "I'm divorced." She started down the steps. "I'll help you get the rest of the things off the porch."

It took only one more trip to bring the tools inside. When Steve nodded to the cooler, Jane felt bad that she hadn't offered him anything to drink. "Would you like a can of soda or something?" He shook his head and pointed his thumbs in opposite directions. Did she want the cooler left here or taken to the car? "God, I'm sorry. I'm so tired I'm not thinking. Let's put it in my car and I can fill it up for tomorrow."

She pulled her key ring from her pocket and opened the empty frame of the screen door. Tattered and rusted scraps of screen hung from the bottom edge of the opening. As she reached in to lock the door, Steve tapped her on the shoulder, raised his hand in a "Wait" gesture, and opened the notebook. "Want me 2 fix screens at home & bring back? Will get buggy without them."

"That would be great." Jane pushed the front door open again. "Front and back?" Steve nodded and crossed through the kitchen to remove the screen door frame. He carried it under his arm, tackled the front screen door and moved them to his truck while Jane locked the door. He reappeared a minute later, picked up the cooler as easily as if it had been a quart of milk, then set it down a foot away. Jane realized he had seen the flat round stone she had removed from the center of the garden, and now knew why his handwriting had seemed familiar. He had scratched those letters into the stone. He nodded in the direction of the garden.

"I'm going to clean it up and put it back exactly where I found it," she said.

Steve nodded his approval, picked up the cooler again and headed for the path to the road. Jane looked back once before she entered the stretch of woods between the house and the road. Her little house looked sturdy in the near darkness. The roof with its ragged chimney appeared solid against the backdrop of shifting clouds that drifted over the stars, winking them on and off.

She turned toward the path and walked into the woods, jumping when an owl hooted nearby. Steve stood at the back of her Jeep, tablet and pencil in hand. The cooler had been stowed in the back and the door closed. He held a piece of paper out to her. She took it, then leaned closer to read what he was writing on another piece of paper still in the notebook. It was almost too dark to see. "My phone #."

"You can use the telephone?" Jane folded the loose piece of paper and slipped it into her pocket.

"Voice relay. Operator types your words to me, I type back, she talks to you. Works pretty well."

"Sounds like a good system. Thank you for your help. And I didn't ask how you would like to be paid."

He flipped to a page near the back of the notebook where he had written "Jane's house" at the top of the page. On the next line were the date and hours he had worked. Returning to the last page he had been writing on, he continued. "Keep hrs here. $10/hr for everything. Little high for hauling, real cheap for carpentry." Compared to New York City prices it sounded "real cheap" to Jane for any kind of work. She shook Steve's hand.

"Do you want me to pay you now?"

The little pencil scratched at the paper, its point dull. "Friday's usually payday. We'll put this on next week, 1st full week. Checks or cash, no credit cards." His broad face was serious but the crinkles at the corners of his eyes deepened with the joke. He started to put the paper away, then wrote one more message. "Wait till I get here for heavy stuff."

"Okay." She would wait if she could. There was plenty of regular cleaning to tackle, and she was too tired right now to think about all that needed to be done. "We'll make the house beautiful again," she said, not knowing if she was talking to Steve or herself. He nodded and walked to the cab of his rusted pickup truck. He turned away from her to check that the trees and trash and mattress were tightly secured, then waved and got inside the cab. He turned his headlights on, and Jane knew he wouldn't leave until she had started her car and headed down the road toward the hotel.

She fought her exhaustion every minute of the short ride to the hotel. In the parking lot, she opened the back of the Jeep to take the cooler upstairs. No way, she thought. She checked inside. Two cans, a banana and a container of yogurt floated in a shallow pool with a few remaining ice cubes. Jane grabbed the banana and yogurt, locked the car, and headed into the hotel.

Back in her room, she thought she would take a bath and order dinner from room service. She stripped off her clothes, and realizing how hungry she was, ate her yogurt with a plastic spoon while the bathtub filled. Jane slid into the water and rested her head on the back of the tub, cold porcelain feeling like the softest feather pillow. She woke hours later shivering in the tepid water.

Jane staggered into bed while the water drained from the tub. She wrapped herself in the covers and fell into a deep and dreamless sleep. In the morning, she woke to the sound of a gentle rain and the roar of a sullen and petulant sea.

Chapter Six
Afflackernd (G.) Flaring Up, Flickering, Wavering

1973 – 1976

The evening after Sister Helena suggested that Jane study with Mr. Lamb, Jane paced beside her father while he phoned his friend, the fingers of her left hand tightly crossed for good luck. She listened as he apologized for missing the rehearsal of the concertino and reminisced about acquaintances and music. Finally, her father waved Jane into a seat and approached the subject of her piano lessons.

Jane could tell that Mr. Lamb hesitated. She closed her eyes and remembered the arc her silver dollar had made as it sailed out her bedroom window the night before, catching the glow from the streetlight and winking out like a shooting star. The Good Folk could do anything, Nana had told her, but it was always a trade. It always cost you something. Jane wondered if they could make her dream of studying with Mr. Lamb come true, and she had bet her silver dollar on it.

Her father told Mr. Lamb about her progress in piano and violin, and she was embarrassed because it must sound so unremarkable to the renowned teacher. She wondered why she had let herself hope he might accept her as a student. Jane began pacing again while Jack listened for several minutes. When her father said, "If you can't take her right now, who would you suggest?" Jane walked to the spinet, closed the music books on it, and tossed the stack of music on the floor. She left the room as her father said goodbye and hung up the phone.

She closed the door at the bottom of the stairs with a force just short of a slam and stormed up the steps to her bedroom.

She flopped down on the bed at the same time her father knocked on the door.

"Jane, can we talk about this?" The door gently creaked open.

"There's nothing to talk about." From her bed, she watched as her father climbed the stairs.

"May I sit down?" he asked. Jane rolled to one side to make room for him. "It sounds like he's got more students than he wants right now, but he suggested some good people who might be taking on new pupils. He even said he'd call a friend of his at Case if we want him to."

"I'll stay with Sister Helena. Or maybe I'll just quit." She had said the word without thinking. Her hands closed in tight fists. The thought of life without the piano hit her with the strength of a physical blow.

"Why don't you get out your violin and work on the Bach sonata for a while? You were making progress last night."

"I can't right now. I've got homework."

Jack kissed her on the head as though she were still five years old. "I understand. But why don't you come pick up your music before your mother sees it." They walked together down the stairs.

After she put her music back on the piano, she went into the kitchen where her mother was pouring gelatin into a copper mold. Jane sat at the table, kicking her foot back and forth, brushing gently but insistently against the leg of the table, waiting for her mother to ask her what was wrong. She didn't know what her mother's reaction would be, probably relief whether she admitted it or not. Jane wanted someone to be angry with, and in the past few months, that person had most often been her mother.

After a few minutes, her mother set the plastic bowl with half a cup of still liquid gelatin and a large spoon in front of Jane. "Cherry Jell-o soup," she said. "Want to tell me what's wrong?"

"Mr. Lamb can't take any more students right now." Nana had always saved some of the mixture for her and so did her mother. Comfort food. "He probably wouldn't want to teach me anyway."

"Can he take you later on?"

"I don't know." Jane drank some of the sweet, thick liquid.

"I know you're disappointed —"

Jane stood up and pushed back her chair with such force that it teetered on its back legs. She gasped and righted it before it could fall. More of Nana's superstition: it was a bad omen if a chair fell when a person stood up. But her mother was right. Nana's stories were nonsense, malarkey. "You're probably glad he's not going to be my teacher. It wouldn't surprise me if you'd called him and told him not to take me as a student."

"Jane, you know I wouldn't do that."

"What do you have against him anyway?" Jane carried the bowl and spoon to the counter and poured the rest of the gelatin into the sink. "He and Dad are friends. He was Dad's teacher."

"Joseph Lamb has a reputation for drunkenness and carousing," her mother began.

"Carousing? I didn't know that anyone 'caroused' anymore. That's something out of English Lit class."

Her mother lowered her voice, as if revealing a secret she didn't want overheard. "He's been involved with drugs and has been in jail more than once."

"He's been arrested several times. I've heard all about it."

"From whom?" her mother asked.

"From kids at youth symphony and lots of people. It's not a big deal."

"It's a big deal to me when my daughter wants to start going to his house for piano lessons."

"Piano lessons." Jane turned on the water and washed the last of the gelatin down the sink. "That's all I want is piano lessons from him." The sound of the water almost drowned out her sobs.

Jane's mother reached out and hugged her. "I know how excited you were about the idea of studying with Mr. Lamb. Maybe in a couple of months he'll have an opening."

"He probably doesn't want to take me."

"I'm sure it's not that."

Jane pulled away but took a tissue her mother offered. "I'm going to read some history and go to bed." She said goodnight to her father and walked upstairs, where she cried herself to sleep as though she were three instead of thirteen.

* * *

The next day, Jane's mother met her at the door after school. "Mr. Lamb called. He said he was able to rearrange his schedule to take you for a half hour lesson."

Had the Good Folk worked their magic as Nana said they could? Jane dropped her schoolbooks, grabbed her mother's hands, and danced her around in a circle. "When do I start?"

"Tomorrow at 4:30."

"Tomorrow? That doesn't give me any time to practice!"

"I think you've been practicing for this for years, but if you don't want to go, you can call him and tell him you've changed your mind."

Still holding her mother's hands, Jane led her to her father's big chair. "Tell me," Jane began, half teasing, half genuinely curious. "Did he sound like a monster?"

"No, he didn't sound like a monster. Actually, he sounded quite charming."

"I told you! Now tell me exactly what he said."

"I don't remember exactly. He said that he had moved some students' lessons and had half an hour open at 4:30. You're supposed to bring whatever piece you're working on, and he'll decide if he can take you as a regular student."

Jane hugged her mother. "I've got to practice, and I don't know what to play for him! Is it all right if I call Dad?"

"Sure, but what about your homework?"

"I don't have very much—just a history quiz." Jane dashed for the phone.

After Jane talked to her father, she began to page through a book of Chopin waltzes her father had suggested she play for Mr. Lamb, hearing the melodies in her head, choosing the one that might most impress her new teacher. She decided on the Waltz in B Minor. It was a favorite of Sister Helena's and one of the first Jane had learned. Now she practiced it over and over, trying to hear it as Mr. Lamb would. She took a break for dinner. Her mother shook her head, and her father smiled as Jane's fingers ran through the waltz's rhythmic patterns on the edge of the tablecloth.

After she had practiced for another hour after dinner, her father sat down beside her on the piano bench. "Your mother says you have a history test tomorrow."

"It's not a big deal, not a midterm or anything. And I have a study hall before the test."

"She's worried that you'll be spending even less time on your homework if you're studying with Mr. Lamb. Let her quiz you on the history and I'll wake you up early so you can go over the music again." He kissed his daughter on the forehead. "The waltz sounds wonderful."

"I want it to be perfect. Promise you'll wake me?"

"I promise. Now go tell your mother everything you know about the Ottoman Empire. And remember, Mr. Lamb isn't expecting a performance. He just wants to get an idea of how well you play."

"Call me really early." Jane grabbed her history notebook and carried it into the den.

Jack had not needed to wake Jane in the morning. The sky was still pink with dawn when the soft sounds of the waltz chased night from the little house.

The day at school passed both too slowly and too fast for Jane. She hurried home, convinced that she could not recall any of the waltz which she had known from memory for months. After racing through the piece once more, she brushed her long dark hair, applied pale pink lipstick, then wiped it off hoping to look more like a serious music student. She checked Mr. Lamb's address twice in the telephone book, grabbed the music books from the top of the piano, and told her mother that she was ready to go.

Mr. Lamb's house was only a few blocks away, walking distance in good weather, Jane thought, and they arrived several minutes early. Jane loved the neat white house with its screened porch, scalloped awning, and maple tree. "Looks safe enough," she joked to her mother.

"I believe that's what Hansel said to Gretel when they found the gingerbread cottage. Mr. Lamb said you should go inside if he was still teaching. Have a good lesson." She pulled a crisp white envelope from her wallet, opened it, and handed Jane a check made out to Joseph Lamb. "I have a few things to get at the store, but I'll be back in half an hour." Jane thanked her mother and, clutching her music books, walked to the door.

From the enclosed porch, she could hear the final measures of a Mozart sonata being played inside, then gentle laughter and singing and shaping of the melody that she knew came from Mr. Lamb. Jane sat on a small sofa and listened as the measures were repeated, this time by the sure hand of the teacher. When the student played again, it was with a new grasp of the structure of the music. The allegro sections were livelier, melody lines delineated. Jane's grip on the books relaxed. Soon the front door opened and a boy of about fifteen walked onto the porch. "Practice the last movement slowly this week. And good luck with your soccer game tonight." Mr. Lamb stood in the doorway. "Come in, Jane."

In front of the picture window, a black grand piano, its lid closed and draped with a tapestry throw, dominated the small living room. Stacks of music and manila folders were piled on it. Two gooseneck desk lamps were positioned to throw a warm light on the music. The piano was placed so Mr. Lamb could watch a student's hands from the overstuffed chair that faced the front door. Beside the chair, a table held a pipe rack, tobacco, and books—novels, books on music theory, several dictionaries. To Jane's left as she entered the room, an archway led to a dining area with a round table, also covered with books and papers. Beyond the sofa, a small hallway led to the back of the house.

"What are you going to play?"

Jane wished that she could sit for a while listening to him play while she breathed in the mystery of this world anchored by the ebony piano and perfumed with the sweet cherry of pipe tobacco. "The Chopin B Minor waltz."

"Good," he said, sitting in the chair. "Play for me."

Jane sat on the piano bench, the unopened music book in front of her. She closed her eyes for a second and found the melody in her mind. She played the piece from memory and after the last chord had faded, sat afraid to look at Mr. Lamb, sure that his silence meant that she had not played well enough to be a student of his. She turned to him. He sat with his eyes closed, and she wondered if she should apologize and leave.

"Go back to the key change in the music. This section was marked *dolce*. Play it sweetly." She began to play again. Before she had played a dozen measures, he was standing beside her at the piano. "Open the music." She found the third page of the waltz. "Here." He pointed to the section she had just played. "Lift your right hand here at the end of the phrase." He hummed along with the music. She played the few notes. "Again." This time he reached out and lifted her hand from the keyboard as she reached the end of the phrase. "Then use the weight of your hand to begin the next phrase." He pressed her fingers into the keys. "Try it."

She replayed the few measures of the waltz, capturing the rise and fall of her hand to sculpt the phrase, but she stopped after a few measures, disturbed by the disruption she felt in the line of the music. Mr. Lamb smiled and sat on the bench beside her. "Now use the pedal to connect the ending note of this phrase to the next one." She was distracted for a moment by his closeness to her on the bench. She moved to the left to give him room and concentrated on his foot on the pedal. The phrase sighed away but remained connected to its next repetition. "Again," he said, moving away from the center of the keyboard but staying on the bench with her.

This time the *dolce* section was alive, breathing, molded by the lift and weight of her hands. When she had played to the end, Mr. Lamb stared at her still hands as though searching for her future there. Jane was suddenly embarrassed by her ragged, bitten fingernails, and hoped he hadn't noticed. She folded her hands in her lap. "May I try it once more?" she asked.

He stood up from the bench. "Of course." Mr. Lamb wandered to the front door and gazed out the window. Jane was quiet for a moment at the piano, listening to the new phrasing in her head, amazed by the contrasts it suggested for the rest of the piece. She was smiling, excited, when she began the waltz again. This time there were mistakes, wrong notes she had not played the first time through, but the music was textured with the discoveries she had made, her approach to the entire waltz colored by new ideas he had given her for the final section. The waltz was alive with a new sense of movement.

When the last note had sounded, Jane spoke softly, as much to herself as to Mr. Lamb. "It's still not right. The second section should be more legato so the staccato notes are even more fun."

The teacher nodded and began calling out the names of scales and arpeggios for her to play. "C minor Dorian."

"I don't know what that means. I haven't had much theory." Now he would surely refuse to accept her as a student.

"Play this," he said, opening a book of music from the top of the piano. It was a Beethoven bagatelle she had never played. Halfway through the piece, he stopped her. "Bring out the melody in the left hand."

She went back a few measures and was lost in the piece, entranced with the interplay of the musical lines. Both she and her teacher seemed surprised when Mr. Lamb's next student entered the room and sat at the round table to wait for his lesson.

"Would you like to work on this for next week?" Mr. Lamb asked, gesturing to the bagatelle.

"You'll really take me as a student?"

"Of course. Same time next week." He smiled at her surprise. "You have a few bad habits, but you've been taught well. You'll probably feel like you're going backwards for a while. I'm going to give you some Dohnanyi exercises to strengthen your hands. Have you worked on the Czerny books?"

Jane said that she had, and Mr. Lamb asked her to bring them to her next lesson. She handed him the check and picked up the book of Chopin waltzes and Mr. Lamb's Beethoven. "Thank you very much. I'll work on the pedal in the waltz." Jane held the music tightly to her chest as she left the house. She could smell the faint warm phantom of pipe smoke that haunted the pages, and she felt that something of him went home with her.

Her mother was waiting in the car. "He's wonderful!" Jane said, sliding onto the passenger seat. "And a perfect gentleman."

Jane was soon at her piano reexamining the Chopin waltz, hearing in it a dozen new possibilities for interpretation. She had rummaged through her music for the Czerny books, had looked up "Dorian" in her father's music dictionary, and was beginning to savor the complexities of the Beethoven bagatelle which she had saved for last, like a much-anticipated dessert.

"How was your lesson?" Her father asked during a pause in her practicing.

"I didn't hear you come home." Jane gave him a quick hug from the piano bench. "He's going to take me as a student every week. I felt really stupid because I didn't know the theory things."

"That doesn't mean you're stupid, just that you have a lot to learn."

"I know, but I felt that way. He helped me with phrasing in the waltz, and he wants me to start working on a Beethoven bagatelle."

"Do you want to play it for me? Your mother says we have about ten minutes until dinner is ready."

"No." Jane's quick reply seemed to surprise both of them. After other lessons, they would sit, Jane at the piano, Jack in his easy chair, while Jane took hesitant first steps with the new music, both of them enjoying the discoveries she made. Jack became involved in the music in a way he would never permit himself when she played the violin. "I need to work on it by myself first."

"Sure. Don't forget your art project is due tomorrow."

"I could use some help with it," Jane said.

"We'll work on it after dinner."

"Great." Jane turned back to the music as her father left the room. She could spend some time with her father and finish the art assignment. There would still be a few hours left for the piano—and, she reminded herself, the violin. She could not explain why the music was suddenly not just hers, but something to share with her teacher. Jane was filled with thoughts of her first lesson with Mr. Lamb, thoughts she didn't want to share as she had shared experiences from her lessons at the convent with Sister Helena. She turned away from the memory of how much he had heard in her playing, of his voice shaping the melody lines for her, of their closeness on the piano bench, recent memories tucked in the back of her mind like violets pressed between the pages of a novel.

* * *

For the next several years, Jane's life began a tightening spiral, music at its core. Time away from music moved at a lethargic tempo, as though meted out under the spell of a rusty metronome. Hours spent practicing or playing for Mr. Lamb vanished at a pace that left her breathless and hungry for more. She kept up with her schoolwork, reminded by her parents that even music schools demanded good grades. Late one night, she heard her parents talking Her mother worried that Jane had few friends her own age, and so Jane spent some afternoons and weekends with classmates who were also musicians. Her mother was thrilled when Jane offered to accompany the school musical. She still took weekly violin lessons and moved to the first chair in the violin section of the youth symphony. She was working with Papa Cohen on a solo piece when he suggested, "Why don't you take the piano part along to your lesson and ask Mr. Lamb to play it with you? He could help you with the phrasing."

"I couldn't do that! It would be like —" Jane sought for a comparison. "Like asking Picasso to frame a picture that I had painted."

Her teacher laughed. "Ask him at your next lesson. He would love that analogy. Now play this *presto* section again and listen to the piano accompaniment underneath."

Jane asked Mr. Lamb, hesitantly, at the end of her next lesson and he had said, "Of course. Bring your violin." After that day, Jane's lesson often ended with a romp, an entanglement, a musical seduction as the violin and piano taunted and teased each other in the air of Mr. Lamb's living room. When her violin was left at home, the lesson expanded to include the theory of music. Mr. Lamb moved his next student to another day and Jane's lesson stretched to an hour; even then she was amazed by how quickly the time passed.

One afternoon, near the end of her sophomore year, Jane went to her piano lesson carrying stacks of extra music and her violin. Her teacher raised his eyebrows in question as she laid some of the music on the sofa and carried the rest to the piano. "Let's start with the scales," Mr. Lamb suggested, settling into his chair.

Jane played a scale and arpeggio that would have sounded proficient to most ears.

"Again. Fourth finger, not third, on the F#. You've done that right a hundred times before." The second time through was better but still rough. "Have you practiced any scales this week?" He selected one of the pieces of music she had brought and opened it in front of her. "Never mind. Play the Khachaturian for me."

She sat with her hands in her lap, not looking at him. "I was hoping that you would help me with something else."

"What 'something else'?"

"I'm playing piano for the spring musical at school." Mr. Lamb was silent. "*Oklahoma.*" Still, he didn't respond. Jane glanced at him and saw he was staring at his hands. "You said that I should start playing more in public."

"So I did." He sat to her left on the bench. "Play me those songs of waving wheat and Kansas City and poor dead Jud." Jane lifted the huge accompaniment score to the music rack and her teacher turned pages as she began to play the music. "For the performances, will it be piano or do you have an orchestra?"

"We'll have the whole senior high orchestra for the last two weeks and the show. Right now it's just me for rehearsals."

"You'll want to emphasize the rhythm here." He pointed to a section of the music. "To bring the strings in together." He circled the measures lightly in pencil. "When do you rehearse?"

"Only four nights a week."

"Only four," he echoed, standing up from the piano bench. Jane felt strangely relieved when he moved away from her. Usually, she secretly treasured the moments he spent close beside her on the bench, as he demonstrated a difficult fingering or pedaling, or especially the times he sat to play a four-hand piece with her. Then she experienced the magic of watching his fingers in a dance with hers, and she imagined she could feel a current between their arms, their hands, their thighs. If they were playing in the dark, she thought, there would be sparks in the charged space between them like the tiny private fireworks that flashed between two woolen blankets when she pulled them apart on her bed in the winter. But now he had closed himself off from her.

He nodded toward the black case leaning against the sofa. "And the violin?"

"I have a solo passage in *Capriccio Espagnol* that we're playing in the next youth symphony concert, and I know I don't quite have it yet." Jane glanced at her watch. "But there isn't any time. I can't stay late today."

"No?"

"I promised to go downtown with my mother. To look at prom dresses." She laid a check for the lesson on a stack of music, not wanting to look at her teacher, embarrassed at how young and silly she must sound to him.

"Do you want to learn to play the piano?"

Jane looked up at him, frowning slightly, confused. "You know I do."

"I know you have the potential to be good." He had never told her how good. "But right now you're scattered, unfocused. You have to decide whether or not you're willing to concentrate and develop your talent or go flying off in a million directions." He handed her the violin case. "You can't do it all. And you've got to decide soon."

Jane couldn't speak. She nodded, picked up her music, and headed out the door mumbling goodbye. She wouldn't let Mr. Lamb see her cry.

She did cry on the walk home, tears of anger and frustration. When Jane reached her house, her mother met her at the door as she always did to ask how the lesson had gone. "What happened?" She took the violin case and held Jane for a second to stop her sobbing. Then she led her to a chair, sat her down, and knelt in front of her. "Did Mr. Lamb do anything to hurt you?" She gently brushed strands of hair away from her daughter's face. "I'm going to call him and find out what happened."

"No!" Jane couldn't talk to her mother about it. She wished her grandmother were there to listen. "I fell on the way home." She showed her mother the grass stains and scrape on her knee. Too angry to pay attention to where she was going, her vision clouded by tears, she had tripped on a curb. "I messed up my knee a little, but I didn't drop the violin."

"Do you want some ice for it?"

"It's okay. But I don't feel like going shopping. Could you take me to the library to work on my homework? I'll fix a sandwich before I go."

Her mother watched as Jane deliberately stacked all the books of music from the piano and put them on the top shelf of the coat closet. Jane was fighting back more tears but didn't seem to be favoring her knee. When the piano had been cleared, Jane closed the cover over the keyboard.

"I thought you told me pianos look deserted or dead like that," her mother said.

"They do." Jane crossed to the small oak buffet that had belonged to her grandmother and carefully lifted out and unfolded Nana's Irish scarf. She draped it over the top of the spinet. "I think I'm going to quit piano lessons." The words came out in a whispered rush, as though if the thought were not expressed quickly, it could not be voiced at all.

"Something did happen at Mr. Lamb's." Jane could see the panic in her mother's eyes. "Did he touch you or try to do something ... not appropriate? I was afraid this was going to happen —"

"Nothing happened! He wouldn't do anything like that." Jane turned to walk into the kitchen. "There's just too much to do. School and the play and everything."

She returned in a few minutes with a sandwich in her hand. "I've got an English paper due tomorrow. Could you take me to the library and pick me up in two hours after you and dad finish dinner?"

Her mother held her by the shoulders and looked into her eyes. "You know you could talk to me if anything happened."

"Mom, nothing happened." Jane picked up her school notebook and headed for the door, needing to leave the piano and the room where she had spent so many hours practicing.

At the library, she sought out the thick quiet of the stacks. The setting sun illuminated motes of dust that swirled and settled without a sound. The thought of life without Mr. Lamb and the joy they shared in music sucked the air from her lungs, and she doubled over, gasping and sobbing. He must be so disappointed in her. He must have so many students to take her place. He must not want her in his life.

Jane wiped her eyes and concentrated on her paper, trying to drive out any music in her head with words that lacked all melody.

Her father was waiting outside in the car when she left the library. "How's your knee? Your mother told me you fell on the way home from your lesson."

"It's a little stiff, but I didn't drop your violin."

"You might want to put the heating pad on it tonight."

"On the violin?" she asked, managing a smile.

"No, silly. On your green knee."

"I will if it still hurts."

They were quiet for the rest of the short ride home. In the driveway, he put his hand on her shoulder to keep her from getting out of the car.

"She also told me that you want to quit piano lessons." When Jane didn't respond, he asked, "What happened at your lesson today?"

"Nothing."

"Is that why you closed and covered your piano?"

Jane bit her lip to keep from crying. "I guess I'm not very interested in it anymore. There are so many other things going on."

"What other things?"

"The musical and violin and school. I'm too scattered," she said.

"Scattered?"

"Scattered. Unfocused. Mr. Lamb says that I'm too scattered and unfocused. I think he wants to teach students who have nothing to do but play the piano, and I have other things to do." Jane opened the car door and got out, leading heavily with her sore knee as if relishing the pain as a diversion from the conversation. "Thanks for picking me up." They walked into the house together.

"I have to finish my English homework," Jane said. She picked up her pile of schoolbooks. "I have to read the rest of *Julius Caesar*, and then maybe I'll still have time to practice the violin."

A few minutes later, Jane's father knocked on the door that led to her attic room. He walked up the steps. Jane sat on her bed in near darkness, staring out the window, a closed book on her lap. "I called Mr. Lamb," he said.

Jane felt a stab of shame and embarrassment. "You didn't need to do that."

"He thinks—and I think—that you misunderstood what he said today."

"He said that I'm not getting anywhere with the piano because I'm trying to do too much. Maybe I wouldn't get anywhere anyway. Mom thinks it's really neat about the school play. There's nobody else in that stupid youth symphony that can play the solo for the concert. And I'm not going to quit the violin." Jane opened the book on her lap but didn't look at the page. "Mr. Lamb has lots of really good students, and he doesn't want to waste his time on someone as 'scattered' as I am."

"Jane," Jack moved closer to his daughter and sat beside her. "Mr. Lamb thinks you have a future as a pianist, and I agree with him. But if that is what you want, you have to concentrate and start preparing to perform. Mr. Lamb thinks you can be ready to enter the new international competition at the Institute of Music. It's a stepping-stone to the Casadesus. He doesn't want to lose you as a student; he wants to really start teaching you."

Still, Jane stared into the darkness outside as if she had not heard. These were the words she had dreamed about for years, words that should have made the almost unbearable hurt from earlier in the afternoon vanish. Her long fingers, white knuckled, gripped the book. Her teeth marked her lower lip as she fought to keep it from trembling, but still, she didn't speak.

"Your mother will understand. She knows how difficult it is to make music your life, but most of all she wants you to be happy. Do you want to play the piano?"

"Yes," Jane whispered.

"Then do it."

She turned to her father, her eyes filled with the tears she had struggled against for hours, and asked the question that had tortured her since she began her love affair with the tiny spinet downstairs. "Then who will play your violin?"

Jack held his daughter in his arms as she sobbed against his shoulder. Jane had been born on the day his dreams died, he had given her his violin teacher and his violin, and she considered it her duty to live out his dream for him. He patted her on the back as he had done when she was a child. When her tears slowed, he took her hands in his. "These are the hands of a pianist. You need to make your own dreams come true. You can play the violin for fun, to see music in a different way."

"What will Papa Cohen say?"

"I think he's known for a long time where your heart is. He would say, 'Go, play your piano.'"

"Mr. Lamb thinks I'm ready for a competition?"

"No, but he thinks you can be ready. We'll have to work out a schedule so you can begin to concentrate on piano."

"To focus." Jane took the handkerchief her father offered and wiped her nose. "The music director can play the score for *Oklahoma*. And I already know the violin part for youth symphony. The performance can be my swan song."

"You're a little young for a swan song." Her father kissed Jane on the forehead. "And don't forget that *Julius Caesar* awaits."

"Can I practice a little first?"

"'May I practice'," Jack corrected. "Yes, you may as long as you save time for Shakespeare. And Mr. Lamb said to tell you that he didn't mean to upset you this afternoon."

"He said that?" He hadn't rejected her. He did want her as a student. She nearly ran down the stairs. She pulled Nana's scarf from the piano and called to her mother, "Mr. Lamb thinks I should try for one of the piano competitions."

Her mother came into the living room and took the scarf from Jane. She folded it carefully and hugged her daughter. "I'm very proud of you."

Jane began to work on her scales and arpeggios, her fingers flying across the keys, *appassionato*.

Chapter Seven
Chamomile (*Matricaria chamomilla*)

April 30, 1998

Jane rolled over on the chilly expanse of the hotel's king-sized bed and pulled the blankets up to her chin. The air conditioning had clicked on in the middle of the night, and she shivered a little, listening to the drip of the rain and the pounding of the surf outside. As she curled up and burrowed under the covers, she winced as her sore muscles complained about the hours of hard work the day before. It was probably a good thing that the rain would keep her out of the garden today. She rubbed the muscles in the back of her legs and began to make a mental list of things she could accomplish until the sun came out again.

She should go shopping for a refrigerator and mattress. Mike had given her several maps and the clerk at the front desk could give her directions. There was more scrubbing to do, but she ought to buy paint now so she'd be ready for that step. Brushes, rollers. She would need sheets and towels and dishes. When she and Alex were married, Jane had created a lifestyle based on a compromise of their tastes, geared to their world of Alex's successful career in architecture and her traveling and celebrity as a performer. Now she felt as though she were courting and setting up a home for some part of herself she was just getting to know.

Jane was warmer. The rain lulled her. Wind whistled off the ocean, caught in the angles of the hotel eaves, and hummed broken measures like breath across the ragged end of a reed flute. Dozing, she thought about McCue and saw him again transformed into a faun in her garden. In her dreams, he shimmered and shape-shifted like a drop of oil in rainwater.

Half an hour later, she woke up and jumped out of bed as the silky voice of the flute abruptly transmuted to the rude brass of her travel alarm. She pulled on her jeans and a tee shirt bearing the faded logo of some symphony orchestra she had soloed with years before and decided this would be a good time to visit the garden shop in Aria. She would need seeds and plants and advice. She wouldn't let herself acknowledge that even though McCue had said he would be away, she was curious to see where he lived and taught.

After a quick breakfast at the hotel, Jane headed for a department store near Wilmington. In two hours, she had ordered a small refrigerator, mattress and box springs, and a set of simple white china dishes; these would be delivered on Friday. She made a trip to the Jeep to load it with brushes and rollers and drop cloths. A young salesclerk followed her with paint for the walls and ceilings. She hiked back into the store to the linen department.

Jane chose white sheets of the softest cotton and white towels. She paused beside one display stacked with designer patterns, running her hand over a bedspread sprigged with tiny rose buds, like the paper in Selena's house, but left it in the pile.

A local station on the Jeep's radio said the rain would continue at least until late afternoon. Jane eased the Jeep onto Route 17 and headed toward Aria.

The little town looked older, a bit shabbier, in the rain, but in spite of the gloom, Jane felt her heart begin to race as she pulled closer to the two-story building beside George Jackson's house. Several parked cars occupied the spaces in front of the once white frame store, so she parked in front of Jackson's house. A wet wind had coaxed the multi-tiered sign in front of his house into a slow undulating shimmy. Jane could hear its metallic complaint under the sound of the rain and wind as she got out of the car. She thought for a moment about paying George a visit to thank him for his help and tell him how much she loved the house. Had the lace curtain at the front door moved? Was he waiting for another visitor? A client? But the house was dark, and Jane's attention was drawn to warm light streaming through the glass of the store next door.

As she walked on the rain-wet sidewalk toward the front door, she felt she had already been caught in the magic of the place. Her footsteps disturbed the sheen of water that reflected the message "Candy Store, Sweets and Such" as though it had been written on delicate tissue paper saved to wrap a special gift. When she looked behind her, the letters had settled and shimmered with a watercolor rainbow swirling lazy spirals on the surface. In the corner of the left window, a neatly hand-lettered sign announced, "A Garden Place, Moira Coinín O'Shea, Proprietor." The cardboard had aged to an uneven ivory, and darker streaks on one edge suggested contact with a long ago leak in the ceiling. The ink had faded to warm brown, a color that reminded Jane of manuscripts penned by monks in flickering candlelight, or old treasure maps hidden away in locked chests. She peered closer at the stains on the sign; through the steamy, scratched glass they could have been maps of rivers and islands and seacoasts. Past the sign, Jane could see several women standing with their backs to her. They were laughing together, and Jane felt a sudden stab of envy and then near panic at the thought of entering the store.

She continued walking past the window. The heavy double storm door centered between the display windows was open wide. Jane paused in front of oak-framed screen doors. She closed her eyes for a second and inhaled deeply. The scent was an intoxicating mixture of earthy herbs, exotic spices, and incense: smoky, piquant, dark, and musky. Holding the air deep in her lungs like a drug she willed to enter her bloodstream and bring calm, she moved to the window at the right side of the doors. Jane exhaled, steaming a lacy circle on the glass. Through the damp scrim, she saw a child standing in the middle of the shop turn to her, as though she were expected, and wave. Startled, Jane glanced over her shoulder to see if someone stood behind her, someone the child might have been waiting for. The sidewalk was empty. When she looked again, the child nodded a mass of reddish curls and opened both arms to Jane.

Jane couldn't help returning the welcoming smile but raised her finger in a wait-a-minute gesture. Raking her hand through her short hair, she walked to the far-right end of the building. She passed a closed single door and paused in front of a square window divided into dozens of panes of wavy hand-blown glass. It must be original to the structure, she thought, and the plate glass of the candy store added later. This window, too, held a sign, one professionally printed and neatly framed. "Flutes. Restoration, Repair, Lessons. M. Cairncross." The message was as straightforward as McCue had been. Only the choice of a delicately shadowed font for the lettering hinted at the artist behind the words.

As the rain lightened to a warm drizzle, the sun wrapped gilt edges around the bottoms of the remaining clouds and began to trace the grid pattern and Jane's shadow on the floor of the flute shop. The thought crossed her mind that perhaps her shadow would stay in the shop, like Peter Pan's with Wendy. Through subtle concentric distortions she could see a scarred worktable where sections of a flute lay on scraps of cloth. Tools lined up neat as a surgeon's instruments along the edge of the table. Further back, two mismatched wooden chairs faced a music stand positioned to take advantage of light from the window. Catching sight of the sheets of music, Jane turned away, not waiting to see if her shadow followed. She returned to the double doors of the garden store and entered as the women she had seen earlier were leaving.

Jane stood inside the door for a moment, soothed again by the scents. She glanced around the room, looking for the red-haired child, but no one else was in the store. Traffic had worn gentle valleys in the wooden floor in front of a massive counter and from the counter to the front door. Jane followed the path for a few steps, then veered off to a table stacked with gardening tools. She chose a pointed trowel with a varnished oak handle and examined a wicked looking claw for working the soil in the garden. "Buy two, get one free today." Jane turned toward the source of the voice. At the back of the store, behind the counter, a woman stood framed in a doorway that had been draped with a dark green woolen blanket. She was several inches taller than Jane; her skin was pale, freckled across her cheekbones and nose; her sun-streaked brown hair was pulled back and tied with a white ribbon. Before the edge of the blanket dropped, through the doorway Jane could see a cluttered storeroom and a stairway leading to the second floor.

The woman moved around the counter and walked to Jane's side. She picked up a single-pointed digging tool. "This is great for uprooting weeds—or discouraging trespassers."

"I'll take it." Jane returned the woman's smile, meeting the direct gaze of her blue eyes.

"I'm Moira O'Shea."

Jane shook the hand she extended. "Moira Coinín O'Shea," she said, quoting the sign. "An Irish rabbit in the garden store. It suits you."

"And Jane Bell suits you."

Jane released Moira's hand. Moira nodded toward the Jackson house. "George is so delighted that you've taken the Nevin place. He couldn't keep still about it. We really cared about Selena and know she would be pleased." She waved her hand in the opposite direction, toward the flute shop. "McCue is thrilled. I recognized you because he has a collection of all of your CDs, and several have your photo on them."

"My hair was much longer then," Jane said lamely, uncomfortable with the conversation. "Did he tell you that I thought he was Steve and made him cut down trees? I felt so bad about the blisters on his hands."

"He thought that was funny. We found some cream for the blisters. The workout was good for him."

Jane felt a flash of jealous curiosity. Were Moira and McCue lovers? She knew it was none of her business if they were.

"McCue said you've cleaned up the herb garden."

"I'm trying." She nodded toward the trowel in her hand. "I'm really new at this. Any suggestions about what I should plant—and when and how?"

"Sure." Moira led the way to the left side of the store. Small square bins with hinged plastic lids lined the wall. Jane realized that the cubbyholes that once held a child's treasure of candies, including Mike Tyler's root beer barrels, had been converted into bulk storage for seeds. Each bin had a tiny scoop chained inside. Moira opened one of the bins marked "Parsley—Curley" and scooped up some of the tiny black seeds. She carefully tipped them into a small plastic bag, fastened the top with a thin metal tie and labeled it with a marker. "The sage, rosemary, and thyme are better planted as seedlings." Jane returned Moira's smile at the folk song reference. "Those are out back." She reached into another bin. "You'll want a couple of kinds of basil. This purple is my favorite." She labeled another bag and handed it to Jane.

They moved slowly in front of the wall of wooden cubes. Moira pointed to an identifying tag and raised her dark eyebrows in a wordless question to Jane, who nodded her agreement with most of the choices. Soon she was juggling a dozen little seed bags.

"Not that one," Jane said. Moira replaced the scoop and closed the plastic lid as Jane explained, "I love Mexican food, but I've never really liked cilantro."

"Silly Aunt Tro, Silly Aunt Tro."

Jane looked up from the bin, searching for the source of the echo. If a tiny silver bell could be taught to speak, it would have this voice, she thought. Balancing on one leg like a crane in blue denim, the red-haired child peered out from the edge of the blanket covering the doorway. At Jane's glance, the face disappeared behind the woolen drapery leaving only the angle of a knee jutting out in front of the doorjamb. "I used to stand on one leg to practice the violin." Jane spoke to Moira but projected her voice so the little girl could hear it.

"Kaeth is shy with new people." Moira moved to another bin and pointed to the label. "Chamomile."

Jane avoided looking at the draped doorway. "For tea? I'd love to try that. My grandmother used to make chamomile tea." She caught sight of movement out of the corner of her eye. Like a reticent shadow, Kaeth was inching her way toward them.

Moira nodded. "Peter Rabbit's mother gave it to him to cure his headache. You're not allergic to ragweed or chrysanthemums, are you?"

"No."

"Then you should be fine with it. You can also dry chamomile for potpourri." Moira printed neatly on another plastic bag and handed it to Jane. "Oh, about the basil seeds. Be sure to curse as you plant them."

"Excuse me?"

"Curse, swear while you sow the seeds. You have to learn some old wives' tales if you're going to have a serious herb garden. Basil is the devil's plant; the more you abuse it, the better it will grow."

"That sounds a bit harsh, but there's usually some truth in what those 'old wives' suggested."

"Absolutely. The basil will grow fuller if you pinch off the top leaves regularly. When the seedlings grow the first six leaves, pinch them back to the first two and keep them pruned like that whenever there are six or eight leaves on a branch."

"'Pinching back' sounds a little better than 'abuse'." Jane heard the sibilant hiss of her last word echoed by Kaeth, who crouched behind an old metal magazine stand. The skeletal structure that had once held comic books chronicling the tales of Superman and Archie now housed a selection of paperback books on gardening and herbs. The soft sound was joined with a high-pitched squeak from the revolving stand as Kaeth's shoulder brushed it into motion. Her giggles punctuated the music. Jane was aware that the rain had become isolated, syncopated drips on a canvas awning outside. "What else should I know about what the old wives say?"

"Well, I've heard that the best parsley crops are sown by pregnant women or witches on Good Friday. And you shouldn't cut parsley if you're in love. I've never been able to figure out where that idea came from." Jane saw Kaeth slip behind Moira. She was still hiding but growing bolder. "Would you like some iced tea? We've got sun tea brewing." As though Moira's speaking the word had conjured the light, a glow filtered in through the rain-streaked front window. Jane remembered George Jackson's offer on another day and guessed that Moira kept her friends supplied with herbs for flavoring tea, chamomile, mint —

"Chamomile, honey and some catnip," Moira said, as though she had read Jane's thoughts. "The way Kaeth likes it." Seemingly brought forth by the same magic that had produced the sunlight, the curtain of Moira's arm parted from her side and Kaeth's auburn curls appeared. Echoing "catnip" in a breathy whisper, Kaeth tilted her face to Jane. Jane stared into the upturned face, held by eyes the color of dark honey, flecked with gold. As she took the tiny hand that was held out to her, she was shocked to realize that the elfin person she had taken for a child was actually a woman of thirty? forty? older? Up close, Jane could see silver hairs shining in the mass of curls; fine lines crinkled at the corners of her remarkable eyes.

"Hello, Kaeth. My name is Jane."

"Jane-I-know." Kaeth responded as if the reply were one word. The little woman in overalls had taken Jane's right hand in both of hers. Beside the pianist's long fingers, Kaeth's hands could have been those of a china doll. The tiny fingers curved into loose fists and tapped Jane's hand. "Singers."

"She means that your hands sing," Moira said.

"Not anymore." Jane withdrew her hand.

Kaeth's brow creased in a frown, a gentle clicking of her tongue suggesting disapproval.

"I would like some tea," Jane said. "If it's no trouble."

Moira brushed her fingers through the mass of curls. "Kaeth, would you get some glasses for iced tea?" The smile was back, and Kaeth skipped toward the blanket-draped doorway behind the counter chanting "Tea" with each bounce.

"I thought she was a child..." Jane felt haunted by the depth she had encountered in the gaze of the golden eyes.

"In many ways she is." Moira handed Jane a verdigris wind chime. A hummingbird suspended over four tiny bells on copper chains of different lengths swung as Jane held it in the air. "Sometimes I think we can learn the most from the simplest people."

Jane stepped backwards and the metal wings slipped from her fingers. The wind chime hit the floor with a clatter that seemed out of proportion to its size, and Jane bumped into the magazine rack, which rotated with a shriek. What did this woman know about her, she wondered. For a moment, Jane wanted to drop the packets of seed on the worn wooden floor beside the downed hummingbird and run from the store and from the anguished memories Moira had stirred up.

Moira picked up the wind chime, and it resumed its pleasant metallic harmony. "A housewarming present. But perhaps we should choose one that won't fly out of your hands."

Jane reached for the wind chime before Moira could replace it on the rack. Thinking of the hummingbird she had dreamed about in the Jackson house, she said, "No. I like this one the best even though it tried to get away. I'll hang it on the back porch outside the bedroom window."

"If the ocean breeze is too strong, try it on the other porch." Moira turned and headed for the blanket-draped doorway. "I think the rain stopped. It's probably still wet outside, but we can have our tea on the porch." Moira placed an apple-sized brass bell on the counter beside a wooden sign. *We're in the back. Please ring.* She held the blanket to one side so Jane could pass through.

The storeroom was much darker than the store had been. Jane paused for a moment to let her eyes adjust. She smelled wood from the boxes and barrels, wool from the blanket, musky and earthy scents that seemed to emanate from the walls themselves. As she walked toward windows at the back of the room where hazy light filtered in, Jane encountered the heady fragrance of lavender and other herbs drying on wooden racks and hanging from the ceiling in twine-wrapped bunches.

"Lavender," she whispered, and she felt that Nana had passed close to her, as though the spires of delicate purple and the chamomile leaves and flowers drying close to them had conjured the spirit of her Irish grandmother.

"There's lavender out back with the other seedlings." Moira's voice, in an answering whisper, surprised Jane, who had almost forgotten that anyone was with her. "We've got several kinds." Moira moved ahead of Jane to open the door to the patio.

A canvas awning covered the irregularly shaped stone patio where it seemed to Jane that huge flat stones had been allowed to choose their own places. At the border of the free-form area, creeping herbs with the tiniest leaves nestled into odd angles. Ceramic pots of all sizes gushed with miniature roses, geraniums, and fuchsias in pastels and primary colors. Now Jane knew the meaning of a riot of color. Pillows and seat covers of mismatched gingham checks and prints brightened old wicker rockers and a love seat. All of the wicker pieces were quite worn. Some were painted white, some a forest green. One small, tired, round wicker table sported its old white paint and the start of a new coat of brick red.

"I love it!" Jane felt the same sense of peace and pleasantly heavy quiet she had sensed in George Jackson's house, where the flowers had been porcelain and crystal but equally profuse. She glanced into his yard. Mary Ellen's garden was brown and tangled with neglect. In her daydream, it had glowed with the colors of Moira's yard.

Moira motioned for her to sit down and called toward a window on the second floor. "Do you need any help with the tea?"

"Tea? Tea?" the silver voice echoed. "No help now, not now."

Jane sat in one of the rocking chairs and saw Mr. Jackson coming out to his back porch. In the light of the sun, he looked more fragile than he had two days before. He waved and called hello over the hedge of roses that separated the two yards.

"George, look who's here to buy some plants for her garden and visit a while." Moira moved toward her neighbor. "Would you like to come over and have some iced tea with us? Kaeth went in to get it."

"Thanks, but I'm feeling a little tired. Always a good time for a nap after the rain." He looked toward the ruins of the garden. "The shower cooled things off." Mr. Jackson shook his head and turned to go back inside. "Take care of each other. Enjoy the tea." The screen door closed behind him.

"Did you know Mr. Jackson and Mary Ellen well?"

Moira looked at her with eyes that seemed suddenly heavier, hooded with sadness, with wariness. "They're very special people." Both women turned at the sound of the back door opening. Kaeth was carrying a plastic cup in each hand, her head bent over with concentration, auburn curls bouncing.

"Do you need any help, Kaeth?" Jane asked.

"Help Kaeth help Kaeth," repeated the echoing voice. "Okay now." She had reached the rocking chairs and handed a cup to Jane and the second to Moira. The cups were filled with ice cubes. Without another word Kaeth nodded in response to their thank yous and reentered the store.

Moira sat in the rocker, her long legs stretched out. She held her plastic cup of ice in both hands, sliding her fingers in abstract patterns in the condensation on the sides.

Jane lifted her cup to her forehead for a second. The air had become hot and hazy, steamy after the rain. She heard footsteps descending from the second floor. "Here is our perfect hostess."

Kaeth, holding a plastic cup of ice in her right hand and a small pitcher of tea in her left hand, was beaming as she joined them on the patio. She poured tea for each of them, tilting her head to better hear the crystal crackle of the ice cubes as the warm sun tea filled the glasses.

Jane declared that the tea was excellent. Moira reminded her that chamomile and catnip flavored it. "And honey," Kaeth added. "Honey."

As they finished their tea, Moira led them to the small greenhouse of stretched plastic that housed rows of seedlings with neat little tags. Kaeth skipped away for a moment and reappeared with a cardboard box cut down to hold the tiny plants. Soon the box was filled with a collection of tomatoes—large and cherry varieties—more herbs, and a few flowers. Jane shook her head when Kaeth brought out a second box. "I promised myself I'd stay out of the garden today and work on painting the ceiling and walls. I want to at least do the kitchen and bedroom if I can. The refrigerator and mattress are going to be delivered tomorrow."

"Sounds like you have everything under control."

"Not at all. I'm making it up as I go along."

"That's the best way to learn. *Is ón saol a thagann an chiall.*"

Jane felt a stab of longing for her grandmother. "Nana used to tell me that."

"Life will teach you what you need to know. When you're ready, you'll understand. It applies to the garden, too. Don't worry about the plants. Keep them watered and they'll be fine for a few days until you get them in the ground." Moira held the screen door open. "Do you need any help with the house?"

"Thanks, but it's really important to me to do it myself." Jane knew what she had just said was true, and she felt that Moira would understand. Jane also admitted to herself that she wondered if McCue might show up even though he had said he would be out of town. "Steve will be coming by to help with the heavy work."

Jane and Moira passed through the fragrant back room and into the store. Kaeth lagged behind. After selecting an herb book that Moira recommended, Jane paid for her purchases at the counter. A humming song came from behind the blanket-draped doorway and Jane watched the bent knee appear as it had earlier in the day. Kaeth was in her crane position, hiding. Her tiny fist thrust a bunch of flowers through the opening in the blanket. Bright pink, yellow, blue and purple blossoms arranged for a second against the wool blanket reminded Jane of another bouquet. "You brought the flowers to my house!"

Kaeth's silver giggle rang out, slightly muffled by the drape. She danced into the room. "My house, my house," she chanted.

"I love the flowers. They're in a little cream pitcher I found in the kitchen. I had no idea who could have given them to me."

Kaeth handed her the bouquet. Jane closed her hand around the stems and felt the bite of thorns in her palm. She winced and Kaeth's eyes narrowed. The corners of her mouth turned up, revealing the points of tiny teeth. Jane ignored the pain and moved to the counter where Moira was figuring the total of Jane's purchases on a lined tablet. "Thank you for these beautiful flowers, too."

As the three women carried the plants, seeds, books and wind chime to the car, Jane glanced at the Jackson house, but it was quiet, napping. "Thanks for the tea and the housewarming present. As soon as the house is a little more presentable, I'll invite you over for lunch."

"We'd love that." Moira stood in the arch of the store entrance. She held Kaeth's hand.

"Love that, love that," whispered the tiny woman.

Moira called out to remind her that it was better not to work in the garden when the earth was wet. It would clump together as it dried and make it difficult for the roots to spread.

Jane nodded and waved as she pulled into the street.

Back at the house, she set the cans of paint and other supplies on the floor of the living room. She added the new flowers and some water to the bouquet in the china pitcher, opened the back door, and watched the ocean for a minute, promising herself a lunch break in the rocker that waited for her.

Jane covered the brass headboard of the bed and the old oak dresser with a plastic drop cloth and began to paint. The ceiling and one wall went quickly; she decided to leave the tedious job of painting the French doors for another day.

She was sitting in the rocker, eating yogurt and an apple when Steve appeared from around the corner of the porch. Under his arm, he carried a new white toilet seat. His hammer hung from the loop on his overalls, and tools weighed down the worn leather tool belt he wore. He grinned a greeting and sat on the edge of the porch.

"Hows it going?" He wrote in the little notebook with a new pencil.

"Great! Would you like some lunch?"

He printed a reply. "Thanks. Have snack in truck for later. Screens, too."

"I can't believe you finished them so fast."

"No problem," he wrote. He nodded toward the open kitchen door. "Wind keeps bugs away now. Might get bad later." He held up the toilet seat. "Will do. Little time today. What else?" He was already standing up and checking pouches for the tools he needed.

"The new refrigerator is being delivered tomorrow —"

Before she could finish, Steve was writing again. "Will take old away when I go today."

"That would be great. But can you move it by yourself?"

Steve surprised Jane with the gravelly but cheerful sound of his laugh. His huge body froze for a second in the body builder pose he had shown her the day before.

"I know, the 'strong, silent type.'"

"With dolly," he wrote in his notebook. Jane gave him a thumbs-up sign and went back to painting the bedroom. She could hear Steve working as he moved from the bathroom to the front and back doors, replacing the screens. When she walked by the bathroom, she saw that Steve had installed the seat and put toilet paper in a new ceramic holder. He must have brought them in one of his voluminous pockets. The old, rusted metal holder was nowhere in sight.

Back in the bedroom, she pulled the drop cloths from the headboard and chest and mopped the hardwood floor with hot water and oil soap, then carefully wiped over the graceful metalwork of the headboard. For a moment, she stood by the French doors, amazed as always by the willow, the expanse of blue sky, the ocean.

The red of the setting sun had turned the new paint in the bedroom to a warm rose. She glanced at her watch and was surprised to see it was nearly seven o'clock. She heard a thumping noise. Steve had disconnected the refrigerator and was moving it down the front steps on the dolly. As she passed through the kitchen, Jane noticed he had torn out old linoleum from the spot where the refrigerator had stood. Above the irregular wooden spot, the outline of the old appliance hung like a patient ghost, only slightly less dingy than the rest of the walls.

Jane went out to the porch to see if she could help, but Steve was wheeling it down the path to his truck. Jane followed behind and thanked him for his help. He nodded acknowledgement. At the edge of the road, Jane was amazed as she watched him wrestle with the refrigerator and hoist it into the truck bed. He brushed his hands together with an exaggerated, cartoon move to signify a job completed. Then he pulled his little notebook from his pocket and wrote, "Clean wood under fridge if you have time. Can rip up rest of floor later. House looking good."

"Thank you." Jane watched perspiration dripping from Steve's reddened face. She was beginning to realize how hot and tired she was, too. "Can I get you a cold soda or water before you go?"

"No thanks," Steve wrote. "But you sit down for a bit." He started to put the pencil away, then wrote more. "Moving in soon?"

Jane had been thinking about it all afternoon. "I don't see any reason why I shouldn't move in tomorrow. There's still lots to do, but by tomorrow afternoon I should have a place to sleep, a working kitchen and a bathroom." Steve smiled and winked when she thanked him for bringing and installing the new toilet seat.

"Remember to wait for me for heavy work. I'll stop by soon." Steve slipped the pencil and notebook into his pocket and climbed into the truck. Jane waved as he pulled away.

She ate the last two apples and some cheese from the cooler. In a few days, she should be able to find time to explore the beach even though she knew it would mean crawling and scooting her way down the hill to the sea. By the light from the bulbs George Jackson had provided, she scrubbed the irregular patch of wooden floor where the new refrigerator would go.

Jane thought about Moira and Kaeth. Soon, she would be able to invite them to the house for lunch and chamomile iced tea. She was glad she had called Ken before leaving the hotel this morning. He wanted to come visit but understood that she needed some time alone first. As she locked the back door, she paused to picture how it would look with all the walls fresh and clean. She ran her hand over the worn oak of the kitchen table, then moved the pitcher of flowers to the center of the table.

The bedroom was already a quiet haven. Smells of new paint and oil soap lingered and mingled with lilac on the ocean wind. Jane closed the one French door that had a screen and had been opened as she worked. She was exhausted, but reluctant to leave. She covered the paint, rinsed out the rollers, turned out the lights, and locked the door.

On the front porch, seedlings in their cardboard boxes nodded in the wind. Jane stuck her fingers in the earth around them, surprised to find it damp. She smiled as she saw a shiny new plastic hose snaked around from the side of the house to the porch. Steve must have also thought of that.

Back at the hotel, she ordered dinner from room service, promising herself that tomorrow she would fix dinner in her house on the ocean.

Jane opened the package her mother had sent and crawled into bed with Nana's book. Tears blurred the words as she recognized Nana's handwriting, the script here so bold and unwavering, so similar to—yet far from—the shaky handwriting of her grandmother years later.

The first pages looked like a school notebook with notations from math, religion, and literature classes. Opening the book to a random page, Jane realized that it contained a diary entry for Saturday, May 13, 1933. *My mother says it's nonsense, but my lover swears it's truth*, Jane read. Lover? She started with the first page and read through the school lessons until they ended and the journaling began.

Thursday, April 13, 1933
Dear diary,
I met a boy, a boy who likes me, and I daren't tell a soul, so I'll tell it only to you, dear diary. Please forgive being put inside last year's composition book. My bratty sister Jenny—Sister? Both her mother and grandmother had told her that Nana was an only child, orphaned before she married and left Ireland for America. She continued reading, *colored all over the cover but it is where you will be safe especially from Mother and Da. They wouldn't even hardly look at it when I laid it open on the table at the end of school. Open to the page, it was, where Sister Alben wrote in red in her perfect script, "Cara is a fine bright girl, and ought to be encouraged to further her education,*

perhaps to enter a teaching order." And who was "Cara"? Her grandmother's name was Margaret.

Mother read it to Da, who ventured that God willing my brain might get me a job, but there was sure no money to send me to college. Mother said the convent would feed me and maybe send me to school, but neither of them looked to me and I feel no vocation, no calling. Except to the lad with eyes so green they dizzy me.

He was in Murtrey's field playing music to a horse when I passed by on my way home from school. I'd seen the horse a thousand times, a swaybacked nag the color of wet peat. The animal leaned to the side and did no more than shudder weakly when the horseflies swarmed in the summer as though his ratty tail wasn't up to the job of swatting his rump.

But today, oh today, there in the field with the boy who likes me, that very same horse danced. I swear to God in Heaven, the roan's hide shone like chestnut leather, his hooves barely marked the earth in the field, and he whinnied and tossed his head like a faerie stallion. The boy kept blowing across his silver flute, though I couldn't hear a sound—or not like I usually hear things—and he didn't see me at all until the horse snorted and swung his great head in my direction, mane flying about in a wind that tied the boy and animal together.

The boy who likes me looked my way, and I don't remember ducking through the fence or moving close to him, but somehow he had looped his arm through mine and was walking me to the oak tree at the edge of Murtrey's property, and the peat-colored horse was wobbling with his tippy gait near the stable again. "I'm Brian," the boy said as he sat me down on the warm grass. I must have told him my name as he split the flute in its three parts, wiped it off as careful as a holy relic, and laid it in a leather case, because the next thing I remember is the sky being scarlet with the sunset. The church bell was ringing the Angelus, and I knew hours had passed since I left school.

At the clanging of the bell, my lips began to pray three Hail Marys, but his mouth was on mine with three kisses and they seemed as sweet as a prayer. "Until next Thursday, Cara," he said, and walked into the west. The sun seemed to eat him up, and I wanted to follow but my legs carried me back to the road that leads to home. Dear diary, keep my secret.

Jane rubbed her eyes, too tired to continue, as though the diary had conjured up the voice of her grandmother, a sweet soprano that had sung her to sleep so many nights in her childhood. She closed the book and turned out the light, wondering how many secrets slept between the pages of the strange diary.

Chapter Eight
Requebrando (Sp.) Flirtatious

1977

The months before the competition passed in a blur of practicing, memorizing, and polishing the Beethoven sonata Jane and her teacher had chosen from the short list of pieces approved by the judges. She was surprised to find her name on the list of ten finalists out of the original twenty-eight entrants. Mr. Lamb just smiled.

"Go out and have some fun with your friends tonight," he told her the evening before the final round. "You know the piece. Go out dancing. Then get some sleep." He was the one who seemed tired. "I'll see you tomorrow, and you will play for me."

She hadn't gone out dancing. She had played through the Beethoven a few times and let her mother fix her a glass of warm milk with a little vanilla and sugar, her grandmother's recipe to guarantee a good night's sleep. After she tried Nana's other remedy for insomnia, walking backwards three times around the room, she lay in bed, the faces and hands and names of her competitors, many from foreign countries, rushing through her mind with disconnected passages of the music they had played in the elimination rounds. Jane wondered if she had chosen the right piece. Four other pianists were performing the same sonata. But she trusted Mr. Lamb's advice.

Mr. Lamb rarely left his home but announced that this was one event he would not miss. He was waiting in front of his house when Jane and her parents pulled up. No one talked much on the drive downtown. Jane and her teacher fingered silent passages on the seat, he in the front, Jane in the back with her mother, in a mute four-hand piano duet.

As Jane crossed the stage to the piano, she looked for her teacher in the audience. He nodded, and mouthed the words, "Play for me."

She did. She shut out the world and pulled herself inside the music and played it for her teacher. Afterward, she remembered little of her performance. She waited backstage with the other pianists until all of them had taken their turns. When her name was announced as the second-place winner, she heard the words echoed by whispers of Nana's voice and stood frozen in place in the wings. A Japanese girl whose playing Jane had particularly admired gave her a hug and pushed her toward the stage.

There were also hugs from her parents a few minutes later. Mr. Lamb hung back from them as Jane accepted congratulations from the crowd around her. She looked around for Gary, a high school friend she had dated a few times. Jane wasn't sure he was serious when he said he would come to hear her play. He appeared at the edge of the crowd and pretended to toss a bouquet of daisies to her as he might launch a football. Gary eased through the group of people, handed her the flowers, and shook hands with her parents.

He gave Jane a quick embrace. She stood with her arms around him for a moment. As she peered around the boy's broad shoulder, she felt a shock of longing when her gaze connected with Mr. Lamb's. It was his arms she imagined holding her. But she also felt a rush of power and pressed against the boy longer than she might have, until Mr. Lamb's raised eyebrows and smile suggested amusement at the game she played. Jane said something to the young man, and they walked toward Mr. Lamb.

Before Jane could hug her teacher, he took her hands—and the daisies—in his and held them, an obstacle between their bodies. "Excellent. *Brava*."

"Did I remember everything?"

"Enough for this crowd." He released her hands and took a step back. "You played beautifully. We'll talk about the little things at your next lesson."

"Mr. Lamb, I'd like you to meet Gary —"

"Lee." Mr. Lamb and Jane spoke the name together.

"Quarterback of the football team. I thought you looked familiar. From sports page photos. You're having quite a season."

"Thank you, sir." He sounded pleased with the recognition. "My mother has been a fan of yours for years. She'll be so excited that I got to meet you."

They shook hands.

"Congratulations again." Gary kissed her on the cheek. "See you in school Monday."

On the ride back, Mr. Lamb reminisced with Jane's father about music they had performed together and musicians they had both known.

Jane talked with her mother, but she watched Mr. Lamb's profile, willing him to look at her, talk to her, make contact with her. "Everyone at school is saying Gary will probably lead the team to state finals this year. A bunch of colleges are already interested in him."

"He's taking you to the dance next week?" her mother asked.

Jane thought she saw her teacher turn his head a bit, as though he had tuned into their conversation. "Yes. But I can wear the dress from last year. He hasn't seen it." Jane was never particularly interested in clothing or hairstyles, but she found herself wishing that Mr. Lamb cared. He seemed not to notice that she had changed from the awkward child who played a Chopin waltz for him four years ago. She angled her body so she could watch his profile as he continued his conversation with her father.

A few days later, her practicing was interrupted by the sound of a car horn honking in the driveway that connected the alleyway to their garage. From the window, she could see her father's car sitting in the driveway. He waved and motioned for her to come downstairs. Jane and Bridget reached the door between the kitchen and the garage at the same time and together opened the garage door for Jack.

He pulled the sedan in slowly, turned off the engine, and leaned out the window. "Did you tell her?" he asked Bridget.

"Not a word."

"A word about what?" Jane had no idea what her parents were talking about.

"I thought my last time driving the Dodge in here should be a bit special," began Jack.

"We're getting a new car?"

"You're getting a new practice room."

It took Jane a moment to understand.

"It's an early Christmas present," Bridget said. "Your father has been making plans for months to turn the garage into a studio for you."

At Jane's next lesson she told Mr. Lamb about the music room.

"Good. Your father and I talked about it some time ago. You need a place like that to practice." He turned on the lights over the piano and rearranged the pencils already lined up in a neat row on a folded linen napkin above the keyboard. "You know that even if it's not time for a lesson, you can still come here to practice any time you want some supervision."

"I'd like that, especially if I do any more competitions."

"If?"

"When." Jane watched as her teacher placed the pencils in yet another order.

"You're still playing on your little spinet?"

"It's all I've got at home for now. But I've been saving my allowance and lunch money, and the school has been great about letting me practice on the concert grand whenever I can."

Mr. Lamb seemed satisfied with the arrangement of pencils and stilled his fingers. "Good." He settled into his chair and Jane began her scales.

Forty-five minutes later, she glanced at her watch, the football game on her mind. She began to speed up the tempo of the Chopin Nocturne she was playing until Mr. Lamb slowed her down with a hand on her shoulder. "It says cut time in here somewhere? You've got the notes but you're running away with the music." Suddenly, she was aware of nothing but his closeness, the gentle weight of his hand on her shoulder. Her lips parted and she drew in a deep breath, surprised at the intensity of the wave of heat that warmed her belly. Jane wanted to turn her head and press her mouth against the back of his hand and taste the salt on his skin.

Mr. Lamb pulled his hand away as if he, too, had felt the heat. He moved away from her. His voice was husky, brusque. "Do you have somewhere to go that you're in such a hurry? That you can't give poor Frederick his due? You're playing it like the 'Minute Waltz'."

"I'm going to the football game tonight."

"Well, you don't want to be late for that." He sounded relieved, glad that she was leaving, breaking the contact.

"I'm going out afterward with Gary and some other kids." Jane didn't know why she had said it. After she had spoken, it sounded so silly. She stacked up her music books and took the check from her pocket.

"You're not thinking about giving up piano for cheerleading again, are you?"

"Not right now." She placed the check on the piano. "Gary wouldn't want that. He's a musician, too."

"Oh?"

"He sings in the advanced chorus and plays in the jazz band."

Jane leaned against the doorframe, holding her music. Usually, Mr. Lamb walked her to the door, but this afternoon he sat in his chair, keeping distance between them. He reached for his pipe, knocking cold ashes into the wastebasket. "Have a good time at the game, and be careful. Musicians can be even more trouble than football players." Before Jane could respond, he began filling the bowl of the pipe with darkly fragrant tobacco. "Next week, practice the Nocturne with the metronome. You need to develop control."

He hadn't said goodbye, but Jane knew she had been dismissed. Mr. Lamb lit a match and focused on the flame burning closer to his fingertips.

The following day, work began on the transformation of the garage into a music room. Jane's father was standing on the oil-stained concrete floor talking to the contractor when Jane ran in waving an envelope.

"It's information on Juilliard!" She hugged her father and ran into the TV room where her mother had set up the ironing board.

"The application for Juilliard came in the mail." She opened the envelope. For a moment, she held the school brochure in her hands as though she were trying to absorb the information through her skin, then began scanning the course descriptions and application procedures.

Her mother froze in place, the iron held above a flowered tablecloth. Bridget cleared her throat and nearly burned her fingers as she aggressively resumed the ironing. "I thought you might decide to stay a little closer to home for the first year or so."

"You went off to New York when you were my age."

"But the city was a lot different then."

"You're going to have to let me go sometime!"

Jack walked in. "Why don't you two come help me make a decision about where the door should go. You don't have to send applications for a while."

Bridget turned away from them to fold the tablecloth, then reached for a pillowcase. "You and Jane can figure it out. I really need to finish this ironing."

Jane picked up the information and envelope and left the room with her father. A part of her wanted to stay and tell her mother that she understood her fears. Another part of Jane—the part that was pulling her away from her family and into her own life—argued that her mother had never understood her or her music.

***

A few weeks later, near the end of Jane's lesson, a red pickup truck pulled up to the curb and parked. The driver's head nodded in time with music from the radio in uneasy counterpoint to the rhythms Jane breathed as she played a Chopin waltz.

When Jane reached the end of the piece, she skipped a repeat, her attention drawn to the truck outside. Mr. Lamb spoke over the fading final chord. "Your ride?"

"It's Gary. He said he'd pick me up before the game." It had been Jane who had asked for the ride. She had wanted to be together with the two of them again.

"Tell him to come in."

Jane closed her music and stacked it on the sofa. After she placed Mr. Lamb's check on the piano, she moved to the front door. She caught Gary's attention and waved him toward the house. She was aware of both of them watching her. Gary ran across the yard with an athlete's unconscious grace, running a hand through his sandy hair to tame it as he reached the door. Jane felt charged with sexual energy, enjoying for an instant the fantasy of welcoming a second lover into a space shared with the first.

"It's good to see you again, Mr. Lamb." Gary extended his hand. He wore an old football jersey, and the muscles of his arm played beneath tanned skin as he grasped the older man's hand.

Mr. Lamb's grip was as strong. Jane knew stories were still told about the strings he had broken on his grand piano practicing Rachmaninoff. She suddenly wanted to be pressed between them, crushed and taken by both, seizing power and control in the taking. She stepped back so she could breathe again.

Mr. Lamb had moved to his chair and gestured to the folded newspaper on it. "Just wanted to wish you good luck against North tonight. Paper says they're going to be tough to beat."

"I think we'll do all right. The team's healthy and I'll have my good luck charm in the stands." Gary put his arm around Jane, who was both pleased and embarrassed by the corny remark. "Did Jane tell you she got her application from Juilliard?"

Mr. Lamb turned away from them and settled in his chair. He unfolded the newspaper and appeared to search for a story, perhaps one he had been reading before Jane's arrival. When he spoke, it was directly to Gary. "I don't believe she mentioned it. What are your plans for next year? Jane says you're a musician, too. Are you going to continue with your music?"

"I'm not a musician like Jane. Just tenor sax in the jazz band."

"The big sax." Mr. Lamb glanced up from his paper, sharing a musician's tired joke with Gary.

"Yes, sir. But not the biggest." Jane knew he meant the huge baritone saxophones, which seemed to rumble rather than sing.

"Big enough."

Jane felt dizzy.

Mr. Lamb ended the exchange by focusing again on the paper. "Good luck against North."

Jane glanced back as she left the house, but her teacher's eyes never left the page.

***

The following Friday, Jane explained to Mr. Lamb that she hadn't made any decisions about where to go to college. Her mother certainly wasn't encouraging her to head for New York. She had hoped Mr. Lamb would want to discuss it, to offer her some advice, but he had simply responded that he would be glad to help her choose and prepare some audition pieces for wherever she decided to apply.

He sat in his chair, calling out different major and minor keys, and she warmed up by playing the requested scales and arpeggios. After a few minutes, he stood and nodded toward the new sonata he had given her the week before. Jane made room on the bench for her teacher, hoping that he would play the piece for her as he often did to introduce music she had never played, but he remained standing.

Jane slid from the right end of the piano bench to the center, experiencing a momentary disorientation until she had aligned herself with middle C. Her teacher moved out of the crowded living room into the kitchen where he could hear her but let her pretend she was alone. She shut out the world, except for the sweet cherry whisper of his pipe tobacco, and heard the first notes in her head. The melody line which had consumed her for the past week, the liquid caress of the harmony slipping under it, was there, and her fingers reached out and caught up with it and she played what she had discovered about the music. It was actually quite simple. The Mozart was sex. It was the masculine and the feminine, the ragged breath and the driving finish, the lace and the sweat, the maddened fingers and the swollen lips.

And then she was there at the end of the first movement of the sonata, beyond the edge. She hadn't pedaled the last note at all. Had actually hit it and dropped it in surprise that she had gone so far. Too quickly she had snatched her hands from the keys as though they had burned her, and her hands lay clenched in separate fists near her knees. The final note still echoed in her head like an aftershock, like the metronome pulse between her thighs. C, she thought without meaning to, the dominant.

Mr. Lamb hadn't said anything. She knew he had come back into the room and had been behind her for the page turn. She had felt more than seen the motion as he reached over her shoulder to turn the page, his hand brushing close enough to her cheek to warm it without quite touching. She knew, on some level, that he had leaned into her to drink in the scent of her skin, her hair. A sweet and secret theft.

She didn't know if he had read the "feathers/ice/warm breath & knives" she had penciled at the top of the page, and he had reacted with an intake of breath, she thought, when she said "Fuck" in frustration at playing the wrong notes. There had been wrong notes, and maybe he was angry with that. But she knew it was more. She was wet and weak and flushed with the power of the music and felt suddenly embarrassed, as though she had spread her legs in front of him and touched herself and he had seen her pleasure.

She waited for him to turn away and tell her not to bring this Mozart next week. But he hadn't turned away.

His left hand brushed the hair away from the back of her neck. "*Accarezzevole*," she thought. "Caressing." Her nipples hardened, and she waited for his teeth to graze the skin at her hairline, an answer and a question. He did not touch her again. She wanted to turn around and open her mouth to him, but she wanted the music more.

She leaned back, relaxing her shoulders against his body. She felt his cock pressed hard against her spine. He started to back away, but before he could take a step she whispered, "Stay." She curved her fingers over the keys in position for the first notes of the sonata. His right hand turned the pages back to the beginning, then both hands rested on her shoulders like listening angels.

"Play it again," he said. The angels shifted easily, languidly. He whispered into her hair. "And relax. There's still too much tension in your hands. Don't rush anything this time. You can't force it. Let the music take you where it wants to go."

She pressed harder against him, letting him support her weight, and resting her head against his chest, she fell into the music.

Chapter Nine
Parsley (*Petroselinum crispum*)

May 1 – 15, 1998

By eight o'clock, Jane had packed up the car and checked out of the hotel. Three hours later, a new refrigerator was humming beside the tiny two-burner stove, Jane had made up the bed and put her clothes away, the box from her grandmother sat atop the oak dresser, and white dishes had been washed and stacked on shelves in the kitchen. A breeze from the ocean played in the hummingbird wind chime.

Each trip Jane made from the car to the house reminded her that a high priority was clearing away the grass that had overgrown the lot and the path to the house. The sun had dried the earth in the garden enough to plant the seedlings and sow the seeds, and Jane chose that as her project for the afternoon.

She gathered her gardening tools and carried the boxes and bags to the edge of the garden. She nestled the roots of the seedling herbs into the hand-tilled soil, then focused on the bricks defining and crossing the garden. The earth had stained black crescent moons at the base of her fingernails. Jane dug her hands back into the ground, searching for the sharp, Braille edge that meant she'd found another buried brick, ripping away the grass that covered it, sensing a pattern emerging in the way she might anticipate the structure of a melody from the first few notes she heard. She could tell that the outer rim, about ten feet in diameter, was almost circular, egg-shaped, really. Pathways in a simple pattern, a single brick-length wide flanked by matching bricks placed end-to-end along the length of the paths, entered from five points, leaving a gap in the center of their intersection. Jane sat back on her heels and brushed her short hair away from her face, striping her cheek with a smudge of the black soil. She looked toward her house.

From where she sat, she could see only the tops of windows and the artificial horizon of the roof. The roofline sagged a bit but most of the weathered shingles were in place. The chimney had lost a few bricks at the top, but, she thought, pointed in the right direction. When she leaned back on her hands and looked up, Jane could see the tangle of branches of the weeping willow playing against the intense blue of the North Carolina sky. The wind whipped a Chopin prelude through the branches, but she didn't want to hear it. She just wanted to feel the early May sun and watch the tree that had called her to the house.

Gradually, she became aware of the rumble of a motor, blended at first with the murmuring of bees in the lilacs, then separating out in the solo chugging of an engine. Jane stood, wiped her hands on her jeans and stared out over the ripples of grass toward the road. She walked to the picket fence and saw an industrial-sized riding lawn mower crawling like a powerful beetle toward her. McCue waved to her from his bouncing perch. A safety flag fluttered from a pole behind him, and he looked to Jane like a knight with his pennant riding into battle. Jane opened the gate and met him in the road.

"I heard you had some grass that needed to be cut," he said as soon as he had turned off the motor. "Cairncross Landscape and Flute Repair at your service."

"Where'd you get that thing? It's great! Not your everyday mode of transportation, is it?"

"I only borrow it for special occasions." McCue dismounted from the lawn mower. "I figured I could start out here and clear some more space for parking. Then we'll ride this thing through the gate and find your front yard."

"What can I do? I'm not one of those helpless Southern belles, you know."

He pointed to Jane's bare, earth-stained hands with his gloved ones, "First, you put on your work gloves. My blisters are better, but it looks like you're working on some beauties of your own. Then you can tackle the wicked work." He handed her grass clippers that had been behind the seat. "You can use these to cut the grass under the fence and trim around the posts. You get your gloves, and I'll start out here."

Jane nodded and headed for the house as McCue revved up the motor. When she returned with her gloves, she watched him for a moment from the porch. He was clearly enjoying the work, and seemed to be whistling a tune Jane couldn't hear. He tapped the steering wheel in a rhythmic accompaniment. Jane crossed back through the yard, knelt down, and began to trim under the picket fence.

In a few hours, the mower and clippers had turned the tall grass into a respectable yard. Jane helped McCue dump the clippings in the woods. "Will you come in and have something to drink? Iced tea or soda or something? And please let me pay you for the work today. I don't know how I could have done it myself."

McCue glanced at his watch. "Sure. I'll have a glass of whatever you're having. I've got two evening lessons to teach, and that mower goes about fifteen miles an hour top speed on the road, but a cold drink sounds good." He put the clippers back behind the seat and followed Jane toward the house. Both of them brushed loose grass off their clothes and left their shoes beside the front door.

"Amazing," McCue said as they walked into the living room.

Sun shone through clean windows. The hearth of the fireplace was swept. "I haven't finished painting, and it's still a bit Spartan," Jane said, "but maybe that's what I wanted." McCue looked around for a place to sit. "I'll have to get some furniture."

"Moira knows every antique store around, if you're interested in that sort of thing. She would probably love to go shopping with you."

"What about the store?"

"She can take time off when she wants to."

Jane led the way to the kitchen and was pleased to see McCue's approval of her work there, too. "You've moved in!"

"Getting there." Jane reached into the new refrigerator for two cold cans of soda. She took them to the porch, and McCue followed. They sat together on the steps that faced the ocean.

"Have you walked on your beach yet?"

"No, but I can't wait much longer. Mike said the stairs were dangerous, and he would send someone out to check the dune and see what should be done. He was worried that I might trip on the vines on the way down the hill, and the last thing I want to do is end up with a broken ankle at the bottom of the hill with the tide coming in."

"Want to go for a little walk before I leave?"

"Do you have time?"

"I have enough time for a quick walk so you won't be tempted to try this alone in the middle of the night." He reached out to help her up, but she pretended not to notice and led the way, walking carefully over the dune. Halfway down the hill, she slipped in the loose sand and McCue caught her before she could fall. He took her hand until they reached the beach.

When they were on level sand, he noticed the tears that filled Jane's eyes. "Did you twist your ankle back there?"

"No. I'm fine." The setting sun behind them had stained the sky an impossible coral pink. The ocean was turquoise except where it reflected rosy clouds. "'There is hope from the sea...'"

If McCue knew the rest of the Irish proverb, "but none from the grave," he didn't finish it out loud. He reached into his pocket and offered her a wrinkled handkerchief. "It's clean. Maybe just a little sweaty."

Jane wiped her eyes. She refolded the cotton square and handed it back to McCue. "This reminds me of when I was about ten and my violin teacher would give me his handkerchief."

"This one has cleaned a lot of flutes—and wiped a few tears, too." They walked without speaking for several minutes. Jane stopped every few steps to pick up a shell, and McCue told her what kind of shell she held. "You might want to bring some plastic bags with you the next time. Usually when I walk on the beach, I carry two bags: one for shells and one for trash."

He splashed into the surf up to his ankles, reached down into the water, and held up a white disc about three inches across that the waves were pulling out to sea. "A sand dollar. But it's broken." He showed her the jagged edge that marred the perfection of the shell and prepared to throw it back into the water.

"Please don't throw it back! I want to keep it."

"There will be lots more," he said, handing it to her. "If you want to keep it, soak it overnight in some bleach so it doesn't start to stink." He glanced at his watch. "I probably ought to head back to return the mower if you've satisfied your curiosity about the beach."

"Enough for today. Thank you. It's going to be hard to stay away from the water." Jane's pockets were full of scallop shells, and she cradled the sand dollar in her palm. They walked together in silence back to the base of the hill. When they started the climb, McCue held out his hand and Jane let him help her this time.

"Thanks again. I'd like to pay you for the work you did today. It would have taken forever for me to mow all that."

"It wouldn't have taken forever. And not another word about payment. This is fun."

McCue reached behind the seat of the mower and retrieved a clean tee shirt. When he pulled the grass-stained one over his head, Jane saw that his shoulder was striped with Band-Aids. Smaller scratches, red and swollen, mapped the areas between.

"You didn't do that cutting down the pines, did you?" She hadn't remembered so many cuts from two days before.

McCue pulled the clean tee shirt over his head. "A friend and I had a bit of a run-in last night."

The woman had scratched with long, red, perfect nails, Jane thought, thrusting her own hands into the deep pockets of her overalls. In a flash of crazy jealousy, Jane wondered if the woman had used her teeth, too. Had McCue?

Her fingers touched the plastic bag of seed in her pocket. She grabbed the seed and the subject. "If I plant this now, will it grow?"

"What is it?"

She felt like an idiot. Of course he couldn't tell, and she couldn't remember which bag she'd dropped into her pocket this morning.

Jane opened the bag and held the twist tie in her mouth. She unfolded the tiny handwritten label that had been nested inside. "Parsley," she mumbled around the plastic-coated wire.

"Oh, yes," he said, taking the tie from her mouth. Could he have come closer to grazing her lips without touching her? With care equal to hers, he reclosed the bag and handed it to her. "Moira's parsley will grow fine in your garden if you plant it now."

"Maybe I can get it in before the sun goes down." She watched McCue climb back on the mower. "Thanks again for your help. And thank your friend for the use of the mower."

McCue nodded and turned the key. The noisy engine sputtered, then began its even rumbling. He turned the key off and ran his fingers through his dark hair. "Have you talked to the phone company about starting your phone service?"

"No. I kind of like the idea of not having a phone. There's a pay phone about a mile away if I need one."

"A mile is an awful long way in an emergency. And what if I wanted to call you—to find out how your parsley is growing or if your grass needs to be trimmed or something. Or maybe I'd want to ask you about going to dinner. Of course, I guess I'm getting ahead of myself. I don't even know if you would be free to see me even if you wanted to have dinner. If you know what I mean." McCue dismounted the mower. "Damn. I think I'm going about this all wrong."

"No. I'm sorry." Jane's voice was nearly inaudible. "It's not you, it's me. I'm just not good at this." McCue started to speak but stopped when Jane held up her hand in a wordless request for his silence. "I'm divorced, so I guess I'm 'free.' I just don't think I'd be very good company."

"Well, we could go to a really bad movie, or we could head for the worst restaurant in Wilmington. Then we'd have such low expectations that no one could be disappointed."

"That might work." Jane couldn't help smiling at the absurdity of his plan. "But I need a little time."

"You can have all the time you want. Besides, it might take me a while to find a bad restaurant around here." McCue climbed back onto the mower seat. "How about that phone? I can call the phone company first thing tomorrow." Jane stood quiet, staring at the sand dollar. "Even convents have phones, you know. Just a plain black phone for emergencies?"

"Okay. Just a plain black phone for emergencies."

Jane pulled a few weeds from the base of the mailbox as she watched McCue disappear down the road, bouncing rhythmically on the mower seat. Before he reached the corner that would take him out of sight, he turned and waved. Jane waved back, clipped a few of the pink rose buds to add to the bouquet on her table, and headed to the house, admiring the neat lawn. As the sky darkened, she planted the parsley seeds in an empty spot in the garden. Nearby, in an old dogwood tree, a round-bellied robin worked diligently, carrying pieces of straw and string to weave into her nest.

As she ate her first dinner in the little house, Jane made a list of furniture she would need. The idea of shopping for antiques with Moira and Kaeth was appealing. The living room needed chairs and perhaps a tiny sofa, and a telephone table for her "convent" phone. A bookshelf and desk or table would turn the smallest room into a charming study. All of the books she had brought along were still in cardboard cartons, except one that now lay beside her bed. As she unpacked, she had found a worn copy of Anne Morrow Lindberg's *A Gift from the Sea* tucked into her suitcase with a note. "Found this first edition at our favorite bookstore. A gift to help you heal by the sea. Ken."

After a long, soaking bath in the footed tub, Jane curled up in bed with the diary.

Friday, April 14, 1933
Dear diary,

Today was Good Friday. At services, I tried to concentrate on asking forgiveness for my behavior with Brian, but the more I thought about him, the more I wanted to be with him again and the less I wanted to repent a single kiss. How could I pay attention to the droning sermon of old Father Devlin with memories of Brian's sweet mouth and music tangling up my thoughts?

Grandmother Reilly visited all day and made us spend most of the day cleaning house. We heard the same old stories about how when she was a girl they not only cleaned inside, but also whitewashed the whole outside of the house on Good Friday. Jenny said she was glad our house was brick, and Mother shushed her and told her not to be disrespectful, but I know Jenny didn't mean any disrespect by it. I was glad it was brick, too.

We had to be quiet from noon to three. Jenny fell asleep, but I couldn't stop thinking about Brian and wishing there was enough money this year for new Easter clothes so I could wear them the next time I see him. Before Grandmother left, she planted some parsley seed to bless the garden even though it was cold and she moved slow with her arthritis. I helped her so we could get back inside. Before Da took her back home, she made Mother promise to trim our finger- and toenails and cut our hair. Grandmother Reilly says cutting your hair on Good Friday keeps headaches away all year, and Mother says it's best not to sneer at the old ways because sometimes there's truth in them.

Tomorrow we'll have the Holy Water blessed and sprinkle it all over for good luck. Is it a sin to hope the good luck means I'll see Brian again?

Jane closed the notebook and set it beside her bed, aware of an almost physical ache in her chest from missing her grandmother. She had so many questions, and she doubted her mother would have the answers. She listened to the ocean and the breeze rustling the branches of the willow tree. Night sounds hummed her to sleep and covered the stealthy footfall of a nocturnal animal. Amber eyes watched Jane through the French doors until the moon rose high over the tiny house by the sea.

*****

Friday morning of the following week, Jane woke to the gentle percussion of rain. Wrapped in an old quilt she had found on her shopping trip with Moira and Kaeth, she sat and rocked on the back porch and watched the unsettled ocean. McCue had been right; Moira was delighted to let a neighbor watch the store while she and Kaeth directed Jane from one antique shop to another. Jane learned about folk art and Brumby rockers and crazy quilts as they piled treasures into the car. Steve had gone back to collect a two-seater sofa for the living room and a bird's-eye maple secretary for the study.

Jane had removed her books from cartons and arranged them on the shelves of the secretary. Inside the desk, the flute rested in its scuffed case. Could the flute have belonged to "Brian" in the diary? Was he her grandfather? Jane left the chair rocking by itself in the breeze on the porch and went into her study. She opened the desk drawer and removed the case, laying it on the desktop. She ran her fingers over the leather as though her touch might conjure up a genie to tell her the story of the flute.

McCue might be home, if she wanted to have him check out the old instrument. She went into the living room, dropped the folded quilt over the back of the sofa, and sat down on the end nearest the phone. Under the plain black telephone, Jane found the card printed in Moira's sprawling script with her phone number, McCue's number, and the number for information on weather and tides. Very important, she had insisted, for anyone living on the beach.

Jane dialed the first three digits of McCue's phone number, then hung up. She clasped her hands together to stop their shaking. She hated calling people on the telephone, wasn't sure what to say to him. Maybe she should just put the flute in the car and drive to Aria. Then, if she changed her mind about taking the flute to him, he needn't ever know.

Jane ran nervous fingers through her short hair. Her eyes had lost what Ken once called their "haunted" look, the bruise-colored circles that had alarmed him. She put on lipstick, realizing she had not opened her small cosmetics case for a month. She wiped it off with the back of her hand as she laid the flute case beside her on the front seat.

Aria was sleepy and gray in the rain, as it had been on her first visit to Moira's store. Driving past the Jackson house, she thought the lace curtain at the front door looked as though someone held the edge back from the frame of the door, but there were no lights on that she could see. The garden store was also dark, as McCue had told her it would be on a Friday. Warm light spilled onto the wet sidewalk in front of the flute shop, and Jane saw McCue bending over the worktable inside. She drove past without stopping.

"This is stupid," she said out loud when she had gone to the end of the block. "Just take the flute to him." She turned around in the next driveway and parked in front of the shop, then grabbed the flute case and got out of the Jeep. Before she could analyze her feelings or reconsider, she found herself listening to the ringing of the doorbell inside the shop.

When the door opened, Jane watched McCue's smile of recognition change to a look of near panic. He turned and took a step back into the room, and Jane wondered if she had interrupted a meeting with some other woman, the lover she suspected of mapping his skin with scratches. At the same instant, she became aware of music playing in the room—a poor-quality recording of a Schumann piano concerto.

"The A minor," she whispered. "I played it here." She wanted to turn around and run back to her car and drive as quickly as she could to the shelter of her house, but the music held her.

"I'm sorry —" McCue moved toward the sound system against the far wall.

Before Jane could ask who was playing the piece, she recognized the late entrance of the strings near the end of the first movement, the *Allegro affettuoso*. "There was no recording made of that performance."

"I'm so sorry." McCue stopped the music. A gentle drumming of rain outside broke the sudden silence. "I recorded it."

"That's illegal and invasive and just wrong!"

"I'll destroy the CD if you want me to."

"Why would you keep it anyway?" Jane was unaware of her tears. "Why would you want to listen to it? It's flawed. I've left behind much better work." She turned to leave.

"Wait." He ejected the CD from the player. "I listen to it because it was the only time I got to watch you play, and because after you lost your concentration in the Adagio, the music became more magical. The flaws made it even more precious to me. But I'll get rid of it if that's what you want."

"Can you just put it away for now?"

He slipped the CD into a case and hid it behind a huge conch shell on top of the bookshelf.

"Trade you," he said, holding out a clean folded handkerchief from his pocket and pointing to the flute case that Jane had forgotten she was holding.

She handed him the case and wiped her eyes and nose. "I don't know what's wrong with me. I haven't cried in years and now..."

"Good thing I've got lots of handkerchiefs. I must bring out the Irish side of you." He carried the worn case to the worktable. "Let's see what your flute looks like."

As Jane turned to follow him, she noticed all six of her CDs lined up on his bookshelf.

"I've been a fan of yours for a long time."

"I think Galway's got me outnumbered." Jane nodded toward a different section of the CD holder.

"Only because Jimmy has recorded more. Would you like to borrow some of them?"

"No." Jane was embarrassed at the sharpness of her reply. "Maybe another time."

"Just let me know." McCue opened the case and Jane moved beside him to look at the flute. "Do you know anything about it?" He lifted the shortest of the darkened metallic tubes out of the red velvet lining.

"It's tarnished," she said half in jest as she tried to decide if she should share her speculation about the flute.

"But look at this." McCue turned the darkened silver so she could see different colored metal surrounding the opening for the flutist to blow over. "It's got a gold mouthpiece. This is no cheap student model."

He handed the section to Jane, and she was surprised at its warmth, at the warmth it must have absorbed from his hand.

"I won't know much about its condition until I take it apart, but it's certainly worth fixing." He looked around the shop at other instruments in various states of repair. "It will take me a week or so to get it in playing condition. Would you like me to do that?"

"I'm not sure. I don't know what I'd do with it."

"I could teach you how to play it."

"I just don't do music right now. I can't explain it."

"You don't need to explain anything." He reached out and took the section of flute from her. "It has claimed you already." McCue nestled it in the case.

"Claimed me?"

He took her hand. She felt herself pulling away from his touch, but he did not let go. When she began to relax, he gently opened the fingers she had clenched into a fist and ran his finger over the tarnish mark on her palm. "It's left its mark on you. That's a good sign." He took the handkerchief that she still clutched in her left hand and wiped at the stain. Then he tucked the cotton square into his shirt pocket. "Why don't I fix it up, and if you decide you don't want to keep it, I'll buy it from you. I always have students who are looking for new instruments."

At his touch, she had been thrust into the past to her first lesson with Joseph Lamb. He had studied her hands and led her into a world of music and love. She felt herself closing off from McCue, and as though he knew she had reached a barrier she could not cross, he released her hand.

"Yes. Please take care of it. Someone in the family might like to have it someday."

She sensed movement in the room, a ripple in the space beside her. A huge cat leaped from one of the top shelves and landed on McCue's shoulder. Pointed ears twitched; amber eyes stared into hers. He draped himself possessively around McCue's neck.

"Be very quiet and try not to look like prey."

Jane wondered if he was serious but caught his smile.

He nodded to one of the chairs in front of the music stand. "Sit there," he said to her, and she did. He stood very still. "This is Duncan." He gently scratched the cat's ears, and Jane was surprised to find herself envious of the attention.

She recognized the white-rimmed eyes, spotted coat, and stunted tail from cats she had watched for hours at the zoo. "He's a bobcat?"

McCue nodded and the dark curls of his beard seemed to tangle with the cat's tawny fur and merge the two of them.

"Is he tame?" As if declaring his independence, Duncan pushed off from McCue's shoulder and landed with a muted thud on the worktable.

McCue winced. "That's how I got those scratches last week. Some things can't be tamed. One can only hope for a peaceful truce with them." Duncan stretched out with his head resting on the flute case. "He likes your flute."

"Maybe I'll have to try it then." Jane had not intended to say it out loud. The amber eyes closed, and the bobcat curled its lip in a silent snarl, revealing tiny, pointed fangs. "I don't think he likes me."

"He just doesn't know you. And he knows he has to go outside when I teach a lesson. He's too unpredictable to keep inside when students are here."

"Does he like flute music?"

"Actually, that's how I found him—or how he found me." McCue sat at the second chair in front of the music stand. Both of them watched Duncan as he cleaned his paws like any domestic cat. "I was involved with a music festival in Ashville a few years ago and was out in the woods practicing —"

"That's something I couldn't do as a kid."

"A major advantage of the flute. I used to spend hours playing a single note, working on tone or breathing."

Jane remembered her first impression of McCue as a reed-playing faun and wondered what her Irish grandmother would have said about that. He picked up a flute that was standing upright in a holder near the music stand and began to breathe into it as though warming it, infusing it with part of himself. Jane felt a stab of panic. She wanted to run, as she had for the past few months, from any contact with music. But no melody emerged to make her flee, to force her to disconnect from the rare ease she felt in his presence. Instead, a ribbon of velvet sound seemed to spin into the air in the room and weave around the dust motes, brush her cheek, enter her belly, hypnotize her. The dark tufts of fur on Duncan's ears began to twitch, and Jane could hear the rumble of a purr from the cat's throat harmonizing with the single note of the flute.

Suddenly, the bobcat leaped to the floor beside McCue. Jane realized a car had pulled up and parked outside the shop. McCue replaced the flute in its stand and rubbed the cat between the ears, eliciting a louder purr. It brushed against his leg, narrowing yellow eyes at Jane, then padded toward a door at the back of the shop and waited to be let out. Jane and McCue stood at the same moment from the music stand chairs. As McCue let Duncan out the back door, Mike entered with a young girl.

"Jane," he said, shaking her hand, "I'd like you to meet my daughter, Emily. Emily, this is Jane Bell."

Emily had inherited much of her father's charm. "I'm so pleased to meet you. My mother has lots of your CDs, and she lets me listen to them. I took one to school when we had students' choice day in music class."

"That's a real compliment."

"Most of the kids brought in rap music, but the teacher was really glad that I brought Chopin."

"I'm pleased that I could be a good influence." Jane glanced at McCue. "You'll call me when the flute is ready?"

"You got your phone then?"

"Yes, a plain black one. Thanks for calling the phone company for me." McCue picked up a pencil from the music stand and a piece of blank staff paper. Jane felt a stab of familiarity as she watched him poise the sharpened point over the waiting lines.

"Do you mind if I write that down, too?" Mike was pulling a small notebook from his pocket. "I'm glad you got that phone.

It's safe out there, but you never know when you might need help with something."

Jane recited the number, and both men wrote it down. She said goodbye to all of them and left the shop, wishing she had been able to spend a little more time with McCue. As she drove slowly out of Aria, she thought she saw—or sensed—the bobcat racing beside her car, a presence that ruffled the grass and parted the thick afternoon air. She was not sure if he provided a protective escort or followed to be sure that she left the shop, departed from the town. She shivered in the heat. A goose on her grave, Nana would have told her.

Chapter Ten
Entruckt (G.) Withdrawn, Removed, Distant

1977 – 1978

The following week, Joseph did not come near Jane. She felt a wall between them; even his voice suggested distance from her, a coldness.

She played through her scales and arpeggios over and over. He stood looking out the front door, as far away from her as he could be in the living room. He stopped nearly each repetition with corrections—she wasn't reaching her thumb far enough under her hand to make smooth transitions from one octave to another as the scale ascended; her hand position had become sloppy; her fingers were not curved enough; several times in a row she had used a fourth finger where a third was clearly called for; she needed to begin paying attention.

She stopped in the middle of a minor scale and sat with her hands folded in her lap. Joseph did not turn to look at her.

"Nothing happened, you know." She spoke softly, as if to herself.

Her teacher did not move.

She repeated, in a louder voice directed to him, "Nothing happ—"

He turned to face her but came no closer. "That 'nothing' should never have happened, and I owe you an apology."

"I wanted you ... close to me."

He turned away from her again. "Would you like to start working on the Prokofiev sonata Mitsuko played at the competition?"

She began playing it. She had been studying the piece on her own, hoping that he would suggest it. "I'm not a child."

"No. You're not a child. But you are the pupil and I'm the teacher, and I shouldn't have let it happen." Before Jane could continue the discussion, Joseph opened his copy of the sonata and placed it on the piano. "Look carefully at the three opening measures."

He moved a few steps away from her, but Jane felt a far greater distance between them. She focused on the music more intently than before, sensing it was the only way to reach her teacher.

Music became a rough diamond passed between two jewelers who obsessively faceted and polished it until it reflected more light than either had thought possible. Spoken words were nearly abandoned by both as though speech had become an awkward second language that neither felt comfortable with. Jane would reach out to her teacher through the music, and he would respond. They joked with each other in Mozart's joyous passages. He challenged her with the physical and mental demands of Rachmaninoff. She seduced him with her uncanny explorations of the intricacies of Chopin etudes and nocturnes.

A few weeks before Christmas, as Jane helped her mother fix dinner, Bridget asked, "When is your application to Juilliard due in the mail?"

"In two weeks, but I didn't know if I was allowed to apply." Jane had filled out the application and read the catalogue dozens of times. Each piece she played for Joseph became a Juilliard audition in her imagination. In her daydreams, she roamed the streets of Manhattan between music classes and rehearsals, but at the end of each piano lesson, she wondered how she could leave her teacher.

"Why wouldn't you be allowed to apply?"

"You don't want me to go so far away. You think the city's too dangerous even though you got to go there when you were my age." Jane was crying. "You probably don't want me to have a career because you couldn't. You never finished your degree, and you don't want me to succeed at anything either." Jane could see the hurt and confusion in her mother's eyes but couldn't stop her attack. "You never understood the music and you never wanted me to take lessons from Mr. Lamb and now you're trying to keep me from learning from anyone else."

"Jane —"

"No! I'm sick of the way you try to control my life, and I'm sick of this whole stupid place." She turned to run out of the room.

"Jane, the check for the application fee has been on your desk for a week."

Jane paused for a second, then headed to her room. She reappeared about twenty minutes later. Her eyes were red from crying and tears began to fall when she spoke to her mother.

"I didn't mean what I said."

"We all say things we don't mean sometimes."

Jane wished her mother would hug her and make everything all right, the way she had when Jane was little, and Bridget might have wished for that, too, but neither seemed able to cross the divide between them that had opened up with Jane's words.

"And maybe you're right. I'm a little jealous of the life you have in front of you, but I do want you to succeed in your career."

"I know that."

"You're under a lot of pressure, applying to schools—and you have another competition next month. Jane, if you think it's too much with the end of your senior year, tell Mr. Lamb that you need some time off."

"You really don't understand, do you?" Jane felt another burst of anger toward her mother. "The music is what makes me get up in the morning and go back to that stupid high school so I can get out of here and go to New York."

Bridget turned to the kitchen sink and continued peeling potatoes.

"I'm just really tired." Jane picked up the pile of schoolbooks on the counter. "Do you want me to help with dinner?"

"Go get started on your homework. I'll finish setting the table." Bridget slipped a casserole into the oven as Jane started out of the kitchen. "Jane —"

Jane sighed and faced her mother.

"I know this is a difficult time for you. I wasn't much older than you are now when your father and I fell in love."

Jane was confused, then alarmed by her mother's comment. Could her mother know about her feelings for Joseph?

"You haven't been seeing much of Gary, and if that's part of the problem and you want to talk about it," she twisted the dishtowel in her hands, "or about anything else, I would be happy to talk with you." Her voice trailed away with a gentle puffed sigh, and Jane was reminded of the thousands of childhood wishes they had sent off with blown dandelion fluff. She moved closer and hugged her mother. It had been a long time since they had talked together. She was far more likely to talk with her father about music than she was to share thoughts with her mother, especially these past few years.

"Everything is fine." She took her mother's hands, which continued to twist and smooth out the dishtowel, and was surprised by how much they looked like her grandmother's hands, the skin thinner than she remembered, revealing slender tendons, and mottled with the hint of age. Her knuckles seemed thicker, and Jane wondered if they had begun to trouble her mother with the pain that Nana had endured.

Bridget seemed suddenly embarrassed and withdrew her hands. "Dinner will be ready in half an hour. I'd be glad to talk if you want to."

Jane knew confessing her feelings for Joseph would only confirm the suspicions her mother had harbored since she began her lessons. It was much easier if her mother thought Gary was the man she wanted. "Thank you for the check. Everything else is nearly ready to go in the mail. If I get to the next step, they'll schedule an audition. Do you think all three of us could go?"

"That would be fun. Your dad and I could show you all our old haunts in the city. Finish your homework, and we'll talk about it when we have dinner."

When Jane told Joseph at her next lesson, he seemed pleased about the decision. Tamping tobacco into his pipe, he said, "Actually, I also have some news. I've been asked to play something for a benefit at the University, and I'm thinking of saying yes." His voice was steady but the flame of the match in his hand quivered. He had not played in public since the single performance of his concertino for a small audience several years before. It had been well received, but after that evening, he had withdrawn even further from contact with the public. "I was wondering if you would be interested in working on one of the Rachmaninoff concertos for two pianos. You're ready for the pieces, and I wouldn't have to be up there all alone." He drew heavily on the pipe and Jane watched the flame bend and redden the tobacco.

"I would love that." She felt a rush of warmth at the thought of the intimate musical entanglement with her teacher. "When is the performance? Do you have the music so I can start working on it now?"

He stood to let her know it was time for her to leave. "I'm not sure they have a date yet. It will be sometime in the spring. I'll find the music, and we'll look at it at your lesson next week."

Jane paused when they reached the front door. "I mailed my application to Juilliard. If I get past that, they'll set up an audition, and I'll need to choose a piece to play."

"Of course they'll set up an audition. We can talk about that next week, too." Their eyes met briefly, and Jane realized how they had avoided that contact for the past few months. Neither of them said goodbye as Jane headed home.

When Jack and Bridget knocked on Jane's bedroom door a few days later and climbed the stairs together, Jane closed the chemistry book she was studying and looked at them with concern. Her father's question made her still more apprehensive.

"We were wondering how much money you have saved toward a new piano." Both her parents knew she had put all of her babysitting money and most of her allowance and lunch money in a savings account for the past several years. "We need to withdraw it tomorrow."

Jane's hands were shaking as she pulled the passbook from her desk drawer. "Is someone sick? Are you losing your job?" She looked at her parents for a clue to the strange request. Neither one of them seemed upset. In fact, her mother's pursed lips, and the deepening crinkles at the corners of her father's eyes, suggested that both of them were trying to hide smiles.

"Oh, no. Nothing like that," her father said.

"But we can't say anything more," her mother added.

Jane opened the book. "One thousand two hundred forty-seven dollars and twelve cents. You can have all of it, but I was going to use a little for Christmas presents."

"We thought this should be a very simple Christmas." Bridget said. "Why don't you make something little for us?"

Jane thought that sounded like they had all regressed to her life in second grade, but she agreed, not letting herself imagine that her parents' real plan might involve a new piano.

Three days after Christmas, she joined Linda for a morning of shopping at the post-holiday sales. Jane knew she would just be window-shopping. She had received small gifts, but no piano had appeared. Jane felt cheated. She slammed the front door shut on her way to her friend's house and felt no better for it, just embarrassed by her childishness. She resented the clothing Linda bought with her Christmas money. Back in the house, she threw her coat over a chair in the living room and yelled toward the den, where her mother was ironing and watching a soap opera, that she was going to practice on her stupid little piano. She had not heard from Juilliard about an audition, although when she thought about it, she knew they had not had enough time and were most likely on holiday break. She had not been able to play the Rachmaninoff two-piano piece with Joseph yet, and the music was more difficult than she had expected. Christmas had been crappy.

She walked into the garage-turned-music room. The tiny spinet had been pushed against a wall and another piano stood in the place it had occupied. It was not the used baby grand she had hoped for, but a new Steinway grand piano. Jane walked toward it slowly, as though afraid it was an apparition that might disappear if she approached it. She stood for a few seconds spellbound by the reflection of the sun on the glossy cherry-wood lid until its grain blurred through her tears. She wiped her eyes, dried her fingers on her shirttail and opened the keyboard cover.

She glanced up to see her parents standing in the doorway to the kitchen. "It's so beautiful," she whispered. "Are we renting it?" Jane knew even with the money she had saved, her parents could never afford to buy a piano like this one.

"It's your Christmas present," Bridget said. "Sorry it's a little late."

"We thought that wouldn't matter since it didn't fit in your stocking anyway." Jane's father had tears in his eyes, too.

"Thank you!" Jane ran to her parents and hugged them. "But how —"

"We've all been saving for this," Jack said. "And your grandmother helped out." He nodded to Bridget to continue the story.

"A few weeks ago, an elderly man with a brogue as thick as Nana's came to the door. He said that an investment she made years ago had matured. He handed me an envelope with a check. According to him, she requested that the money be used for your music if you 'still had the gift,' and the piano seemed the best way to do that."

"Still had the gift?" Jane asked, but Bridget only shrugged in response.

"Mr. Lamb helped choose the piano and negotiate a price with Elgin's, and here it is."

"I should call Mr. Lamb," Jane said, moving to the keyboard and adjusting the piano bench in front of it.

The phone rang as she sat down, and both her parents laughed. "That's probably him now. He has already called twice to see if you were home yet." Before they left the room, Jane began to play the Chopin waltz she had played for her first lesson with Joseph.

A little while later—she had no concept of passing time as she played but had now moved to her part in the two-piano Rachmaninoff—a knock at the door to the backyard broke her trance. Joseph stood outside in a snowstorm, his hair, graying at the temples, was windblown and silver with melting flakes. He clasped a worn leather portfolio under his arm as if afraid the gusts might carry it away. When he smiled, desire for him squeezed the breath from Jane, and for a second, she feared both her teacher and the new piano were part of some dream she would wake up from.

"May I join you?" Joseph asked, walking in and nodding toward the Steinway.

"Thank you so much!" She threw her arms around him and felt the tension in his body, as though he were as cold to her as the snow melting on her cheek. Then he put his free arm around her shoulder, and she felt him relax slightly. Jane took a step back. "It's beautiful."

Joseph handed her his coat, opened the portfolio, and removed his part of the Rachmaninoff. "From the beginning? You were taking that a little fast."

Jane wondered how long he had stood outside listening. She took her music off the new piano and started toward the spinet.

"No, no, that's your piano." He nodded toward the Steinway. "I'll play the little one." He took his seat on the bench of the older instrument, making it look even smaller than it had. When he warmed up with some scales and chords, he drew more sound from it than Jane thought possible.

"You should try the new piano."

Joseph winked at her. "They let me break it in for you at Elgin's. Let's take it from the top."

***

Spring passed for Jane like an etude practiced with the metronome set at far too fast a speed. She traveled with her parents to New York City for her Juilliard audition and received an acceptance the day before the performance of the Rachmaninoff. Bridget reacted with a slight frown of disapproval when she read a review out loud that compared the pianists to lovers, caressing, chasing, giving in to each other.

***

The snowy winter transitioned to one of the hottest springs Jane could remember. On a Saturday in mid-May, the temperature hovered in the nineties. Through the open windows in her mother's Chevy, a breeze swept in, tangling Jane's hair and pretending to cool her as she drove to a Saturday lesson. As she waited on the porch for another student to finish, the pounding out of an early Mozart sonata seemed to add weight and heat to the air.

Finally, the lesson was over, and a young boy and his mother left.

"Have you been keeping cool?" Joseph stepped close to the old fan slowly swiveling between the piano and his big chair.

"I just came from swimming with some friends." As Jane walked from the porch into the living room, she wondered if Joseph could tell she wasn't wearing a bra under her white tee shirt. Drops of water from the shower at the pool stuck the white cotton to her chest between her breasts. Her legs were a warm tan from the sun. She was wearing short cutoff blue jeans and the faded threads of the frayed edge of the shorts tickled the sensitive skin of her inner thigh. She sat on the piano bench, placing her music in front of her.

"Play for me," her teacher said, sitting in his chair.

Jane chose the Chopin she had been working on for a few weeks. She had mastered the piece quickly. Joseph leaned back. He stared out the front window, not looking at her hands; Jane knew he could detect a wrong fingering of the notes just by listening to her playing. She began well, taking hold of the music and leaning into it. Midway through the etude, she began making careless mistakes in passages she had mastered. The delicate thread that held the piece together, that made it soar from one idea to another, was broken. She stopped in frustration, her hands draped lifelessly on the keys.

"I'm sorry." She shifted on the piano bench to face him. "I'm not concentrating." She couldn't tell him that the erotic rhythms of his breathing in time with the music—the quickened and shallow breaths driving into the climax of the phrases, the deep sighing away of the decrescendos, the captured, withheld pressure of a *ritard*—were all that she could hear sometimes when he sat a few feet away behind her right shoulder. In those moments, she mentally left the music and wanted to sit on his lap and steal the breath from his mouth and then go back and play the notes with his rhythms in her body.

She felt naked in front of him and supposed that was what she had wanted from the moment she planned the swim party for her best friend's birthday celebration. They had timed it so Jane would have to go directly from the pool to her piano lesson, bypassing her mother's scrutiny of her outfit. She had wanted to look grown up to him, but now she felt more childish, even though Joseph never seemed to notice what she was wearing.

As Jane twisted to face him, her tee shirt caught at her waist and her small breasts, swaying with the movement of her body, pressed against the fabric, her nipples texturing the cloth. Joseph looked away. He rose quickly from his chair and crossed to the archway between the living room and the little dining area. "Play it again. And this time concentrate on the music."

He sounded so impatient, so annoyed with her. Jane's long hair was heavy and hot on her back, and she worked it into a single braid that she draped over her left shoulder. At least that way she could feel the whispered breeze of the fan on her neck. She knew she could play the Chopin. She tried to block Joseph out of her mind and focused on the etude, determined to prove to her teacher that she could play the piece.

She was aware that he stood staring out a side window waiting for her to enter the music. He was sweating from the oppression of the summer-like heat in the air. Soon his gaze returned to her, watching her from across the room. Joseph's restless fingers no longer tapped out their mute songs but were curled into white-knuckled fists that left half-moon marks in his flesh, like a hieroglyphic warning that no one could remember how to read. He closed his eyes tightly, and when he opened them, there was no music, only an intense and heavy silence hotter than the space they shared.

He looked at Jane. A cryptic smile played around her mouth, and she watched him with eyes that cut through his desperate and angry facade.

"Do you know what it does to me when you look at me like that?" he asked.

"Yes."

"Play the etude again," he said. "Just the opening measures. It needs a clean attack, no hesitation."

"I still don't know what's the best fingering for the third measure."

He moved to her side, picked up a pencil, and leaned in to mark the music. She slipped her right arm around his neck and drew his mouth to hers.

He tried to laugh it off and said, "No tongues," when her open mouth met his, as if he would kiss her and be done with it. He slipped his fingers against her lips to stop her tongue, but she sucked at them and teased them with her tongue, and Jane knew that he was lost.

He moved with Jane to the floor. He stretched out over her, thrusting his tongue into her mouth, cradling his hard cock between her thighs, reaching under her tee shirt to fondle her breasts. Her hair had come undone from its loose braid and spread out under her shoulders.

Joseph pulled away from her. "Are you a virgin?" He knew she had been dating Gary for months.

But Jane had responded, "Yes. I want you to be my first lover."

Joseph moved further away and sat trembling beside her. "We can't do this. I'm going into the kitchen to get a drink —"

Jane reacted with a panicked expression.

"A drink of water. When I come back, I want you to be seated at the piano, ready to play the Brahms for me." She reached for him, but he gently evaded her touch and walked into the kitchen.

Jane stood beside the piano and thought about leaving his house, abandoning the music on his piano and never coming back. But she sat down instead, closed the Chopin, and opened the Brahms.

Joseph came back into the room, and she began playing the piece before he could say a word. Jane played brilliantly, hauntingly, slashing at him with every note for rejecting her.

Chapter Eleven
Flowering Dogwood (*Cornus florida*)

May 18, 1998

It was early afternoon. Jane sat on the porch and watched storm-swollen clouds bank like a phantom mountain range over the sea. She had already weeded the herb garden and ventured down to the ocean for a morning beach walk. After a landscape architect had pronounced the dune stable and Steve had repaired the steps to the sand, she found it hard to let a day go by without a trek along the water's edge.

She sat in the rocker with a cup of coffee as the mother robin ventured out for bits of straw for her nest. A piece of thin ribbon that Kaeth had tied around a package from the garden store was tangled in the grass. Jane planted her feet on the porch to steady the rocking chair and sat as still as she could. The robin made several swooping passes over the ribbon, then landed close to it, both feet flat in the stubbly blades, mirroring Jane's stance.

The robin looked around as though searching for the ribbon's owner. She took a few hops toward Jane, then, bobbing her head, picked up the ribbon and flew heavily to her nest in the dogwood tree. She swayed a bit in flight, unbalanced by the eggs she carried. Jane remembered watching for the first robin of the season with her grandmother. They were sacred, Nana would say, for it had been a robin that pulled the sharpest thorn from the forehead of our Lord on the cross, reddening her breast with Christ's blood.

Jane thought about the diary sitting beside her bed. Reading it felt like spying on her grandmother, uncovering secrets that Nana had kept hidden for most of her life, but she couldn't help reading another entry.

Moving slowly so she didn't disturb the nest-building robin, Jane went inside to get the composition book. The ringing of the phone made her jump as though she had received a physical shock. It was the first time anyone had called her and broken the silence of the house with a piercing ring. "Hello?" Her voice was hesitant and hoarse, and she realized she hadn't talked to anyone for several days.

"Is this the Little-Convent-by-the-Sea?"

Jane recognized McCue's voice. Sisters of Chopin, she thought, remembering a joke she had shared with Joseph many years earlier. "Just us novices here."

"I wanted to let you know that I've finished repairing the flute. Would you like to come pick it up?"

"Could I come over tomorrow?"

Now McCue was silent for a moment. "I won't be around tomorrow. But I'll be here all afternoon today and most of the day on Wednesday."

Jane had forgotten his strange arrangement with Moira. "This afternoon around three?" She realized her hands were white-knuckled, gripping the phone cord, and she tried to force herself to relax. I'll pick the flute up and come home, she thought. I don't have to touch the flute or listen to him play it. Before she could reschedule the trip to his studio for a later time, she heard a relieved sigh from his end of the phone.

"Perfect. See you at three," he said and hung up.

She glanced at her watch. There was time to read more of the diary before she headed to Aria. Notebook in hand, she returned to her rocker on the back porch. The robin was gone, but the shiny ribbon was woven into the nest, one end waving in the breeze. Jane reentered her grandmother's story.

Sunday, April 16, 1933
Dear diary,

The day started like any beautiful Easter. Mother called us at sunrise, and Da held a pail of water so Jenny could watch the sun's reflection dance in it. We colored some eggs. When we went upstairs to dress for church, we found new blouses from Mother and Da. They said the clothes must be a magical present and, even though I knew better, I pretended to believe for Jenny's sake.

Something most strange happened in church. The priest chanted the Mass like always, and I opened my mouth to sing the response soft as I could in what Ma calls my foggy alto voice, but the sound that came out was—and I mean no bragging or pridefulness—tones so sweet like from an angel when the Lord passed by. Ma dropped her prayer book and her beads. The beads didn't break away from the tiny chains that link them, but in my mind, I could picture them bouncing and tap-tapping right to the feet of Father Devlin.

Ma shushed me when I wanted to sing out with my new voice. The whole McKinney clan turned around as soon as I got a few notes out, and Shannon McKinney, who is a senior in school this year, asked if I would try out for the chorus. As soon as the service was done, Mother grabbed my hand and rushed me straight home. Till supper my palm was pocked with dents from the rosary beads wrapped between her hand and mine.

I stayed up as long as I could, hoping Mother would tell Da about it, but she didn't say a word. Jenny was asleep when I got to our room. I tucked her doll back under her arm and sat on the floor with my ear pressed against the door.

I was dozing myself, and my left ear almost numb, when I heard their voices like a buzz of wasps from the next room. Mother was saying that it just wasn't natural, and I knew she had to be talking about my singing. She didn't seem to think it was any kind of Easter miracle. I can't stop thinking about Brian's music all twisted up with my new voice. Mother hushed Da when he said something about her superstitions and the Good Folk, but she didn't have to quiet him down much as he seemed afraid to talk about it in a very loud voice.

He said lads' voices change when they reach manhood. Maybe that could happen to girls, too. Ma told him I'd been having my periods for two years now since I was thirteen and why would my voice change now? I crawled back in bed with Jenny, wishing I was a little girl like her again, ashamed to hear my mother talking to Da about those things, so ashamed.

Jane nodded in the chair. Nana's beautiful voice had surprised the whole family when she was fifteen? Jane related to her grandmother's shame, remembering her own desperate need for privacy as a teenager. Reading the diary seemed to have a spell-like effect on her. She fell into a sound sleep, listening to a remembered silver soprano voice crooning Irish lullabies.

A crack of thunder and a cold spray of rain shocked her awake. She moved around the house, closing windows. It wasn't until she sat for a moment in the living room and glanced at the phone that she remembered McCue's phone call. It hadn't been part of her dreams. Her watch told her she had half an hour to get to his studio. She grasped at the storm as a perfect excuse to cancel the meeting and picked up the paper on which his phone number was written. She lifted the receiver as another flash of lightning lit up the room and more thunder rumbled. The phone was dead. Jane listened as the low hum of the refrigerator became a silence, which was quickly filled by the drumming of rain on the roof.

"A sign, Nana?" Jane asked out loud. Grabbing her purse, she ran through the rain to her car and headed for Aria.

The streets were wet and nearly deserted. The rain had slowed, but the afternoon sky was still dark, as were the buildings she drove by. She saw McCue watching the road from his window. He waved as soon as she came into sight, and Jane knew she couldn't drive past the house this time without his knowing.

She parked in front of the studio and watched him set down a lighted candle. Shadows danced in the room as McCue disappeared from sight, and Jane wondered what music the shadows might be hearing. A second later, the front door opened and McCue appeared at the car door with an umbrella.

"Very gallant," she said.

"But hardly dry." The rain intensified and a gust of wind drove heavy drops under the flimsy shelter.

Inside, Jane couldn't help glancing at the top shelf where the huge conch shell was no more than a fat shadow in the gloom.

"It's still there." McCue struck a match and cupped his hands around it as the tiny flame sputtered, then burned. "I'll destroy it if you really want me to."

Jane thought it might be the jade green shirt he was wearing that made his eyes look as green as her own. The flickering light hollowed his cheeks and caressed the planes of his cheekbones, and Jane thought of Nana's mysterious Brian.

"Leave it there for a while. Maybe I can listen to it someday."

"Shit!" McCue dropped the match that had burned him and stuck his finger in his mouth. "Sorry. Way to spoil the mood."

"Are you all right?" Jane reached out her hand for his, then withdrew it before he could touch her. He held up a reddened forefinger.

"It'll be fine. But I may have to take it easy on the grace notes."

"Maybe I should come back some other time for the flute." A huge clap of thunder shook the studio and sheets of rain pelted the window. The bobcat launched himself from his hiding place on the shelf, and, teeth bared, shredded the space between them. They heard the thunder's crash decrescendo seamlessly to Duncan's growl, and Jane stepped back from McCue and the cat. The narrowed feline eyes glowed, and pointed teeth flashed in the candlelight.

"Duncan!" McCue picked up the cat. Lightning exploded again as he opened the door to put Duncan outside, and Jane felt a tug of sympathy for the animal. She started to suggest a reprieve when she sensed a wicked animosity in the narrowed amber stare directed at her.

"He'll find shelter outside. I'm sorry he scared you."

"Maybe we ought to do this some other day."

"You shouldn't be driving in this." As if to reinforce McCue's point, the rain pounded harder on the roof and front window. "Let me make some hot tea."

"Can you?"

"Cooking with gas."

Jane followed him into a room off the studio. A kerosene lantern flickered on the square oak table, leaving much of the room in shadow. In the lightning flashes, she could see that this room was as neat and spare as the rest of the house, an interesting contrast to the confused muddle of Moira's place.

Both of them were quiet as McCue puttered around the kitchen, putting spoons, napkins, and a pot of honey on the table. When Jane reached for the filled mug he offered, her hands were shaking.

McCue opened a cupboard door. Affecting a heavy Irish accent, he asked, "Might I offer you a drop of this in your tea?" When he turned around, Jane saw that he waved a bottle in the air. Even in the unsteady light, she recognized it.

"Tullamore Dew," she said. "My grandmother's favorite."

"My grandmother's favorite, too. It will take the chill off."

Jane held out her cup, and McCue fortified both mugs of tea with some of the excellent Irish whiskey.

"Let's go look at the flute."

Back in the studio, they sat in chairs in front of the now empty music stand. McCue opened the leather case, and Jane gasped with wonder at the beauty of the instrument. All the tarnish had been polished away, revealing intricate carvings that twined about the flute, encircling the gold lip plate.

"It's a treasure." As McCue lifted the head joint from the case, the gold flashed in the candlelight. "I had to replace the pads. They were so full of holes they looked like a moth had been nibbling at them. But there wasn't any rust on the rods or pins, which is really unusual in an instrument that's been ignored so long."

"I'm sure the case wasn't opened in over forty years."

"That's another strange thing. Usually, a case closed so long has a musty smell for a while, but this one has a clean smell, almost sweet."

For a second, Jane thought she caught the scent of her grandmother's roses. "Maybe you should keep it here and play it."

"I thought this might be a good time for your first flute lesson. You can take it home and practice on it. It wants to be played."

Jane felt a wave of panic and anger at McCue. She didn't want a flute lesson, didn't want to be seduced again by the music she had fought so hard to separate herself from. But if McCue realized how close she was to running from the room and not returning, he chose to ignore it. He took her hand to keep her from standing up and placed the shortest silver section in her palm. When she tried to hand it back to him, he closed her fingers around it. "The head joint with the mouthpiece. This one has been elaborately, lovingly decorated." He kept his voice pitched low, like an objective lecturer focusing on the beauties of a particular instrument, fascinating Jane with what she might learn without involving her in the music itself.

"We won't even put the pieces together," he said, as though anticipating the whole instrument would be more threatening than the smallest section alone. "Head joint, body, foot." He pointed out the pieces nestled in the case. He picked up the head joint and positioned it under her lower lip. "Blow over the embouchure hole like you're cooling a cup of hot tea or blowing over the top of a pop bottle."

"Or a whiskey bottle?"

"Would you like a little more in your tea?"

"If we're really going to do this, yes."

McCue carried one of the candles into the kitchen to light his way. In the undulating darkness, Jane examined the section of flute in her hand, tracing her finger around the opening, the embouchure hole. She heard McCue in the kitchen, pouring more water from the teakettle. Settling the embouchure plate against her lower lip, she blew hesitantly over it. "Louder," McCue called from the kitchen. "Just pretend I can't hear you."

"That's what I was trying to do." Jane blew with more force. A silken tone reverberated in the room. "A."

"Exactly. God, that's a beautiful instrument." McCue carried a small tray in one hand and the candle in the other. He sat beside her, poured more tea in both cups and laced them with the whiskey. "The gold mouthpiece makes the tone darker, sweeter, especially when you get to the upper octaves. Try it a few more times."

The tension Jane had felt at approaching music again began to evaporate as she closed her eyes and let the sound spin out on her breath.

"Twinkle, Twinkle, Little Star."

Jane opened her eyes at McCue's mention of a song.

"Put your finger inside the head joint and slide it to change the pitch."

Within seconds she had figured out pitches for the simple melody.

"It's like shortening the length of a violin string with your left hand to raise the pitch," McCue noted. Jane wondered if his not alluding to the shorter length of piano strings for the higher notes was a conscious omission.

"Let me show you how to put the pieces together." He aligned the three sections of the instrument. "Try not to grab the keys when you pick it up. The exact alignment depends on the size of the player's hands." He seemed to already have taken the measure of her long, slender fingers. Before she had time to object, he opened an elementary flute studies book and placed it on the music stand.

The whiskey in the tea had relaxed her, and the gentle cadence of McCue's voice guiding her through the lesson kept at bay the rejection with which she had greeted any contact with music for several months. He handed the flute to her and positioned her fingers on the keys.

"Now blow across the opening." The tone rang in the shadowy room.

"G." Jane, with her gift of perfect pitch, recognized the note.

"Try a few more of them."

She repeated the note several times, becoming more comfortable with the instrument in her hands. Gradually, her eyes sought the music notation on the page on the music stand. She changed her fingering and lowered the pitch of the note she played to F.

"Sure you've never done this?"

"Positive." Jane nodded toward the diagram at the top of the page. "It's got pictures."

"Then go for the E."

They worked through several pages in the book, McCue picking up his flute to illustrate his instructions.

"You've got those fingerings. Now we need to work on breath support. Go back to G and hold the note as long as you can."

Jane returned her fingers to their original position, inhaled, and began to play the note.

"Breathe from here. From your diaphragm." McCue pressed the palm of his hand low on her ribcage. Surprised by the contact—and by the rush of warmth she felt at his touch—Jane inhaled sharply, then exhaled forcefully.

He turned toward the music stand. Jane couldn't read his expression but sensed his amusement. "You've definitely got the lung capacity. We'll just have to work on control." The storm had dwindled to rumblings and syncopated drips. The lights flickered on at the same moment McCue reached toward her again, his fingers close but not touching her. "You should feel your rib cage expanding."

Both were startled by the guttural snarl behind them. They turned to face the front window. Duncan crouched on the windowsill, staring at them through the rain-striped glass, his tawny eyes narrowed to slits. His raw cry violated the peace of the studio, rising to a demonic screech before it tapered off like the thunder. Banshee, Jane thought, hearing the word in her grandmother's thick brogue. But there was none of the anguish of the banshee's loss in the sound; instead, the cat's cry seemed to rattle the pane with pure malevolence.

Some of the flickering candles, which had embraced her with a warm light, now guttered out, shapeless stubs in the sudden glare of the electric bulbs. The promise of the music they had been making still echoed in the room but grated in painful disharmony against the remnant of the bobcat's wail. The whiskey backed up raw in her throat, and she thought she might gag or vomit or pass out from the sudden lack of air in the room. She was struck, as though physically kicked, by the pleasure she had begun to feel in the sounds she made, and her hands released their grip on the flute.

McCue caught it and set it on the table beside him. Jane stood, jarring the music stand, which McCue managed to steady before it could fall.

"I'm sorry. This was a bad idea," Jane said. She started to move toward the door, but hesitated when she realized she would have to pass by the bobcat to get to her car.

"It was my fault. I'm the one who should be sorry. I thought you would enjoy trying it." McCue moved to her and took her hands, but she shook her hands free and stepped away from him.

"That's because you don't know a fucking thing about me."

"Do you want to tell me anything?"

"I can't."

"That's okay. Want to sit for a minute, and I'll show you how to clean the spit out of your flute?"

"The spit?" Jane found it difficult to stay angry during a discussion of what sounded like a kindergarten playground topic.

"It's not as neat as wiping the rosin off a violin bow. But look inside your flute."

Jane peered into the open end. Drops clung to the inside.

"It's not really spit, just condensation." McCue picked up a slender rod from the flute case and threaded the corner of a clean cotton handkerchief through a slit in the rod, wrapping a section of the cloth over the end so the metal wouldn't scratch the inside of the flute. "Take the flute pieces apart, run this through them, and voila—It's ready to put away."

Jane followed his instructions and laid the sections of the flute in its case. McCue folded the handkerchief and handed it to Jane. "One free with every first flute lesson."

"What if I really don't want to do this?"

"Then don't." They both stood again. "But take this book just in case you want to try."

When she asked, he named a low price for the repairs of the instrument and added that the fee included one flute lesson. As she handed him the money, her mind flashed to checks for piano lessons she had left for Joseph. She turned to leave, carrying the flute and the music book.

"Use a 'tuh' or 'duh' sound on the notes. Play around with it. Leave the head joint out for the week and practice the basic sound." She was near the door, and her back was toward him. "Feel like you are filling up with air all around, from here." The instant he placed his hands on her lower back, they both heard a scratch against the glass, amplified in Jane's mind as loud as the thunder had been.

The bobcat clawed at the front window. Marks from his nails, as though they had been made of a substance hard as diamond, marred the pane. Rainbows of color, shattered sunlight bouncing off the gouged glass, splashed on the studio floor.

"Duncan —" McCue's voice was low and threatening. He stamped his foot on the floor, and the bobcat, ears twitching, pounced from the window ledge and disappeared toward Moira's garden store.

Jane hesitated at the door, and McCue walked her to her car. She drove away with neither of them saying another word.

Chapter Twelve
Vaporoso (It.) Very Light, Airy, Transparent

1978

"Do you want to talk about this?" Jane's doctor rested his elbows on her open chart and looked at her over the top of the half glasses that had slipped to the end of his nose. At her appointment for her college physical, just a couple weeks before heading to Juilliard, she seemed to have surprised him with her question about birth control. "If you're not comfortable talking to me, I could recommend a woman gynecologist here in town."

The calendar on Jane's desk at home was scarred with inked exes marching over the days of summer until she was scheduled to depart for Juilliard. Each night before she went to bed, remembering the stolen kiss with Joseph, the kiss she felt she had stolen from him, the marks seemed more difficult to make. If her virginity were the obstacle it seemed to be to taking Joseph as her lover, she would attack it with the same determination with which she approached a particularly difficult piece of music.

"I'm not uncomfortable talking about it. I'm eighteen, I've thought about it, and unless there's a medical reason against it, I want to go on birth control pills."

He nodded and signed a prescription form. "Betty will give you some samples."

"But my mother and dad don't need to know, right?"

"Right. Good luck at Juilliard." He nodded toward the prescription in her hand. "Take care of yourself."

Her plan would be delayed somewhat, though. She didn't realize that she needed to be on the pill a few days before it was effective. That didn't give her nearly enough time before she left.

***

Gary had been accepted at Ohio State. He and Jane had not talked much over the fall semester, but when he called over Thanksgiving break and asked if she would help him prepare for a test in his freshman music theory class, she agreed immediately, sensing that she had found the last clue to a puzzle she was trying to solve.

As he drove her home from a study session at his house, they parked, and she asked him to make love to her.

"Why now?" he asked.

"Why not?"

"You should wait." They were still close friends, even though both of them realized they would move on to other people. "Wait until you find someone you love as much as you love your music. Have you met anyone at school?"

Jane slipped out of her unzipped jeans. "I don't want to wait. Please, let's just do it."

***

Just a few weeks later, Jane returned home for a damp and cold holiday break and a lesson she had requested with Joseph, just to brush up on a few things. Her piano lesson was over, but she didn't want to leave. She took forever gathering her music, stacking it with exaggerated care in the crook of her arm. Then she rummaged through her coat pocket for the check her mother had put there when Jane ran out of the house for her lesson. She let the piece of paper slip through her fingers several times like a goldfish eluding capture in a net, finally withdrawing it from her pocket.

Even with her back to Joseph, she knew he had already settled into the big chair. In a few seconds, he would open a can of tobacco and start to fill his pipe. Jane was his last student that Friday, and he must wish that she were out the door. But if she could stall for a little while longer, she would hear the crack of a match, inhale after his deep draw on the pipe, and carry home in her hair the ghost of cherry smoke.

"Why did you stop composing?" She unfolded the check and handed it to him. He hadn't written anything since his concertino, and that had been his only new work for several years.

He rhythmically sucked air through the pipe stem, igniting the tobacco, then took the pipe from between his teeth and held it, as if looking for the answer—or another world—in its glow. He stood to usher her to the door. "When I was writing and performing, I drank. A lot. And got into some trouble —"

"Lots of it. I know."

"You do?"

"My mother says you were the town's most famous drunk and you ended up in jail."

"She's right." He drew on the pipe again. "What does your father say?"

"He says that artists have demons, and you've paid more than you should have for any trouble you caused."

"But your mother wouldn't know about things like that?"

"My mother wouldn't know." Jane felt they were, against all laws of physics, occupying the same space at the same time, wrapped in the same skin, breathing the same molecules of sweet and heavy air.

"I'm happy now that the fire is out," he said, as if to conclude the discussion. She sensed in his comment an absolute truth that concealed a deeper and contradictory truth.

The cherry smoke had tied them up with faint and floating ribbons. "There are other fires," she said.

Joseph's hands were on her shoulders, and she couldn't tell if he meant to pull her closer or push her away. She could feel on her left cheek the warmth of the pipe he still held and knew it must be burning his hand.

He placed the pipe in the ashtray, spilling embers that winked a message and erased it in ash. "I told you I couldn't do this."

"But I'm not a virgin anymore."

"Jane, just stop this and go home."

"I let Gary make love to me because you wouldn't."

He must have known by the look in her eyes that she was telling the truth, and his hands gripped her shoulders as if to shake her, but he just held her close. "You're crazy. You know that?"

"So are you." She tilted her face to his. "You know that?"

He kissed her gently, tenderly, and she felt the strength of his desire not so much in his mouth as in his hands as they tangled in her hair and pulled it away from her face. "Call your mother and tell her you're going to be late."

She put her music and coat on the sofa, picked up the phone, and dialed her number. He walked into a room at the back of the house, and she heard him closing Venetian blinds. The telephone rang in a strange counterpoint to the metallic strumming sound of blinds being lowered that she supposed must be coming from his bedroom. "Hello?" Her mother sounded annoyed and Jane could hear the theme from her mother's favorite soap opera in the background. Jane had always despised the shows, but not nearly as much as she resented their prostitution of melodies like the Tchaikovsky that ran under her mother's voice.

"Mom, it's me. If it's okay, I'm going to stay here a while longer at Mr. Lamb's because I really messed up the timing on the Bach piece and he thinks I need to work on it." She hadn't told a lie, and she knew that her mother had lost interest in the conversation as soon as she knew that Jane was all right.

"That's fine. Mrs. Jeffers called to say that they don't need you to baby-sit tonight." Jane could hear the music swell as her mother adjusted the volume on the TV set. "Tell him you'll pay him extra next week." The bastardized music faded into a laundry detergent commercial.

He was back in the room. "I don't think he's going to charge for the extra time, but I'll offer. I'll be home as soon as we get the rhythm figured out." Jane saw him raise his eyebrows, amused, but preoccupied. "Bye, Mom. I love you."

"I love you, too, dear." Her mother hung up as voices rose in scripted passion in the background.

Jane replaced the receiver. She was aware that her hand had warmed the black plastic a few degrees, that the newspaper beside the telephone was three days old and was opened to the sports section, that the small brass clock on the table had stopped at 10 (a.m. or p.m.? she wondered) and the cord had been pulled out of the wall and lay coiled like a sleeping snake on the carpet.

She had no idea what to do next.

In her fantasies, they had always been thrown together in a fiery, irresistible whirlwind of passion. They had ripped the clothes from their sweating, panting bodies as the last note of a perfectly and passionately played Beethoven sonata vibrated in the heat—the way it would have happened on her mother's favorite show. But now it was chilly in the room and the music had been put away and both of them had all their clothes on and time had stopped moving as surely as movement had stopped in the brass clock. She knew this was the only way that he would let it happen. He was giving her time to think about it, to reconsider, a pause, *caesura,* before they moved to the next phrase of this most ancient of duets.

She turned to face him and began to unbutton her shirt, but her hands were shaking too much to get past the second button. He walked to her and held both her hands. "Are you sure you want to do this?" She answered him with her open mouth on his.

He released her hands and tried the button, but his hands were no steadier than hers. Jane pulled the buttoned shirt over her head and gasped as he circled the bare nipple of her left breast with his tongue. Heat filled her belly, and she would have fallen if he hadn't held her up, pulling her hips to his.

She reached between their bodies to unbuckle his belt.

"Wait." He moved to lock the front door, took her hand, and led her into the bedroom.

The room was almost dark, and Jane felt like they were under water, moving through an atmosphere thicker, more resistant, than air. He had left his pipe in the living room, but wisps of smoke had drifted in and stripes of sunset behind the nearly closed blinds had infused the haze with a rosy glow. Piles of scores were stacked against the walls, and it was as though she had entered a chamber of his heart, a space lined with music, beating with both their pulses.

He pulled down the covers on the double bed. She slipped off her shoes and socks, unzipped her jeans and let them fall to the floor. He had stripped to his shorts and slid under the covers; then he took her hand and brought her into his bed. She still wore her underpants; he was giving her another chance to change her mind.

He placed the bed's only pillow under her head and touched her hair, her cheekbones, her lips as if he were a blind man intent on creating a portrait of her in his mind. "Close your eyes," he whispered to her. As she did, he began to brush his fingertips over the flesh of her neck, feeling her pulse, timing his touch to its beat. He explored the shallow pools above her collarbones. To gauge the effectiveness of her practice, he had, during her lessons, traced with his fingers the muscles in her forearms, strengthened by endless repetitions of scales, arpeggios and Dohnanyi exercises she had played until her arms ached. Now he brushed his fingers there for the pleasure it gave both of them; he caressed her hands, and the strangely secret and sensitive spaces between her fingers.

Removing his hand from hers, he laid his palm flat against her belly. She moaned, a feral growl from deep in her throat, and he kissed her and drew the sound deep into his chest. When he moved his mouth away from hers, she started to open her eyes, but he closed them again, kissing her eyelids. His hand began to stroke the satin flesh of her inner thigh.

She had begun humming an animal song again, an ancient, haunting hymn of hunger and need as she raised her hips upward toward his hand, seeking release. Trembling, unable to lie still any longer, she whispered, "Please," and moved his hand to the elastic at her waist. She raised her hips and slipped out of the pants.

"Turn over."

She languidly turned to lie on her stomach and her song became a purr as he slid his hands like hot breath over her back. She wished that she could stay here for days, for weeks, discovering what gave them both pleasure, letting him teach her things she didn't yet know about her body, like he taught her the music. But she knew that she would have to leave. Soon. But not yet. Now Joseph memorized the angles of her shoulder blades that jutted slightly away from her body like folded wings, whispered his fingers over her hips, and tongued the hollows at the back of her knees. Her breathing had become heavier again, and she had spread her legs a little, welcoming his touch. She turned on her side to face him.

"I want you to be inside me. I need you to be inside me." He kissed her on the lips, almost sadly, she thought, as though he were afraid he might be losing something he had come to treasure. He slipped off his shorts, and she reached out to touch him.

"God is going to punish me for this," he said.

"I'm going to punish you if you don't do this."

She spread her legs as he stretched himself over her. He moved as gently as he could until he could no longer control the thrusts. Then they lay together damp and entangled and amazed by where they had gone.

After a few minutes he pulled out of her and turned on the light at the head of the bed. In the dim glow they noticed at the same time the stain of blood between them. It marked the white sheet with the scarlet shape of a continent she had never seen before, a place she thought she might have visited once in a dream.

"You said you weren't a virgin." He did not sound accusing so much as appalled at what he might have done.

"I'm not. I swear Gary made love to me." She felt suddenly embarrassed and ashamed. "I might have started my period." She had never asked her mother about anything like that, had just assumed that people didn't have sex at that time of the month. "Do you hate me?" She tried to turn away from him. She wanted to pull the sheets over her body but was afraid to stain them more.

He pulled her head against his chest and cradled her in his arms. "You're such a child," he whispered, as though reminding himself. After a few minutes he gently slipped his hand between her thighs, then smeared a pattern on his chest with her blood. "I'll wear you," he said, a knight-errant off to battle, proudly sporting his true love's colors. She ran her fingers from the marks toward his cock, which was beginning to stir again.

He stopped her hand. "You have to get home." He slid off the end of the bed, and stood beside her. "There are some pads and things in the bathroom closet." He handed her a worn flannel robe that smelled of soap and smoke, and she walked to the bathroom. She knew he had been married, and she wondered who else had been here with what her mother called the "women's things."

Jane showered with one of his towels around her hair and dressed. He had folded her clothes and laid them on the sink. He must have washed and dressed in the darkened kitchen, and he sat in his chair, lighting his pipe. He stood when she came into the room and handed her the music. The check from her mother was folded and lay on top. "I want you to have both movements of the Bach memorized by next week," he said. She knew that he couldn't talk about what had happened.

"I love you." She pressed the check into his hand. "And this is for the piano lesson, unless you don't want to be my teacher anymore."

He kissed her on the forehead, turned back to the piano and laid the folded check in his appointment book.

Jane left the house and closed the door, but paused on the front porch as she heard him play the first notes of a new melody, a dance that whirled from his fingers, *vaporoso*, very light, airy, transparent. And as whispering snowflakes began to fall, she walked home, humming the first measures of a waltz that was just being born.

Chapter Thirteen
Sea Oats (*Uniola paniculata*)

June 25, 1998

Ken stretched his legs, pale from their New York encasement in long pants, and rocked gently on the back porch of the beach house. "I had to be sure you were really all right." He spoke loud enough to be heard over the clatter that Jane was making in the kitchen.

"I told you I'm fine, but I'm so glad you came to see for yourself." She opened the newly screened door, balancing two glasses of iced tea on a small tray. "Sure you can't stay for a few days?"

"I have to fly to Charleston tonight. But I figured I'd better go by way of Wilmington and get that deli order delivered."

Ken had called the day before to say he had a brief layover in North Carolina and he was coming for a visit whether Jane wanted to see him or not. Jane had given him directions, then closed the conversation by assuring him, "Of course, I want to see you. I miss you more than anything—except maybe New York cheesecake."

Right after she hung up, before she could lose her nerve, she called McCue to ask him to lunch so he could meet Ken.

"I'm sorry, but I've got lessons to teach—out of town ones."

Jane had forgotten Ken would be visiting on Thursday, McCue's day out of town. "I'll give Moira a call and see if she can come."

"She and Kaeth are out right now," McCue said, and Jane wondered how closely he followed their activities. "I'll put a note under her door and have her call you first thing tomorrow morning."

Neither of them seemed comfortable continuing the conversation. During Jane's lessons at the studio, they focused on the puzzles of the flute music, breath control, and octave shifts that fascinated Jane with their connection to flow of breath over the carved mouthpiece. "The octave exercise —" she began, trying to fill the silence.

At the same moment, McCue started to thank her for the invitation. Like teenagers embarrassed by bumping into each other, they said quick goodbyes and hung up.

Now Jane sat with Ken while they waited for Moira and Kaeth to arrive.

"You look great," Ken said. "This break has been good for you."

Break, Jane thought, sounds like something I'll return from. She didn't know how to respond to his comment.

"I couldn't believe those first pictures you sent me of this place. You've done wonders with it." He set his iced tea beside the rocker and walked to the edge of the porch. He watched the ocean for a while; when he spoke again, he didn't look at Jane. "Houston contacted me again about your schedule. They want to know if we're going to honor your agreement to perform with them in the spring."

"'Honor my agreement'?" Jane echoed the words that sounded so unlike Ken.

"I've postponed this as long as I could, but they need to know when they can expect an answer."

"How much time do I have?" She spoke in a strained whisper as though Ken's question had consumed most of the oxygen from the air.

"I think I can stall them a month or two. Right now, they're advertising you as a surprise guest, but they're going to need some time for publicity."

"Then let me have the rest of the summer to decide. I'll let you know by the end of August."

Ken faced her, but before he could reply, Jane continued. "If you need an answer now, the answer is no."

Ken turned again to stare at the ocean.

"Is that why you're here? To find out if you still have talent to represent?" It came out crueler than she had intended, but she was too upset to back away.

"No. I told you the truth. I was worried about you and had a chance to fly through Wilmington on my way to Charleston. I'm setting up a southern tour for Carrie Templeton."

Carolyn Templeton had been two years behind Jane at Juilliard. She hadn't experienced Jane's superstar fame, but her name was mentioned more and more often as Jane withdrew from the New York music scene.

Before she could react to Ken's news, knocking at the front door interrupted them. Moira's cheerful, "Hello?" was followed by Kaeth's softer echoes as they opened the never-locked front door and walked through the house to the back porch. Moira carried a bowl of potato salad. She had joked on the phone that it was her duty as an Irishman to do something with potatoes. Kaeth, tugging at a bow in her hair, ignored greetings from Jane and headed for the herb garden. Moira shrugged an apology.

"Moira, I'd like you to meet Ken Witten." Jane paused for an instant. She had, for so many years, introduced him as her friend first and agent as an afterthought. Now, stung by his new alliance with another concert pianist, she continued, "My agent when I was working out of New York. Ken, this is Moira O'Shea, my new friend in Aria."

If Moira felt the tension between them, she ignored it and took charge of setting up a picnic lunch in the back yard. She and Ken carried the kitchen table outside while Jane made a buffet of the boxes of deli food Ken had carried, packed in ice, from their favorite spots in the city. Kaeth was finally enticed to the table with a promise of cheesecake.

Moira, Jane, and Ken lingered over dessert and iced tea, as Moira and Ken chatted about all the work Jane had put into the house and yard. Suddenly, the three of them focused on sounds from inside the house: soft, syncopated beats, accompanied by high-pitched giggles, rose to a crescendo punctuated by the crash of breaking glass. "Kaeth?" Moira pushed away from the table and rushed through the back door. Ken and Jane were right behind her.

In the living room, the diminutive guest whirled, swatting at a dozen flies that swarmed around her. Fragments of a vase lay shattered in the midst of flowers Jane had collected from the garden. Kaeth's curls danced as her tiny hand, gripping the book of flute music, smashed at the buzzing insects, her peals of laughter sliding to a sibilance that mimicked the voice of her bluebottle targets.

Moira and Jane rushed to pull Kaeth away from the shards of glass while Ken began picking up pieces of the vase.

"I'm so sorry." Moira wrapped her arms around Kaeth to calm her. "I hope it wasn't an antique. I'll replace it."

"Don't worry about it. But, Kaeth, are you all right? You didn't cut yourself, did you?"

Kaeth opened her doll-like hand and dropped the music book. The page was streaked with red, and dotted with bits of broken wings, and it took Jane a few seconds to realize that Kaeth's blood was not mingled with that of the insects. Jane lifted the book by the corner and put it on the desk, but not before Ken noticed the single line of notes on the music page.

"Violin?"

"Flute, but it's a long story." Jane picked up the scattered flowers and dropped them into the wastebasket Ken held.

"No more," Kaeth whispered, taking Moira's hand and leading her to the front door.

"I think Kaeth's had enough visiting for today." Moira looked embarrassed.

"It was good to see both of you," Jane said.

She and Ken stood on the front porch, waving as Moira's car pulled away. "Thanks for bringing the deli picnic. I'll let you know what I decide about the spring schedule. I just can't promise anything."

"I don't want to push you, but you've worked so hard to get where you are. I'd hate to see you throw it away."

In the intense afternoon sunlight, Jane could see Ken seemed to have aged more than a few months since she had seen him last in New York. "Are you all right?"

"Fine. Just tired. You know the city in summer—meetings, brownouts, garbage strikes." He stared at the breeze-stirred branches of the willow. "I'd understand if you never wanted to leave here." Ken checked his watch and took car keys from his pocket. "I really have to get to the airport."

"Plan to stay longer next time." They hugged briefly, mechanically, the momentary closeness emphasizing how far apart they felt. "Thanks again for making the trip."

She watched as Ken's car disappeared down the same hazy road that had swallowed Moira and Kaeth. She opened the new screen door and felt a sharp scratch on her leg. The metal mesh was damaged; a jagged flap had scraped her skin, and probably allowed the flies to enter the room. She was sure the damage had not been there earlier in the day. The solid wooden door slammed louder than she had intended, and she locked it with a jerk of her wrist, feeling separated even more from her friends.

The sky was still silvered with the end of the daylight when she finished cleaning the kitchen and sweeping up the last of the glass in the living room. Smeared streaks from the crushed flies, and the black pellets of their bodies scattered across the floor, were depressing reminders of the afternoon, so different from the way Jane had imagined it would go. She wandered through the house feeling chilled in spite of the leftover warmth of the summer day.

Wrapped up in a quilt on the living room sofa, she tried for hours to lose herself in a novel, but the words kept escaping comprehension. Finally, she took Nana's diary into the kitchen and dropped it on the square oak table. "Sorry, Nana," she whispered, "no Tullamore Dew." But Jack Daniels seemed a good second choice, and she poured some into a tumbler and raised it in a toast. "To screwing things up," she said, opening the diary.

Wednesday, April 19, 1933
Dear diary,

I've watched for Brian every day on my way from classes. Mary Margaret and Sophie hardly speak to me, saying as they do that I'm putting on airs and feeling too good to pal with them like we used to. But it's just that I want to be alone with him even though it's the kind of thing Mother would say gets good girls in trouble.

All that's been in the field is the lop-eared rabbit, and the swayback horse rubbing against the oak tree and looking around for the same boy I'm missing so bad.

It's only Wednesday, and he said to meet him Thursday. But the days are dragging by.

Nights are flying swifter than ever, full of dreams where I almost see him. I hear his music and wake up out of breath and wanting him, as I know I shouldn't.

Tomorrow, dear diary, is Thursday.

Jane woke at the table about two in the morning, massaging her neck as she lifted her head from the pillow of the notebook. She fell into bed wiping away tears she refused to acknowledge. Disquieting dreams enfolded her.

***

Jane sat on the floor in front of the screen door; she had repaired the hole in the wire mesh with a neat whipstitch, and she hoped for a breeze to cool off the room.

The music book, crumpled and soiled, was another reminder of the unpleasant end to the picnic. She carried it to the kitchen and dampened a paper towel to try to erase the evidence of Kaeth's insect massacre. The red smears of yesterday had dried to sepia stains that resisted her attempts to remove them. They tracked along the staff lines like macabre, unruly grace notes.

Maybe she should take the damaged book as a sign to forget all about the flute lessons. She closed the cover and laid it on the counter. Indentations in the upper right corner of the cover caught her eye. Lifting the book, she tilted it in the sunlight, but the impressions were faint, and Jane wanted verification of the name she thought she saw there.

She carried the book to the living room and grabbed a pencil from the telephone table. Rubbing the pencil lead over the imprint, she watched letters appear like clues in a Nancy Drew mystery. "Selena Nevin" materialized, presenting more questions. Had Selena been a student of McCue's? Had Selena been a better student?

Taking the music book to the study, she opened it to the page after the stained one and leaned it up on the desk. She took a deep breath, then lifted the lid of the flute case and assembled the instrument as McCue had shown her. She marveled again at the intricacy of the carvings that swirled around the mouthpiece. Filling her lungs even more deeply, she began to exhale, focusing her breath over the embouchure hole and picturing the air as it wove its way around the tiny room in patterns like those etched into the silver and gold.

After a period of time, which she could not gauge, lost as she was in the luxuriant sound, she began to concentrate on the page in front of her, realizing there were fingerings she was not familiar with. She had missed instruction on several notes.

Jane flipped back one page, now more fascinated than repulsed by the dried bloodstains. She studied the diagrams at the top of the page and fingered the new notes. Why not, she thought, play the carnage? She read through the exercises, ornamenting the simple melody with the quirky grace notes of sepia spots and darker flecks on the bar lines. Mentally apologizing to Selena for the violation of the book, she turned the page and began a long tone on the new note.

As one might be aware of a growing wind in the background presaging a storm, Jane heard an answering flute dancing around the note she played, pausing a third, a fourth, a fifth above it, gliding from disharmony to delicious harmony with her notes. As she played the first exercise on the page, the distant instrument joined her in a clever duet. She wandered to the open front door, holding the next note illustrated on the page.

McCue sat on the front porch with his flute, his back to the door, a backpack on the floor beside him. With only a brief, deep intake of breath, Jane continued the note and sat in front of the screen door with her back to him. Their improvised duet continued until McCue's whimsical dancing around her notes caused Jane to sputter, then laugh out loud.

"It's not fair. No one could ever break me up on the violin or piano!"

"That's why good flutists have no sense of humor. You can't play and snicker at the same time."

"Flutists or flautists?"

"Flautists have to have a sense of humor or they wouldn't let themselves be called that."

"Agreed. We could just call you 'one-who-plays-the-flute.'"

"You can call me anything," McCue said with an attempt at a Mae West accent, "Just so you call me."

"Well, I'd have to call you a tad flat. And you never showed me how to tune my flute to yours."

"I never argue with perfect pitch. How about if I show you how to raise the pitch of my flute." He pressed his nose against the screen. "Mind if I come in for the rest of the lesson?"

Jane opened the screen door. McCue walked in and sat on the sofa.

"Moira told me what happened yesterday. She felt terrible about the broken vase." He rummaged around in the backpack he had carried in with him and pulled out a small package wrapped in tissue paper. "She asked me to bring you this."

Jane unwrapped a small bud vase with a plump body and the ruffle of a fluted edge at the top.

"She said it was her grandmother's."

"Another Irish grandmother?"

"Everyone should have one." He seemed to sense her reluctance to accept the gift. "Moira really wants you to have it."

"It's lovely. Please thank her for me. I'll send her a note tomorrow." Jane set the vase on the fireplace mantle. "Now—about your flute that's out of tune."

McCue showed her how to raise and lower the pitch by pushing in or pulling out the head joint. When both flutes were in tune, he reached into the backpack and retrieved another music book.

"Want to try a real duet?" He opened the book of easy duets to the first one and looked around for Jane's music stand.

"Sorry. I don't have a real stand yet." She nodded toward the study. "I've been leaning it against the secretary." McCue started to speak, but Jane anticipated his offer and interrupted him. "I'm really not sure I even want one."

"Leaning works." McCue followed her into the small side room.

Nearly an hour passed while they sight read the elementary duets, McCue embellishing his musical line, pausing to teach her a new note, making her laugh again with silly comments.

In the middle of a simplified version of a Mozart piece arranged for two flutes, Jane felt a sense of panic pressing like a physical force against her chest, squeezing the air out of her lungs and creating a vacuum she could not fill. The playing had ceased being a puzzle and had become real music. She released the flute onto the desk as though the silver had burned her. "No more." Her voice was as hoarse and high pitched as Kaeth's. She stood and walked away from McCue and the music.

"You shouldn't leave it with the spit inside."

Jane didn't react to McCue's attempt to lighten the mood.

"I was going to give this to you later," he said, rummaging again in the backpack he had carried into the study. "But I think you can use it now." He took out a device with metal legs and a wooden peg, about four inches high, set it on the floor, and stood Jane's flute on the peg. "Want to go for a beach walk?"

Nodding her assent, Jane headed out the kitchen door and down the steps to the ocean without waiting to see if McCue followed her. They walked side by side in silence for a few minutes, the closeness of their footprints in the low-tide sand contradicting the distance Jane seemed to be trying to put between them. She stopped to pick up a scallop shell and rinsed it in a wave. "You gave me Selena's flute book. Was she a student of yours?"

"Selena wanted to try everything. She hadn't learned to read music as a child and taking up the flute as an adult was harder than she thought it would be. She only took a few lessons and gave up on it." He took two plastic bags from his jeans pocket and opened one so Jane could drop the shell in. "I didn't think you'd mind a slightly used music book."

"Of course I don't mind. I was just curious about her."

As they walked, McCue began to fill the second bag with rusted cans and other trash that had washed up on the beach. Jane slowed her pace when she heard muffled sounds of voices ahead of them.

"Around that curve in the shore is where the edge of the city beach starts. Actually, all the wet sand beaches are public, but at high tide your section is pretty well cut off from the rest. Not too many people wander down your way."

Jane stood still, unwilling to move closer to the more populated area. She seemed hypnotized by the rhythmic lapping of the waves.

"The tide's coming in now." He followed as Jane began to walk back toward her house.

When the distant voices had faded and transitioned to the inhale and exhale of waves against the sand, she stopped again, pulled off her sandals, and waded into the water. McCue kicked off his shoes and stood with her.

"It's so beautiful," she said. Tiny slivers of silver darted around her ankles. She felt the easy slip of sand beneath her feet with each pull of the waves. The sun, hot on her face, was tempered by every breath of ocean breeze.

"It's a dangerous beauty."

"I'm not afraid of drowning."

"You don't think you could drown?"

"The concept of drowning doesn't scare me."

"Now that is frightening." McCue took her hand. She neither resisted nor responded. "You have the phone number for weather and tides, right?"

"Moira wrote it down for me."

"You need to pay attention to it, living this close to the sea. You have to respect the water."

Jane turned around and walked back to the beach, letting her hand slip out of his. She sat on a piece of driftwood and nodded for him to sit beside her. Nearby, a tall stand of sea oats rustled, and a small, concealed animal scampered away from them. "What do you think of rabbits?"

"They're cute?" McCue sounded baffled by the question.

"Lop-eared ones."

"Even cuter, I guess."

"Magical?"

McCue stood up and wandered back to the edge of the ocean.

"I'm reading a diary my grandmother left me. She seemed to think there was something weird about a rabbit she saw in Ireland."

"What would I know about that?"

"You had an Irish grandmother, too."

"My Irish grandmother would probably have agreed with yours. There were lots of stories about special animals."

"Special?"

McCue shrugged and handed Jane her sandals. "It's getting late, and the tide is coming in. If we don't head back now, the water will be close to that vegetation line, and we'll be scrambling back through it in the dark." He offered her his hands, and she stood up from her seat on the driftwood. "May I kiss you?"

What surprised her most was the quaint gallantry of the request. She closed her eyes and let him interpret her response, as she was not sure of her own answer. His mouth, sweet and cool, lighted on hers for only an instant. Then he was pulling her by the hand across the beach toward her house.

Part of the way up the stairs that stretched over the dune and into her yard, McCue turned to her. "What do you think about rabbits?"

"Definitely cute. But I guess I'd have to agree with my mother that all the magical stuff is nonsense."

"Hokum. Malarkey." He seemed to agree, but the rising wind shredded his words and diffused the meaning behind them.

Inside the house, McCue packed his flute into the backpack and politely refused Jane's offer to fix them supper. They were silent at the front door until he left with an awkward reminder to practice her flute and listen to the weather reports.

Long after darkness had fallen, Jane stood at the French doors in her bedroom, brushed by the breeze through the screens. A swath of moonlight paved a path from shore to horizon and lit the waves as though with neon strips that swelled then melted into the sand. "Malarkey?" she whispered, clutching her grandmother's diary. "What are you trying to tell me?"

In bed, she opened the book.

Thursday, April 20, 1933
Dear diary,

He was there! Brian was there in the field, but I didn't see him at first. I ran from the schoolyard into the road before the dismissal bell had stopped ringing. I was singing a song and running so fast that I tripped and fell and scraped my knee. The song turned into a sad one. I sat with my back against Murtrey's fence, wanting to keen and wail because the field was empty. Even the horse was gone.

And then I heard his fluting—silver sounds that could have been a bird or wind twining around my voice, lifting it, the two melodies dancing together—and he was standing just behind me.

"I didn't see you," I said.

"You must have nodded off."

I told him I must have done but knew that wasn't the truth of it. All I wanted to think about was that he was there, helping me to my feet, linking his arm in mine, walking across the field with me.

The afternoon was turning darkish with rain clouds while I waited by the road, but with every step we took together, the sky turned brighter and the grass greener. I tried to keep our path in my mind and listened for the striking of the hours so as not to be late getting home. But time made no sense. My head felt full of dreamy cobwebs. When the Angelus rang, the bells sounded as far away as Rathclooney Lake, the distant noise was like a hand on my shoulder shaking me, waking me up, and I fought to stop my feet from dancing closer to the edge of the rise of earth in front of me.

Brian stopped his fluting. His mouth looked pouty and disappointed, and the sun flashed off the silver like lightning from the black clouds that were forming again. "We'll just go a little further," he said, taking my hand and nodding toward a whitethorn bush at the top of the embankment in front of us.

But I knew where we were and I knew what he must be. I pulled my hand away from his, and the flash from his eyes must have been a reflection of real lightning because it had started to rain great splashes of water. I slipped and slid down the hill and across the field, and when I reached the road, the

Angelus rang again. It couldn't happen, I know, dear diary, the bell for sunset twice in an evening, and my clothes were dry, my knee unskinned. Brian stood across the field, the flute teasing his sweet lips. His voice whispered in my ear, "I'll be here next week."

I don't think I can stay away.

Chapter Fourteen
Avec Delices (F.) With Delight, Happily

1978 – 1979

When Jane returned to Juilliard for spring semester, she spent hours staring at the calendar, counting down the weeks remaining before she was to leave New York again. When she practiced, she saw in the music all the questions she still wanted to ask Joseph, thought about all the pieces she longed to play with him. When the end of the school year finally arrived, she stopped by her advisor's office.

After Jane returned home and the three of them were seated at the dinner table, Jane made her announcement.

"I've changed my mind about returning to Juilliard this fall. There's a lot more that Mr. Lamb can teach me, and it would be nice to spend a year close to home."

Her father put his fork down, and her parents looked at each other.

"You were so excited about Juilliard," her mother said. "I thought you enjoyed the classes, made friends. Are you going to give that up?"

Jack was quiet. Jane had the feeling he knew why she wanted to stay.

"I spoke with my advisor before I left. They understood why I want to study with Mr. Lamb this year. It must happen all the time. I can take classes at Case and work with him and then return to Juilliard the following year without another audition."

"Case has probably admitted everyone they plan on taking. How are you going to get in there?"

Jane could not interpret the tone in her father's voice. She knew what she had been thinking about, knew her daydreams, but could not voice them here. For several years, maybe since she began her lessons with Joseph, she had imagined living in his house, taking care of him, planting flowers, hanging sheer curtains at the windows, and—always—making music with him. But these were her secret dreams, never shared with anyone.

"I talked to admissions at Case. They knew my name from the competitions and said they'll be glad to make a place for me this fall. I can get credit for the extra time I spend with Mr. Lamb, and all my credits will transfer to Juilliard next year."

"Sounds like it's all settled." Her mother still held her fork suspended above her plate.

"I thought you would be pleased. You didn't want me to go away last year. You said New York had changed."

Jane's mother raised her eyebrows and looked at Jack.

"What does Joseph know about this plan?" he asked.

"He doesn't know anything. I'm going to tell him at my lesson Friday, and I don't want you to say anything to him before that! He had nothing to do with it."

Her father laced more spaghetti around his fork. "It will be good to have you home for another year. We'll just have to cancel our plans for renting out your room again."

***

Jane was almost late for her lesson the following Friday. She changed shirts three times and tried on several shades of lipstick. Over and over in her mind she had played out the way their next encounter might occur.

She arrived at Joseph's house as the student before her was leaving. She nodded to the boy, whom she had known casually for a few years, and wondered if she looked different to him, older, more mature. She hesitated on the front porch, watching until the other student pulled his car out of the driveway. She heard Joseph improvising on the waltz theme he had found the last time she saw him.

Jane stepped into the open doorway and listened. She had decided on a shirt of pale blue cotton worn soft and thin. She knew that the blue of her shirt, reflected in her green eyes and turned them turquoise. She posed there, cradling her music in her arms, aware that the daylight behind her would outline her body. Would he run to her, lock the door and carry her to his room? Should she approach him? He repeated a few measures of the waltz over and over, varying a few notes of the phrase each time.

"What do you think?" he finally asked, focusing on the keyboard, not looking up at her.

She moved to the piano and sat beside him on the bench, both of them watching his hands instead of each other. "I'd flat the third the second time through."

He tried her suggestion. "Jazzy."

"But I'd drop the trill. It's a little too cute." Jane stopped the trilled note by taking Joseph's hand in hers.

He looked at her. "Your eyes..." he said.

"Weird eyes, my Irish grandmother called them. She said they meant I had ties to the Other World." Jane closed her eyes and leaned toward Joseph to kiss him. But he kissed her on her forehead and stood up from the piano bench.

All week she had imagined their making love again, trying to decide the best time to tell him that she would not be leaving for New York again in the fall. Now it seemed that he didn't want to touch her or respond to her at all. Had she not pleased him the last time they saw each other?

"Do some scales to warm up."

"I'm warm." She sat with her hands clasped in her lap. "Was last time so awful?"

Joseph's eyes grew wide when he realized what she meant. "It was wonderful." He sat back on the bench at her left side. He began an early Mozart four-hand piano sonata that was the first piece they had played together. Jane sat still, refusing to join him until he had reached the twelfth measure; the bass part alone, robbed of its treble half, sounded empty, hollow. He sustained a trill with an even, patient repetition until Jane joined him with a statement of the melody. Joseph continued, as if the music allowed him to speak and her response assured that she was listening to him. "But you're leaving again this fall, and I don't think you understand how this can get in the way of your music."

"I'm not going back. Not for another year. It's all arranged." Now Joseph stopped playing, but Jane continued, embellishing the simple melody. "And now I don't think you want me." She skipped to the third movement and began a racing *Rondo*, flying through the measures with a verve and genius that might have made the composer laugh out loud. Joseph leaped into the music and flew with her to the end of the piece. His foot depressed the damper pedal, letting the final chord fade to silence as he took her in his arms.

"The music still has to come first," he said, after a long kiss. He left the piano bench and sat in his chair. "Second movement of the Brahms. Put that passion into it."

***

Jane enjoyed her classes at Case, except for a math class that her mother was pleased to help her with. Most important to Jane, her parents didn't question the long hours she spent at Joseph's house. They could hear progress in her intense practice sessions in the studio at home.

At Joseph's house, he insisted on the music, and not their new relationship, as the focus of their time together. He forced her to concentrate intently on each piece she played, closing her mind to the distraction of his presence and her desire.

In February, Jane won another piano competition. Her parents had flown with her to Chicago, and they all stayed a few days to see the city, and, Jane knew, to provide a forced break from her playing. She had experienced some pain in her wrists from the strain of preparing for the competition. Her professors at Case had suggested she avoid practicing for a while. When they returned, Jane went as soon as she could to her teacher's house for a lesson.

She knew from his embrace that he had missed her, but he seemed distracted. Jane played through a scale and arpeggio and waited for Joseph's reaction. She hadn't played it well. Her hands felt cold and stiff.

"That was fine."

It hadn't been fine, and she turned to look at him. He was facing away from her, gazing through the tiny breakfast room and out the window. She waited. "Should I play it again?" She was sure he hadn't heard it the first time.

"Yes, play it again."

Jane shifted from the C# major she had just played to E minor. The original key still vibrated in her head, only minutes old. He should turn to her at the first note, laughing at the capricious modulation to her favorite key. But he stood silent, staring, until the minor had also faded away.

She stood up and crossed to stand behind him. He tensed as she leaned against him and rested her head on his right shoulder. She slipped her arms around him and felt him relax a bit as he took her hands in his, caressing them as if they were small frightened animals he could calm.

"What?" she asked, in unconscious imitation of his one-syllable questions to her.

He brought her hands close to his mouth. She could feel his breath on her palms and knew how hard it was for him to talk to her. She waited.

"I had a dream about you last night," he whispered into her hands. "I had an erotic dream about you last night."

"Do you want to tell me about it?" She longed to pull her hands away from his and slip her fingers into his mouth or slide her hands down over his chest and across his hips and between his legs.

"I don't think I can." He kissed her hands gently, then released them.

"Can you play it for me?"

"Play it?" He finally turned to face her.

"Major or minor key?" she questioned, leading him to the piano bench.

He sat down and leaned into the keyboard. "Major. It began in a major."

Joseph began a D major arpeggio, waves thrusting in through his left hand, and Jane heard gulls calling from his right even before he whispered, "I was at the beach. And there was a sand castle." A melody began to emerge in the right hand, structured and angular but touched with dreams. "I pushed something out of the sand with my foot, and I realized it was silverware, buried around the sand castle." Jane heard glints of sunlight reflected in the polished metal, and silver grace notes accented and shaped the melody as it shifted and climbed.

"I picked up one of the spoons in my hand and walked closer to the castle." He played with the delicate theme he had found. The music was warm, sun and sea interlaced, but the rhythm of the waves was building, pushing. "I realized that you were sitting in the middle of the castle. You were naked, sitting cross-legged in the castle and you couldn't hear me when I called to you." Joseph inverted the melody line, turning it upside down, and Jane felt the tension rise like wind blowing a storm to shore. "I started to dig with the spoon to get through the wall of sand to reach you, and when I did, you smiled at me, and I knew that everything would be all right. But you still couldn't talk to me."

His voice was quiet for a moment but the music continued to sing the story to her until he could talk again. "I touched your hand and saw that your fingernails were pink seashells, and the shells dropped into my hands and there were new little shells underneath. When I whispered to you, shells fell from your ears, and I could hear the music of the ocean when I leaned close to you. You were so beautiful and warm and I started to lick the sand from your body, but it wasn't sand but something sweet like crystals of honey. I realized that your crossed legs formed a bowl full of the sweet liquid that had crystallized on your skin. I knew it would make me crazy, and I wanted to be drunk on it, and I bent over you and drank all of it." The music had whirled and reeled and peaked with his telling of the dream. Now Joseph's voice became so soft that Jane had to lean in to him to follow his words. "And I woke up with the most intense erection."

The music had shifted to a second theme, this one in a minor key, a lyrical passage full of longing and hunger. Jane was sure that the piece would return to the sun of the original major key in completion of the same cycle that pulled waves to shore and sent them back out to sea.

Jane knew how desperately Joseph wanted her then, but he couldn't let go of the melody. He sifted the notes through the fingers of his right hand like grains of sand, enjoying their warmth, aware of their sharp edges. She reached for a blank sheet from the pack of staff paper she always carried to her lessons for theory notes, put it in front of him with a pencil, and gently kissed him. "I don't think we need Dr. Freud to figure that one out." He smiled but stared at his hands, unable to look at her. "Write it down," she told him, getting up from the piano bench. "I'll be right here when you're through." She stretched out on the couch, closed her eyes and tried to fall into the dream he had painted for her. But her sleep was light and dreamless, wrapped in the silk of Joseph's music.

She awoke to the warmth of his breath on her neck and his weight against her. In her sleep, she had turned to face the back of the sofa, and Joseph had wrapped himself around her. Like a shell, Jane thought. She had always hated when excited high school dates thrust a wet tongue in her ear, but now, as Joseph ran his tongue around the curve of her ear and grazed the lobe with his teeth she felt a sharp stab of desire. He was humming the new melody into her with his breath as though whispering an ocean sound back to the shells he had found in her ears in his dream.

Joseph slipped an arm under her shoulder, reached to her face and brushed his thumb across her mouth. He traced the outline of her lips, and as she opened her mouth to him, he thrust his thumb inside, scraping his nail against the ridges of her teeth and meeting her tongue. She closed her lips around him and sucked the salt from his skin. With his other hand he caressed her hip, then slid his hand over her and unzipped her jeans. He stroked her belly, hardly touching her at first, then moving with increasing pressure and pace until she grabbed his hand and pushed it between her legs.

As Joseph thrust his fingers inside and moved his hand against her, he slipped his tongue deeper into her ear and moved his thumb harder against her teeth and tongue. Jane felt as though she had been taken by a dozen lovers at the same impossibly sweet moment. Joseph sustained the climax that rushed in waves through her body, then cradled her until she lay still.

When she started to turn to face him, he gently pressed his hand on her waist to stop her. He stood up, and Jane closed her eyes and let him pull her shirt off over her head and slip her underpants and jeans from around her ankles as she lay on her side. She heard his clothing drop to the floor. He gently lifted her by the waist and slid her body off the couch so she knelt in front of it, her hips pressed against the edge, facing away from him. Playing a new melody, he brushed his hands over her bent neck and feathered them down her back. She bit into her lower lip and tasted her own blood as he kissed the small of her back and traced along her spine with his tongue.

Jane felt Joseph pressed hard against her, and she moved her knees apart so he could kneel between her legs. As he reached to cup her breasts, Jane angled her hips and Joseph thrust inside her, moving deeper within her than she had thought possible. They came together and lay for a minute draped like rag dolls tossed half on, half off, the couch. Joseph kissed the back of her neck and gently pulled out of her. He helped her up, then sat on the couch while she stretched out with her head in his lap. Joseph wrapped the afghan around her as she hummed the ocean dream song in her mind and he mutely fingered the music on her shoulder.

***

Jane sat for hours on the couch in Joseph's living room studying her English textbook while her teacher composed additional music for the dream cycle of songs that seemed to flow from the pleasure he found with Jane. Often they would analyze points discussed in the advanced music theory class that Jane had been admitted to, the only sophomore accepted into the upper level class.

"Is Mueller still hounding you about your interpretation of the bagatelle?" Joseph asked one afternoon after a two-hour lesson on a Chopin Etude. He sat beside her on the piano bench.

As usual they spoke as much through the music as with words.

"I'm focusing the paper on dynamics." She played through several measures. "I've found a dozen editions that support separation here." The notes rippled like staccato giggles. "But Professor Mueller is so tied up in the biographical stuff." The same measures moved as though slurred together with the sticky weight of molasses, *legato*, mournful. Jane continued to play the melody with her right hand, exaggerating the funereal quality, while she pretended to stroke a beard with her left hand. She mimicked her professor's voice. "Ve must keep in mind, Fraulein Bell, in dis moment of Beethoven's life, September 23 of 1820 at seven forty-two in the evening, he was burdened by the anguish of his unrequited luf for his next door neighbor's new upstairs maid."

Joseph smiled at her impersonation while Jane played through the bagatelle with dirge-like intensity. When she had played the last note, she put her hand in his lap, needing to touch him, closing her eyes. His mouth brushed hers as he whispered, "Not yet," against her parted lips. He took her hand and placed it back on the keys. "The Chopin one more time. You'll hit the F# more surely," he said, his voice husky, absentmindedly caressing her hand as he had a thousand times to remind her to curve her fingers, "if you switch to the third finger in the measure before."

He returned to his chair and, only after Jane had performed the etude flawlessly, nodding agreement as she played the new fingering, did he take her in his arms.

Before Christmas, Jane confirmed that she would return to Juilliard for the next fall semester. Neither of them mentioned Jane's leaving, but their lovemaking became more desperate, *accelerando*, as spring melted into summer.

One weekend in July, Jane walked the short distance to her teacher's house and let herself in the back door that Joseph left unlocked for her. She walked through the living room where she imagined that the grand piano still throbbed with the music they had played there.

In the bedroom, Joseph was lying on his back, his eyes closed, and Jane couldn't tell if he was really asleep or just pretending until his mouth warmed in a smile and he reached out and pulled her on to the bed. "Don't wake me up," he mumbled. "I'm having a wonderful dream."

"An erotic one?"

"An incredibly erotic dream."

"You're lazy today." She began to lace her fingers through the silvered hair on his chest. She knew that he was usually up by five or so to practice, especially when it was so hot. "Do you feel okay?"

"I feel great, and I'm not lazy. I've already put in several hours at the piano and planted two rose bushes in the backyard and showered because I was all sweaty. Now I'm going to rest until my crazy student who insisted that she needed an early Saturday lesson gets here." He still had not opened his eyes.

She ran her tongue lightly across his shoulder and over the muscles in his arm. "You're getting sweaty again."

"You're making me sweat." She could tell that he didn't mind at all.

Jane slipped her tee shirt off over her head. "What if your crazy student gets here and wanders in the back door because you happened to accidentally leave it unlocked, and she comes into your bedroom and sees you lying on the bed naked except for a sheet draped over your ... privates?"

"My 'privates'?" he asked, opening one eye, then closing it again in a slow wink. "Sounds like a dreadful scenario. She might be shocked."

"Yes, your 'privates.' That's an anatomical term I learned in health class." She stretched her hand over the bulge in the sheet and stroked him. She could see the muscles in his thighs tense as he pressed his hips upward to control the pressure of her hand. "What if she wasn't shocked? What if she just wanted to kiss him?" Jane began a slow trail with her tongue from his left nipple down his chest toward his navel. "Everywhere..."

Joseph stopped her. With a hand on each side of her head, he tilted her face to his. "No." His eyes were open now.

"I know about oral sex," she said, trying to sound casual, sophisticated.

"How do you know?" He wasn't laughing any more.

"I read about it."

"Wonderful." He rolled his eyes and turned onto his stomach.

She was quieter now. "Don't you like it?"

"Jesus, Jane! You're making me crazy! Yes, I like it!" The anger she sensed in his voice struck her with the force of a physical blow.

"But not with me." Jane felt all at once cut off from him, floating unattached, unable to remember why she was in his house, embarrassed to be sitting here without her shirt. Cold in the humid warmth of the room, she shivered, pulled away from him, and reached for her tee shirt.

"No. Not with you." Joseph seemed to hear the tears in her voice and realize how she had misunderstood him. He grabbed her wrist to keep her from leaving. "Jesus, Jane," he repeated, this time with tenderness and apology. He sat up at the head of the bed and pulled her down to sit beside him, draping the sheet over both of them. "There's nothing that I wouldn't want to do with you. But someday you're going to meet a man your own age who will want to discover things with you."

She thought he sounded awfully old fashioned. "I'll never love anyone else," she said, hating how young she must sound to him.

"Jane, I'll probably be dead by the time you're thirty."

As though she had considered the possibility, she didn't contradict him. "Then I'll wear black all the time and join an order of musical nuns —"

"Sisters of Chopin," Joseph suggested, wiping her nose with a corner of the sheet.

"We'll play Gregorian chants with jazz rhythms on tinny upright pianos."

"Ah, speaking of jazz..." He scooted her off the bed and wrapped the sheet around his waist. "How is the Gershwin coming?"

Jane shared her teacher's passion for the syncopated, improvisational form, and during the past year, they had spent hours enmeshed in the intimate language of jazz. "It's impossible. There's not enough time..." The statement ended in a sob as Jane realized how fast the summer was ending, how soon she would be leaving her teacher, her lover.

Joseph held her in his arms and stroked her hair. Then he gave her a gentle nudge toward the living room. "You warm up. Let me get dressed and you can show me where the problems are."

Soon they were entangled in intricacies of the *Rhapsody in Blue*, concentrating on rhythms and fingerings and dynamics that diverted both of them from the coming separation.

As the date approached for her to leave for New York, Jane found herself angry at her teacher's apparent indifference to their parting. At her final lesson, Joseph ignored her careless playing and lack of concentration, and lectured her on focus, the opportunities New York could offer for the start of her performance career, and learning all she could from her professors.

"What if I fuck my teacher at Juilliard?" she had asked, wanting to hurt him, then turning away before she could see his eyes.

He spun her around to face him and gripped her shoulders so tightly that she wore the bruises for days. He stared at her for a long time. "Do it if you have to," he said. "But be sure that you're willing to pay whatever it might cost you."

She had started to cry then. He kissed the tears from her cheeks as he laid her on the floor. Her lips were salted with the tears he shed as he saw the marks on her shoulders. She tasted blood as their teeth met in a brutal kiss and he thrust into her as though he wanted to break both of them. She arched her body to meet his and crossed her legs behind him, seeking a pain to drive away the emptiness and numbness she feared in front of her, like monsters lurking just off the edge of the earth.

Chapter Fifteen
Indian Blanket (*Gaillardia pulchella*)

July 14 – 17, 1998

Moira and Jane sat in the grass at the edge of the garden circle, chatting and weeding. Both of them glanced frequently at Kaeth, who seemed quite content to stack up piles of shells, then knock them down.

"Are you getting used to the heat?" Moira looked as cool as always, the wide brim of her sun hat shading her eyes as she glanced at Jane.

"It gets pretty hot in Manhattan during the summer, and we don't have the advantage of this ocean breeze."

As if called up by Jane's words, a gust brushed across the yard and tangled the wind chime into fractured metallic song. Kaeth glanced toward the sound, and her gaze focused on the mother robin rearranging her wings over the single egg in her nest.

"There's an egg in the nest, Kaeth." Jane pointed into the small tree. "Remember the ribbon you gave me at the store? Do you see how the robin used it to make her nest?"

Moira stopped weeding. "We don't touch the egg, Kaeth."

Jane could not read the expression in Moira's eyes concealed by the floppy brim.

"Touch the egg, Kaeth," the childlike woman echoed. Her amber eyes stared at the nest.

"Look at the pelicans, Kaeth! Over the water." Moira pointed toward the ocean where five of the huge birds soared in formation.

They were quiet for a few minutes except for Kaeth's uncanny mimicking of the seagulls' cries. She so accurately captured the sound that the surprised birds swooped and banked and shrieked in answer, wheeling over their heads.

Moira tilted her hat back on her head and closed her eyes. "Are you enjoying your flute lessons?"

"The flute's interesting, but I have no desire to get back into music."

"McCue says you could be good."

Jane focused on perfecting the edge of the garden oval, pulling out a few blades of grass at a time. How much, she wondered, had McCue told Moira about their lessons, their walks by the ocean? She wanted to know if they were lovers, but asked instead, "How long have you known McCue?"

"Years."

Before Jane could learn more, both women were diverted by Kaeth's giggles, which rose to shrieks as she lobbed seashells at circling gulls. One of the largest birds pulled up sharply. A white feather caught in the wind and looped like a toy glider toward the back porch.

Moira sighed and stood up, brushing grass from her long skirt. "I think we'd better head home." Kaeth had begun a tuneless humming song that rose in pitch as she leaped into the air to catch the feather. Sticking the feather into her wild curls, she dashed up the stairs and into the house, closely followed by Moira and Jane.

She was out the front door before Moira and Jane reached the living room. On the porch, Kaeth pivoted to face the screen door as it slammed shut, her eyes focused on the hole that Jane had patched in the screen. As though pushed by invisible hands, she continued backwards, slamming with an alarming crack into one of the wooden posts that held up the porch roof. Kaeth sat slumped at the base of the square column.

Moira and Jane rushed to the tiny woman.

"Are you all right, Kaeth?" Moira sounded much calmer than Jane felt.

"Should we take her to the hospital?" Jane shivered with a sudden frisson, the "goose on her grave" chill. Looking into Kaeth's eyes, Jane sensed she was laughing at both of them.

Kaeth seemed unharmed except for a scratch on her arm, which she must have held behind her as she smashed into the post. Before Jane could go inside for a towel and bandage, Kaeth tilted her head to the wound and licked at the blood with her tongue.

Moira sounded suddenly exhausted. "I think she's fine. I'll take her home and get her cleaned up."

The three of them walked to Moira's car. Moira looked back and nodded toward the house. "She may be less damaged than your porch. I'll pay for the repairs."

The peeling paint on a pillar at the left side of the porch was veined with cracks where Kaeth had rammed into it. "Don't be silly. I'm just glad Kaeth wasn't hurt. The wood must be completely rotten."

As Moira's car pulled away, Jane saw the gull feather sail out the open window, catch in the wind, then dive into the dust of the road. Kaeth's echoed, "Rotten, rotten, rotten," followed Jane into the house.

***

The next day, the gusts had not abated. By evening, a constant wind had driven the warmth from the air and replaced it with a damp chill. After dinner, Jane poured a few fingers of Jack Daniels into a glass and carried it into the bedroom. Her bedside light shining through the drink danced a tawny faerie trail across the diary. What a perfect place for the faeries to march, Jane thought, on the journal of a woman who would brook no skepticism about those on the Other Side.

Jane remembered late fall evenings in her childhood. As she practiced the violin, her grandmother often insisted on rocking in her chair nearby, her arthritic fingers tatting doilies, bookmarks, Irish lace collars so hopelessly out of date that even her doting granddaughter would not wear them. The weaving magic of the crochet hook would halt occasionally while Nana took a sip of whiskey, Irish or otherwise, from a bone china teacup. As Jane's music improved, Nana's strange humming accompanied her practice more often.

Nana, who had perfect pitch and a soprano voice that never showed the signs of age evident in her silver braid or swollen knuckles, would croon odd melody lines so out of tune with the music Jane played that the jarring pitches were almost physically painful to her.

"Nana," she said one night, at the end of her patience with the abrasive sounds. "You're making the music ugly."

Her grandmother smiled and nodded. She raised her cup in a toast as if to acknowledge success and sipped the warming whiskey.

Jane laid the violin in its case and knelt at her grandmother's feet. "Why?"

The rocking stopped and Nana leaned closer to her granddaughter. "They can hear, you know."

Jane's parents had gone out for the evening, but perhaps Nana had forgotten.

Before Jane could remind her grandmother, Nana said, "Not your mother and father." She looked around, as though searching for something or someone in the corners of the room and dropped her voice still lower. "They can hear you. Them on the Other Side. They can give you the music gift, but sometimes they want it back. They can take you away to get it."

"Oh, Nana..." She had heard her mother complain to her father for years about the superstitions she feared would rub off on her daughter. Her father had smiled and diffused the annoyance by insisting that Nana meant well, and Jane was a sensible girl.

"Sometimes they steal the prettiest babies and leave changelings in their place. The ones they leave in the cradle can be fearsome strange, but the strongest can love them anyway and redeem the odd little ones." Nana's hand was shaking as she lifted the cup to her lips. "I protected your mother, and I kept you safe, but I worry about your music. It can draw them right to you, you know."

Jane could see the love and fear in her grandmother's eyes. "Don't worry, Nana. Keep humming. They won't find me." Jane had returned to her music, practicing not only the violin but also the concentration she brought to the concert stage years later.

Now she raised her own glass of whiskey in tribute to her grandmother and read the words Nana had written so long ago.

Monday, April 25, 1933
Dear diary,

Lettie came in late to school today—in the middle of music class, the only hours worth living through except for the time with Brian. Sister Meghan thinks the change in my voice is "surpassing strange," but she gave me the solo for next Sunday in spite of her misgivings. We were just into work on the anthem when Lettie snuck into the room. Her eyes were red and puffy, and her face, usually pale and smooth as the Blessed Mother's (I've had to confess to envy of her skin more than once) was blotchy as old parchment from her crying.

At lunch she told us that her sister had been stolen away by her aunts from Ennis. They took her to the Laundry because she let her boyfriend take liberties and now she is expecting a baby. "I'll never see her again," Lettie kept crying. We tried to tell her different and calm her down, but the nun in charge of lunch duties heard her and rapped Lettie on her knuckles. Then her poor hands were as splotched as her face. "You oughtn't to be talking about what you have no knowledge of," Sister said, and her voice was shaking and a blush crept up and reddened her face from collar to wimple.

I asked Mother about it tonight before I came upstairs to bed. "Be a good girl and you won't have to worry about it," was all she would say. She sounded angry, but I couldn't tell if she was mad at me or herself or the aunts from Ennis. I know I'm not a good girl. I don't want to be a good girl. I waste my prayers asking God to let me see Brian again, and I go to sleep longing to hold him in my dreams.

Jane was still awake—it was the first time she had not been lulled to sleep reading her grandmother's diary—and was curious about the mention of the Laundry. Would McCue know anything about it? Could Moira explain the reference? Jane read another entry.

Thursday, April 27, 1933
Dear diary,

Today was Thursday, and I saw Brian in the field. I ran to him singing in the sweet voice I still don't know as my own. The notes from my song danced and twisted with the music from the flute, and then we were in the grass as tangled together as the melody. I know it was wrong. The Church says it is wrong. My mother and father would say it is wrong. But the song is mine—is ours. And what would they know of our music?

The next morning Jane sat in front of the open flute book propped against the glass doors of the secretary. She had been practicing octave shifts for an hour, marveling at the subtle distinctions in tone shaped by her lips against the gold mouthpiece, by her breath exploring different angles over the opening in the flute.

The Zen-like repetition of the notes, the distant, rhythmic rush of the waves to shore, the hypnotic drone of bees in the nearby lilacs lifted her away from the music she played while an unconscious part of her mind continued the exercise. Had this really been her grandfather's flute? She thought about the passages from Nana's diary she had read the night before. Her grandmother had never been the proper, stuffy character of children's stories, but thinking about her as a rebellious and passionate girl, making love in the Irish fields with a young man she hardly knew, added a new dimension to Jane's understanding of her grandmother.

A reverberating thump on the front porch startled her. She laid the flute on the desktop without taking time to upend it on the flute stand and rushed to the front door.

Steve stood there looking as sheepish as a man his size could. At his feet lay several small pieces of plywood and the eight-by-eight square column that had caused the crashing noise. He pulled a clean handkerchief from his pocket and wrapped it around his right hand.

"Splinter?" Jane asked.

Steve nodded. Jane reached out and tied two corners of the white cotton square together to keep it around his hand.

"Want a Band-Aid?"

Steve shook his head. He reached into his overall pocket for the notebook and pencil. "Sorry," he wrote. "Was trying to leave this QUIETLY so not to bother practice." He shrugged apologetically.

"That's okay." Jane nodded toward his hand. "But are you sure your hand is all right?"

Steve nodded again. His pencil scratched softly on the lined page. "M wants to fix porch tomorrow. Asked me to bring post & saw."

"M" must be McCue, not Moira, Jane realized, and felt the flash of an emotion uncomfortably close to jealousy. Once more, the news of events at her house had traveled through Moira to McCue with remarkable speed. "Will you come in and have some iced tea with me?"

"More flute to do?" Steve wrote.

"I need a break."

Steve nodded to the porch step and sat down. "Tea sounds good."

When Jane brought two glasses of tea to the porch a few minutes later, Steve was sitting with his hands folded in his ample lap. He reminded her of Buddha dressed for a day of carpentry. As she watched him through the screen door, his features became more sad than meditative.

"Thinking about Selena?"

Steve smiled and nodded, but the smile made the expression in his eyes seem even more melancholy.

"Tell me about her."

He reached into a back pocket in the overalls and pulled out a worn leather wallet. "Beautiful," he wrote, then opened the wallet and pointed to a photo of two women. His rough index finger seemed to caress, then rest below the picture of the woman on the left, but Jane's attention was drawn to the figure beside her, whose hand she held. Even caught beneath the haze of plastic, her image was unmistakable, blue eyes, poppy-red lips, the woman who had spoken to her in a dream at George Jackson's house on her first day in Wilmington.

She forced herself to break the magnetic pull of her gaze and looked at the woman Steve pointed toward. "She is lovely." *Gamine* was the word that came to mind. Pixied hair, huge brown eyes, a wide smile revealing perfect teeth except for a lower one, that hid slightly behind another. She might have looked far too wise as a child, Jane thought, and young at seventy. "What happened to her?"

Steve laid the open wallet between them and reached for his paper and pencil. He sat without moving for so long that Jane thought he might have forgotten the question. When he finally began to write, he stared into her eyes and not at the blue lined notebook. "We lost her."

"She died?"

Steve looked down at what he had written and closed the notebook. He put the pencil in his pocket, and she was afraid he would leave.

"I'm so sorry. I hope she would be pleased with what we've done with the house."

He tilted his head as though listening to a message only he could hear, then he nodded an affirmative. The only sound Jane could perceive was the jingle of the wind chime.

Jane reached out, her hand and nails nearly as rough as the carpenter's, and pointed to the woman on the right. She took a deep breath before asking, "Mary Ellen?"

Steve nodded again, closed the wallet, and stood up, slipping it back into his pocket. He did not seem surprised that she recognized Mary Ellen.

"They must have been good friends."

As though in response, he opened the notebook again. It was nearly filled, the first three-quarters of the spiral-bound book jammed with pages slightly crinkled from the pencil's indentations. Jane imagined he must keep them, journals of all his past communications. He flipped two blank pages, then wrote, "Like it here?"

"Do I like it here? I love it." She searched her memory for the Irish word for "good." *Maith.* "It's *maith.* It's a good place."

Steve nodded as though something important had been settled. He finished the iced tea, smiled his thanks, and turned to leave.

"Steve —" She followed him a few steps down the path to the road. "Are McCue and Moira ... close?"

He shrugged.

"Are they lovers?" Jane couldn't believe she had asked the question out loud. She felt a blush warming her face.

Steve, however, seemed delighted with this second question. "NO!" he wrote. "He likes you." He punctuated the last comment with a pencil jab in her direction.

Jane reached out and threw her arms around him. It had been so long since she had hugged anyone. A breeze jarred the wind chime again, and Steve stepped away from her. "Thank you. For the wood ... and everything."

He waved and started toward the road.

After the loose-muffler roar of Steve's truck had transitioned back to the usual quiet of her yard, Jane wandered around the house toward the garden. Over the rhythmic brush of waves caressing sand, she heard faint chirping sounds. Standing back a few feet from the dogwood tree, she could see the beak of the hatchling opening and closing hungrily. The adult robin flew over the scene several times before landing in the nest and tending to the little one, reassured by Jane's stillness that she presented no threat.

***

The following morning brought McCue and the return of summer weather. Jane had awakened early, damp with sweat, sheets kicked to the bottom of the bed. She opened the French doors, closed the night before against the chill in the air, but no breeze stirred. The strip of ocean she could see from her room was flat as a freshly ironed ribbon; even the solitary gull in the sky flapped his wings listlessly in the oppressive heat. Only the mother robin, darting her beak into the loose soil of the garden in search of earthworms, seemed energized.

McCue appeared at the front door at nine, toolbox in hand. He wore jeans and a tee shirt that was already darkening with sweat. The hair at the nape of his neck curled in damp ringlets.

"Thanks for doing this," Jane said, joining him on the front porch.

McCue shook his head as they looked at the damage to the post. "I'm surprised the whole porch roof didn't come down."

"Tell me what to do."

They worked for nearly an hour, measuring, sawing, checking the support on the right side of the porch to be sure it was sound. The sun baked the life out of the air and seemed to leech color from everything in the yard. McCue pulled off his shirt and wiped his face.

"Let's take a break," Jane suggested. "I'll get some iced tea."

When she returned with the tea, she sat beside him on the porch step. "You were born in Ireland?"

"I'm betrayed by my bit of a brogue?"

"It's lovely. Reminds me of my grandmother."

"I was four when we came over. I still remember the passage." His body tensed with a slight shiver, and Jane thought it might be from the chill of the iced drink.

"Was it terrible?"

"It is always harder for some of us than others." He stood up, put down his glass, and went back to the damaged post.

Jane joined him. "Do you know anything about laundries in Ireland?"

"My mother always did our wash in a tub in the cellar. Or do you mean the infamous ones?"

"Those, I guess."

"Some convents took in young girls who were pregnant and kept them there after they had their babies. Sometimes, the girls hadn't done more than flirt or act out. The places were called Magdalene laundries. Guess they thought the girls would wash away their sins while they cleaned the local priests' clothes."

"Sounds barbaric."

"It went on until a few years ago. Where did you hear about them?"

"They were mentioned in a book I was reading." Now it was Jane who seemed eager to change the subject. "Next step?"

McCue nodded toward the rotten wood, then picked up a metal pole that was lying in the grass. "This will be a temporary support." He raised it in a javelin-thrower stance. With his flexed muscles, sweat-slicked torso, jeans riding low on his hips, he reminded Jane of a Greek statue. A rogue wind tested his hold on it. He broke the pose and handed the pole to her. "When I raise the porch roof, wedge the support under the edge. We'll knock the old post out of the way and put up the new one."

She noticed that the scratches on his shoulder were nearly healed. She wanted to run her fingertips or her tongue across the slightly raised scars they had left on his skin. Instead, she tightened her grip on the warm metal of the support.

McCue moved to the front edge of the porch. He braced his hands above him and raised his arms to assess the weight of the roof. The shingles crackled, the small porch roof lifted, and the damaged square column tumbled into the yard as though it had not been attached at all, merely held there by the weight pressing on it. Jane wedged the support into place and stepped back as McCue reached up to slide the pole to a more vertical position. Jane heard a ripping sound and saw the pole had penetrated the ceiling.

"Plywood," McCue said, but Jane had already grabbed a square piece from the materials Steve had brought. As McCue inched the roof higher, she held the pole upright with one hand and slipped the board between the support and the ceiling with her other. "I don't think two musicians equal one good carpenter," he said, adjusting the board to distribute the weight of the roof on the support pole. Their bodies were nearly touching, with only the metal post between them. McCue's banter was light-hearted, and he seemed focused on centering the board, but Jane was aware that his breath had quickened, deepened with their closeness.

She sat down on the porch floor in front of him, wrapped her arms around his legs, and rested her head and chest against him. She smelled his skin and the sheen of sweat on her own, salt from the ocean, the clean, baked scent of sun-dried grass. She could no longer distinguish the sound of his breath from hers. She sensed a slight trembling in the tensed muscles of his thighs that matched the unsteadiness in her arms; she felt the warm pressure of his erection against her cheek and turned her head to press her mouth against him.

Suddenly, fingers were tangled in her hair, tilting her face upwards. McCue glanced towards the porch roof. His voice was husky. "It's not going anywhere." He took her hands and led her inside the house.

In the living room, he kissed her gently and held her face in his hands, tracing the fullness of her lips with his thumb. She pulled her tee shirt off over her head and he followed her into the bedroom.

The air was hot and still, but Jane felt a chill; her nipples hardened even before McCue caressed her breast, as though their bodies might be superheated and any breathable air a few degrees cooler than their flesh.

She unzipped his jeans, then her own, while he kicked off his shoes. They lay on their sides, bodies pressed together. For a long time, his fingers whispered over her arms and back so lightly, they might have been ghost strokes reaching her from another dimension. She let him turn her onto her back, but when his hand brushed over her belly, she pulled away.

"Let me just hold you," he said. "We don't have to do this."

She sat beside him, and said only, "Please," as she pushed his shoulders flat against the bed.

He reached over, pulled his wallet out of his jeans that had fallen on the floor, and quickly retrieved a thin silver disc.

It had been so long since she had even seen a condom. A minute later, she straddled his hips and guided him inside her. She matched his rhythm as though he were a conductor intimate with a song she had long ago forgotten. His eyes closed, and he gripped her shoulders when he climaxed, but she gazed at him, unblinking, savoring his pleasure while denying her own.

He wrapped his body around hers, stroking her arms and the curve of her waist and hip. When she was nearly asleep, she murmured, "Six weeks to decide if I'll play again."

"You'll know when you're ready." The sun was setting as McCue slipped out of bed and pulled the sheet over Jane's shoulder.

He was gone when she awoke an hour later. A dozen Indian Blankets from her garden, their crimson daisy-like petals tipped with yellow, were spread out on the pillow beside her. They seemed to reflect the sunset that tinted the front porch pink and blushed the wood of the new pillar that held up the porch roof. Slipped between the lumber and the floor was a note: *Be back soon to nail it in. Didn't want to wake you.*

The robin swooped over the roof toward the dogwood tree, and Jane could hear the hungry cries of the nestling.

Chapter Sixteen
Alejandose (Sp.) Dying Away, Becoming Distant

1982

Jane rushed down West Sixty-Fifth Street clutching a letter to Joseph. Near the end of her third and final year at Juilliard, Jane felt as at home in New York City as she had as a child at the piano when she first slid onto the wobbly bench of the spinet. She waved hello to the hot dog vendor chopping onions for the Manhattan lunch crowd that would soon be issuing mustard and ketchup requests. Jane was on a break between class and practice session, and the rhythm of the vendor's knife on the scarred cutting block was absorbed into the music in her head. Her left hand gripped the envelope and marked the rhythm against her blue-jeaned thigh, while her right hand mimed the melody line of a Bach cantata.

She slid the letter into the mailbox, aware that her letters to Joseph had become less frequent. During the first weeks back at Juilliard, she had written long letters to him, which were often composed during theory lectures on subjects Joseph had taught her years earlier. When she wrote to him with questions, he would respond in penciled messages peppered with his neat musical notation on sheets of staff paper.

Jane slowed down as she passed the recessed doorway to the jazz club where she played some evenings and weekends for tuition money. "Jane Elizabeth," her father had said, employing the rare evocation of her full name, evidence of his concern, "Can't you find a ballet class to accompany?" But Jane suspected that if her grandmother were alive, she would have loved to join Jane in the smoky bar.

Jane usually ignored the contents of the glassed showcase beside the door, but today she was drawn to her image reflected there. While measures of a Thelonious Monk recording drifted through the open door, marking time until live jazz signaled an end to slow hours at the bar, she peered into what seemed to be the Irish Other World. Behind the reflection of her face—high cheekbones scrubbed free of makeup, green eyes flashing color even on the smudged glass, hair caught carelessly in a barrette—hung her black and white publicity photo. The photographer had caught her intensity as she leaned into the piano keyboard, a mature formality in the gown she wore and with her dark hair swept up in a French twist. For a second, she felt she was watching both her present and her future.

In the letter to Joseph, she told him that when she saw him in a few weeks, she would bring him something special. She had already signed a copy of the photo for him, but the real surprise was a manuscript of her first major composition.

Jane pulled herself away from the glass and hurried back to school. In a tiny practice room, she raced to complete the third movement of her piano suite. It was more than a final project; it was a gift for Joseph Lamb.

At home for spring break, she spent a little time with her parents, then, clutching a portfolio with the photo and her music score, she borrowed her mother's car for the short drive to her teacher's house. "I might be late," she called over her shoulder as she left. "I hope Mr. Lamb will have some ideas for the legato movement."

On the short drive, her focus was split between the new music blossoming in her mind and the desire building to a crescendo in her body.

She stopped the car in his driveway, barely letting it come to rest before she tucked the portfolio under her arm and started toward the house. It was after six, and his last student would have finished his lesson and left. She heard Joseph reveling in the near excesses of Rachmaninoff's Second Piano Concerto. She paused for a moment, holding her breath, awed as always by the genius of her teacher, and her need for the man whose hungers fed both his music and hers.

As the final note of the haunting second movement faded, Jane knocked and walked through the front door. She saw the surprised look in Joseph's eyes. When she moved toward him, he raised his right hand from the keyboard as though to stop her. She felt like she had tripped on his panic and her desire, and she drew closer to the piano, a trapeze artist falling to the ground, knowing there was no net to catch her but unable to halt her descent.

"Jane, I didn't know when you were coming home."

"I wanted to surprise you."

Joseph rested his head in one hand, avoiding her eyes. For a second, Jane felt the Other World again, saw that everything was wrong. A woman not much older than Jane stepped through the bathroom door. As though running a film backwards in her head, Jane realized that this world had changed. The garden she had run past was weeded now, blushing with roses. Over the roses, wooden birdfeeders swayed in the yard. Jane could hear a cardinal replacing the Rachmaninoff with a simpler song. The young woman's blond hair hung in damp ringlets, and Jane could smell the fragrant steam that followed her from the shower. She wore Joseph's bathrobe, the one he had offered Jane the first time they made love. A Persian cat rubbed against the woman's legs, then draped itself over the back of the sofa where Jane had slept while she waited for her teacher to find the first of his dream songs.

The woman smiled and pulled the robe tighter around the pregnant swell of her belly.

Jane took a step backward, and Joseph stood up from the piano bench as though to keep her from falling. "Jane, I'd like you to meet Anna."

The woman started to extend her hand, but Jane held her hands tightly clasped around the portfolio. "I'm so pleased to meet you," Anna said. "Joseph talks about you all the time. I think you must be his most famous pupil." She ran slender fingers through her hair and Jane saw the glint of a small diamond on her left hand. "We'll be eating in a little while. Would you join us for dinner?"

"No." Jane felt suddenly sick. "No, thank you." She reached into the portfolio and pulled out the publicity photo. One corner was bent and Jane wished the whole picture had been ruined. "I just came to give you this," she said, handing the photograph to Joseph. "My parents are expecting me at home."

As she turned toward the door, she saw Anna shrug, scoop up the cat in her arms, and head toward the bedroom.

Joseph followed Jane through the front door. "Did you finish your suite?" She ignored him and rushed faster toward the car. She could hear his heavy breathing as he tried to catch up to her. She laid the manuscript folder on the roof of the car and found her keys. When she started to open the car door, he pushed it shut and turned her around to face him. She did not struggle when he put a powerful hand on each of her shoulders, but she wouldn't meet his eyes.

"Have you finished it?" he asked again, his voice pitched lower but even more insistent.

Jane wanted to answer him, wanted to scream that yes, she had finished it for him and how could he do this to her, how could he bring another woman into his life? She wanted him to feel as empty and gutted as she did. But she could not speak.

"I couldn't tell you about Anna until you finished composing. I didn't want to stop the music." He caught her wrists when she reached out to push him away. "You won't be coming back here to live. You've got to move on with your life and your music."

"I'm here now."

"For how long?"

She didn't answer him. Months ago, she had written to tell him that her second concert tour was scheduled to begin the week after graduation from Juilliard. The first series of performances had occupied most of the summer before.

"I didn't intend for you to find out like this." Joseph held Jane's hands and stared into them as he had at her first lesson. "I didn't want to tell you until you finished writing the suite."

Jane felt the sun-warmed metal of the car pressed against her back, and the heat from Joseph's hands as he held hers. She smelled bread baking inside the house and roses opening in the garden. In her mind, the third movement of the piano suite smashed and clattered with a fevered dissonance the music had not contained. It shifted from ordered, predictable harmony to a pounding cry of loss. She held onto the new sounds she heard and shut out the pain.

Joseph released her hands. He lifted the portfolio from the roof of the car, held it for a moment as though hoping to absorb the new music through his touch, then handed it to Jane.

"It's not finished," she said, opening the car door. "It's wrong. I thought it was a love song." She backed out of the driveway without looking at her teacher.

Jane drove with no thought of a destination. She found herself on the expressway, following the route she would take to return to New York. The sun glared off the hood of the car. She wished for weather to reflect her mood: lightning, the manic percussion of thunder, a driving rain to slick the highway. If she lost control of the car and died, crushed in the wreckage, pages of her music soaked with the rain and her blood and scattered about like macabre confetti, Joseph would be sorry he had abandoned her. She turned on the windshield wipers. They beat and squeaked on the dry glass, their thump an unrelenting metronome.

Gradually, Jane's tears slowed, and the anger at Joseph, the furious things she wished she had said to hurt him, were incorporated into the insistent pulse of a new third movement. The original glib and predictable melodic lines transmuted into compelling dissonance. She suddenly hated the controlled breath of the music, formulaic in its rise and fall, and heard in her mind the gasping, panting, wailing sighs the movement now begged for. In counterpoint, she felt the melody of her grandmother's whispered, *"Is ón saol a thagann an chiall."* Nana was right. It had taken life to teach her the meaning of her music. Now she was ready, and she understood it. Her hands ached with desire to pull the new composition from the keyboard. Her fingers tensed and tapped on the arc of the steering wheel. She realized she had turned the car around and was nearing her house and her piano.

She spent the next week listening to the new music in her head and translating her loss and fury into notes on the staff paper, which seemed barely able to contain this wave after wave of passion. Her parents did not ask about the sudden frenetic immersion in revision of her work or about her break with Joseph. They took turns bringing sandwiches to the music room when she seemed unable to abandon the music long enough to eat with them.

***

The jazz club was dark and smoky, a cave anchored by the ebony gleam of the grand piano. A pungent haze hovered like anguished genii in the candlelight. It was the first time Jane had played there since returning to the city from spring break, and she leaned over the keyboard, shoulders hunched as though she sought to become one entity with the instrument, isolated from anyone else in the room. She inhaled the odd, sweet sadness of jazz-flattened thirds. She played nothing but blues, her fingers digging into the ivories and drawing out heartrending melodies like an injured patient worrying a wound because the pain reassures her that she is alive.

Gradually, she was aware of slurred comments directed toward her from a table not far from the piano. "Lighten up, honey. This ain't a funeral parlor." The voice rang with a drunk's assurance that he speaks for everyone in the room.

Jane responded with a few chords of the Volga Boat Song, accentuating the mournful melody.

"Come on, doll. You can do better than that. How 'bout something cheer —"

His comment was cut off. In the dim light, she saw two men slide their chairs away from a round table and approach the heckler.

Jane heard the thump of a glass as it was placed heavily on a table. Whispers. The scrape of a chair being moved. She glanced at the door and saw the bouncer in his usual pose, legs apart, arms folded over his chest. He nodded silent approval as the three men moved through the front door and only two returned.

After another hour, the gentle weight of a hand on Jane's shoulder broke her trance at the keyboard.

"Take a break, Jane." The owner of the jazz club looked at her with concern. "Your heroes over there want to meet you." He nodded toward the table where the men sat. "Drinks for the three of you on the house. Want a glass of wine?"

Jane sat up, surprised by the tension and stiffness in her shoulders. Her hands shook when she lifted them from the keys. "Jack on the rocks."

She moved toward the men's table as the vacuum caused by the end of her playing was filled with rising murmurs of conversation. She passed couples lighted by flickering candles and tried to shut out the hum of whispered seductions.

Both men stood as she neared the table. The taller one extended his hand. His handshake was firm and businesslike, but Jane immediately warmed to his open gaze and his shy smile under a ginger moustache.

"I'm Ken Witten. We've been enjoying your playing but were worried you might be chained to the piano or held there by some evil spell. Glad you could take a break." Jane looked into his eyes, startled by the reference to a curse. Nana, driven by her

Irish superstitions, had warned her about the conjuring enchantments of music that could snare the unwary. But Ken seemed totally grounded in the realities of a smoky New York jazz club.

"Thank you for rescuing me from spells and from drunks in the audience."

"Our pleasure." Ken nodded toward the second man at the table. "My friend, Alex Holt."

Alex nodded. Jane was charmed by his serious brown eyes and prematurely silver hair. He didn't shake the hand she offered him, but rather held it in his hands as though protecting a fragile treasure. "I don't do music, but I know you're amazing." They sat down as two beers and a tumbler of whiskey arrived at the table.

"To the blues," Ken toasted, and they clinked glasses. He kept up a lively conversation about the city music scene and surprised Jane with his knowledge of her own career, mentioning the prizes she had won and her first concert tour.

When the candle on their table flickered out in its pool of wax, Jane realized she had taken a far longer break than usual. "Thanks again for the rescue. I've got to return to my chains for a while."

The men stood as she pushed back her chair, and Ken held out a business card. "I don't know if you have an agent, but if not, I would love to represent you."

"Do you have many clients?" Jane wasn't sure of the questions she should ask. She hated dealing with the business aspects of her career and had arranged the upcoming tour through Juilliard contacts.

"You would be my third, but I can promise you lots of attention."

"I'll think about it." Jane impulsively slipped the card into the front of her cocktail dress. "It was good to meet you." She headed back to the piano, warmed by the unaccustomed drink and the men's company.

After another hour, she finished her last set, which had become decidedly less gloomy than those earlier in the evening. The table where the men had sat was empty, and Jane tried to deny her disappointment. Outside, she recognized Alex as he stepped from the shadows beside the door. He had been staring at her picture in the glass case.

"May I walk you home?"

"I'd like that."

He was an architect in his thirties, and he entertained her with stories about the buildings they passed. They sat outside the door to her apartment house and watched dawn rise over Manhattan, both amazed that the night had passed.

Seven months later, between a concert tour and recording session that Ken had arranged, Jane married Alex Holt, relieved to be so loved by a man who didn't do music.

Chapter Seventeen
Pansy (*Viola x wittrockiana*)

August 6, 1998

Jane drove the Jeep slowly into Aria. It was not the most direct route to the grocery store, and today was one of McCue's teaching-out-of-town days, but she found herself drawn to his studio like a teenager cruising the lockers for a glimpse of a football player on whom she had a crush.

Several cars were parked in front of Moira's store. Jane pulled up in front of George Jackson's house and was surprised to see him sitting on the front porch, waving as though he had been waiting for her. His right hand transitioned from the wave to a patting motion in the aluminum chair beside his. As she approached, she sensed a change in him. The ethereal, translucent quality she had noticed when they met was even more pronounced, as though time were slowly erasing him.

"I have something for you," he said as Jane settled into the metal porch chair, warm from the sun. He looked at the small stacks of objects arranged at his feet, bent over, and picked up a red book. He held it for a moment like one would hold the hand of a friend one might never see again. "I'm divesting myself of things and this was calling your name."

Jane took the book, noting its worn corners and the old-fashioned scalloping of the page edges. On the inside cover, *Mary Ellen Jackson* was written in fading ink. Although most of the gold had flecked off the spine, she could read the title, *Lore of the North Carolina Sea Coast*. "It's beautiful, George, but are you sure you want to give it away? I could read it and return it to you."

"I'm at an age where it's a pleasure to share my things and know that I don't have to dust them another year."

"Thank you. I'll take good care of it." Jane and George watched as cars pulled in and out of the parking spaces in front of the garden store. "I've never seen it so busy at Moira's."

"Ah. It's the end of summer sale. Always draws a crowd." He nodded in the direction of a woman leaving the store with a flat of flowers, bright with yellow and purple. "It's time to plant fall pansies, you know. They grow all winter here." They were both quiet for several minutes. "Will you be putting some in, do you think?"

After a few more minutes of silence, Jane shrugged. "I have three weeks to let my agent know if I'm returning to my concert career."

"And?"

"I don't know what to tell him."

"Three weeks is ever so much time, Jane." His eyes were closed, his head nodding, as they sat together in the sun. "You'll know the answer when you need to know the answer."

When the shadows had slipped a bit further on the porch, and George Jackson was napping soundly, Jane patted his hand, took the book he had given her, and walked next door to Moira's.

She paused inside the double doors, put off by the presence of a dozen women and several men, shopping, chatting, at ease with one another. She turned to leave.

"Jane!" Moira spotted her from across the room. Nodding an apology to two women at the counter, she wove her way through customers to Jane's side. "Have you come to do some shopping?"

"I stopped to say hi, but I can tell you're busy."

"Just give me a minute."

While Moira settled accounts, Jane wandered to the sidewalk outside the store. Hardy pansy plants in baskets created mounds of jewel tones and pastels. Flanking the doors to the store and McCue's studio, square stone planters glowed with newly planted color, and Jane wondered whose hands had dug in the rich potting soil, Moira's or McCue's. Just as Jane turned to begin the short walk that would allow her to glance through McCue's window, Moira called to her from the store's open door.

"Jane." Moira sounded breathless, more agitated than Jane had heard her. "I saved a flat of pansies for you in the back." She turned to take a quick look into the store, and both women saw Kaeth pacing inside. "Want me to get them?"

"I can pick them up later. You have a full house in there. I stopped to ask if you and Kaeth would like to come to dinner. Looks like you could use a break."

"That sounds great, but we just can't do it tonight." Moira took Jane's arm and led her into the store. "Stay around for a minute while I wait on those women at the counter."

Moira's attention seemed split between counting plants, making change, and watching Kaeth, whose pacing had transmuted to a twitchy step that looked to Jane like an Irish clog dance pounded out on the deck of a wave-tossed ship. Her sharp features were constricted with concentration on a rhythm she alone could hear; her pale eyes squinted so tightly that only the obsidian slits of her pupils showed. Her hands pressed palm-first against the air, her fingers curled.

Jane watched, fascinated, afraid to break the trance that held Kaeth.

Moira sighed as the last of the customers at the counter exited with their purchases. She nodded toward the dozen people still milling about the store. "Thanks for the invitation, but we'll have to stay here for a while 'til closing. I'm taking Kaeth to the cabin tonight. It will do her good to run around while I look for herbs."

"Where is the cabin?" Jane had wondered for weeks about Moira's late-night treks.

The Irish woman nodded again, letting her hair veil her face, but the gesture was vague and unfocused. "You know, up Burgaw way."

"I'd love to come along some night —"

"The storms will be here any day now. It's rough up there. We know the way, but you might fall and break a leg. We couldn't have that."

Kaeth's dance stopped as suddenly as a marionette abandoned by the puppeteer. Only tiny glitches haunted her steps as she moved to Moira and Jane. "Break your neck, break your neck," Jane thought she heard Kaeth whisper in a perverted echo of Moira's warning.

Moira pulled Kaeth close to her and slipped her hand over the smaller woman's mouth. The gesture was playful, but her expression was cold. Moira's eyes widened. She jerked her hand away and Jane saw three red dots where Kaeth's teeth had drawn blood. Kaeth spun away from them. She ran to her quilt in the corner and curled up, her face to the wall. Jane sensed that laughter rather than sobs shook Kaeth's narrow shoulders.

Jane wanted to ask Moira if her hand was all right, but Moira had slipped the punctured fingers into the pocket of her jeans.

"I'll pick up the pansies in a few days," Jane said, turning toward the front door where three women entered, exclaiming over the profusion of plants blooming outside. "Take care of yourself."

Moira nodded, glanced at Kaeth, who, shoulders stilled, seemed to be asleep, then turned to greet the new customers.

Jane felt a sense of lightness and release when she walked outside. She relaxed her grip on the book George had given her. She had forgotten she was holding it, and now her fingers ached with the tension in her hand. She resisted turning toward McCue's studio but started to raise her hand to wave at George. He was no longer on the porch. The seat of one metal porch chair bounced a few times as though recently vacated, or as Jane knew her grandmother would suggest, it was occupied by a presence she could not see. She completed the wave before sliding onto the car seat and heading for the grocery store.

Back home later with her groceries, she paused in the yard a moment to study the line of the porch roof. Satisfied that it now hung parallel to the porch floor, she entered the house, warmed by thoughts of her afternoon with McCue the day they had repaired the roof. She put the food away, picked up her grandmother's diary, and carried it with the book from George Jackson to the porch facing the ocean.

Settled in the rocker, Jane opened the diary and found where she had stopped reading.

Thursday, May 4, 1933
Dear diary,

A week has passed. Only Thursdays seem worth writing about. For all the weird shortening of time when we are together, the hours when we are apart stretch to many times their length like taffy at the fair, but without the sweetness.

I lied to Sister Catherine about being needed at home and ran from school early. The sweet lop-eared rabbit was gone. The field was empty except for the horse. He wandered up to me with his rickety walk, and we stood together, waiting, watching the fields for Brian. The horse's eyes were clouded and weepy. I ran my fingers through the mat of his mane, prickly with burrs and tag-along hay. Blue-green flies worried his ears, but he seemed too tired to flick them away.

Then the sun came out from behind a cloud and reflected off the horse's hide, which was suddenly as sleek and glossy as Father's boots on Sunday morning. My fingers slid through the silk fringe of his mane. He rolled his eyes, pricked up his ears, and his hooves danced a pattern as fine as any lady's at a ball. He arched his neck and whinnied, then bowed his proud head to—Brian. Brian had appeared from nowhere it seemed.

"I've brought us a picnic supper," he said, nodding to a wicker hamper in his hand. He turned his green eyes to the horse, now pawing the grass as though impatient to gallop into a battle I was afraid to think about.

I backed off from them—the changed horse and my otherworldly lover.

"What are you?" I was sure he couldn't tell me the truth I had suspected from our first meeting.

His eyes turned gray and stormy. "You know," was all he would say.

I did know. I'd heard the stories; everyone had heard the stories since we were little. Stories our grandparents whispered about the Others, the Good Folk, names that skipped around their real meaning like the feet of step dancers tapping around a tripping spot on a wooden floor.

"I won't go off with you and never see my family again." I must have been crying because the horse, the boy, the sun, the field all looked blurry and far away.

"I won't take you if you don't want to go."

"And I won't eat your food." Everyone knew that was a trap. He swung the basket over his head three times and when he let it go, it disappeared. Or maybe I was blinking back the tears and didn't see where it landed.

"I love you, Cara," he said. His eyes were the beautiful green again.

I let him put his arms around me, and we were lying in the grass, but I pushed him away because I had to know. "Can I keep my pretty singing voice?"

He laughed and that was the loveliest music. "If you sing for me."

"What will it cost me?" It was always a swap with the Good Folk.

"Only what you are willing to pay." And the world grew quiet and dark in his arms.

Jane felt the familiar effect of the diary and fought against the desire to fall into a deep well of sleep. As she read the last words in the entry, her head had become heavy, resting against the high back of the rocker, which might have been made of down pillows instead of its red oak. She dropped the diary to the floor and reached for the book George Jackson had given her as though it were a lifeline to continued consciousness.

She stood up and stretched, looking out over the ocean, the book in her hand a red flag that startled the robin in the nest. "Sorry," Jane whispered, settling back in the rocker as the bird returned to dropping pieces of worm into her baby's wide open beak.

The book bore an 1893 copyright. The title page announced in an ornate typeface that the author was Miss Julia Whitfield. Jane read several chapters with their quaint Roman numeral titles, drawn to the information Miss Whitfield had accumulated but even more fascinated by notes penciled in the margins in Mary Ellen's handwriting. *Piper's Cove?* she had written beside the mention of a location identified only as a nineteenth century beach town. Facts about Wilmington landmarks featuring gardens, and every comment about locations close to Aria, were underlined and highlighted by arrows and exclamation points.

Jane looked up from the book and was surprised that the setting sun already blushed the ocean waves. A red sky at night was supposed to mean a clear day tomorrow. She had overheard several comments in conversations at Moira's store about big storms on the way, but if sailors' lore held true, the next day should be beautiful. She laid the red book on top of the diary beside the rocker and went inside, returning a few minutes later with a sandwich.

After her supper, she reached for the book. A small piece of paper stuck out from the leather spine. She began to tuck it back, concerned that the hand-sewn binding was not as well preserved as it had appeared. The paper slipped further, revealing a blue line, thin as a vein. Jane carefully pulled the folded piece of lined tablet paper from its hiding place in the binding.

It took her a moment to orient herself to the pencil-drawn map in her hand. From a starred location in the center, arrows pointed away toward Burgaw, Wilmington, and Aria. At the same instant that her mind took in the words "rat's vein, wintergreen, witch hazel, wild ginger," each with an arrow pointing to a spot near the star, she noticed "M's cottage" written at the bottom of the page in Mary Ellen's careful script.

Jane realized the paper must be a map to Moira's cabin. Jane had never heard of rat's vein, but assumed it was another herb. She had been curious for weeks about where Moira and Kaeth disappeared with such regularity. Her friend had not seemed eager for company tonight, but what if her hand had been hurt worse than it seemed? What if Kaeth was acting out even more and Moira needed help dealing with her? Jane knew she was manufacturing excuses to follow the map and solve the mystery of Moira's outings away from Aria.

The top edge of the sun hung on the horizon, then slipped away leaving clouds smeared crimson. But before Jane could convince herself that it made no sense to traipse around unknown terrain in the dark, the silver arc of a full moon began to rise from the ocean, tracing a rippled path to the edge of the sand. She tucked the map in her pocket and went in the house to find a flashlight to supplement the natural beacon.

Although the map was not drawn to scale, it mentioned enough landmarks to make it easy to follow.

Jane drove with all the windows and the sunroof open, watching for the buildings and side streets Mary Ellen had noted, checking her odometer against the *5.3 mi* or *12.2 mi* distances between locations. Moonlight glinted off the dashboard, and for a few moments she allowed Beethoven's sonata to play through her mind, its melody as sinuous as the silver light. She gripped the steering wheel and silenced the music memory when she realized her fingers had begun to pantomime the keyboard patterns that would have created the music. As if echoing the emptiness, the moon slipped behind a cloud.

Things had changed, Jane realized, since the map was drawn. Stretches of road lined on both sides with Mary Ellen's sketchy triangular icons, which must have symbolized expanses of scrub pine, now had been cleared for housing developments with names like Tide Ponds and Sea Branch.

After half an hour, she knew she must be close to the turnoff from the main highway. Few cars were on the road. She slowed down, looking for a cutoff to the right. On the map, Mary Ellen had printed *Sandy Trail*, but Jane couldn't tell if that was a description or its official name.

She pulled off the highway into a cracked asphalt parking area in front of an abandoned shop. It was half past ten. She probably ought to postpone her adventure and try to find it in the daylight.

Jane got out of the car and paced across the parking lot. Flattened soda cans had rusted to filigreed scrap metal. A used condom lay partially buried beneath a pile of cigarette butts. She stepped over the sad lump of a dead gull, its once white feathers as dark and defiled as the rest of the litter. She looked at the debris and then up at the moon that shook off a cloud and winked into sight in another part of its arc through the sky. Before the next full moon, she had to let Ken know if she would perform in the spring.

She had reached the boarded-up shop door. In the moonlight, she could read letters nearly worn off a sign that leaned like an exhausted messenger against a cracked window: Jonah's Custard Stand. She ran back to her car as quickly as she could without tripping on the uneven surface of the blacktop. A glance at the map verified the custard stand as one of Mary Ellen's landmarks. She had missed the turnoff.

Before pulling back onto the highway, Jane studied the map. Sandy Trail had to lie between Jonah's and a little square on the map marked Hardware. Heading back in the direction from which she had come, she missed the side road again, but found a ramshackle building whose flickering neon sign and row of wheelbarrows identified it as the hardware store, apparently still in business in spite of competition from the huge chain home improvement stores not too far away. Sandy Trail must be in the half-mile stretch between the two landmarks.

She turned around in the hardware store lot and reentered the main road. It was after eleven, and if she couldn't find it in one more pass down this stretch of highway, she would turn back and head home.

Jane had nearly passed a graveled area to her right when her headlights bounced off the reflector of a dented station wagon pulled off the road and partially hidden by thick bushes. It winked red. Jane slammed on the brakes and her car slid a few feet, fishtailing slightly before coming to a stop. She took a deep breath, checked behind her, and backed up. She pulled in beside the concealed vehicle. It was Moira's battered station wagon with A Garden Place stenciled on the driver's door. Through the rear window, she could see empty cardboard boxes for carrying plants back to the store.

Sandy Trail was just that, not a road at all. A narrow path of gravel and sand led from the parking area, through the woods, and over a rise. Even in the moonlight, Jane could not see further than a few feet. She retrieved the flashlight from the floor where it had landed after her quick stop and got out of the car, realizing she had not decided how to proceed if she found the path to Moira's place.

Mary Ellen's neat notation suggested a half-mile walk to the cottage. Jane let the arc of the flashlight beam sweep the ground at her feet. Kaeth's "break your neck" chant sounded in her head. She could think of a dozen reasons why she should turn around and go home.

She devised a quick plan. She would walk a short distance up the path, and if it were passable, she would continue to the cabin. If there were no lights on and it looked like Moira and Kaeth were asleep, Jane would leave and maybe visit them tomorrow. If there was a light on ... then Jane realized she would have to make some more decisions.

She hiked about four yards, swinging the flashlight beam to illuminate the path. She avoided a few vines that coiled into the trail, but the neat clipping of most plants suggested that the path was frequently cleared. Her light glanced off the hubcap of another vehicle parked on the opposite side of the path from where she and Moira had left their cars. She knew from the moonlit outline that it was McCue's truck. A quick sweep of the flashlight beam verified its identity. She felt an intense rage and the desire to smash his windshield with the heavy metal in her hand. She dug in her toe and kicked sand and loose gravel at the truck in what she realized was an infantile gesture. Her foot caught in a coil of kudzu, and she fell to her knees, making her angrier.

Suddenly, there were new pictures in her head, not Moira puttering around alone in the moonlight gathering herbs, but moonlight reflecting off sweat-slicked limbs, Moira and McCue intertwined; Kaeth, with her animal voices, and the bobcat, sounding his preternaturally human cries, joining in a wicked counterpoint to their lovemaking.

Jane grabbed a sapling beside the path and pulled herself to her feet. She ran, hurting from this betrayal and old betrayals and losses, dashing up the incline toward Moira's cottage. She stumbled on a loose rock and lost her balance, pitching forehead-first against a low tree branch. The flashlight rolled from her hand and winked out. She tumbled several feet down a hill beside the path and lay still.

A minute later, she sat up, rotating her wrists and ankles, checking for broken bones. The worst damage seemed to be scrapes and bruises. She raked her fingers through the leaves and twigs around her but couldn't find the flashlight. The moon had ducked back behind a cloud. As quickly as the light was snuffed out, the night sounds, insects, frogs, a distant owl, ceased their music as though hushed by the baton of an invisible conductor. In the vacuum, Jane heard one sound. The paws of an animal skittered through dry leaves, coming closer. She searched the ground again, this time closing her hand around a baseball-sized rock. She tried to remember what she had read about predators in the woods of North Carolina. Cougar? The animal sounded too small to be a bear.

She scrambled up the slope to the trail, gripping the rock. It would be better to see what was approaching than have it pounce on her from above.

The rustling moved closer, then further away, and back from another angle as if playing with her, teasing her. Jane held her breath, concentrating on other sounds so soft she might be imagining them. It seemed at first as if the black night itself exhaled the simple melody of an Irish folksong her grandmother had sung to her. Then footsteps approached, marking the rhythm of the whistled song.

"Hello?" Jane was sure it must be McCue, but things seemed so strange in the woods that she couldn't be sure.

The footsteps and whistling stopped. Clouds thinned over the moon and Jane could see McCue's silvered outline on the path. "Jane?" He took a step closer to her. "Did you follow me?"

"I followed Mary Ellen's map to Moira's place." But had it actually said "Moira," Jane wondered. "Are you lovers?"

"Moira and I?"

"Well, hell, maybe Mary Ellen, too."

"Mary Ellen was thirty years older than me."

There had been thirty years difference between Joseph and Jane. "Are you fucking Moira—and me?"

Jane heard a feral hiss. McCue stamped his left foot hard on the ground. Duncan stopped mid-crouch. Eyes flashing red in the moonlight, the bobcat dashed into the woods, snarling.

"Moira and I aren't lovers." McCue sounded tired and sad.

"I'm going to talk to her."

"She won't be there."

"I parked beside her car."

"Full moon. She'll be out —"

"Gathering herbs." Jane finished his sentence with more than a little sarcasm.

"I'll take you to the cabin."

"No." She turned to go up the path and winced when she put full weight on her left ankle.

McCue took a step toward her and saw the scrape on her forehead. "What happened?"

"Nothing." Jane tested her ankle and decided she could walk on it. "I slipped."

He reached into his shirt pocket and handed her a clean, folded handkerchief. "Let me help you."

"No," she snapped, as though he had been the one who pushed her off the path.

He took a small flashlight from his jeans pocket and gave it to her.

She did not look back at him but sensed that he watched her climb the gentle rise in the path that led to the cabin.

It took her about ten minutes to reach the clearing and cabin at the slower pace she took to favor her ankle. It was a few minutes after one. The moon was out again, now tangled in the treetops as it began its descent in the night sky. The cabin was tinier than Jane had imagined, about fifteen feet square. It was sided with boards weathered to silver under the lunar sheen, which would revert to aged wood in the daylight. Jane saw no one. The insect song was silenced again but the owl, closer now, continued his nocturnal lament.

Jane walked to the door and knocked softly. There was no answer from inside, but a nearby woodpecker echoed the rhythm. She tried the door. It was unlocked. She pushed it open a few inches, touched the key on the chain around her neck, then closed the door.

She started back toward the path, unwilling to break the silence by calling Moira's name. She tried to remember the areas on the map marked as herb locations. Rat's vein? Witch hazel?

Her throbbing ankle reminded her that it was dangerous to try to find Moira in the dark woods.

But she had found and followed the map, and, although she had no right to demand an explanation of a nighttime meeting between Moira and McCue, she needed to ask Moira about it. Jane turned around, walked to the door, and opened it, whispering Moira's name. Silence. She ran her hand along the wall inside the doorframe searching for a light switch, but there was nothing on the rough plaster surface.

She turned on McCue's flashlight and danced the beam around the room. Along one wall, a narrow cot was draped with a clean, nearly threadbare sheet. A few quilts were stacked in a corner. Two stools sat under a small square table in the center of the room, and a single lightbulb swung in a gentle arc over the table, nudged by a breeze through the front door. After pulling the light switch chain and turning off the flashlight, she closed the door and sat on a stool to wait for Moira and Kaeth.

The room was warm and still, filled with the earthy scent of herbs planted in tiny pots on the windowsills; cut twigs with odd leaves sprouted tangled webs of roots in milk bottles; flowers in drying racks suspended from the ceiling hung heads-down like children on a playground. She tried not to think about McCue, who must be on his way back to Aria.

She didn't remember folding her arms and laying her head down. In her dream, she was a little girl, hiding in the closet in her grandmother's room. She could smell lavender and talc and linen dried in the sun. She peeked into the room through the sliver of open space. In front of the dressing table stood a woman Jane knew must be Nana in her late teens, a laughing girl with long red hair who slashed at her arms with a shard of broken mirror as though trying to cut herself in two.

Jane heard knocking and woke from the nightmare, sobbing her grandmother's name. Realizing where she was, she called, "Moira? Kaeth?"

Still shuddering from the dream, remembering that there had been no blood, no pain in the images in her sleep, she opened the cabin door. The yard was empty. She heard the knocking again and looked up to see a woodpecker hammering for grubs in the peeling bark of a cottonwood trunk.

She checked her watch and turned out the light. It was half past two when she closed the door and started down the path to her car.

The flashlight beam bisected the trail and exaggerated shadows of stones and tree roots underfoot. The call of a bird raised the hairs on the back of her neck, and she glanced quickly behind her, half expecting to catch sight of someone or something following her. The only thing there was her shadow dogging her footsteps. She thought of her grandmother in the dream, trying to split away from herself.

She heard McCue before she saw him. He was still whistling, or was whistling again, this time the melody from the second movement of a Carl Philipp Emanuel Bach flute concerto. She wondered if he had started with the *Allegro di Molto* movement and planned to whistle to the end of the piece. Near the same spot where Jane had headed off by herself, he sat with his back to a tree, legs stretched across the path. He stood up when she reached him.

He didn't ask if she had found Moira. She didn't ask why he had waited for her. On the way back to the parking area, she stumbled, and he took her hand. She didn't resist.

At her car, he opened her door and nodded goodnight. As Jane backed the Jeep out, she saw McCue open his passenger door and heard a single piercing whistle. A streak of tawny fur pounced into his truck.

Chapter Eighteen
Cantellerando (It.) Humming, Singing Softly

1996

Jane rushed into the Manhattan bistro, pulling off her winter gloves. She paused to let the flickering candles, the muted jazz from the trio in the corner, and the whispers of intimate conversations drive away the rhythms pounding in her head after hours of rehearsal. She waved to her favorite waiter and headed for the quiet table in the corner where she knew Alex would be waiting. His back was to her. She saw him check his watch. As she took her seat, Jane noticed a glass of red wine had been poured for her. Alex motioned to the waiter to refill his own empty glass.

"Sorry I'm late. The rehearsal went on longer than I expected, and it took forever to get a cab."

"It's a mess out there."

Jane lifted her glass to taste the wine, but Alex stopped her. After the waiter refilled his glass, he nodded to Jane, and they toasted each other. "To something special?" she asked.

Alex pulled a large envelope from his pocket and laid it between them. "To getting away from winter madness in the city." He pulled brochures from the envelope and fanned them on the table. Colorful pictures of Caribbean resorts promised sun and blue water. "Last week, Ken said your April schedule was light." He took a drink of his wine. "I've cleared my calendar for the last two weeks. I think we need some time together." He took another swallow of wine before setting the glass on the table.

"It sounds wonderful, but I can't do it then. I signed a contract yesterday to play in North Carolina at the end of April."

She pulled a small appointment book from her purse. "March. I might be able to get away for four or five days around the tenth of March if I shift a few rehearsals. Would that work?"

He ran his finger around the edge of the wine glass and looked at her.

"F#," she said, identifying the note sung in the clear crystal voice. It was a game they used to play.

"Actually, it doesn't work. I have to be in Copenhagen then. We got the museum contract."

"Alex, that's wonderful. When did you find out?"

"Yesterday. I was going to tell you at dinner last night."

Jane had cancelled their dinner plans when a recording session rehearsal had to be rescheduled. By the time she arrived home, Alex was asleep. "I'm sorry."

"Doesn't matter." He pushed the brochures aside and opened his menu. "It was just a thought."

During the meal, the silence between them was broken by small talk. Had anyone been listening, they would have sounded like casual acquaintances, exchanging mundane details of their day. When they left the table, neither seemed to notice the candlelight through Jane's wine throwing sunset colors on the picture of an idyllic island.

When they toasted each other next, a month had passed. Alex raised his glass of wine and clinked it against the glass of milk that Jane held. "To our baby," he said.

"Our baby." Jane whispered her response and heard warning echoes of Nana's voice. She set her glass down and her fingers traced a symbol on the tablecloth, the cross with a circle in the center, the Celtic cross, to protect children from agents of the Other World. Then her fingers returned to miming the music that ran through her head. She thought Alex seemed as hopeful as she was that the baby might close the distance that was growing between them.

***

Alex took the paintbrush out of Jane's hand, balanced it on the top of the can, and wrapped his arms around her thickening waist. "You can take a break, you know. The baby's not due for another four months."

"But I'd like to get the painting finished before the tour starts."

He led her to a rocking chair and seated her in it as though she were a fragile doll. "I believe the doctor said that at thirty-five you are an elderly *prima gravida* and ought to be resting."

"And what does that make you?"

"An even older first-time dad. Maybe we should both take a nap."

The buzzer from the door downstairs interrupted their banter. When Alex pushed the intercom button, a distorted metallic version of a familiar voice announced, "Uncle Ken is here." Alex buzzed him in.

"Ken, tell Jane she should lighten her performing schedule and leave the painting to professionals."

Concern showed on Ken's face. "Is anything wrong?"

Jane stood up and hugged him. "Everything is absolutely fine. Alex is just nervous. I think he'd be happiest if I stayed wrapped in a cocoon for the next few months, but the doctor says moderate exercise is good for me."

"We could cancel the North Carolina tour." Ken looked at Jane, then Alex.

"Wilmington is supposed to be beautiful this time of the year. And playing the Schumann is hardly stressful. I've done it a dozen times." Jane's eyes took on a distant focus and her hands began a pantomimed ballet as new music entered her mind. She was unaware of her own soft humming. "Excuse me for a minute?"

At the piano, the fingers of Jane's right hand danced out a melody. Her left arm draped protectively across her stomach. This abundance of inspiration was as much a surprise as the pregnancy had been. She and Alex had both wanted children, but after so many years of trying, they had stopped talking about the possibility, both of them filling their lives with their respective careers. They had stopped talking about most things; more and more, music was the only voice with which Jane was comfortable. News about the baby had brought a rush of inner song that filled Jane day and night. Every street noise or birdcall or child's laugh she heard blossomed into melody.

Alex hadn't accompanied her on tour for years, but two weeks later, both he and Ken flew with Jane to Wilmington.

April in North Carolina was a gift following the damp early spring of Manhattan. After settling into the hotel, the three of them walked along the beach visible from their rooms.

"Where am I playing?" Jane always checked out the piano and performing space before meeting with the orchestra.

"Thalian Hall downtown."

"New or old?"

Ken understood her theory that the venue she played in colored her performance. "I've seen pictures. You'll love it."

"You may never want to leave." Alex held Jane's arm to steady her as she pulled off her sandals and wiggled her toes in the warm sand.

She laughed as a wave surprised all three of them. Alex and Ken jumped toward drier sand above the tide line, protecting their street shoes. Jane let the water soak her jeans up to her knees as it splashed and receded. "My God, it's cold!"

She linked arms with them, and they watched the waves turn pink and gold from the setting sun.

"Let's get you back to the hotel before you get chilled," Alex said, wrapping his jacket around her shoulders, but Jane hesitated.

"Cold enough sea for Selkies and seals." Jane's whisper was nearly blown away by the rising breeze from the ocean.

"Selkies?" Ken asked.

Jane smiled and shook her head. "Nothing." But it was something—the murmuring of her grandmother invoking creatures from Celtic legend. Far down the beach, a tiny woman raised her head as if listening to Jane's musing, then reached into the crazed mirror of a tide pool and pulled out a shell. She slipped it into her dripping pocket and disappeared down the beach, moving away from them with the speed of the sandpipers she seemed to be chasing.

Jane did love the hall. The following morning, she and Ken arrived as the concert grand was being tuned. While her agent attended to business matters, she sat in the back row with her legs propped up on the seat in front of her. Usually before a performance in a new location, she paced the entire hall, checking acoustics, listening for echoes or dead spaces. During rehearsal with the orchestra, she relied on Ken for advice about resonance and balance, but she enjoyed immersing herself in the unique sound quality of each auditorium.

Now she sat with unaccustomed stillness in the opulence of Thalian Hall, its fluted columns, gilt plaster moldings, and profusion of red velvet cushioning her in the luxury of the 1850s when it was built. She closed her eyes and let the "tuner's song" wash over her, as the waves had undulated at her feet the day before. From her seat at the back of the house, she listened with the technician as he played the notes in the middle of the keyboard, notes that would establish temperament, the template for tuning the rest of the piano. He tuned fourths and fifths, then focused on minor thirds and major sixths. She opened her eyes when he moved to chromatic major thirds. His left hand fell with consistent weight on each key while his right hand adjusted the pitch of the strings with a wrench. As he trued the unisons, making more than one string hit by the same hammer sound as one, Jane wandered to the stage to thank him. Rehearsal went well with only a few stops to adjust tempos.

The Schumann was scheduled for the second half of the concert, and during the first part of the program, Ken and Alex sat backstage with Jane. The briefcase at her feet, which usually held music scores, bulged with skeins of yarn. The muted metronomic click of knitting needles accompanied music pouring from the stage as pastel pink, white, and blue variegated wool grew into a baby blanket.

After intermission, the audience greeted her enthusiastically as she walked on stage and shook hands with the concertmaster and conductor. Both had seemed a bit in awe of her at rehearsal, but by the end warmed to her sincere praise of the orchestra's preparation and comprehension of the concerto.

She moved to the downstage edge of the instrument's familiar ebony curve and nodded to acknowledge the applause from the house. Always, the glare from stage lights obliterated any real view of the audience, but now it blinded her with a dizzying bank of shimmering suns. She gripped the security of the piano's edge and followed it to the bench. She bowed her head for a moment, her hands resting on the keyboard until a wave of nausea passed. Then she dove into the joy of the A Minor concerto.

After a few measures, she and the other musicians settled into an appreciative give and take, presenting passages to each other like generous children at a birthday party. Jane had not thought of individual notes in the piece for years; they were fixed in muscle memory, engraved in her mind. She was enveloped in the music, unaware of the passage of time; even the slightly late entrance of violins near the end of the first movement did not shake her concentration.

The audience was unusually attentive during the pause between the first two movements. There was little of the squirming, shuffling, and throat clearing that sometimes erupted. Jane and the orchestra slid comfortably into the *Intermezzo,* moving together like old lovers who have danced in each other's arms a thousand times.

Suddenly, the ascending four-note melody line from the piano abruptly stopped and Jane's hands hovered like perplexed butterflies over the keys. For a moment, the orchestra seemed to pause, their sound suspended by the unmoving baton of the conductor. He held for a moment waiting for her to find her place and return to the music in her head. But Jane was distracted by the first perceived flutters of the baby inside her. She imagined a tiny foot kicking for attention, perhaps dancing to the rhythms of the Schumann, protesting confinement.

She glanced up into the panicked eyes of the conductor. In the wings, Alex and Ken stood ready to rush to her side. She smiled at all of them, sharing a lovely joke with the new life inside her. Back in the music, the bewildered butterflies regained their bearings, and Jane nodded to the conductor who sighed with audible relief. As Alex and Ken maintained watch offstage, Jane entered the music with focus and delight that had the audience applauding for several minutes after she finished playing the last note of the final movement.

As she stepped out of the bright lights of the stage, she kissed Alex. "I felt the baby move!"

"I love you," Alex said.

Ken whispered an awed, "Cool," and they gently pushed her toward the glow onstage as the audience called her back for another curtain call and encore.

After the musicians filed out and the last patrons had left the hall, while Jane signed programs in the greenroom and a stagehand in overalls covered the piano and wheeled it to the corner of the stage, a bearded young man slouched in the back row where Jane had sat the day before. When the auditorium was empty, he retrieved a small CD recorder from behind a potted palm on the edge of the stage and slipped it into his pocket. He wandered out of the hall, his footsteps marking the beat of a softly whistled flute sonata.

Chapter Nineteen
Dotted Horsemint (*Monarda punctata*)

August 17, 1998

The first knock at the door was so gentle, Jane wasn't sure she heard anything at all. She held the flute away from her lips and listened, then returned to practicing. The knocks that followed were quiet, but the rhythm more insistent. She upended the flute on the stand McCue had given her and went to the door.

Steve stood on the porch. His hair recorded each ridge left by the teeth of his comb. He was dressed in a dark gray suit, a little too short in the arms and legs, and frayed at the right cuff. He had unbuttoned the collar of his white shirt, which stuck to his chest like damp tissue paper, and he carried a rumpled silk necktie and painter's overalls draped over his left arm.

"Steve, come in. You look like you could use some iced tea." He nodded his thanks and entered the living room without the hesitation he had shown on his first visits. Jane gestured to the couch and Steve eased his massive body onto the furniture as though testing its capacity to support his weight.

"I'd almost forgotten about painting the fence," Jane said when she returned from the kitchen carrying a tray with glasses and a pitcher of tea. "Our Tom Sawyer project."

Steve sipped the tea she had poured for him.

"You're dressed up today. You look nice. We could put this off until another time."

He reached into his jacket pocket for his notebook and pencil. "Mr. Daley's funeral this morning. On my way back from cem."

"I'm sorry. I know he was a good friend of yours. We can do the painting some other time."

"Now is best. Work makes sad times easier." He gestured to his work clothes, then to the bathroom.

"Sure, you can change in there. I'll meet you on the front porch." She took the tray to the kitchen and returned with tools. "I've got my trimmers to prune the roses at the mailbox, and two brushes so I can help with the fence."

They started painting at opposite ends of the fence and, in a few hours, met in the middle. Steve worked on the gate while Jane put on gardening gloves and clipped at the roses around the mailbox. Steve had replaced the rusted mailbox with a shiny plastic one that perched on the old post.

"Steve," Jane hesitated before asking the question that had bothered her for weeks. "What happened to Selena?"

Steve painted the last board on the gate and tamped down the paint can lid. He bent over and traced the letters *S. Nevin* still visible on the mailbox post. "Gone," he wrote in his notebook.

"Did she die?"

Steve put his brush on top of the paint can and walked away from the house to his truck parked in the street. He sat on the running board and Jane squeezed in beside him. Neither of them spoke for several minutes. Steve turned to a blank page and wrote, "Cops said drowned."

"You don't believe it?"

"S body gone. Part here I think." He slipped the notebook and pencil into the pocket of his overalls.

Part? "Her spirit, you mean?"

He gave a slight nod, collected the paint can and brushes, and headed to the house. As they reached the porch, Steve stopped her with a hand on her shoulder. His other hand pointed to a bush Jane had planted a few weeks earlier. The horsemint was in full bloom. Slender apple-green leaves reached protectively around pink flowers tipped with green. The iridescent flash of a hummingbird's wings dashed from flower to flower, and Jane remembered the scene she had dreamed on her first visit to George Jackson's house.

"On my first day in Aria, someone—I think Mary Ellen—mentioned Selena to me in a dream."

Steve seemed pleased. "Someone must have said their names & you got to meet them in dream."

Jane nodded agreement and leaned closer to the hummingbird, which flitted to another flower. The key on the chain around her neck slipped from her shirt and she quickly hid it, but not before Steve noticed.

His pencil made a sound like the whirr of the hummingbird's wings. "What did you lock away?"

Jane turned from him and started up the porch steps. He stopped her and wrote, "You ask me hard questions."

"My music," she whispered. "I locked my music away."

He followed her inside the house; retrieved his folded suit, shirt, and tie; and penciled a final note on his way out the door. "Good thing you still have the key."

***

Exhausted from the sun and the painting, Jane crawled into bed early and reached for Nana's diary. She had poured two fingers of Jack Daniels into a glass and raised it in a toast to her grandmother. "What can you teach me tonight, Nana?"

Saturday, May 13, 1933
Dear diary,

My mother says it's nonsense, but my lover swears it's truth. There's not a soul I can tell the tale to who might help me untangle the riddle of it all. I tried with the priest—not old Father Devlin for sure—but the priest newly come from Kilkenny, the one with the teasing smile and the hands that shake a bit when he puts the communion wafer on the tongues of us young girls, although I'm sure, truth be told, he's not thinking impure thoughts. It's probably just nervousness he's feeling at his awesome responsibilities. I tried to broach the subject at confession just last Saturday, in hopes of his offering some advice on the entanglement I find myself in.

I hid in the far back pew and watched old Father Devlin finish his last confession of the morning and hobble out the door to the rectory. That cursed gossip Mary Katherine McCain slithered out of the confessional grinning like a wicked tabby cat with stolen milk dripping from its whiskers. I wondered what bit of juicy slander she had managed to leak into her confession this week. "Father, forgive me for I have sinned. I listened in on my cousin Fiona's fight with her boyfriend from Cork—and him a Protestant and all—and she said she might be with child—and her unmarried and the news would most likely kill my Auntie Margaret. What penance must I do for my transgression? Surely listening in is a sin," and the nasty girl herself gloating there behind the sleazy veil of her piety.

Finally, she slipped out the front door of the church leaving not so much as a penny in the poor box. I could just imagine her rolling her skirt up above her knobby knees and unfastening a button or two on her blouse before she walked by the boys gathered outside Clancy's pub.

The church was empty for a few minutes, and I must have nodded off because the next thing I knew, Father William from Kilkenny was closing the middle door. Quick as I could, without being unseemly, I got myself into a confessional and down on my knees. I don't even remember what sins I laid before him, even though it was this very morning, but Father William was lenient with his Hail Marys.

Just as he was closing the little sliding door that meant confession was over, I grabbed up my courage and squeaked out, "Father, can you tell me about the Other World? Are there people—well, not real people like us—but changers who look like us, here on earth? Is it a sin to believe in the Otherness?" I wanted to ask about souls, too, and if they might have them, but there was no answer from the priest's side of the screen, as though it were in a different kind of Other World. There was sort of a gasping, choked sound, and the screen clicked shut. I knew Father William was there because the whisper of his own prayers for protection leaked through to me like smoke in a burning house. I sneaked out of the church afraid that I had spoken of things so awful there was no penance he could think of to absolve the sin of mentioning them.

Jane fought the usual soporific powers of the diary and read on.

Tuesday, May 16, 1933
Dear diary,
My monthly is late. I lied to Mother that I was crying because of the cramp pains. I dare not even pray about it to God or the Blessed Virgin lest a bolt of lightning strike me for bothering Them with a situation born of my own sinning.

Jane reached for the glass on the bedside table, realized that it was empty, and walked to the kitchen to refill it. Back in the bedroom, she closed her eyes and savored the sweet, soft kick of the whiskey. Dear God, what was her grandmother telling her?

Thursday, May 19, 1933
Dear diary,
Today is Thursday. I waited until dark in the rain for him, but no one came, not even the rabbit who seems to look at me sometimes with Brian's eyes. When I got home, Mother and Dad and Jenny were all frantic with worry, and I'm sorry for that. Mother said I could catch my death of cold. That doesn't sound so bad. Forgive me, God, for thinking so.

Saturday, May 27, 1933
Dear diary,

I won't tell Mother. The Sisters in school look at me like they suspect something. I don't know how soon I'll be showing. I'll run away rather than go to the Laundry. I'll go to America.

Thursday, June 1, 1933
Dear diary,

Brian was waiting for me! I know he loves me. I told him about the baby that is on the way and that I want to run away to America. "We just need money for tickets," I said. I saved last Sunday's newspaper that lists the sailing of the boats from Dublin.

He held my hands. His face was pale as the beaten hay in the field. "The money's no problem," he said. "It's the getting away from here." And even as he said it, the sky seemed to grow heavy and press on us, and the wind groaned in the oak tree. "But we'll try, if that's what you want to do."

I'm to pick a day and tell him next week.

It will kill me to leave Mother and Da and Jenny, but they would send me away with the baby. I don't want to give it away or have it in the Laundry.

Wednesday, June 7, 1933
Dear diary,

I'll see Brian tomorrow. A boat sails this Saturday. It's a market day and Mother won't miss me until evening. I'll leave her a note, but I don't know what to tell her. I can only take a dress or two and you, dear diary.

Saturday, June 10, 1933

Oh, God, dear God, I am on the boat to America by myself. Brian met me in the field like we planned. He looked so frightened to be leaving, and weakened somehow to be out on a day not a Thursday. We took the horse. Brian left money far greater than the worth of the broken-down animal the farmer had owned. They say that the Good Folk have riches beyond measure, and it must be true.

Brian was so sweet and treated me like a fragile piece of glass while he helped me into a cart for the horse to pull. He dropped a leather satchel, his only luggage, to the floor, and tapped the reins on the horse's sides. The horse was magical once again. We laughed as he danced down the road, carrying us away from all we knew.

The further we got, the tighter Brian's hands gripped the reins. The horse slowed and I could almost watch the burnish fade from his coat. He stopped a few miles from Dublin, swinging his head around and blinking rheumy eyes in apology. Brian released him from the cart and turned him toward home. We walked a few miles before a farmer stopped for us and carried us into the city.

The docks were a madhouse. We barely had time to buy our passage and line up in front of the gangplank before we were scheduled to depart. I should have seen that Brian's steps grew more hesitant, but I was afraid of losing our place in line and excited about a new life in America.

Sailors reeled in the rope that kept the crowd on the dock, and hundreds of passengers pushed us toward the boat. I felt Brian's hand grip mine even tighter as he pulled us away from the water's edge. His green eyes were panicked. Suddenly, I remembered my grandmother's advice. The only way to escape the Good Folk was to cross running water because they could not follow. Brian was willing to cross the ocean to be with me in America. "Try!" I begged him. And I think he did. But the crowd pulled our hands apart. He threw his satchel to me and the waves of people separated us, and he disappeared as though below the sea itself.

I have a little cabin for the journey. His money bought us that, and the leather bag contains more than I could spend in years. His flute is in it, too. I'm so sick and so tired. I can't write more. This part of my story is done.

Jane turned the page, but it was blank as was the one after that. She closed the diary and let the waves of sleep pull her under.

Chapter Twenty
Desconsolado (Sp.) Grief-stricken, Downhearted

1996

Jane inked the final measures of the sixth piece in her song cycle. Each featured a different instrument entwined with piano, celebrating milestones anticipated in her baby's life. The series sailed from "Glint in Your Father's Eye," a gentle waltz for tenor sax melting into sexy swing, through a bouncy piccolo march in "First Steps," into the just completed cello-crooning "Forever Lullaby." A sudden knifelike pain shocked her hummed melody to a gasp. Her hand jerked across the structure of the staff paper, graphing a several octave arc as though the pain sang its own terrible melody.

She tried to control her breathing and waited for the pain to subside, but the sharp pain transitioned into a cramp that left her doubled over on the piano bench.

When it relaxed enough for her to move, she phoned Alex.

"I'll call an ambulance right now."

"No," Jane said, remembering stories about her mother's emergency trip to the hospital the day of her own birth. "It's easing up a little. Can you take me to the hospital? Just to be sure everything is all right."

"I'm leaving right now, but it will take me at least twenty minutes with this traffic. I'll call Dr. Kreidler and ask her to meet us at the hospital. I'll see if Ken can pick you up sooner, and I'll go directly to Mt. Sinai."

A few minutes later, Ken raced up the stairs, making a very poor attempt at appearing calm. "Sure you don't want an ambulance?" Jane shook her head. He took the overnight bag

Jane had packed and offered her his free arm as they went downstairs. In the car, Ken tried to divert her with small talk about orchestra gossip but stopped after a few minutes of her silence.

Alex and Dr. Kreidler met them in the emergency room. Jane tried to wave off a wheelchair, but the nurse was insistent.

"This is probably nothing," the doctor said. Jane was always calmed by the presence of this soft-spoken woman who had followed her through her pregnancy. She wanted to believe her now. "We'll take you for an ultrasound. If there is a problem, you're close enough to term that a C-section will be safe for you and the baby."

Alex and Ken tried to look reassured, but Jane could sense their fear. Another cramping pain overwhelmed her. Liquid gushed from between her legs, and the nurse propelled the chair toward the delivery room.

The next hours were a blur of pain. After a final agonizing push, Jane felt the baby slip from her body. She waited to hear its first cry, to feel the baby in her arms.

A terrible silence, as palpable as a wall of ice, filled the room. Alex turned from Dr. Kreidler, who held the small body in her arms, and moved to grip Jane's hand. His eyes were haunted with uncomprehending agony. The doctor tenderly handed the baby to a nurse, who wrapped it in a warmed blanket, then moved away from Jane to another part of the room.

"I want my baby!"

The doctor nodded to a nurse, who began to fill a syringe. "We're going to give you something to relax you." The doctor's eyes were filled with tears as she approached Jane's side. "There is a problem with your baby."

Jane tried to move her arm away from the nurse, but Alex gently restrained Jane and she barely felt the prick of the needle. "What could be wrong?" She looked from the doctor to her husband and back again.

"It's called anencephaly. Her brain didn't ... develop. I don't know why we didn't see it on the ultrasound weeks ago."

"I want to hold her." The baby was a girl. Her secret wish had come true. But a cotton drug cloud was pushing itself between her brain and the world. "Hold her..."

"You sleep for a little while, and we'll bring her to you." The doctor spoke, but Jane did not hear. And she did not feel the tears that Alex shed as they dripped on her cheek.

When she woke a few hours later from a dreamless sleep, Alex and Dr. Kreidler were conferring quietly in a corner of her hospital room. Her brain slipped slowly to consciousness, trying to make sense out of the random whispered words she heard. Damage, a few days, support. She struggled to sit up in the bed. "Where is my baby?"

"The nurse will bring her in, but first we have to talk." The petite physician sat on the edge of the bed. "Your baby was born with anencephaly. Sometime early in your pregnancy, probably in the first month, the neural tube failed to close properly, and her brain was not able to develop."

"Did I do something wrong?" Jane was barely able to pose the question and pulled back as if afraid to hear the answer.

"We don't know why it happens. I'm sure that nothing you did caused it."

"Can we take her home?" Jane was suddenly aware of a muted chorus of sounds in the hospital room. A cheap clock on the wall opposite her bed clicked the seconds with a tin heartbeat. A chattering family passed down the hall, complaining about maternity ward visiting hours. Dr. Kreidler tapped her heel against the metal edge of the bed. Alex seemed surprised by the sob that escaped him like a hiccup.

Dr. Kreidler reached for Jane's hand. "Most of these babies don't survive the birth process. The ones who do rarely live for more than a few hours. Some a few days. I think you should stay here and hold her for as long as she's with us."

Jane pulled her hand away. She didn't want sympathy or attempts at comfort. "Please let me have my baby."

The doctor left the room. Alex helped Jane get out of bed and sit in a rocking chair. He draped a blanket around her and tried to embrace her, but she was unresponsive, as though she had been as damaged as their child.

Dr. Kreidler brought the baby to the room and placed her in Jane's arms. The baby's head was enveloped in a pink cap, which covered the malformation in her skull. Jane thought of the changelings, the shape-changers from her grandmother's stories and wondered at the transformation in her child.

"Have you named her?" Dr. Kreidler asked.

Alex started to explain that they had been considering several names, but Jane broke in. "Deirdre." It was the name of a legendary Irish heroine and meant broken-hearted.

Alex touched the baby's limp hand. "Does she know we're here?"

"She can't see or hear, and she feels no pain," the doctor explained. "But I think she may know that you're here."

Alex brushed his fingers against the baby's cheek, and both he and Jane gasped when Deirdre's tiny mouth pursed in a sucking motion. "She's hungry. She's fine!" Jane felt a rush of milk swell her breasts, and she held the baby closer as though to protect Deirdre from this doctor who had so misjudged her.

"That is one of the cruelest things about her condition. Sucking is such a primitive reflex. She doesn't feel hunger, but there are special bottles you can try to feed her with. I'll have the nurse bring one in." Jane didn't respond, but Alex thanked Dr. Kreidler and said they would like to try.

The doctor turned to leave, then asked, "Do you have family who would like to see her?"

"A friend is picking up Jane's parents at the airport right now. They'll come directly here."

Jane knew it would be Ken who had gone to the airport. He'd prepare her mother and father for the news.

"You can try to feed her with this." The young nurse entered so quietly that Jane hadn't heard her. She reached out to pick up the baby, but Jane would not relinquish her. "My name is Erin." She spoke softly as she loosened Jane's grip on the limp body. "I may look too young to be a nurse, but I am one, and I helped raise three sisters." She held the baby and showed Jane and Alex how to use the bottle. "Don't worry if she doesn't drink much. She can't feel anything bad." She handed Deirdre and the bottle back to Jane. "I think these little ones are angels even before they're born."

It took only a few minutes for Jane to realize the baby could not drink. She rocked and Alex sat quietly with them.

A gentle knock on the door announced the arrival of Bridget, Jack, and Ken. Her father's reddened eyes and Bridget's smeared mascara suggested that they had been told about their grandchild's condition, but her mother tried to sound cheerful as she greeted them. "You'll get through this, you know." She kissed Jane on the cheek. As she bent to caress the baby's unresponsive hand, Jane's whispered "I'm so sorry" seemed to break Bridget, and she began to weep for all of them.

"Please take them to the apartment," Jane said, addressing both Alex and Ken. "You should all probably get some dinner."

"I want to stay with you," Alex began, but Jane's look to him was one they had all seen. It was a closing off, a retreat to a place where they could not follow. Usually an escape to her music, now she seemed to leave them for a sanctuary she shared with her daughter, where she would hide and protect her as long as she could.

"I'll be back soon," Alex said as he and Ken walked Jane's parents out of the room.

Jane rocked and held her baby. Gradually, the murmured creaking of the chair began to whisper with her grandmother's voice, retelling stories from Jane's childhood.

"Love the strangest things," Nana had told her. "They might be the most treasured of beauties in the Other World." She had never been able to explain exactly how to find that mysterious place but swore that she knew it existed. "There are things that can't be talked about, but sometimes you can write them down or tell them in a story or sing about them, and the Good Folk will be fooled into thinking that they still guard their secrets."

She would tell Jane little more than that, but most nights, as Jane was falling asleep, her grandmother would spin tales she had heard as a girl in Ireland. Now Jane's thoughts, numbed with the pain of losing the baby in her arms, slipped into a world of shapeshifters, and leprechauns, and selkies, who transmuted themselves from seductive women to seals as quickly as Jane's hope had turned to heartbreak.

Alex came back to sit with her and was replaced by her parents and then Ken, and still Jane rocked, silent, except for occasional moans that escaped from her lips, prolonged exhalations that seemed part Irish lullaby, part keen.

After twenty-six hours, Jane fell asleep with Deirdre in her arms. When she awoke, her arms were empty. She cried out, still held by a dream, and feared that she had dropped the baby. But Alex was there, and she could tell by the tears he wiped from his cheeks that the baby was dead and had been taken from her, as though Deirdre could only escape the desperate pull of her mother's love when Jane slept with exhaustion.

Bridget had arranged for a simple memorial service in the hospital chapel. Alex, Ken, Bridget, Jack, Dr. Kreidler, and Erin, the nurse, wept for the baby who had been with them such a short time. Jane did not cry.

"Jane." Dr. Kreidler approached her outside the chapel. "I've made an appointment for you in a few minutes with Maureen Hankins. She's our staff psychologist who specializes in helping parents who have lost children. Alex spoke with Maureen while you were with Deirdre."

"There's nothing I want to say or hear about it." Jane started to walk away.

"Please, Jane." Alex had joined his wife and the doctor. "You need to talk to someone about this." He knew Jane's silences, her shutting off from the rest of the world. "Maureen is easy to talk to. You need to be able to mourn, to cry about this." Alex's eyes filled with tears again. Jane knew how badly he, too, had been hurt, and she did not have the strength or the will to argue with him. She nodded her assent.

She could see his relief, and sense in his slight smile, her husband's constant optimism that—somehow—everything would turn out all right. "Good, then. Ken has gone off to get some food for dinner. Your parents and I will come get you when your session with Maureen is over. An hour and a half?" He looked to Dr. Kreidler for confirmation. She gave it with a nod, checked her beeper and said goodbye, again expressing condolences to both of them.

Maureen Hankins' office was decorated in soothing seashell colors. Jane thought of entering the shelter of a huge conch shell that confined her in a swirl of ivory, sand, and palest pink. Had the only sound been the breathy murmur whispered by a shell held to her ear, she might have been able to sit and talk with the calm woman who met her at the office door. But underlining the words of condolence and welcome, Jane heard the recording of a Mozart four-hand piano sonata, the one she had played with Joseph, a piece she had daydreamed about playing with her daughter. She felt herself withdrawing, assuming a psychic fetal position, putting up barriers between herself and the psychologist. Part of her wanted to talk, to cry, to scream until her lungs were empty and she collapsed, but she was as deaf and blind and unresponsive as her baby had been.

After about ten minutes of gentle questions from the psychologist that elicited no answers, Maureen handed Jane two business cards. "This is how you can reach me at any time." She pointed to one of the cards in the same sea shades as her office. "This other one is for a colleague of mine. I think you and Alex should make an appointment with him soon, when you're able to talk about this." She placed her hand gently on Jane's arm. "The healing process is hard, but we can try to make it a little easier for both of you."

Jane could not speak but nodded and left the room. She went to the front door of the hospital and hailed a cab, forgetting that Alex would be arriving in an hour to get her.

At her apartment building, the doorman's somber greeting told Jane that he had been told about the baby. Before he could express his sympathy, she rushed through the doors. Behind her, she heard him say that Mr. Holt and Jane's parents had left a few minutes earlier. Jane pushed past several other people to enter the elevator.

In the apartment, she paused in front of the door to the room that had been Alex's study, listening for sounds that weren't there. The door handle was cold to her touch. She opened the door and saw that her father and Alex had removed the crib and changing table. At the window, she released the cord on the Venetian blinds with a jerk that sent them clattering to the windowsill. Grabbing the edge of the valance, she pulled it down, cutting her fingers on the rod that bent in her hands. Primary red streaked the pastel balloons that floated on the fabric.

Stuffing the material into the wastebasket, she jostled a bookshelf emptied of Alex's design books, now holding *Pat the Bunny* and Dr. Seuss. A Pooh Bear music box played three notes of a lullaby before Jane threw it into the corner. It shattered into yellow fragments. Springs vibrated, then stilled.

Jane collapsed cross-legged in the center of the room. Beside her on the floor was the blanket she had knit between rehearsals and before concerts, busying her fingers with yarn before her hands flew across the keyboard. Now she bit into a corner, severing the yarn with her teeth.

Stitch by stitch, she began to unravel it, watching the colors as they slipped through her fingers. Pink, blue, white. Pink, blue, white.

When Alex and her mother and father came home, they found her there, the rewound ball of yarn resting in fingers that were finally still.

Bridget and Jack left for Florida a few days later, saddened, frustrated, and exhausted.

At Alex's urging, he and Jane sat for hours in a succession of therapists' offices. But words, which had always been less adequate than music to articulate her thoughts, seemed to abandon her, and she could not express her sadness and anger at losing the child with whom she had hoped to share her music.

Appointments with grief counselors transitioned into tense, silent sessions with marriage counselors. She took to sleeping on the sofa beside the piano she would not play. By day, she spent hours there, drapes closed, reading music theory books. She took walks in Central Park with Alex when he insisted that she get some exercise and fresh air, returning in the evening to read until she fell asleep on the sofa.

Eight months after the baby had left their lives, Alex woke to muted sounds from the piano room. It was two in the morning. The piano did not sing with heartfelt melodies of Chopin, nor did it throb with the power of the driving bass of a Beethoven sonata; it dutifully plodded through a pedestrian series of scales, then moved to the calisthenics of Dohnanyi. Jane repeated the exercises with the uncomprehending robotic intensity of an *idiot savant* whose mis-wired brain has conquered the notes, but not the soul, of the music.

Jane fell asleep at the keyboard, her head resting on the wooden ledge of the music rack. Alex awakened her and led her to their bedroom. They had made love only a few times since Jane had returned from the hospital. Even though she sensed Alex hoped the return to music might mean a change in her, this attempt to engage her was no different from the others. She was compliant, acquiescent, but totally without the sexual energy that had enriched their relationship since they met in the jazz bar.

"I'm sorry," replaced the usual breathless, "I love you," that Jane had whispered for years after lovemaking.

A few weeks later, Ken took them to dinner at their favorite Italian restaurant. When the first bottle of Chianti had disappeared, and the woven rattan cover of the bottle had been nearly unwoven by Jane's fingers, Ken brushed aside loose bits of wicker. He cleared a space in front of Jane and took her hands, as though that were the only way to assure her attention. "St. Louis needs to know if you will perform in the spring. They understand if you can't and will release you from your contract, but they need time to find a replacement soloist."

Jane pushed the slivers of rattan into tiny equal piles as if reading clues to her answer. "I can't play the Chopin —"

Ken cut her off, as if anticipating her inability to return to her signature music right now. "Tell them another piece you want to perform. They have plenty of time to prepare."

Jane traced cryptic designs in the mess of slivers in front of her. "Scriabin," she said, naming a composer she had first studied at Juilliard. The waiter's hand reached down and swept the fragments off the table like a god bored with the divination conceit of humans. Jane noticed the look that passed between the two men who loved her, each in his own way, a look that signaled hope in them that her decision to perform again might hint at recovery from her loss.

"Excellent." Ken motioned the waiter for another bottle of wine with which to toast Jane's decision. "Choose the piece you want to play and let me know in a few days. I'll tell the maestro, and we'll set a rehearsal schedule."

That night, after many glasses of sweet ruby wine to numb the pain of facing music again, Jane returned to the architectural purity of early Bach and played until her hands ached and her mind craved the silence of sleep.

She chose Scriabin's Piano Concerto in F Sharp Minor to play in St. Louis and focused on preparation, rarely leaving the music room.

***

"Jane, we need to talk," Alex said, as they cleaned up a supper of soup and sandwiches that he had prepared in their apartment. Jane hadn't wanted to take time to go out to dinner so she could return to the piano for several more hours.

"Could we talk later? I'm finding some new dynamics in the Allegro."

"Now. Later you'll be too tired, or you'll play until I've fallen asleep. We need to talk now."

In the living room, Jane realized she could not remember when they had last sat here and talked to each other. Then, she did remember. Before the baby was born, they had spent hours there, speculating about how wonderful their child would be, imagining their offspring wandering from piano to drawing board, soaking up knowledge, absorbing inspiration from both of them, their talents magnified in this original creation they had made. Jane remembered and pulled her knees in and wrapped her arms around them to make herself as small and insulated as possible, like a novice fighter who realizes he cannot defend himself from anticipated blows and hopes only to provide the tiniest possible target.

"I can't do this anymore, Jane. Unless you can help. Will you help us get through this?"

She wanted to say she understood, that she wanted to help, but she felt choked by the silence that so often kept her from speaking when she most wanted to.

"I'm talking to a lawyer tomorrow. Maybe we can have a separation for a while. I don't know how any of this works." He passed his hand in front of his eyes, but Jane didn't know if he was crying, or just tired. "Do you want to come with me?"

If she had been able to say, "Yes, I'll come along," they probably would never have divorced. If she had been able to say that much. But she shook her head and felt the possibility of response shutting down until it had vanished.

"There's no one else." Alex responded as if she had asked the question. "But I'm lonely. I'm so sorry about the baby, but I don't know what to do about it."

Still, she couldn't say anything. She couldn't cry, and she couldn't let him hold her.

"I guess that's it," he said. Jane heard him dropping ice cubes into a glass in the kitchen as she returned to the music room and the discipline of Bach.

Fifteen years after Ken had introduced them in a smoky New York jazz club still echoing with the blues Jane played, he brought her the papers to end the marriage to his best friend. Now there was only silence, the faintly pulsing vacuum following the last movement of a symphony forever unfinished.

Chapter Twenty-One
Crape Myrtle (*Lagerstroemia indica*)

August 25, 1998

A crack of thunder startled Jane from an afternoon nap. It sounded so close she wondered if the willow tree had been struck by lightning. Rain beat down on the roof and was blown in staccato spurts against the windows. She reached for a quilt draped over the arm of the sofa and unfolded it to wrap around her shoulders, its scent of old cotton and lavender tempering the sharper smell of falling rain outside. A gentle thump, barely audible in the noise of the storm, drew her attention to Nana's diary, which had dislodged when she reached for the quilt.

She wondered if she could believe anything she had read in it. Her grandmother had been pregnant and unmarried when she left Ireland? Had Nana actually believed the boy she loved was from the Other Side? Could the diary be truth, or just a young girl's fantasy, the musings of a troubled Catholic teenager who found herself pregnant and afraid, running away from the shame she would cause her family, escaping the rumored horrors of the laundries?

"My mother says it's nonsense, but my lover swears it's truth," Nana had written. Jane knew her mother had also branded the Irish myths as nonsense. Jane had been the one her grandmother entrusted with a legacy of Irish legends. In the diary, had she passed along more myth and fancy, or the truth?

She sat on the edge of the sofa and reached for the slim book. As it fell, it fanned past the blank pages on which she had sought more of Nana's story. Jane grabbed it and stared at the entry penciled near the end of the book.

Saturday, January 13, 1934

She was born this morning. A perfect baby girl with big brown eyes. I told the hospital my name is Margaret O'Rourke, I'm 21 years old, and my husband, Brian, died on the trip from Ireland. The same story I told them at Ellis Island. God knows there was more than one body carted off the ship, and a few buried at sea, and no one seemed to care.

I'm Cara Reilly no longer. A new life has begun for little Bridget and me.

No wonder her grandmother had discouraged Jane's interest in tracing her Irish roots. Nana claimed there was no family to find, no relatives to contact, and that was true for the invented Margaret O'Rourke, "widow" of Brian.

Jane continued through the book, page by page, examining the ones she had skipped over. Three pages from the end, she found the final entry.

Tuesday, November 17, 1960

Bridget's daughter was born last night in the middle of the dead month, at 12:30 am, the middle of the dead hour of the night. The nurse tried to tell me that a newborn's eyes often change color in their first year, but I bet Brian's granddaughter's stay as green as his were.

It had been written the day Jane was born, in handwriting that was the decades older echo of the girl who had begun the diary in Ireland. Jane's eyes had remained a startling green.

The storm subsided, but the decrescendo of the background noise of rain and wind was suddenly filled with the alarmed cries of the mother robin. Jane ran to the back porch.

At first, she could distinguish little through the rain. Gusts pummeled the branches of the small tree, which seemed to cower in the middle of the garden. With softer cries, the robin swooped past the porch to the branch where she had built her nest. The nest hung at an odd angle; the side that the ribbon had decorated dipped low, its drenched ornament half buried in mud beneath the tree. The bird circled a few times as the rain increased, then flew into the woods.

Jane stared at the ribbon as the downpour beat it further into the wet soil. A black sadness filled her, and she held her breath as she recognized the small, feathered object on the ground. Seconds later, she expelled the air in a drawn-out anguished moan.

With the dazed intensity of a sleepwalker, she moved barefoot into the garden. Empty except for sodden bits of down and shards of sky blue eggshell, the nest mocked her. Pelting rain and lightning in her eyes rendering her as blind as Deirdre, Jane swept the nest from the branch, raking her arm against the rough bark, and sending the nest flying toward the ocean. She dropped to her knees beside the tiny form, whose wings seemed spread as though it practiced flight. In her mind, in her heart, she saw her own damaged newborn, and she cried now for the loss she had never acknowledged.

Jane clawed at the earth, willing herself to become part of the garden faerie cyrcle that blossomed with new life. She pressed her fists against her belly and curled up in the mud. The rain soaked her clothes. Her hair stuck like wet feathers to her forehead and the nape of her neck. Wind whisked her cries from her lips and dragged them in counterpoint against its own songs.

She did not hear the knock at the front door, or Moira's voice calling her name. Another rattle of thunder drowned out Moira's cry of alarm, the slam of the screen door, the rapid clatter of her sandaled feet down the steps from the porch. She knelt beside Jane and wiped mud from Jane's face, from her mouth. "Are you sick? Did someone hurt you?"

Jane jerked away from the contact. "I lost—I lost—I lost—" Her voice rose three times from a harsh whisper to a cry of anguish that choked and strangled in her throat. Lightning seared the darkness, glinting off the feathers and the black bead eye of the nestling. "Oh, God! I lost my baby." Jane reached for the tiny body, but Moira caught her hands before Jane could pull the bird close to her.

"When did it happen, Jane?" Moira stroked Jane's shoulder to calm her. "Did you lose the baby today? Do you need to go to the hospital?"

"I lost her in a hospital. Three years ago. My baby would be almost three now." Moira leaned closer to hear Jane over the noise of the rain and rising wind. Jane's voice and body shook with her sobs. "They stole her away from me."

Moira tried to lift Jane to a sitting position. "We need to get you inside and warm. Then we can talk about the baby."

"The Good Folk took my baby like Nana said they could." Jane lay back down, and Moira stretched out on her side, facing her friend in the rain-pocked mud. In a singsong whisper made jagged by her sobbing, Jane said, "The Others took my baby and left me one of theirs. She was broken. She was —" Again she spat out the word that choked her, "Ugly. She was ugly and she wasn't made right. But I held her, and I wanted to love her."

"It's all right. You didn't do anything wrong." They were both shivering as the temperature dropped and the rain continued to fall. "Come inside," she said, and this time Jane let Moira help her to her feet and they stumbled up the stairs and into the house.

Moira pulled out a chair and seated Jane at the kitchen table. She sat straight, staring at her hands clasped together in her wet lap as if she were not sure to whom they belonged or what their purpose might be. Moira grabbed a sweater from its hook on the wall and draped it over Jane's shoulders, then she started the burner under the tea kettle. She kicked off her sandals and walked to the bathroom. A few seconds later, hot water was splashing into the claw foot tub.

When Moira returned to the kitchen, Jane was still in the chair, her arms crossed over her stomach, her body pulsing with sobs. She moaned and whispered the story of her baby, oblivious as Moira pulled off her muddy clothes and dropped them in a heap on the floor. Then Moira led Jane to the bathroom and helped her into the tub. Moira sponged away the dirt and rinsed the mud from Jane's cropped hair. She could not wipe away all the tears and let them fall as freely as the rain had fallen on both of them.

Jane was still shaking as she sat, wrapped in her terrycloth robe, on the edge of the bed. Minutes after the tea kettle whistled, Moira brought her a steaming mug. "Hot toddy," she said. "Drink it while I get some of the mud off myself. I couldn't find any lemon, but the extra Jack Daniels ought to make up for it."

When Moira returned, a little cleaner, dressed in a sweat suit Jane had left hanging on the back of the bathroom door, the toddy cup was empty and Jane had stretched out on the bed. She had not stopped shivering or crying.

"It wasn't your fault," Moira told her, sitting on the edge of the bed.

"I took the music. I used the gift. Nana said there was always a price with the Good Folk."

"With all respect to your grandmother, they'd not do that. Move over." Moira tucked the covers around Jane's shoulders and lay down on the bed beside her. She wrapped her arms around Jane. "They wouldn't take your baby."

"Deirdre."

"They wouldn't take Deirdre."

When the shivering stopped, and regular breathing replaced the sobs, Moira slipped off the bed. She leaned close to hear Jane whisper so softly that she might have been eavesdropping on dream dialogue. "I thought if I gave back the music, they might let me have Deirdre again."

Jane heard Moira leave the bedroom. She seemed to pause for a few minutes in the kitchen. Then Jane heard more footsteps and the click of the door to the front porch. As the rain slowed to random taps on the roof, she expected to hear Moira's station wagon chug to life and pull away.

Jane's head throbbed from crying and the whiskey, and she walked into the kitchen to take an aspirin. She was startled to see a narrow beam of light raking across the yard that separated the house from the ocean. She sat still in the dark room and watched as Moira moved like a silver shadow in the cloud-filtered light outside. Her friend, carrying a flashlight and garden trowel, walked around to the garden, ignoring the mud that spattered her sandaled feet. The light, like an artificial moonbeam, reflected a deceptive wink off the jet-black bead of the bird's eye. Cradling the limp feathered body in her hand, Moira dug a shallow grave for it at the edge of the woods. She piled a cairn of small rocks to protect the spot. Before she left, she skittered the light over the earth of the garden under the limb that had held the nest and smudged with her muddy feet the paw prints that the rain had not quite erased.

Finally, Jane heard the rumble of the car's engine before it faded away. She went back to bed. As she fell asleep, she hummed a song that was sad and inevitable, its timbre so like the wind that ordinary ears could not distinguish between the sounds.

Chapter Twenty-Two
Allein (G.) Alone

1997 – 1998

From the moments before the St. Louis performance began, it was different from any Jane had played. The notes that usually danced and raced through her mind, an ecstatic rush of music eager to engage the audience and members of the orchestras with which she played, were there, but subdued and ordered. As she entered the stage for the Scriabin concerto, the air between Jane and the massive concert grand seemed too thick to penetrate. The piano loomed like an invincible opponent rather than the comforting refuge it had always been. She managed to reach the bench and sat for a moment longer than usual. Glancing up, she saw Ken standing just inside the proscenium arch, watching her with concern. She heard a whispered, "Miss Bell?" from the conductor, and she nodded to him, signaling that she was ready to begin.

Jane flew through the three movements, listening to it from the outside as though she overheard the music through an open window in a house she feared to enter. Usually during a performance, she had no sense of time passing; she pulled her breath from the rise and fall of the notes and was surprised when the audience seemed to sigh in unison and then signaled the end of a performance with their applause. Now she held her breath, aware of each note.

Throughout the piece, she kept the waving end of the conductor's baton in sight. As long as it measured time, time must be passing, she must be playing, her heart must be beating. The music flowed from her brain and her muscles trained by countless hours of lessons and rehearsal. Her mind sought her grandmother's Other World, a place to escape from this one.

Finally, they reached the end of the piece. Jane took her bows and shook hands with the concertmaster and conductor. The audience, with whom she had always connected at the end of a performance, felt distant and tentative to her. They seemed to accept her offering as palatable while sensing that it lacked a spice so exotic as to be unnamable, as guests might sense something missing at a wedding feast prepared by a heartbroken chef.

On the plane ride back to New York City the next morning, Jane sat beside Ken. She had not slept the night before, and she closed her eyes, relaxing in the tuneless, monotonous drone of the engine. When she woke up, Ken folded the newspaper he had been reading and slipped it into his briefcase.

Jane gestured toward the folded newspaper. "Review?" she asked. Usually, she didn't care about the reviews, but she knew Ken clipped and saved each one in a scrapbook documenting her career. This time, she sought reassurance that what still seemed like a vague bad dream had been an acceptable performance.

"She says that you were technically brilliant."

Jane continued to hold out her hand, and Ken handed the paper to her. "Flawless technique," she read. "Sharp-edged as cut glass... Melody lines interwoven with superhuman precision... Crystalline flawlessness... A multi-faceted presentation..." Jane refolded the paper and handed it back to Ken as the flight attendant brought their coffee. "Sounds like she was reviewing a jewelry show or an antique auction."

"You need to give yourself time to get back into it. Schedule another performance. Each one will be easier."

Jane closed her eyes again.

Circling New York, waiting to land after the two-hour flight, Jane announced to Ken, "I've got to leave."

"Better wait. It's a long way down." Jane's expression made clear that she was in no mood for jokes. "Where do you want to go?"

"I don't know."

"Your mother keeps asking you to spend some time with them in Florida."

"Oh, God, Ken. I love her, but she would smother me. I need to get away from everything." Her slender, powerful hands were shaking as they gripped the armrest between them.

Ken covered her hand with his. She tried to draw away, but he held her hand tight. When she began to relax, he asked, "Where were you happy?"

Jane stared out the window at a sky as blue as the ocean had been a year ago when she performed in Wilmington. Sun, waves, the moment in the Schumann concerto when she first felt the baby move inside her. Peace. Promise. As the wheels of the jet touched down at JFK, Jane whispered, "North Carolina."

"Go back there," he said.

***

The cab ride to Jane's apartment seemed designed to reinforce all negative stereotypes about Manhattan. Horns blared, trash danced like junk puppets manipulated by a mad wind, irate drivers shouted at pedestrians who returned curses with angry hand gestures.

"How do I do it?" Jane asked as the cab pulled up in front of her apartment building.

Ken got out with her and waved the doorman away so they could talk for a minute on the sidewalk. "We'll find someone to sublet your apartment —"

"Without the piano room."

"Yes, we could do it that way. You have two other rooms for bedrooms." Jane had kept the Manhattan apartment after the divorce and converted Alex's study to a guest room.

"I can't play again right now."

"You've got nothing scheduled for months," Ken reminded her. "Get away for a while."

Jane hugged him. "I need to."

"I'll start working on subletting the apartment tomorrow. Get some sleep tonight."

But Jane couldn't sleep and began storing her music books and sheet music in the antique oak ice chest that held hundreds of scores. When it was full, she called the night manager at the desk who found sturdy cardboard boxes to hold the rest of her music.

She sat on the floor, quickly packing some music like the new pieces written for her child, unwilling to let the melodies enter her mind. She thumbed slowly through a worn book of Chopin etudes. It was embellished with Joseph's penciled fingerings, notations and reminders to his favorite student. Jane ran her fingers over the notes. She understood how he had fallen in love with the young woman who was now his wife. He needed someone to be there with him and Jane had already embarked on the career that would keep her far from her Cleveland home.

She put away Beethoven and the rest of the Chopin, the pieces that had become her signature. Finally, she removed the Scriabin from the piano, the last piece she had been practicing. She knew that the "crystalline flawlessness," the sharp-edged perfection, the superhuman technique were what was left when the heart and the passion were torn from her music. She could not return to the piano as long as she was so empty, so dead inside.

Jane poured a tumbler of Jack Daniels, raised it in a mute toast to Nana, and went to bed with a paperback romance she had picked up in the airport. She wanted to drive away all serious thought, all music, all musing.

Within two weeks, Ken had found a couple to sublet the apartment. "He's a physician at Mt. Sinai, and she's a cellist, a new client of mine." Jane and Ken were having lunch, sitting at a sidewalk café in the Village.

"What about the piano room?" Keeping it locked had to be part of the deal.

"They understand completely. And they're willing to go with a month-to-month lease while they finish building their house in New Jersey."

"I guess that's it then." Jane toyed with the lettuce on her salad plate. "When can they move in?"

"As early as two weeks. But I told them you might not be ready quite that soon."

"I'm ready."

"What do you need for your trip?"

Jane shrugged. "I haven't thought about it."

"Are you going to fly there and rent a car?"

She hadn't thought about that either but now made a decision. "I still have my driver's license. I'll buy a car and drive to North Carolina."

"What kind of car? We'll go shopping."

Jane looked up and saw a Jeep SUV looking invincible in mid-Manhattan traffic. "One of those. Can you get one for me?"

"Don't you want to take a test drive? You should really try a few different ones. That's the fun part."

"I want a car just like that." Jane made it clear she didn't want to discuss it further. "In black," she added before Ken could pose the question. "And plain. Like a sturdy nun."

"I bet I can find one for you." After a few minutes, he asked if she would like to meet the couple that would be subletting the apartment.

"No. Please just handle it." She spoke as though the idea terrified her. She was no more able to endure introductions to these people than she was capable right now of suffering through the ordeal of purchasing a new car from a high-pressure salesman.

"I'll take care of it."

On the last night in her apartment, Jane slept on the small sofa in the piano room. In her mind, she had turned over the other rooms to the new tenants. Now she closed the wooden doors to the ice chest, running her fingers over its brass hinges, over the levers that locked the doors, over the raised grain of the old oak, as if she were blind and sought reassurance by touch that all the notes on all the pages were secured in the chest. She slid the cardboard cartons containing the rest of her music into the closet. Before closing the closet door, she took a worn box from the top shelf.

Opening it, she took out the fringed shawl that her grandmother had brought from Ireland. It had been unwrapped and rewrapped so many times through the years that the tissue paper nearly crumbled in her hands. She put the shawl over her shoulders and curled up on the sofa. She closed her eyes and began to dream of the magical creatures with which Nana had peopled her stories. There was music in her dream, music that faded, note by note, and Jane could see each note as a separate, living entity that hid from her in an enchanted wood, like faeries playing a game she did not understand. And then it was morning. Jane woke up. She closed the lid of the piano and the cover of the keyboard. She gently shook the scarf as though it might contain loose creatures that had not yet found a hiding place, and let it float downward to drape the grand piano. It seemed cocooned, protected. She closed the blinds and left the room without looking back.

It took her little time to dress and put last-minute toiletries in her suitcase. Everything else she needed for the trip was stacked beside the front door. She made one last go round of the apartment, assuring herself that all was in order for the new tenants. She walked toward the music room and rested her forehead against the door that separated her from a bruised and aching silence.

Chapter Twenty-Three
Salt Cedar (*Tamarix ramosissima*)

August 26 – 27, 1998

The ocean was black. Waves that had teased and caressed just days before, now tumbled over each other in a foamy race to scar the beach with vicious, raking hits. Jane ran down the steps toward the sea in spite of the rain that had begun to veil the sand. She moved with long strides, her arms open to embrace the air, feeling for the first time in so long that she ran toward something, not away from it.

She had slept late and dreamlessly but woke with the sense that songs lapped around the edges of her mind. The events of the night before might have been a dream except for the pile of her mud-stiffened clothes on the floor. She let herself think about her song-filled pregnancy, Deirdre's birth, and her death, and she was comforted by the absolution she had heard from Moira in echoes of her grandmother's brogue.

It was late afternoon, but as she ran, her heels kicking tiny plumes of sand behind her, the sky darkened, and the wind whipped and whistled louder as if trying to knot the sea grasses that bent in its wake. Jane stopped when she heard the sound that rose from the gusts, from screeching gulls, from the buried memory of Nana's stories. It was the keening of the banshee for Deirdre, and she raised her voice with it in a mad duet.

A hand grabbed her shoulder, and she swung around, not knowing whether a human being or something from the Other Side had touched her.

McCue stood there, wild-eyed, angry, or perhaps frightened for her, rain dripping from his hair and beard. Jane could not hear his shouts over the driving gusts until he leaned close to her, and she caught the word "hurricane."

He took her hand and half led, half dragged her back in the direction she had come. The beach was nearly covered by angry water, higher than she had ever seen it. Sand, so recently a tranquil beach where shells were offered up like jewels at a bazaar, now shifted and sucked at their feet. Jane's legs ached with the effort of lifting them in waterlogged jeans. The water was no higher than her knees, but she felt like desperate hands grasped her ankles and pulled her away from shore. The last wave to hit them before they reached the edge of the water pushed both of them to their knees, and they crawled and stumbled through the grasses and stunted vegetation. A crack rang out like a gunshot over the clatter of tree limbs whipping together, and McCue jerked Jane out of the way as a heavy limb crashed two feet from them, scraping both of them with branches.

Scrambling sideways on the incline that grew steeper toward Jane's section of beach, McCue released her hand so they could grab bushes and rock edges to keep from being blown into the waves that reached for them, spewing rabid foam.

Blinded by the rain and salt spray blowing needle-sharp into her eyes, Jane smashed her forehead against the railing that led up the hill to her house. She felt the palm of her hand make contact with the wood, but the surface was slick as ice, and she lost her handhold and tumbled into the churning surf. Waves smashed into her, rolled over her. Undertow grabbed her legs and wrestled her down to the bottom. She panicked, kicking her feet and flailing her arms.

She heard Nana's voice, crooning a story that reached her over the screams of the wind, the crash of the ocean. "Oh, the selkies, they were things of beauty in the water. They would slip and slide, laughing and dancing through the sea. They were one with the water." Jane stopped struggling. She let the next surge pull her to the surface. She gulped in air, then held her breath and thought of the creatures, beautiful, tragic women on land, sleek swimmers when wrapped in magic seal skins in the waters of Orkney. Another wave lifted her, and she pictured giant hands propelling her toward land. Jane held her arms in front of her, protecting her face from the sand, and smashed into McCue, who pulled her up from the water. They struggled through the surf that tried to reclaim them both and held fast to the wooden steps that led to Jane's house.

Now the wind pitched its voice impossibly high, screeched its fury, battered their bodies so Jane felt she would be plucked from the hillside and tossed back into the water that roiled below them. McCue followed close behind her, bracing his arms on either side of her, and she pulled herself up to the top, grabbing for one aching handhold after another. He paused for a second, and Jane turned to see his gaze focused on a tree that had stood about his height. They watched as its branches bent torturously, then snapped and sailed into the driving wetness that surrounded them. He nodded to her to keep climbing. She dragged herself up a few more steps, fighting the weight of her soaked clothing.

Three steps from the top. The ocean grabbed the bottom steps and shook them, like a dog that had been hit once too often with a stick he now held in his teeth. McCue pressed tightly against Jane to keep her from being flung off, then gave her a push that sent her scrambling up the last steps and onto the ground. As her feet left the top step, she felt as much as heard the crack and ripping of wood as the bottom section of steps was torn away and tossed into the waves churning below.

Jane lay in the soaked grass, gasping for breath, praying for a glimpse of McCue. The mad dog in the sea gave another shake of his head. Jane watched in horror as the railing disappeared, her scream eaten by the racket of the wind. She crawled to the edge and stared blindly into the torrent. His hand grabbed her knee. For a second, she could see blood on his hand before rain washed it away, then his blood was on both of them as she struggled to help him to the edge.

He took her hand as they staggered toward the house, leaning against the wind as though it were a solid object put in place to keep them from shelter. Shingles, ripped from the roof, sailed off in drunken spirals, chased by branches as long as small trees. The willow that had arched so protectively beside the house now bent over it like an old hag, slashing and whipping at the roof and windows.

The glass in the ocean-side windows was intact, in spite of one shutter that chattered against the panes. McCue pointed toward the door and gently pushed Jane closer to the porch. He nodded in the direction of the storm shutters and began unfolding and latching them. Jane dashed to his side just as a gust of wind wrenched the louvered panel from his hands, and they wrestled the shutter in place. Together, they circled the house, protecting every window until they reached the back porch again. The rocking chair had blown away.

They crawled through the back door, used the weight of both their bodies to shut it, and sat on the floor of the kitchen, backs resting against the door that the storm threatened to batter down.

"I heard the banshee," Jane said.

"But you didn't hear the hurricane warnings? That banshee could have been keening for you."

"I didn't have the radio on."

"We left you a note last night."

"We?"

"Moira. I asked her to be sure to tell you to prepare for the storm early." Water and sand dripped from his hair into his eyes, and McCue brushed his hand across his forehead. A crimson smear of fresh blood streaked his skin.

Jane reached out and took his arm. A gash several inches long marked his forearm. "We've got to get this cleaned up." As she stood, the lights flickered. "Let me get a flashlight before —"

The room went dark. In the wavering gray streaks of light that showed the location of shuttered windows still pelleted with rain, she found the flashlight and helped McCue to the bathroom.

She eased his tattered shirtsleeve over the wound and dropped the shirt on the floor. Bathing his arm in warm water, she watched the dirt and blood swirl blackly in the darkness of the sink. She ripped a clean sheet into strips, and he leaned back against the wall while she wrapped his arm with a touch that became a caress. His breathing deepened, and he reached for her, but she gently pushed his shoulders back against the wall, unbuckled his belt and unzipped his jeans. The denim, heavy with rain and ocean water, slipped to his feet.

Jane leaned in to kiss him, but McCue put his hands on her shoulders and backed her against the wall, reversing their positions. He wiped her face, patting the washcloth over the purpling bruise on her forehead. Slowly, deliberately, he began to unbutton her shirt, but she grabbed it from the bottom edge and pulled it over her head. He started to pick her up. The pain in his arm made him wince, and she pulled away from him, stripping off the rest of her clothes. She carried the flashlight and led him to her bedroom.

McCue's first caresses were gentle, tentative, his fingers brushing over the scrapes and bruises that water-colored Jane's arms and legs. Fear and pain were submerged, then drowned in waves of desire she had denied for years. She opened herself to him. Their cries of pleasure and release were swallowed by the drumming of rain that continued to beat on the roof.

Suddenly, the world went quiet except for their ragged breathing. "Is the storm over?" Jane asked.

"Half." McCue got out of bed and pulled the sheet over Jane's shoulder. "We're in the eye. We'll get hit from the other direction in about twenty minutes." He walked into the bathroom and returned, zipping his rain-soaked jeans. "I'm going to check outside to make sure the shutters will hold."

"Not without me." Jane was up and slipping into dry clothes. When McCue started to object, she silenced him. "It's my house." He nodded, handed her a sweatshirt, and picked up the flashlight as they headed for the back door.

Damp air brushed through as McCue opened the door, teasing the corner of a piece of staff paper out from under the refrigerator. Jane picked it up. *Get some sleep. We'll check on you tomorrow. The real storm will hit late afternoon. Secure the storm shutters and keep your radio on! You're not a real North Carolinian until you've weathered at least one hurricane. PS. Deirdre's death wasn't your fault. You need to let yourself grieve and be sad. It is easier with friends to share your loss.* "Moira's note," she said, pushing the paper into her pocket. McCue led her outside.

They stood on the porch. The silence was as huge a force as the roar of the wind had been. Seconds after a single birdcall broke the quiet, the tentative chirp of tiny frogs joined the chorus. McCue reached out for a branch that blocked their way down the porch steps, his hands interlocking with the stripped twigs as though they were the fingers of a friend he had been unable to save. He pulled it off the steps and into the yard, studying the ragged edge of the limb. He nodded toward the embankment where they had watched the wind rip the branch from its trunk. "It was the last salt cedar on this part of the beach."

"Could the tree survive?"

McCue shrugged. "They're tough, but we're not going to check it out tonight." He took her hand to help her over smaller branches scattered across the yard. They circled the house. McCue focused the flashlight on each shutter and together they tested the clasps and hinges that had held fast against the ravages of the wind. He looked at his watch every few minutes. As Jane double-checked the last window, McCue stepped further from the house to the edge of the woods and swept the flashlight beam across the roof, checking for damage.

As the circle of light slipped over the willow, twin pinpoints, red as reflections from sharply faceted rubies, flashed from a branch where the bobcat crouched. McCue shouted a warning to Jane as he bent to pick up a stone from the cairn that covered the robin's body. But Jane had heard a scrape of claws as the cat launched himself from the willow tree, and the hiss that ripped through the silence. She instinctively covered her throat with raised arms. Ignoring the needle-sharp pain as Duncan's teeth pierced the sweatshirt, she flung the cat away from her and watched as the soaked animal landed on its feet and prepared to pounce again.

McCue hesitated only a fraction of a second. Powerful hind legs had propelled the bobcat's body several inches from the ground when a rock struck just below its left ear with enough force to knock it to the ground. The cat raised its head. Amber eyes stared at McCue. Duncan shook his head and turned slowly, testing his balance, then streaked into the woods. As though he had created a whirlwind that sped up the return of the storm, rain began to pelt them like pebbles propelled by a demonic wind.

The muscles in her legs tensed and throbbed in her struggle with McCue to reach the door. Her voice rose in a cry of fear and frustration as McCue pulled with all his weight against the door held tight by the gale. He couldn't budge it more than an inch before the wind slammed it again. Exhausted, Jane crouched down in the corner of the small open porch. McCue tried to shield her body with his. They were both shivering uncontrollably, assaulted by the rain and wind-driven debris. Suddenly, a dripping wet giant stood between them and the storm. Steve jerked the door open and held it for the seconds it took McCue to help Jane inside. The wind caught the door and pinned it open. Rain poured into the kitchen. The wind blew chairs across the room. Steve and McCue wrestled the door closed, and the three of them collapsed on the floor. Jane crawled to the door and reached up to lock it, wondering if anything could protect them from the gale that seemed more furious than before the eye had passed over.

Jane hugged Steve. "Thank you. But it was crazy to go out in this."

He searched the pocket of his soaked overalls and pulled out a soggy notebook. Jane went into the study and brought back a piece of staff paper and a pencil.

"HAD to see if you were OK," he wrote.

"I was stupid and didn't know the hurricane was coming. McCue found me on the beach and got me back here."

Steve turned away.

Jane reached out and touched him on the shoulder. "We'll be fine. You built a sturdy house."

After a moment, he turned back to them and wrote, "It's stronger now. So are you."

Jane knew he was right.

McCue looked with concern at her shoulder where the bobcat had raked her with his claws. "We have to clean that up."

Steve seemed too exhausted to pick up the pencil and ask a question.

"Duncan was crazy with the storm. And jealous. He attacked Jane."

Steve nodded. He pointed to Jane and McCue and, with a slight smile, to the bedroom where the unmade bed was visible through the open door. He pointed to himself, gestured to the living room, and moved slowly in that direction.

"Wait." Jane brought two quilts from the bedroom and handed them to Steve. "You ought to take your wet clothes off and wrap up in these."

He nodded again and, in a few minutes, emerged from the bathroom swaddled in the quilts, and stretched out on the floor.

In the bedroom, McCue checked Jane's shoulder and washed the shallow scratches. "I'm so sorry."

"Do you think he'll come back?"

"It's probably better if he doesn't. Wild things should be left in the wild."

"Steve shouldn't have made the trip out here."

"I think he had to."

"Why would he have to?" Jane asked.

McCue stretched out on the bed and Jane lay down beside him. "Selena was lost in a hurricane like this one. Steve was in town and couldn't get here until the storm was nearly over. The house was empty, and they never found her. The police speculated that she went for a walk on the beach to see the storm —"

"Like I did."

"Yes. Exactly. For two days after the hurricane went out to sea, Steve paced the beach calling her name. He lost his voice from the shouting, and no one has heard him speak since. He felt responsible. Losing you would have been too much for him."

A candle flickered on the bedside table, swaying in scraps of wind that the storm still pushed through cracks in the house. Brass leaves sculpted on the headboard seemed to wave with the movement of the light, as though, Jane thought, faeries hid there. She pulled an extra quilt over them, and McCue found a way to cradle her in his arms that was comfortable in spite of their scrapes and bruises. He closed his eyes and was soon asleep.

Jane lay awake, her mind full of questions. In her grandmother's world, there would be no doubt about the magic of Aria; McCue and Moira, who never appeared in the same place at the same time, would be revealed as shapeshifters. Jane was growing used to the idea. If she fell asleep with McCue, would she wake up in Moira's arms? Duncan and Kaeth must be a second pair of the mystical creatures. When Duncan fled, had he taken Kaeth away, too?

In the memory of Kaeth's laughter, music flowed, and as Jane concentrated on its melody, a new song muted the ebbing noise of the hurricane. Beneath the rhythmic cycle of McCue's inhalation and exhalation, pulsed a largo movement, and Jane welcomed the music. It was the second section, she realized, *pacato*, a calm, tranquil moment between the pounding storm-driven fury of the first movement and a sprite-dance of Kaeth's giggles that would end the piece. She fell asleep filled with new music.

She awoke to the smell of coffee and sounds of Steve moving in the kitchen. She could tell from the arms around her that McCue still held her. Clearly, she still didn't understand all the rules.

"I'll get breakfast for us." Jane stood up stiffly and folded the quilt. "I want to check the house and yard, and we need to see if everyone is safe in town."

The three of them, Steve and McCue dressed in still damp clothes, went together into the yard. The wind had lifted shingles and littered the yard with branches, but quickly opened shutters revealed no cracked or broken glass. The small amount of damage to the house could easily be repaired. Her stairs to the beach lay in splintered sections buried in sand. The beach itself stretched flat; all the swelling dunes of accumulated sand, the sea oats and green vines whose name Jane had not yet discovered, the shells—whole and fractured—that she loved, were gone. But the ocean, tamed for now, exhausted, murmured promises of a return to the peaceful waves she had known in her house by the sea.

They shared cups of strong coffee and listened to the sound of chainsaws as power crews worked to clear the roads and restore electricity. Steve had stuffed a few sheets of paper into his pocket until he could get a new notebook. His borrowed pencil scratched out a new message. "Going to check on Mrs. Daley. Meet you in town." He put his cup in the sink and went out the front door, waving his goodbye.

"Do you think George stayed through the storm?" Jane asked.

"We'll go see."

The phone startled them with its ring. "That was quick," McCue said. "Sometimes it takes days to get the lines repaired."

Jane lifted the receiver and heard Ken's voice before she could complete her "Hello."

"Jane, I've been frantic. The news made it sound like the hurricane made landfall right on your house. Are you all right?"

"We lost a few shingles, but we're fine."

McCue nodded toward the door and left to check the truck.

"So you'll be staying there to take care of things?"

Jane knew Ken was asking, in as gentle a way possible, if she would remain at the beach rather than returning to her concert career. "I need a little more time here. But tell Houston I'm honoring my contract."

"God, Jane, that's great. That's just great." She could hear the relief in Ken's voice and picture the smile on his face as he continued, "Should I tell them you'll play Bach? Or Scriabin?"

"Chopin," she whispered. Then louder, so he could hear, "Chopin, the second piano concerto for the first half of the program. And I'll premiere a new piece, a sea sonata, to end the second half."

"You're sure?"

"Absolutely. But I have to go now. We need to check on our friends in town."

"Good. That's good. I'm going to call your parents to let them know you're safe, and then I'll call Houston. A sea sonata?" He paused. "I'm so glad you're okay. Call me when you're ready to head home."

"I promise." Jane hung up the phone, thinking that she now had two places to call home.

The drive into town showed that the damage was mostly limited to downed tree limbs and shattered signs. Power company trucks had converged on the area from several states, and citizens armed with chainsaws helped neighbors clear fallen trees.

A few shingles littered the sidewalk in front of the garden store and flute studio.

George Jackson stood in his front yard beside the once-swinging multi-tiered sign that lay in the mud like a decked prizefighter. In his right hand, he held a hand-lettered sign, FOR SALE BY OWNER, in his left, a hammer.

"George, are you all right?" Jane asked, jumping from McCue's truck as soon as he pulled it to the curb.

"Weathered the storm just fine. Got my hatches battened down. Pulled my outdoor chairs inside. Rode it out." He gave the sign post a punishing whack with the hammer. "But enough is enough. Come inside. There's hot tea brewing." He held the front door to the house open, warning them to be careful of the porch chairs jammed inside the vestibule.

Jane stopped in the doorway and stared at a framed photograph on the wall. Two young women, their arms draped around each other's shoulders, smiled at her from the picture. Behind them, a garden bloomed.

"Are you all right, Jane?" George asked.

McCue put his arm around her waist to steady her. "You've had a wicked night. That bump on your head might have been worse than we thought."

"No. I'm fine. But George, has that picture always been there?"

"Not always, but for the past fifteen years, yes." He lifted it from the hook on the wall and dusted it with the hem of his cardigan.

"It's Mary Ellen and Selena?"

"It is, Jane. I wish you could have known both of them."

Jane let McCue lead her into the next room. "The first afternoon I was here, I thought Mary Ellen visited me while you and Mike were in the kitchen."

"She might very well have done that," George said. "She comes here all the time." He settled into the velvet love seat.

Jane and McCue sat across from him in the parlor surrounded by flowers of wallpaper, fabric, and crystal that had not been battered by the driving rain. Jane picked up a delicate porcelain dogwood blossom from the table and ran her finger around the edge, still feeling Mary Ellen's presence. The door to the kitchen opened and Moira came in carrying a tray with steaming cups of tea.

Jane gasped and released the figurine. McCue caught it before it hit the floor.

"You can't be here!" Jane whispered.

"We're fine." Moira set the tray down and Kaeth appeared beside her, a sugar bowl clutched in both hands. "We had a few rough hours, but we're here."

"No. I thought —" Jane looked from Moira to McCue. "I thought you couldn't be in the same place at the same time. I never saw you together. And Duncan —"

At the mention of the bobcat, Kaeth whimpered, and Moira wrapped her arm around Kaeth's shoulders.

McCue reached for Jane's hand. "Well, we're together now."

"Those storms do curious things," Moira said. "You'll feel better after some tea."

Jane sat with her hands clenched in her lap. "So Nana's stories were all lies. There is no magic."

Moira, George, and McCue all spoke at once.

"You can't believe that," Moira said.

George shook his head. "You ought not be talking that way about your grandmother, Jane."

"And what do you mean, 'There's no magic'?" McCue's brogue was heavier than Jane had ever heard it.

"I found my grandmother's diary. She let all of us believe she was orphaned in Ireland and married my grandfather, and she said he died on the boat trip to America. But in the diary, she admits that she was unmarried and expecting my mother when she left Ireland. She wrote all sorts of garbage about how my grandfather was part of the Other World and couldn't cross moving water to come to this country. He was probably just a flute-playing neighborhood kid who got her pregnant and dumped her at the dock."

"She was a brave young woman," Moira said. "Believing in the magic in the stories carried her through a rough ocean voyage and gave her strength to start a new life alone and pregnant in a foreign country." Moira leaned closer to Jane. "And if you're talking about magic in Ireland, that's a different story altogether." The others nodded their agreement.

Tears of confusion and exhaustion in Jane's eyes blurred the colors and objects in the room. "I don't know what's real anymore."

Jane thought she heard her grandmother's hushed whisper entwined with the voices of her friends as they murmured, "*Is ón saol a thagann an chiall.*" When she was ready, she would understand.

Jane knew Nana's stories about the selkies had saved her from the riptides that fought to pull her under during the hurricane. It was not quite supernatural, but had her grandmother reached out to rescue her?

"So your beautiful flute probably belonged to your grandfather in Ireland." McCue squeezed her hand. "No magic there?"

"Close your eyes," George said. "What do you hear?"

Jane did as he asked and knew he did not expect her to listen to the muted sound of voices and chainsaws outside. She heard new music, songs in the voice of her piano, a voice she thought had been stilled forever after Deirdre died. Her grandfather's flute, and McCue's gentle guidance, had led her back to music.

"Let's hear nothing more about a lack of magic in the world," Moira said. Kaeth echoed "magic" in an otherworldly whisper. "But, George, what's this about selling your house?"

"I'm too old for the weather and this house and the yard." He held up his hand to stop Moira's contradiction. "I might try that lovely assisted living home in Wilmington, the one with the big front porch and all those rocking chairs. Or I might do some traveling to a place I've been away from far too long. Of course, I won't be able to take all these things, wherever I go," he continued slowly, his glance taking in the room he and his sister had loved. "Jane, I want you to have the piano."

"I couldn't take it. It's Mary Ellen's piano."

"That's precisely why you should. She wants you to have it."

Jane didn't question the present tense. She could picture it in the small room at her beach house; the room she had called the study had been waiting all along to be a music room. "I would be honored to have the piano. I'll take good care of it for both of you."

"One condition." George Jackson sighed as though a very important issue had been settled to his satisfaction. "We would like you to play us a last piece in the garden room."

As Jane stood and walked toward the piano, she was drawn to it with the same magnetic attraction she had experienced on her first visit to Aria, but this time, she did not fight it. The book of Chopin preludes was open as before to the B minor, like a friend waiting for her, and Jane sensed that the final note that Mary Ellen had played, which was also the first note of the prelude, still vibrated in the strings. Jane sat on the bench, her eyes closed, her slender fingers curved over the keys. The prelude's haunting arpeggio welled up from the rosewood heart of the piano, and she caught it in mid-flight.

The End

About the Author

Libby Jacobs holds master's degrees in education from Virginia Commonwealth University and in theatre from the University of Michigan. A theatre director and playwright, her works have been staged in prominent venues, including Lincoln Center and Off-Broadway in New York City, as well as in Cleveland, Boston, and Valdez, Alaska. Her critically acclaimed collection of short stories, "WOLF NOTE," showcases her talent for capturing the nuances of human experience. Jacobs served as the managing and artistic director for Coach House Theatre in Akron, Ohio, for seven years and founding Actors' and

Playwrights' Theatre, where she focused on producing new works. Additionally, she has guest directed at Weathervane Community Playhouse, collaborated with various chamber music groups, and contributed to a live WKSU (Kent State) production of *War of the Worlds*. Jacobs is excited to share her debut novel, *Sea Sonata*.